MW01243104

Wichita KS 67226-3438

Also by Catherine Nelson

The Trouble with Theft
The Trouble with Murder

The Trouble with Greed

A Zoe Grey Novel

By Catherine Nelson

Copyright © 2015 Catherine Nelson
All Rights Reserved

Cover and photo Copyright © 2015 Catherine Nelson
All Rights Reserved

Cover design by Sabrina Mullison

This is a work of fiction. The characters, entities, and events in this story are entirely fictitious, or used fictitiously. No character or event is intended to represent any real person or event, past or present.

For Nancy.

Zoe wouldn't be the same without you, and neither would I. You're a wonderful person with such a unique spirit. And you're a great friend.

Thank you.

1

"How was the vacation?"

Amy Wells and I left Texas Roadhouse and walked over to the Cinemark movie theatre. It was August, and evening temperatures weren't dropping off yet. It was still close to seventy degrees.

Amy and I have known each other since we both wore diapers. At this point, she's more like a sister than a friend.

"Fun," I said. "It was a lot of fun."

She eyed me as we walked, her caramel brown eyes seeing right through me, as they usually did. "I sense a *but* coming. Did something happen at the wedding?"

My boyfriend, Detective Alex Ellmann, and I had been in Malibu for his father's wedding. We'd stayed several days after the wedding, and spent the time playing on the beach. Our relationship had started under stressful circumstances, and we'd had more than our fair share of stress since. It had been really nice to spend the time together doing nothing more serious than guarding against sunburns.

"No, the wedding went fine. Vince actually looked happy."

She tucked a strand of light brown hair behind her ear. She'd chopped it to shoulder length for summer, but I'd always liked it longer. I didn't tell her this, though, because she wouldn't have cared.

"Then what gives?"

I sighed. "It's Ellmann. He . . ."

She nodded. "He's perfect, I know. How troubling."

I glared at her. "Ha ha. This is serious, Amy."

"I don't know what *this* is."

"He told me . . . he said . . . he loves me."

She blinked at me. "And?"

"And? Amy, come on! What am I supposed to do?" Even now, just thinking about it, I could feel the knots in my stomach.

She laughed. "You say it back, and you enjoy it. He's a great guy. By the way, what did you say?"

I squirmed a little and fussed with my shirt, straightening it unnecessarily. "Uh, I didn't really say . . . anything."

"How many days has it been?"

"Four."

"Zoe. He's not going to wait forever."

"I know. And he shouldn't have to. I just . . ."

She nodded. "You're in love. And it scares the shit out of you."

I sighed and looked at her. "Yeah."

I shouldn't have been surprised anymore that Amy could practically read my mind. Maybe I was just surprised by what she'd read there.

"Congratulations," she said with a smirk.

"You're enjoying this just a little too much."

She put her arm through mine. "My life is small and boring. I have to take amusement wherever I might find it."

"Hilarious."

It was a short walk to the movie theatre. At eight o'clock on a Wednesday, the parking lot was mostly full. The glassed-in lobby was crowded, though the line wasn't spilling out the door.

A Fort Collins Police Department patrol car was parked out

front, and a uniformed patrol officer was lingering on the sidewalk. Since there had been a few incidents of people with firearms at public places like movie theaters, the police department had taken to posting an officer on site during the busier hours of the day. The officer was likely meant to serve as a deterrent, but it would also mean help was a hell of a lot closer should anything actually happen.

I knew this officer. He was a younger, blonde-haired guy named Brooks. He was still new to the force, but he'd already had the pleasure of arresting me. Even before that, I couldn't say I'd been very fond of him.

As Amy and I neared the door, a giant man with a long beard and sagging gut crossed the street and stepped onto the sidewalk ahead of us. A tall woman with short brown hair walked beside him, her arm in his. They were both freshly groomed and dressed a little too well for a Wednesday night movie. I guessed they were on a date.

Almost immediately, I noticed the bulge in the man's pants at the small of his back. It was an unholstered pistol. I couldn't think of many good reasons for a guy to carry a gun around, especially one just shoved into his waistband. I mean, that's how the bad guys do it.

I glanced at Amy, but she didn't seem to have noticed the gun. And Brooks was now facing the other direction, talking to a group of college-aged girls who'd just come out of the theatre. My instinct told me the big guy was on a date, and didn't harbor malicious intentions, but people didn't carry guns around on dates for no reason.

Before I could decide what to do, a tiny, rough-looking, fifty-something blonde woman in jeans and leather jacket hurried onto the sidewalk, her hand under her jacket, and her eyes locked on the big guy. She blew past Brooks and the college girls without drawing their attention. She waited for a group of people to pass then planted herself on the sidewalk and drew a .38 special from under her jacket, aiming straight at the big

3

guy.

"Freeze, James!"

Several things happened at the same time. Her shouting drew the attention of everyone in the nearby area, including Brooks. A woman screamed at the sight of the gun. And James immediately reached for his own gun.

"Shit," I hissed under my breath as I charged forward.

James had gotten the gun out of his pants. I jumped and collided with him from behind. Catching him by surprise, he stumbled forward and went down. He landed hard on his knee, and I pushed him over, landing with my knee between his shoulder blades. The impact with the pavement knocked the wind out of him, and he dropped the gun.

James's date screamed in surprise when I tackled James, and she lunged at me, swinging with her purse and shouting. But then Amy was beside us, and the woman was on her knees and immobile with her arm locked behind her back.

"That's enough of that," Amy said.

Amy's been practicing martial arts since she was in grade school. She's taught me most of what I know, and knows more still.

I pushed my hazelnut-colored hair out of my face and took a breath.

Brooks ran over, gun drawn, the equipment on his belt jingling. He stepped on the gun James had dropped and addressed the blonde.

"Drop it!"

The tiny blonde barely glanced at Brooks, and she didn't seem to notice the gun he held on her. Or maybe she just didn't care about it.

"Don't let him up," she said to me as she reached into her back pocket with her left hand, gun still steady on James.

"Hands!" Brooks cried.

The blonde rolled her eyes. "What am I gonna do, pull another gun?" She shook her head in annoyance and held up a pair of handcuffs. "Put those on him," she said, tossing me the cuffs.

"Wait a minute!" Brooks said. "You can't just run around pointing guns and handcuffing people."

The woman reached into her jacket, this time pulling out a piece of paper. It was one I recognized. I clamped the cuffs on James and stood.

"Actually, I can," she said. Now that James was secured, she holstered her weapon. "Bond enforcement." She smiled at Brooks and walked over to James.

"Bond enforcement?" James's date said, staring at the blonde. Then she glared at James. "You said that was taken care of!" She struggled against Amy's hold, trying to kick him. "You lied to me!"

"It's a mistake, buttercup!" James said. "Don't be mad!"

Brooks holstered his weapon and picked up the one James dropped. He ejected the magazine and the round from the chamber. Then he eyed me.

"One of yours?"

I shook my head. "No."

"Then why the tackle?"

This time I rolled my eyes. "He had a gun, Brooks. I thought it best if only one person was waving a gun around out here."

"Hey," the tiny blonde said, reaching into her jacket again. This time she brought out a pack of cigarettes and shook one out. "I wasn't *waving* anything."

I had to give her that. Her hold had been pretty steady.

She put the cigarette in her mouth and fished a lighter out of her pants pocket. Then she looked from me to James and back again.

"Well, get him up already."

I just looked at her as she lit the cigarette.

"What's he worth?" I asked.

She shrugged. "What's it to you?"

"Twenty-five percent, I'd say."

She scoffed, exhaling a puff of smoke. "You hit your head or something there, princess? He's mine. I tracked him down, I'm bringing him in."

The blonde was five-two and weighed a hundred and twenty pounds, maybe—including the gun on her belt. James was six feet tall, and weighed two hundred and eighty pounds, easy.

"You're right," I said. "He's all yours."

I nodded to Amy then stepped over James and started for the theatre.

"Brooks," I called over my shoulder. "Next time, less flirting, more surveilling."

"Always a pleasure, Zoe!" Brooks called.

"Geez," Amy said. "Can't even take you to a movie."

2

After the movie, I went home to an empty, quiet, clean house. Until shortly before leaving for California, Ellmann had been more or less living in my house. His family had been visiting from out of town, and they'd more than made themselves at home in his house.

I'd arranged for Amy's girls to scrub down both my house and Ellmann's while we were out of town. Amy is co-owner of a commercial and residential cleaning company called Clean Sweep, which I take advantage of often. It was nice to come home to a clean house. And an empty one. I don't mind having Ellmann over, but I don't always want company. Like tonight.

I shuffled through the stack of mail I'd picked up from the neighbor as I crossed into the kitchen. Most of it was bills and advertisements, none of it pressing, but I spotted the beige envelopes easily. There were four of them, the orange trim making them easy to identify. The word SCREENED stamped on the front as familiar now as the handwriting beside it.

I left the rest of the mail on the table and carried the beige envelopes to the last drawer in the kitchen counter. I stuffed them inside with the others and left, flipping out the light.

I went upstairs to my bedroom. My suitcase was sitting at the end of the bed where I'd dumped it earlier. I switched on the local news and listened while I unpacked.

The main story was about a woman named Maria Rodriguez. The broadcast flipped to a live feed of a young, male reporter standing in front of one of the more impressive buildings on Colorado State University's campus.

"Maria Rodriguez, eighteen years old, is originally from New Mexico, and hers is a tale of triumph over tragedy. Her parents emigrated here from Mexico in 1991, settling in Las Cruces and working multiple jobs to make ends meet. Maria, an only child, earned a place in an International Baccalaureate high school and then a full scholarship to Colorado State University here in Fort Collins. She's a freshman, preparing to begin her second semester studying veterinary medicine, and will no doubt make the Dean's list again this term . . ."

While the reporter talked, photos played on the screen. Some of Maria as a child with her parents, a good one of her high school graduation where she stood in a cap and gown proudly holding a diploma, then to more recent photos of her with her friends around campus.

"Maria was reported missing to campus police this morning by her roommate. She was last seen Saturday morning when she returned to her dorm room after a visit to the local emergency room. Apparently suffering from food poisoning, Maria was instructed to rest and stay well hydrated. When her roommate returned to the dorm later Saturday afternoon, Maria was gone. She left no note and was not reachable by cell phone. She has not been seen or heard from since.

"Anyone with information about this young woman is encouraged to contact either the Fort Collins Police Department or the Colorado State University Police Department at the numbers below. Reporting live from CSU in Fort Collins, Colorado, . . ."

I wondered how the joint investigation was going. The law enforcement agencies in this area are like rival high schools. There is a lot of competition, and cooperation is difficult.

I also wondered why they were investigating jointly at all. The fact that they were indicated to me the police had more information than was being shared through the media. Either

Maria was known to have gone missing somewhere other than CSU campus, or her case was connected to something else the FCPD were working on.

Of course, this was just idle speculation on my part, and my attention quickly shifted with the news, which jumped to weather. A woman came on and gave a mostly useless report from outside the studio, forecasting that the weather would be hot for the next seven days. That was about as specific as she could be, weather in Colorado being what it is.

I scooped up a pile of dirty laundry from the floor and went downstairs to the kitchen. As I dumped the clothes into the washer, I heard a car stop outside. Out of habit, I glanced at my watch. It was nearly ten thirty.

I switched off the light in the kitchen and started for the stairs when someone knocked on the front door. I altered my course, wondering who was visiting at this time of night.

Rather than use the peephole in the door, I went to the window and peeked around the blinds. Had I been smarter, I would have been terrified rather than relieved to find my late-night visitor was Mercedes Salois.

I pulled the door open, and Sadie stood staring in at me, one hand on her perfect hip, one perfectly waxed eyebrow raised.

"Hi," I said, knowing exactly why she was standing on my porch, and why she was irritated with me. "Want to come in?"

Without one word, she stepped into the house, her heels clicking sharply against the tile of the entryway. Her subtle and expensive perfume gently wafted past me.

I closed the door and turned to face her. She stood in the darkened living room with her arms crossed over her chest.

"I was planning to come see you first thing tomorrow morning," I told her.

Sadie is gorgeous. Tall and thin with blue eyes and long legs. Her blonde hair, double-Ds, and full lips are all natural. I always feel like a slob standing anywhere near her. She always looks polished and perfect; I usually don't. I smoothed an unconscious hand over my unruly hair.

Sadie is three years older than me, and we'd met eight years ago when we'd both been working as CNAs in a nursing home. Sadie had been on a nursing career path, and she'd stuck to it, now working in the emergency department of Poudre Valley Hospital. For a brief time, I'd been on the same path, but a bad relationship set me on a new one. Sadie and I had remained friends anyway.

Tonight, she wore jeans and a lacy top and carried a designer handbag on her shoulder. Her hair was curled, and she had on extra jewelry and makeup; I guessed she'd been out.

"So you haven't forgotten I need to speak with you?" Her southern drawl was heavier now than usual. It always is when she's angry.

Shortly before I'd gone out of town, I'd been treated in the emergency room for a half dozen minor injuries inflicted upon me by a mentally unstable woman with a penchant for kitchen utensils and duct tape. Sadie had taken care of me that night, telling me she needed to talk to me about something important.

After I was discharged, there was a whirlwind of legal activity between the police, the attorneys, and the courts. There just hadn't been time to get back to her before I'd gone to California. Then, once I was in California, whatever Sadie had wanted to tell me, along with all the rest of my problems, were the furthest things from my mind.

Sadie had told me it was important, but I had a hard time believing it was so important that all this anger was directed at me. So I took a wild guess.

"How'd the date go?" I moved over and flipped on the lamp near the sofa.

Even before the light came on, I saw my question hit home.

It always surprised me to hear Sadie talk about bad dates. If she were so inclined, she could have more than one date a night, every night of the week. Men practically fell all over themselves in order to ask her out. But by and large, she just wasn't interested. While Sadie had gotten in line twice when they'd handed out good looks, she'd gone back a third time for smarts. It took a very intelligent and interesting man to keep her attention. And as every woman on the planet knows, intelligent and interesting men are hard to find.

She heaved an enormous, irritated sigh and flung her arms. "He wanted me to pay for dinner! Can you *believe* that?" Her accent was really coming out now. "What kind of man asks a woman on a date, takes her to an expensive restaurant, orders the most expensive items on the menu and a *bottle of wine*, then asks *her* to get the check? And he's supposedly some kind of mechanical engineer! Engineers make money. And I know he has money somewhere—the car, the clothes, the watch. Plus, he paid for all our drinks the night I met him." She scoffed again in complete confusion.

Of course, this wasn't an issue of money for Sadie. Sadie has money, more than I probably know about. Born and raised in New Orleans, her family is in the oil business. When she was seventeen, her grandmother died and left her a small fortune. She'd taken a hefty chunk of the inheritance and bought herself a portion of the family business. And business is good.

This was an issue of pride, and, more importantly, manners, which, Sadie often tells me, Colorado men don't have.

"You met this guy in a bar?" I couldn't keep the disbelief out of my voice. Sadie has a strict policy to never date anyone she meets in a bar.

"I know," she said, flipping her hair back over her shoulder absently. "But he was so charming and funny and sweet. And persistent. And funny." She looked at me, her blue eyes pleading with me to understand.

11

And I did. Humor is probably the most important quality to Sadie. If a man could make her laugh, it would make up for almost any other shortcoming, and she'd be genuinely interested.

"I get it," I said.

She sighed, and a lot of the energy fizzled out of her.

"What a prick," I said. "You didn't pay for dinner did you?"

She scoffed. "Of course not. I gave the waiter enough cash to cover my meal, and I left. And I told the guy to lose my number."

"Good for you. Did you throw a drink in his face?"

She chuckled. "No. But I seriously thought about it. And I kind of wish I had. But I enjoy that restaurant; I wanted to be able to go back without too much embarrassment."

"Well, that makes sense."

Sadie seemed to be aware of her surroundings for the first time. She quickly took in the darkened lower levels and the light and TV on upstairs.

"Is Ellmann here?"

"No. He caught a case about nine minutes after we deplaned. He called me a while ago and said he'd probably be tied up for the next day or so. I was just unpacking."

I indicated she should follow me, and we went upstairs into my room. I switched off the TV as Sadie dropped her expensive bag to the floor and sat on the bed, propping a pillow up behind her and leaning back against the headboard.

"How was the trip?" she asked. "Any juicy wedding drama?"

I laughed as I pulled my toiletry bag out of the suitcase and went to the bathroom. "No drama," I said. "Well, not much, anyway. Hard to believe, but even Vince seemed to have a good time." I set the bag on the counter and went back into the room. "It was really nice to have some time with Ellmann away from both of our jobs."

"You guys have been through some crazy shit, that's for sure. Speaking of, any word on Humpty Dumpty?"

That was Sadie's nickname for the woman who had duct taped me to a kitchen chair and tortured me a couple weeks ago. Desirae Dillon's fractured mind had finally broken that night, and while I don't excuse what she'd done to me, or any of the other people she'd hurt and killed, I did understand her better than most. Her history hadn't been so different from mine. But her righteous anger and frustrated hurt had morphed into something dangerous and deadly.

"She's still in the psychiatric prison awaiting trial," I said. "Of course, with the evidence against her, she'll live out her days in that prison. Dani says there hasn't been any change to her mental state."

Danielle Dillon, Desirae's twin sister, had been the woman I'd actually been trying to track down when my path crossed Desirae's. That night, Danielle had saved my life, and since then, we'd sort of become friends.

"At least she's getting the help she needs now," Sadie said. "Even if it is much too late."

"Yes, indeed."

We were both quiet for a moment, and I zipped the empty suitcase and lifted it off the bed. I carried it across the room and left it by the door to be carried to the basement later. Then I sat on the end of the bed and looked at Sadie.

"What did you need to speak to me about?"

Sadie's flawless face suddenly turned serious, determined. She'd obviously reached a decision.

"I want to hire you."

I stared at Sadie. "Hire me to do what?"

"Investigate," she said. "Privately."

"I'm not a private investigator."

She waved a hand—a typical Sadie gesture. "What's the difference? You basically do the same thing."

I am a bond enforcement agent. In the movies, we're called bounty hunters. I work for bond companies tracking down people out on bail who fail to appear for their court dates. In exchange for locating the skip and dragging his butt back to the pokey, I'm paid a percentage of the bond. Bonds vary, but the recovery fees can be in the high six figures. The most I'd ever made was eight hundred, but I'd only been doing it six weeks. I aspired to break the thousand-dollar mark in the near future.

"Do you want me to find someone?" I asked. "Because that's what I do; I find people."

A lot of it is luck, even *dumb* luck, but I get results either way. And I have the record to prove it. So far, I'd never failed to track down a skip. Of course, a good part of the time that's because the skip walks right by me, but it's a record all the same.

"Not exactly," Sadie said. "Look, there's this woman I work with. Something's off with her, I know it. I need you to help me look into it."

"What do you mean 'off'?"

She shrugged. "I don't know. I just get this . . . *vibe* from her. She's . . . not right. I think she might be dangerous."

"Dangerous? What makes you think that?"

"This woman, Karen, she just moved here about six months ago. I just recently found out her neighbor went missing shortly before she moved. Karen's been posting all over Facebook about this missing woman, asking for people with information to come forward, demanding the police do something, and pointing the finger pretty strongly at the husband. Something about the whole thing is . . . weird."

"With Karen, you mean."

"Yeah. Listen, I know it sounds crazy, but I'm telling you something's going on with her."

Sadie did have a flare for the dramatic, but it was never this kind of drama. And her instincts about people were pretty good.

"Is Karen a nurse?"

"Yes."

"And where did she move from?"

"Boulder. In February."

"What else do you know about her?"

"She's about thirty, maybe thirty-five. She's not a very good nurse, and she's weird."

"Okay." I got up and went across the hall to my office. I picked up a notepad and pen and went back into the bedroom. "I need some details about this Karen person—name, address, phone number, birthday, anything you might know."

"So you'll help me?"

"I'll look into a few things. We'll go from there."

She reached down and pulled her designer bag onto her lap. She pulled something from an outer pocket and handed it to me. "A thousand to get you started. We'll square up at the end."

I took the check. "Something tells me you've hired private investigators before."

She just smiled. "You're going to love this. No one to chase, no one to tackle and haul off to jail. This will be a walk in the park."

It was such a happy thought. Could I actually be that lucky?

3

The following morning I sat in my 1978 International Scout II sipping a perfect mocha and waiting. It was an act of charity, really, that my favorite coffee shop opened at five a.m. on weekdays. And I was grateful for it.

I was dressed in my usual jeans, t-shirt, and running shoes, and I also wore a sweatshirt, because though the sun was now beginning to rise to my left and would undoubtedly bring another hot day with it, it was almost chilly.

Stakeouts are one of my least favorite pastimes. And while this wasn't, strictly speaking, a traditional stakeout, I was bored all the same. I would have preferred to sleep in, done some preliminary work on Sadie's case, and then headed into the bonds office for some new cases. But I knew I would need help with Sadie's case, so my timetable for this particular errand had been pushed up, and here I was.

I knew I'd gotten here way too early, but I found it preferable to be early. I wanted to ensure I saw the occupant of the house and his guest leave.

The neighborhood was beginning to wake now; lights were coming on in windows as people began to move through their morning routines. By six thirty, the first of them began to leave, headed for work and their desks and important meetings and whatever else they had waiting for them. By seven thirty, the kids were pouring out. Some of them walked down the street to meet the bus while others climbed into cars with their parents.

I had never had occasion to spend much time in this neighborhood near Rossborough Park. This was my second visit, and I decided it was a pleasant place. It was all single-family homes with detached garages built in the fifties, and they were all filled with hard working, middleclass families. These weren't the homes of first-time buyers, so the kids were all a little older and the cars all a little nicer.

I was playing Words With Friends, trying to decide the best place to play my *x*, when my phone rang.

"Good morning," I said.

"You're up early," Ellmann said.

"Yeah, I had a couple things I needed to do."

"Are you working a case already? You're barely unpacked."

"Something like that."

Ellmann groaned softly, but he took my response like a champ. He didn't ask any more questions; he didn't try to tell me I ought not be doing whatever I was doing, even though he knew it.

"I took some time for a shower and some clean clothes," he said. "I stopped by your place, hoping I'd find you in bed."

He said that with just the right amount of suggestion, and I wished to hell I'd been in bed for him to find.

"Boy, that sucks," I said.

"Tell me about it. I'm not sure when I'll be free again. Will you be home tonight?"

"I think so. Your case turning out to be bigger than you thought?"

"Not necessarily big, just messy." He sighed, and I easily imagined him dragging his hand back through his hair like he does when he's stressed. "Very messy. I can't make any promises about tonight. Maybe we can grab dinner."

"Sounds good to me. Now go kick some bad guy butt."

I heard him smile. "Will do. Whatever you're doing, just be careful, okay?"

"I always am."

"Uh-huh. I'll call you later. Love you."

In another point-scoring move, Ellmann simply hung up; he didn't wait for me to say anything in response. Which saved us both from an indeterminate amount of time during which a long and awkward silence would have stretched between us while I failed to give him the customary reply.

Ever since Ellmann had first said those three ridiculous little words . . . Who would have thought such small words, on their own innocuous, together would cause such enormous upheaval?

Amy had hit it on the head: I was in love with Ellmann, and it did scare the shit out of me.

My relationship history was, well, it wasn't pretty. I'd had a lot of bad experiences, and I'd made a lot of mistakes. I knew more about dysfunction and leaving than I did about happiness and longevity. Ever since Ellmann had told me he loved me, I'd wanted to run. But I found I couldn't; I couldn't leave him. I knew my only option was to stay and see this whole love thing through. I just couldn't seem to take the first step in that direction.

To his credit, I think Ellmann understood this on some level, because he hadn't pushed or pestered me. And he didn't seem hurt that I hadn't returned the sentiment. I wondered how long he'd wait.

I was saved from any further emotional exploration when finally, at nearly eight a.m., the first person left the house. At eight thirty, the homeowner himself finally emerged, climbed into his car, and motored away.

To be on the safe side, I waited a few minutes longer before I grabbed my bag and climbed out of the truck. I didn't think there was anyone else in the house; I was worried the guy might turn around and come back for something forgotten. But he never did, so I got down to business.

I'd been here once before, a couple of weeks ago, on a reconnaissance mission. I knew the layout. As I neared the house, I did a quick scan for neighbors, but I didn't see anyone. Everyone was off to work by now. I walked up the driveway, went to the fence, and let myself in like I had every right to be there.

The fenced area between the detached garage and the house had been paved and served as a sort of courtyard where the owner had patio furniture and a grill. There was also a small, built-in water fountain that trickled peacefully. It appeared the occupant spent a fair amount of time out here, and I had to admit, while unusual, the space was nice.

I pulled a pair of latex gloves out of my pocket and put them on as I crossed to the front door. Then I retrieved my keys from my pocket and selected the one I wanted. Next, I slipped off my shoe. I inserted the key into the lock, gave it a small but firm tap with the heel of my shoe, and twisted. The lock popped open.

I put my shoe back on and went inside.

I hadn't always been on the right side of the law. I'd been a bad kid, and I'd picked up a few tricks over the years. Since starting this whole bounty hunter gig, I'd been dusting off a lot of those old skills. Which just goes to show it's funny how things work out sometimes.

Lock picking was one of those skills, and bump keys one of the tricks. Bump keys are extremely easy to make, and I always carry at least one. They open most locks and leave the least evidence. I also carry lock pick tools, which I know well how to use, but those always leave marks that betray their use.

Not that I planned on today's activities being investigated by police, but you never knew what might happen or when it would be most inconvenient to leave evidence behind.

19

Experience had taught me that when it came to extralegal activities, it was best to plan ahead, and plan for the worst.

The house was cool and dark, the windows covered against the sun that would soon beat against them. The place was a two-story affair, with a living room, kitchen and dining room, master bed and bath on the main level. Upstairs there was another bathroom, a guestroom, and an office.

The whole house was tidy, but lived in, and pleasantly decorated. It was nothing showy or overwhelming, but rather simple colors, matching or complimenting furniture sets, and nice, subtle decorative items like vases, pictures, and mirrors, done by someone who took time enough to care. Actually, I liked most of the furniture.

I paused in the living room and listened hard. There were no sounds in the house, and I knew I was alone.

The first time I'd been in this house, I'd done a thorough search of the place. I hadn't been looking for anything specific anywhere apart from the bedroom, but I'd found nothing of interest. Everything was fairly straightforward and expected.

Today, I knew right where I was going. I cut through the living room and made my way down the hall to the right. The door at the end was open, and I went into the master bedroom.

This room was as neat and well decorated as the rest of the house, and the faint scent of cologne clung to the air. The furniture was a matching set that had caught my eye immediately. I wondered again where it had been purchased. Maybe I'd ask someday.

For now, I turned my attention to the task at hand. The first time I'd been here, I'd been scoping things out, checking out angles and lines of sight, and comparing the various objects around the room to those contained within a box that Dean Amerson had entrusted to me a short time ago. Now, I reached into my bag and retrieved a screwdriver.

Electronics are smaller and more sophisticated than ever. They make cameras so tiny they fit in everything—teddy bears, alarm clocks, water bottles, smoke detectors, iPod docks, Kleenex box covers, picture frames, lamps, air fresheners you plug into the wall. Some of these devices are wireless, and automatically relay live feeds or download files to specified destinations via wireless internet. Others have DVRs that simply record everything for playback and review later.

From being in this room previously and reviewing the contents of Amerson's box, I knew most of what he had given me would not work here. Fortunately, there was a smoke detector in every room. The smoke detector in this room wouldn't give me the best angle, but I was sure it would serve my needs.

I kicked off my shoes and climbed onto the bed, which someone had taken the time to make. I used the screwdriver to remove the existing smoke detector. Then I pulled a second smoke detector from my bag and worked to install it.

Of course, this wasn't any regular smoke detector. This one contained a night-vision camera with a heat-activated sensor. This particular camera operated a DVR, which I'd outfitted with a 32GB SD card, which I hoped proved to be far more than I'd need.

I just had to cross my fingers that I'd get lucky on the first try.

When the camera was in place, I cleaned up and made my way back out of the house.

4

I drove to the gym and put in my time on the treadmill. I hate running, and I'm not good at running, but this fugitive apprehension thing requires a lot of running. More than one of my fugitives had escaped because they could outrun me. So it sort of became an adapt-or-die kind of situation. I'd started a running program.

Sam, my physical therapist and the Ironman triathlon winner, had recommended a program called "Couch to 5K." I'd been doing it for the last two and a half weeks and could already tell it was working. As an added bonus, my jeans fit better.

After a shower, I headed to Sideline Investigations and Bail Bonds. The thing about the fugitive apprehension business is I don't make any money unless I bring in FTAs. There is no paid time off, no sick days, no vacation time, no retirement package. I'd been on vacation for a week. My bank account wasn't empty, but I wanted to get back to work all the same.

Sideline Investigations originally began as a private investigating agency run by former cop Wesley Meeker and former investment banker Mickey Sands. Both men were officially retired for about ten minutes before they were bored to tears. Meeker started snooping into things for friends here and there, just to keep busy. Sands jumped at the opportunity to do something and proposed a joint venture with Meeker, establishing an official PI office.

Both men were exceptionally good at what they did. The office grew quickly, and they had to hire other investigators, first as part time and then full time, to help handle the growing caseload.

Sands was the one to suggest branching out into bail bonds. Meeker objected on principle. It was hard for the lifelong cop to wrap his head around helping criminals get out of jail. Bail bondsmen weren't as low as lawyers, but they weren't much better, or so Meeker believed.

Ultimately, Sands spearheads the bail bonds side of the business, while Meeker manages the investigations side. They have two full-time bondsmen, a couple of part-time guys, and a few freelancers, like me, who pick up cases here and there.

A couple of months ago, after I'd completed the weekend fugitive apprehension training course the state offers, I'd taken my certificate and gone around to several of the bail bonds companies in town. Most weren't willing to take a shot on a girl with no experience and very little training. However, then manager of Sideline, Dean Amerson, had been willing to do so, for reasons that still weren't clear to me. He'd paired me up with longtime Sideline bounty hunter and old school cop and PI Roger Blucher. Blue, as everyone called him, let me tag along for almost two weeks, passing on to me some of the tricks of the trade, all of which have proved invaluable since.

Sadly, Amerson no longer managed Sideline. He'd fallen head over heels for Ellmann's sister Natalie, of all people, and had picked up and moved to California, where she lives. Amerson, former Navy S.E.A.L., has incredibly marketable skills. He hadn't needed his job at Sideline, and had multiple job offers before his plane ever touched down in California. I thought it would be only a short time before it became clear just how badly Sideline needed *him*.

Amerson and I had become some kind of friends. He'd passed his box of gizmos on to me when he left, saying he hoped they might help me stay out trouble, since he wouldn't be around to watch my back like Ellmann had asked him to. I'd asked him if that was his way of saying he'd miss me. He hadn't answered, but I believed it was.

I parked in the main lot and used the front door. There was a back entrance, and after hours that was the only way to access the building, but during business hours, I typically didn't bother.

As usual, the lobby had people waiting, sipping water and coffee and flipping through magazines. Some looked bored, some looked worried and anxious, and some looked excited. People had all sorts of reasons for seeking the services of a private investigator, and Sideline had someone to help with any kind of case.

I smiled at the receptionist, who was busy with a phone call and working at the computer. She smiled back as I passed, and I made my way to Amerson's former office, located at the back of the lobby. The door was simply marked OFFICE MANAGER; Amerson's name had never been on it, but it was obvious he was gone.

The large window overlooking the lobby was closed, the blinds drawn. Amerson had always left this window open; he'd wanted to have a visual on the front door and those coming and going. I had not seen the window open once since Amerson had left.

The door was shut, but the light was on inside, so I knew the office was occupied. I knocked sharply and resisted the urge to just walk in.

A very long minute later, just as I was about to knock again, the door finally opened. Amerson's successor, Cal Stevens, stared out at me.

"Zoe," he said. I couldn't help but note his tone wasn't entirely friendly.

Stevens was just over six feet tall, thin, closer to forty than thirty, and had brown hair. I thought he looked a lot like Jack Lord, right down to the swept- back hairstyle and teeth.

"Cal. Got a minute?"

Stevens glanced back at his desk, as if trying to decide if whatever he'd been working on could wait for my interruption.

"Uh, sure," he said, finally stepping back. "I didn't realize you were back in town."

I hadn't given Stevens the particulars of my travel itinerary, as he'd requested, because I didn't think it was any of his business. Technically, I wasn't an employee; it made no difference to him where I was or when. Stevens hadn't taken my refusal well. And apparently he was still a little sore about it.

"Got back yesterday," I said, walking into the office.

Stevens went behind his desk and sat. I took a chair opposite him. He leaned back and folded his hands in his lap, eyeing me across the desk. I draped one leg over the other and returned his stare. For a moment I had the distinct feeling we were playing chicken. Whoever blinked first was the loser.

After only a couple of seconds, the phone rang, abruptly ending our standoff. Stevens reached for it.

"Yeah," he said by way of greeting. He listened for a beat then said, "Right. I'll call you later." He hung up. "So, Zoe, what can I do for you?"

I resisted the urge to smirk. Stevens was a prick. He took pleasure in asserting even small measures of authority and dominance of people, especially the people who worked in or for this office. He knew perfectly well why I would have come to see him, but he wanted to hear me ask.

I'd met Cal Stevens a week before I'd left for vacation. He'd set off about a dozen red flags for me from the start, and I'd taken an instant dislike to him. I'd hoped the stressful events that had occurred just before Amerson's departure and Stevens's arrival were coloring my judgment and that a week's vacation spent on the beach would improve my outlook.

Clearly, no such transformation had occurred. If it was possible, I thought I liked Stevens even *less* now.

"I'm selling Girl Scout cookies. Wondered if you'd buy a box or two."

Stevens sat forward and laid his clasped hands on the desk.

"You know, Amerson told me about you before he left. He said you were a hell of an investigator, even if your methods are a bit unusual. He said the best thing I could do for both of us would be to more or less stay out of your way and let you do whatever it is you do. He said trying to police you would only give me a headache."

I couldn't help but grin. Amerson was a smart guy. I missed him. I knew he was ridiculously happy with Natalie, so I was happy for him. But boy, Natalie's visit had messed up a lot of things. I really hoped she didn't visit again any time soon.

"I don't know what kind of an operation Amerson was running here," Stevens went on, "but I run a tight ship. I know what all my people are doing, and when they're doing it. I don't let them run around causing trouble all over town."

I suddenly had the impression Stevens had been doing some research into yours truly. The faint beginnings of unease blossomed in the pit of my stomach, and I wondered just how much digging he'd done and what exactly he'd learned. And I couldn't help but wonder what he planned to do with that information.

I bit back the response that immediately formed on my tongue. I'm not one to tolerate being browbeaten, but I didn't think this was the time or place for a confrontation. I took a deep breath and spoke with forced patience.

"Have you got any cases, Cal?"

He reached over to one of two upright wire filing racks that now sat on the far corner of the desk and fingered through a thick collection of files. Amerson had always kept his desk neat and tidy. Probably a career in the military had done that to him, and I could only assume he also folded his underwear and matched his socks. Stevens did not labor under any such habits. His desk was a disarray of reports, files, printouts, phone messages, and the newspaper. And I'd never seen so many FTA files pending. Why weren't these in the hands of the recovery agents? Surely everyone hadn't been on vacation this week.

He found the file he wanted and handed it to me. I accepted it and opened it.

"This guy's a murder suspect," I said, glancing first at the list of charges.

"He's also FTA."

What would Wesley Meeker have said if he'd known someone from his agency had bonded out a man charged with murder? That was one charge Sideline bondsmen more or less stayed away from. Even if they hadn't been officially mandated to do so, they understood well how Meeker would feel about such a thing. The fact that these guys come up for bail at all is a testament to how overcrowded the jail is.

"I don't get mixed up with murder suspects." I put the file back on the desk. "I've been pretty clear about that."

This wasn't me on a moral high horse. This was simple self-preservation. I make it a practice to keep well away from known murder suspects. I sometimes get mixed up with them unknowingly, but I strive not to walk into those kinds of messes intentionally. And when you deal with murder suspects, that's all that you get: a mess.

Stevens smirked. "You get a little more than mixed up with murder suspects, don't you?"

The cold fingers of unease whispered along my spine, and I wondered again just how much Stevens had dug up about my past.

"I learn from past mistakes. What else you got?"

He tapped the file. "As far as you're concerned, this is the only available case. Once you catch him, I'll give you your next assignment."

"One assignment at a time? That's how you're doing things?"

That explained the files. And it also spelled bad news for Stevens. I hadn't been a bounty hunter very long, but I knew the guys around here. No one worked just one case at a time; it wasn't an efficient use of time. When every FTA found meant money in the bank, it literally paid to be efficient.

"That's how every skip gets caught," Stevens said, tapping the top of the desk with his index finger for emphasis, "and no cases fall between the cracks."

"Amerson used to—"

"In case you haven't noticed," he cut in, his tone sharp, "Amerson isn't here anymore. He chased some skirt to Arizona or something. Thinks he's in love. I'm running things now. And my way works."

I stood. Wisdom told me to keep quiet, but I just couldn't do it. I didn't like his tone.

"Oh, we've all noticed Amerson isn't here anymore. How long before Wes and Mickey notice, too?"

I pointed to the enormous collection of files as I turned for the door. He winced slightly, and I knew I'd hit a nerve.

"You're not worth the trouble, Grey!" he shouted after me, drawing the attention of most the people waiting in the lobby.

I just smiled and kept walking.

5

Sideline Investigations and Bail Bonds isn't the only game in town. Since establishing myself with them and beginning to earn some kind of reputation in the bonds community, I had twice freelanced for other agencies. It also helped that Blue had been willing to vouch for me.

Whether by design or coincidence, a great many of the bail bonds outfits in Fort Collins, Colorado, are located very near the detention center. Sideline included. After exiting the building, I slid my sunglasses on and cut through the parking lot for the sidewalk, angling east.

Front Range Bail Bonds was about three blocks from Sideline, and was one I'd worked with before. They were a smaller agency dealing primarily in lower end bonds. And the husband-wife owners did most of their own recoveries. The wife, Patty, could find anyone, and the husband, Tim, could talk anyone in. They had little use for freelancers. But they were the nearest, so I dropped in.

Patty was at the front desk and smiled when I pushed through the door. She invited me to sit and called Tim out of the file room in the back. We chatted for several minutes before I turned the conversation to business. The long shot proved bust. They didn't have anything they could give me. After chatting a while longer, I left, and they both promised to keep me in mind if they had anything they couldn't handle on their own.

My next stop was Skip's Bail Bonds. I had no idea what Skip's real name was, or how he'd gotten the nickname Skip, but I'd always enjoyed the irony in him calling his business Skip's Bail Bonds. Skip worked out of a storefront between a women's workout club and a Subway. There was always the faint scent of yeast in the air and the distant thump of high-tempo music in the office.

I arrived to find Skip's daughter-in-law, Jenny, working alone in the office. A radio tuned to a local Top 40 station playing on the front desk almost covered the music from the workout place next door.

"Hey, Zoe. What's shaking?"

Jenny was a smart, no-nonsense kind of girl, and I'd liked her from the moment I'd met her. She was pretty in a plain, unconventional way, and she carried a concealed gun at all times, which a person either found hot or terrifying. She was working at one of six five-drawer filing cabinets along the back wall.

"Nothing much," I said. "Wondered if you had any cases I could take."

"Not at the moment, but I probably will this afternoon." She slid the last file into place, shut the drawer, and came over to the desk. "I've got four guys scheduled for court today. Odds are, at least one will no show. They're mostly small bonds, though."

"That's okay. I just need something."

"Sure. I'll call you if anything comes up. Jake's out of town picking up a guy in Texas, and Skip's tracking some woman who fled the area. He thinks she's in Denver, but he's not positive. They'll both be back in a few days, at most, but I like to know where my fugitives are as soon as possible. I'll be happy to have you track them down and bring them in."

Jake was Jenny's husband and Skip's oldest son. I'd met him once and known immediately he was in the right business. He was one scary-looking dude. He was about the size of a Mack truck and wore a lot of black. Probably the guys he went after just wet their pants and fell to their knees with their wrists together. I certainly did not have that effect on my fugitives.

"Sounds great," I said. "Thanks."

"Sideline not got enough work for you these days?"

The bonds community was a fairly small one, all things considered. The news of Amerson's leaving and of Cal Stevens replacing him would have been common knowledge by now. But I didn't know what else might be going around about Sideline these days. I didn't want to start any new rumors.

I shrugged my shoulders lightly and said, "I've been out of town for a week. I just got back yesterday. They just don't have anything to pick up right now."

She raised an eyebrow. "They don't? I find that hard to believe."

"Why's that?"

"My sister, Carrie, you know she works at the courthouse."

I didn't know that.

"People fail to appear in court every day," she went on. "It's the nature of this business. Anyway, you know she's dating Felix Allen."

I didn't know that either.

But I did know who Felix Allen was. He was one of Sideline's two full-time recovery agents. He'd been doing the job a while, and he was good at it. And he made good money doing it, because he tracked the high-dollar bonds.

"Felix has had quite a bit to say about that new guy, Cal Stevens."

"Oh, really?" I said. I tried to keep my tone neutral, noncommittal.

"Oh, yeah, him and all the other guys, apparently. No one's really happy with Cal's one-at-a-time policy. At least that's what Carrie's been telling me. But I have to wonder, if everyone is just tracking one guy, there must be cases left over that you could take."

See what I mean about Jenny? Smart. And apparently well informed.

"That's a good point," I said lightly. "I'll have to ask Cal about that when I check in with him again."

"You know, he's going to need to be careful."

Yes, I did know. But I said, "Why's that?"

"Well, none of those guys have contracts; they're all freelance. They just stayed with Sideline for all those years because of Dean Amerson. Dean made sure there was enough work for those who wanted it; he got the higher bonds to the guys who'd been there longer. They respected him. They probably have some loyalty to Sideline itself, but with Amerson gone and Stevens's new policy in place, they won't have much incentive to stay. And there is plenty of work for skilled guys like that anywhere they want to go."

Which Mickey Sands and Wesley Meeker had to know, too.

"We'll have to see how things work out," I said, moving toward the door. "I think there are more changes to come for Sideline."

Jenny scoffed. "No doubt."

"Let me know about those FTAs, okay?"

"Will do. Take it easy."

I left with Jenny's thoughts bouncing around my head and wondering how much longer Stevens would last.

6

I returned to the parking lot and climbed into my Scout. The Scout is a thing of beauty. It's hunter green with an Army tan interior. The original hardtop is white, though I had replaced it with a sailcloth soft top for summer. That was one of the only modifications; almost every other detail was original. And everything was in pristine condition.

With the sides rolled up, I listened to the radio as I cruised through town, the wind tugging at my hair and the sun threatening my skin. My gut told me my days at Sideline were over. At least, for the time being. And as Sideline had been my primary gig the last couple months, that left me without an income.

Whatever I might pick up from Front Range Bail Bonds or Skip's would be infrequent and nominal. I needed to make the rounds again and get set up with some other agencies in town. It should be easier now that I had some working references and some experience to go with my state certificate, but it would still take time and legwork.

I needed to return home to put some things together first. While I was there, I would start looking into Karen Brickle. Sadie had given me some basic information she'd been able to obtain through coworkers and from Facebook. I had no idea what I might find, but Sadie was paying me, and since I had no other paying jobs at the moment, I thought it best to turn my attention to the case, if indeed it developed into a case at all.

I live in a rented three-bedroom, three-bath house located in a relatively quiet neighborhood just north of Front Range Community College. The neighborhood is mostly first-time homebuyers and couples just starting families. There are lots of kids that play in front yards and the street of the cul-de-sac I live on. I'd only moved in about two months ago, but I was getting settled, and I liked the neighborhood.

When I returned home this morning, I found a kid-sized volleyball net had been erected in my next-door neighbor's yard, and several parents were out supervising a sizeable collection of swimsuit-clad children still too young to attend school. In the next yard over, a couple of sprinklers and a kiddie pool had been set up.

I also found a sleek, black Ford F-250 parked in my driveway.

I parked and waved to the neighbors as I went up the driveway. The tiny blonde woman from the movie theatre was sitting on the lowered tailgate, smoking a cigarette and swinging her legs. She was wearing jeans, black biker boots, a tank top, and a leather biker vest. Her blonde hair was pulled back in a ponytail, and in the harsh light of morning, she looked closer to sixty-five, but between the smoking and the suntan, her wrinkled, weathered skin would not be an accurate measure of her age.

"Didn't think you'd be home so soon, princess."

Being that she and I were in the same business, I didn't find it surprising that she'd been able to find my address, though I knew it would have taken her some work to do so. What I found surprising was that she would bother. I was very curious to know what she wanted.

She lit a fresh cigarette with the stub of the last and tossed the butt onto the driveway with a dozen others.

"For my neighbors' sakes, it's a good thing I am. If I was any later, they'd all have lung cancer from the secondhand smoke."

She exhaled a very deliberate plume of smoke as she eyed me seriously.

"You're fucking hilarious," she said.

"Oh, thanks, but you're a great audience."

"All right, all right," she said on a stream of smoke.

"What are you doing here?"

"Not going to ask how I found you?"

"I figured that part out already. What I don't know is *why*."

"Smart, huh, princess? I always hated the smart ones."

"And yet here you are."

"That idiot cop told me he arrested you."

I waved a hand in a futile effort to clear away some of the smoke and took a step back.

"Highlight of his career, I'm sure. If you don't want to tell me why you're here, you could tell me your name. I can figure out the rest from there."

"That cop, he said you had a mouth on you."

I could only imagine what else Brooks had told this woman about me, or what she'd been able to pry out of him.

"I certainly hope you have the sense to check your facts. You know how cops are about telling the truth."

She actually chuckled at that. "Personally, I like a little sass. Don't got much use for a woman as quiet as a doormat."

"And what use have you imagined for me?"

She exhaled a huge cloud of smoke, appraising me through the haze.

"Turns out, I got a job opening."

"Is that so?"

"What I hear, you got something going with Sideline. But I'd be seriously surprised if you were happy working for Cal Stevens."

35

Whatever else this woman was or wasn't, she had a remarkable acuity for sizing people up.

"I thought you might want a change."

"Does your job come with a sign on bonus or paid vacation or something?"

She smirked. "I can offer you your choice of bonds, no doubt bigger fees than you're making at the bottom of the totem pole over at Sideline."

"Let me see what you've got."

Her eyes flashed briefly then she pulled a business card out of her pocket and handed it to me. "Come on down to the office. You can look through the files, take whichever you want."

My turn to smirk. "You came here to hire me. On the off chance I agreed, you'd want to put the files in my hands before I had time to change my mind. So you've got them with you. Let me see them."

She sat smoking, staring at me for a long moment while she reached some internal decision.

"You know, that idiot cop sold you short. He didn't mention anything about your smarts."

"I'm shocked and devastated."

"I'm sure."

She put the cigarette between her lips and hoped off the tailgate. She went to the driver's side and leaned in the truck with the help of the running board, coming out with a stack of files. She hefted them over and set them on the tailgate with a *thud*.

There was a concerning number of files. I didn't believe for a minute this woman ran a half-assed operation. So I couldn't immediately explain why she had so many current FTAs. The stack of files did explain why she'd made the effort to track me down, however.

I moved over to the tailgate and caught a face full of smoke. I coughed and waved a hand to dissipate the cloud.

"Either put that out or go stand over there," I said, pointing to the street downwind of me.

She mumbled something under her breath as she moved away. All I made out was the word "princess."

I opened one file after another, glancing at each one briefly, and arranging them into three stacks. When I was finished, I picked up one of the stacks.

"I'll take these three for now," I said. "All these deadlines are four to seven days away; they're the most pressing."

"What's with the other stacks?" she asked, taking a few steps forward.

I put my hand on the larger of the two remaining piles. "This one is cases I'll take, when I'm through with these, if they're still available. The deadlines are more than a week away." I touched the other stack, which held three files. "You'll need to find someone else to work these. I don't track murder suspects, or people with past murder charges."

She blew out a stream of smoke. "You really are a princess, aren't you?"

I pulled her card out of my pocket and read her name for the first time. Mary Margaret Lewicki.

"You go by Mary Margaret or something else?" I asked, indicating the card before I tucked it back into my pocket.

"Marge."

"Okay, Marge. I see capture paperwork, current photos, and notes on the initial inquiries you've made in all the files. I'll call you when I've got body receipts. Oh, and I want fifteen percent on all three of these." I patted the files I held.

Marge scoffed. "You're dreaming, princess. Standard ten percent."

I smiled as I took a few backward steps up the driveway. "If you were in a position to negotiate, you wouldn't be waiting for me to come home. I'll be in touch. Be sure to pick up your butts before you go."

I went inside, leaving her standing in the driveway.

7

I fixed a cup of coffee and went upstairs to my office. Before I did anything else, I ran a search of Mary Margaret Lewicki. I quickly found that she was who she claimed to be. She'd been in the bail bonds business for close to forty years, and she and a man named Rick, who I learned was her husband, had owned Sure Bonds for more than thirty years. They'd operated out of the same storefront on Riverside Avenue since they opened, though they did not own the building.

A search of public records told me that Marge was fifty-five, she and Rick had been married close to twenty-five years, and that Rick had passed away about two years ago. According to his obituary, he'd died of lung cancer. (I'm sure you're as shocked as I was.)

I hadn't been in the bail bonds business long, but I hadn't heard anything about her or Sure Bonds, which led me to believe hers was a small operation. Probably because it was near the end of the alphabet, it hadn't been one I'd tried before I got on at Sideline. I made a mental note to ask around and see what people knew of her.

In the meantime, I turned my attention to other things. Probably out of habit, I opened the first of the new files.

Ruben Medera, twenty-six, was charged with assault with a deadly weapon and worth more than five grand when I dragged him back to the pokey, the second-largest fee in the bunch. But after three minutes on the computer, I knew three things. One, finding Medera would be more difficult than I would like. Two, once found, capturing Medera would be more difficult that I would like. And three, if I managed to both find and capture Medera, I would have earned every cent of the five grand.

Medera was an ex-Marine who had been deployed overseas at least twice, according to his Facebook page. There were no notes in Marge's file about why he'd beaten the snot out of some guy downtown, ultimately pulling a knife, but war messed people up, and none of those who participate in it ever came back the same. Marge did note this was Medera's first arrest, however.

She'd accepted the deed to his condo as collateral, and the address was local. There were also local addresses for his mother and sister, and Marge also noted his three brothers were all Marines on active duty.

Of course, I would go to Medera's place and look around, but he wouldn't be there. Even in this urban setting, Medera wouldn't be found unless he wanted to be. I would have to hope to get lucky and happen across him somewhere. Then I'd have to hope he was either injured or willing to come with me, because he could probably kill me in a fight.

I probably should have thought twice about taking Medera's file, but I kind of enjoy the challenge of a hunt like this one, and I'd seen dollar signs when I'd looked at the bond agreement. Strange, because I'm typically not motivated by money, but I guess I'd been experiencing a moment of unease at the uncertainty of future income as the result of my now questionable status at Sideline and the lack of ready work with my other connections.

Robert Hapner, forty-two, had a slew of drug-related charges. His address put him smack in the middle of Timber Ridge Mobile Home Park. According to the paperwork, this was the third time Marge had bonded Hapner out.

The bond was fifty thousand, and Marge had written it accepting a classic 1931 Studebaker 54 R Roadster as collateral. I immediately wondered how a guy with a piece of vintage automotive history, perfectly and meticulously restored and maintained, according to Marge's notes, also lived in a trailer park. Or why a guy would put a car like that up as collateral against a bond when he usually missed his court dates. But then, that just went to show these criminal types don't have real sound thinking.

I logged into Sideline's database and punched in Hapner's name. I wasn't surprised to find they had a record on him, too. Hapner had used Sideline to bond himself out of jail no fewer than four times in the last eight years. A real stand-up guy, this Hapner.

It looked like he was routinely arrested for drug-related offenses, primarily possession with the intent to distribute, with an assault charge thrown in every now and again just for fun. I double checked the notes Marge had already made regarding Hapner's known addresses and associates, and I made a few others based on info I was able to pull from Sideline's database. Hapner didn't seem like he'd be hard to find, but according to everything I was reading, Hapner was hard to bring in; he never came in quietly.

I started to regret accepting the case. Even at fifteen percent.

The last of the files belonged to Jamie Vollmer, thirty-four, charged with solicitation and possession, like all her previous arrests, of which there were many. As far as I could tell she didn't have a permanent address, and her list of known associates turned up basically bupkiss.

Marge had written the bond accepting a 2008 Kia Rio as collateral, a car worth little more than the standard *recovery fee*, certainly not the entirety of the bond. What the hell had Marge been thinking? She couldn't have been thinking this woman always showed up for court, because even according to the Sure Bonds history, she did not. And Sideline's database confirmed this.

I had absolutely no interest in writing bonds myself, mostly because I thought the idea of letting known criminals back out onto the streets was stupid, but also because the entire process gave me a headache. So I couldn't claim to understand the finer aspects of that part of the business, but I couldn't understand accepting a car as a collateral. Yes, cars are easier to liquidate, but they are infinitely harder to *locate*, and you can't sell a car you can't find. At least with a house, or some other kind of real estate, you know exactly where it is. So if you can't find your fugitive, you can at least locate your collateral.

Anyway, I checked DMV records on the car and found it registered to Jamie Vollmer. I made note of the address they had on file, which differed from the one on her Sure Bonds agreement, which differed from the address listed in her arrest report, which differed from every previous address in either Sure Bonds or Sideline's records. When I checked property records, I found none in Vollmer's name.

The address listed with the DMV belonged to someone named Janet Taylor, purchased five years ago. The address on Vollmer's Sure Bonds agreement was an apartment complex, and according to Marge's notes, a call to the property management there found Vollmer was no longer a tenant and that she had left no forwarding address. The address on her arrest report was owned by William Tolliver, and a bit of searching turned up his name in association with one of her previous arrests; Tolliver was a john.

I added some notes from the Sideline database, as Vollmer had also used their services in the past, then I closed the file. Vollmer would be a pain in the ass to track down, and the deadline was four days away. I didn't have high hopes. Hell, I might have stood a better chance of tracking down the Marine.

I put the FTA files aside for the moment and turned my attention to Karen Brickle. I started with a public records search, but came up blank. Karen Brickle did not own any property or have any birth, marriage, divorce, or death certificates on file in Larimer County.

I checked the Colorado Department of Regulatory Agencies and found Karen Brickle did indeed have a current nursing license, and that she had no discipline against that license. It had originally been issued in Ohio in 2007, and was also valid in Washington State and Utah.

I Googled her name, but nothing really interesting came up, just lots of social media and people-finder hits. When I narrowed the search to Colorado, I got a hit for the *Boulder Daily Camera*. The article, published in February, detailed the disappearance of a high school teacher named Theresa Walling. Walling, a mother of two adult sons, reportedly went missing shortly after a public argument with her ex-husband, Frank Walling. According to a police spokesman, Frank Walling was a person of interest in Theresa's disappearance and had been cooperative with police. Karen was mentioned because she had organized a search party, and volunteers were asked to coordinate with her.

I searched for more articles on Theresa Walling's case, but the news had fizzled out quickly, and the single follow-up article I found just rehashed the details of the first. I Googled Theresa Walling's name, but didn't get much more information. So I turned to public records.

Theresa had no birth certificate on file in Boulder County, but she had a marriage license, a divorce degree, and she was listed on her sons' birth certificates. She also owned a house in Boulder. It was the same one she'd owned since 1995, so I assumed she'd gotten it in the divorce.

In the spirit of thoroughness, I also searched records for the husband, Frank. His name was listed on the same marriage certificate, divorce degree, and on the birth certificates of the same two boys. He had a more recent marriage certificate, and he owned a second house, also in Boulder. He'd purchased the house the same year of the divorce, 2008, and remarried in 2012.

I wasn't sure what that got me, so I returned to Karen. I ran her name through a credit check and discovered the first obvious sign something was amiss. Her credit history only went back seven years. According to Sadie, Karen was in her thirties.

I turned to Facebook. It became immediately clear Karen spent a great deal of time on Facebook, and that her privacy settings were rather liberal. According to her profile, she was thirty-five years old. Which meant "Karen Brickle" was not her real name. No one's credit history begins at the age of twenty-eight.

Returning to the credit report, I also found there were only addresses for Karen in Colorado. There was nothing in Washington State, where she currently held an active nursing license, or Ohio, where her nursing license had been issued.

There weren't a lot of reasons to change your name. And I really couldn't think of any that were innocent. Maybe Sadie was on to something with this Karen Brickle thing.

I returned to Facebook and scanned Karen's page. Most of her attention lately had been focused on Theresa Walling's disappearance and the incompetence of the Boulder Police Department. From a few of her posts, I pieced together that Karen and Theresa had been neighbors. Karen was certainly passionate and outspoken, and she was fixated on the idea that Frank Walling, Theresa's husband, had something to do with Theresa's disappearance. Almost too fixated.

My gut told me Sadie's sense that something was off about Karen was right. I could only hope and pray that whatever this thing with Karen turned out to be, it had nothing to do with Theresa Walling's strange and unexplained disappearance, because that was the kind of thing that could get messy in a hurry. After the trouble I'd found myself in the last few weeks, I was keen to avoid all things messy.

8

My driveway was clear of tiny blonde women, Ford pickup trucks, and cigarette butts when I emerged from the house. The kids were taking a snack break next door; they were all sitting in the yard, eating popsicles. Well, mostly eating. They were also wearing some.

I climbed into the Scout and motored off. As I drove, I dialed Sadie. She answered on the second ring.

"Hey, girl. Dig up any skeletons yet?"

"Not exactly," I said. "Know what Karen's work schedule is like for the next few days?"

"No. But I can find out. I'll call you back."

I made a right onto Shields Street and cruised north. Ruben Medera's condo was located in nice area near Shields and Prospect Road. I turned into the lot and searched for the number I needed, noticing parking places weren't marked.

I found Medera's place and eyeballed the cars in the lot. I had no way of knowing which cars belonged to which units, so I wrote down information for the six vehicles parked closest to Medera's door, knowing it was a long shot.

No one answered when I rang the bell, and I couldn't see any movement through the curtains on the window. I knew he wasn't in there, but there was a chance something in there might give me some kind of clue as to where he was.

The capture paperwork I had in my bag authorized me to enter and search the condo. I could have scared up some kind of property manager with a master key, but to save time I just used my bump key and let myself in.

The place was a bachelor pad, but it was tidy. The minimal furniture was new, and neither expensive nor cheap. There was no overall decorative theme and few personal affects. I guessed Medera had moved in here recently.

It was a two-story, two-bed, two-bath setup, with the living spaces downstairs and the bedrooms upstairs. Only the master suite looked occupied. The bed was made, and the floor was clean. Dirty clothes were in the hamper, shoes lined up neatly on the closet floor, and towels hung up in the bathroom.

Not only had Medera likely moved in recently, he just didn't have a lot of stuff. What he owned filled less than half the closet and only two drawers in the dresser, though it could have all easily fit into one. The same was true of the bedside table and the medicine cabinet and drawers in the bathroom.

From my search I also learned Medera had a girlfriend. A third dresser drawer held a few of her clothing items; one bedside table was hers, as was a drawer in the vanity, where she had a bit of makeup, a few hair items, and a couple pieces of jewelry. There were two toothbrushes on the sink and girly stuff in the shower.

Whoever Medera's girlfriend was, I could find no picture, no name, nothing to identify her.

There was a small desk in the second bedroom, but I'd noticed a laptop computer on the bar in the kitchen. There were very few things in the desk drawers, and absolutely nothing of help. Medera obviously didn't use this room or the desk.

Back in the kitchen, I tried the laptop but it was password protected. Which was a real shame, because I had found absolutely no personal papers in the house, so I guessed all of his bills were delivered electronically. A phone bill or a credit card statement would have been extremely useful. Medera didn't even have a landline phone so I couldn't check caller ID.

A quick peek in the fridge and cupboards told me Medera hadn't spent a lot of time here lately. I could only guess when he might be coming back.

I rummaged in the drawers for a spare key. Most of them were empty, and none of them held any keys. So I locked up and headed for his mother's house.

I didn't think he would be there, either, but in my experience mothers typically knew where their children were, even when, or perhaps *especially when*, they were in trouble. I could believe Medera to be an exception to this rule, though. He came from a military family and was now in some kind of trouble. He may very well stay away from his family, either because he'd be ashamed or because he'd want to keep his trouble away from them.

Lupe Medera lived near Poudre Valley Hospital. When I arrived, she was outside, dressed in shorts, tank top, and wide-brimmed visor, mowing the lawn. She was five feet tall and had classic Spanish features. Her thick, black hair was tied up on top of her head, and she wore no makeup. She was in her fifties, but she didn't look it, and she was absolutely beautiful.

She stopped the mower and smiled as I walked up, her face warm and inviting.

"Good afternoon!" she said in Spanish-accented English. "It's beautiful, no?"

I couldn't help but smile and nod my head in agreement. "It is."

She removed the bag from the mower and dragged it over to a waiting trashcan. It was overflowing with clippings and too heavy for her to carry. She struggled to lift it.

I helped her lift and dump the bag. She smiled at me.

"Thank you."

"Sure," I said.

47

I pulled one of my generic fugitive apprehension cards out of my pocket and handed it to her.

She set the bag on the lawn near her feet and accepted the card.

"You must be here about my son."

"Yes, ma'am. I am."

She smiled again and retrieved the bag, carrying it over to the mower.

"Do you know I have four sons? And one daughter." She laughed. "We were just sure she would be a boy, too. We had a boy name all ready for her. Imagine our surprise."

I smiled. "And your delight, surely."

I liked Lupe Medera, and I sincerely hoped her son didn't break my heart.

She beamed at me and nodded. "We were very excited, yes." She said something in Spanish and shook her head. "My goodness, we spoiled her. So did her brothers."

"She's very lucky."

"She is, yes." She reattached the bag to the mower and stood. "All of my sons are Marines. Their father was a Marine."

"It's a lot of work to raise five children," I said. "And it must be hard having four sons in the Marine Corps."

"I've been blessed. All four of my sons have come home, and they're healthy."

"That is a blessing. I'm glad to hear it."

"Thank you. All five of my children are good people."

"I don't doubt it. But even good people get into trouble."

She said something else in Spanish and sighed. "That's true, isn't it? And now he's gotten himself into more trouble. That's why you're here."

"Ruben missed his court date. I need to find him so he can reschedule. I'm not looking to make things worse for him."

"He would never hurt someone without a reason," she said. "A *good* reason."

"I'm not here to question your son's character, Mrs. Medera. I'm not even here about the charges pending against him. My only concern is that he missed his court date, which is a violation of his bond agreement. Nothing more."

She looked at me for a moment then seemed to decide I was telling the truth. A bit of her defensiveness was gone then.

"If he violated the agreement, he did so willingly. Ruben has always been very deliberate, very meticulous. He would know you would come looking for him, so he wouldn't come here. He wouldn't involve me. He has always been very careful to keep his problems away from the people he loves. I'm sorry, I don't know where he is."

I got the distinct impression loyalty was paramount in the Medera family. I wanted to ask Mrs. Medera for names, phone numbers, and addresses of all Ruben's friends and associates in the Fort Collins area, wanted to ask her about his girlfriend, because I had a feeling the girlfriend would lead me straight to him, but I sensed that would do more harm to my efforts than it would benefit them. Instead, I took a step back.

"My number's on the back of that card. You could give it to Ruben, if you hear from him."

She looked at me. "You're not going to ask me to call you myself if I see him?"

I shook my head. "No. Tell him I only want to help; I'm not looking to jam him up."

I thanked her and turned to leave.

"I will tell you this," she said, causing me to turn back to her. "Ruben never would have missed court unless he had a good reason. He's a good boy; he does the right thing, follows the rules, takes care of his responsibilities. But he's not afraid to break the rules, if it's warranted. You understand?"

I felt something vaguely like annoyance forming in my belly.

"Yes, I do."

I was beginning to understand Medera all too well.

"Thank you, Mrs. Medera. And thank you for your family's service."

She smiled and nodded, then turned her attention back to the mower.

9

My next objective was to start working through the list of addresses I had for Jamie Vollmer, and I wanted to start with the one listed with the DMV. I cruised south on College Avenue. Traffic is never good in Fort Collins, but this morning I made good time.

Jamie Vollmer's address listed with the DMV was in a neighborhood west of College Avenue. This is a more expensive neighborhood; the houses are bigger, the yards are smaller, the cars are nicer.

I spotted two cop cars on my way through the neighborhood, one from the Fort Collins Police Department and the other from the Larimer County Sheriff's Office. I knew the only reason they could afford to live in this neighborhood was because their spouses also worked; a cop's salary alone could not support living here. To that end, I wondered how Vollmer could afford it, if she did indeed live here; her credit history indicated she hadn't had a job for most of the last ten years.

I found the house and parked, jotting down nearby license plate numbers. This was a trick Blue had taught me. It didn't always pay off, but when it did, it tended to break a case wide open.

I climbed out of the truck and went to the door. A well-dressed, attractive forty-something woman opened it. She had blonde hair and long legs, and with one look I knew she was comfortable being admired.

"Can I help you?"

I handed her another generic business card. "My name is Zoe Grey. I'm a bond enforcement agent. I'm looking for a woman named Jamie Vollmer."

The woman seemed slightly surprised and mildly confused. "I have no idea who that is. My name is Jan Taylor. This is my house."

She was also guarded, so I wasn't ready to totally believe her.

"I see," I said. "How long have you owned the house?" Pleasant classical music drifted out of the open door, and behind Taylor I could see the place was opulent.

"Oh, I've been here about five years."

I heard a car behind me and saw Taylor look at it over my shoulder. I glanced back as an Infinity sedan turned around in the cul-de-sac and parked across from us.

I held up Vollmer's latest booking photo. "Do you recognize this woman?"

Taylor looked at the photo then shook her head. "No. Is that her, the woman you're looking for?"

"What kind of car do you own, Ms. Taylor?"

The abrupt change in direction surprised her. It was mild and brief, but it was the first genuine reaction she'd had. "A Mercedes. Why? What's that got to do with anything?"

"Do you also own a Kia Rio? Or have you owned one in the past?"

"No. Now, really, what's this all about?"

Taylor was losing patience, ready to go on the offensive now. I wouldn't get any further with her.

I pointed at the card she held. "My number's on the card. Thanks for your time."

She didn't even glace at it. "Of course."

I walked off the porch as the man from the Infinity cut across the street and started up the driveway. He nodded politely to me as we passed one another, but I saw a flash of fear on his face. I heard Taylor greet him from the door. The man, dressed in a tailored suit, looked vaguely familiar, and I couldn't help but wonder what he'd been afraid of.

As I returned to the Scout, Taylor invited the man in and they disappeared when she closed the door. I added the man's plate number to the others on my list and left. I'd just turned onto College when my phone rang.

"Hey, Sadie. What's the word?"

"Looks like Karen works tonight, has tomorrow and Saturday off, then works Sunday, Monday, and Tuesday. If you're planning to break into her house, I expect a full report."

"Naturally. You're financing this exercise in madness, after all."

"Condescend to me now," she said, "but just wait until it turns out that I'm right."

"Actually, you may be right about her."

"Ha! I knew it! What did you find?"

"Nothing concrete, and I don't want to speculate."

"But your Spidey senses are tingling."

"I don't have Spidey senses."

"I want an update. Tomorrow at the latest. Even without anything concrete, I want to know what you've found."

"I hope you don't become a pain in the ass to work for."

She totally ignored me. "I also work tonight, and I'm in charge. Shall I make sure our target stays and works her whole shift?"

"Target? You're enjoying this a bit too much. But yes, that would be helpful."

"Got it covered. Don't forget about my report. It needn't be typed; a verbal report would suffice."

Now she was just having fun. So I hung up.

10

Marge had called the apartment complex Jamie Vollmer had provided on her bond agreement. The management there had told her Vollmer was no longer a tenant and that no forwarding address had been left. I wasn't sure I'd have any better luck, or, if I did, that it would amount to anything useful, but I wondered if I'd get farther than Marge had if I asked some questions myself, one property manager to another.

Before my recent career change to bond enforcement, I'd had a successful career in property management. I'd gotten into the business young and pretty much shot straight to the top. I'd been highly motivated, and I was good at the work. I started with a large company in Denver, but moved back to Fort Collins a few years ago, taking a position with Mark White at White Real Estate and Property Management.

White now had three offices in Northern Colorado and was at the top of the real estate game in the area. He kept asking me to take over the Fort Collins office. Or any of the offices, actually—he'd said more than once I could have my pick, if I'd only accept the promotion. But I wasn't interested. That work reminded me of a life I had tried very hard to leave behind, a life I no longer wanted.

But my announcement to leave White Real Estate a couple months ago had resulted in near disaster. A whopping eighty-five percent of the accounts I'd managed had threatened to walk. White and I had offered them their pick of replacements, anyone in any of the offices, but to my sincere surprise, none of them found that acceptable.

That put both White and me in a serious bind. My accounts were the bulk of White's Fort Collins business; if he lost them, he'd take a hit neither of us were sure he'd recover from. He couldn't let that happen. And while I wanted out, I didn't want to tank his business. White begged me to stay, offering me whatever I could possibly want.

Ultimately, we agreed I would stay on a very part time basis, working one day a week. I would manage the accounts I already had, but I would not take on any new ones, apart from the occasional referral that refused to work with anyone else. In exchange, I got to keep my office and set my own schedule. And I had nothing to do with the daily business around the office. So far, it was an arrangement I could live with.

I parked in a visitor spot outside the leasing office of Vollmer's former apartment complex and went inside. A bell tinkled when I opened the door, announcing my arrival. A young woman in a skirt suit quickly emerged from an office to the left. She smiled and walked toward me with her hand out.

"Welcome to Somerset Apartments," she said. "I'm Angela."

I shook her hand. "Zoe Grey," I said. "Nice to meet you."

"A pleasure. Please, come in and have a seat."

She indicated one of two desks sitting unoccupied in the large lobby. Like most leasing offices, this one was well appointed with new furniture and modern designs. This wasn't the most expensive complex in town, not by a long shot, but you'd never guess that by the office. But then, if the office wasn't appealing, why would anyone want to live in the apartments?

As far as I could tell, Angela was alone. And she was young, perhaps still in college. That might make things easier.

She sat behind the desk and crossed her legs, smiling at me again. She opened a pamphlet on the desk as I sat.

"I'm so excited you're considering Somerset for your new home," she said, and by golly, she sounded sincere.

"Actually, I'm afraid that isn't why I'm here."

I pulled my White Real Estate card from my pocket and laid it on the desk. She may not have recognized my name, as those in the business longer sometimes did, but she knew the name of White Real Estate.

"Okay," she said, fingering the card. "I'm not sure what I can do for you. This isn't a White Real Estate property."

"Oh, I know that. I'm actually here because I need your help."

Her perfectly, if heavily, painted eyes pinched in confusion. "I don't understand."

"A woman named Jamie Vollmer has submitted an application for one of my properties. In processing the app, I've discovered there are some inaccuracies. For that reason, I'm looking into every detail very closely."

I leaned back and crossed my legs. I continued my fairytale as if I was one professional confiding in another.

"I'm inclined to deny her, of course, but she was referred by a longstanding client. If I am to deny her, I must be able to illustrate beyond a shadow of a doubt that she falsified her application and that she was too great a risk for our company. That is my only hope of maintaining my current client, you understand."

Angela nodded, and I saw her softening, warming to me and my made-up predicament.

"According to her app, Ms. Vollmer was once a tenant here. I wondered if you could give me a little information about her, perhaps even let me peek at the application she submitted to you. What was her payment history like, did she cause any disturbances, what condition was the place in when she vacated—that sort of thing. Do you remember her?"

Angela shook her head as she stood. "I'm sorry, the name doesn't sound familiar. Come into my office; I'll look her up in the computer."

I followed her into the office she'd originally come out of and sat while she tapped at the keyboard. This office was decorated even better than the lobby. The desk was real mahogany, the chair real leather, and new, because I could smell it. I usually thought leasing offices were decorated like model homes, all show and no substance. Not so in this office. This one was the real deal. But then, the rental market was booming in Fort Collins. The average cost of rent was higher here than anywhere in the state and the vacancy rates some of the lowest.

"Okay, looks like she was a tenant here for about six months, from January of this year to June." Angela flinched slightly. "It looks like she was evicted." She looked at me.

"That doesn't bode well for her," I said. "What was the reason?"

"Nonpayment. I also see notes in here that management suspected she had others living with her, though she was the only one on the lease." She looked at me again. "Not that we care, of course, we just like to keep track of those kinds of things."

"Of course." What that really meant was that management wanted a piece of the pie.

She turned back to the computer as she scrolled down. "It looks like she denied it every time management asked her about it. Discreet inquires with neighbors also revealed there was a lot of traffic in and out of her apartment. No one complained, but one of the other managers did make a note of it in here."

"Anything else about her stay here?"

Angela did some more scrolling, but ultimately shook her head. "No, that's it. I'm sorry. I don't know if that helps you or not."

"Oh, it very much does. Thank you." I shifted, as if to go, then looked up at her. "Would it be possible to see her app?"

She wasn't objectionable to it, I noticed, but she was curious. "Why? I mean, what good would that do?"

I shrugged. "I want to be thorough, and I wonder if she put equally inaccurate information on the app she submitted here."

Angela stood and moved around the desk. "I wouldn't think so. We check out all apps very carefully. If anything came up as false, we wouldn't have leased to her."

Good. Maybe they had a real address for her.

Angela moved for the door. I stood and fell in behind her.

"I'm glad to hear that," I said. "Perhaps she falsified information on my app because she wanted to hide her eviction here."

"That would be my guess," Angela said.

She led me through the lobby to a back hall where she used a key to open a door on the left. She went in and flipped on a light. It was a storeroom. There were a couple of boxes and miscellaneous furniture items, as well as three large filing cabinets. She used another key to open one of them then pulled open the drawer second from the bottom.

She squatted delicately in her skirt and fingered through the files until she found the one she wanted. She stood, pulling it out and opening it on a nearby lamp table, likely replaced during the last redecoration. She flipped through the stack of forms, which I could now see were applications, until she found the one she wanted. She lifted off the top of the stack, turning it over on the table, then picked up Jamie Vollmer's application. She glanced at it then handed it to me.

"Thank you."

The application had been done in blue ink and a firm hand, yet the script was rather flowy. A quick look at the listed rental history yielded three addresses I didn't have for Vollmer. And the voided check stapled to the top of the app gave me bank history I would have had no way of obtaining. I pulled my phone out of my pocket.

"This is very different from the information she submitted to me," I said, laying the form on the bottom of a chair upturned on a small dining room table.

I snapped a photo of both sides, including the check. Then I returned it to Angela.

"Thank you very much."

Angela returned the form to the pile, put the stacks back together, then returned the file to the drawer. "I'm glad I could help. Unreliable tenants are the bane of our existence, but you already know that."

"Indeed I do."

She closed the drawer and relocked the cabinet before leading me back to the front lobby.

I offered her my hand again. "Keep my card. If you ever need a favor, be sure to call me. I can't thank you enough."

She smiled. "I'll do that. Thank you. And good luck."

I chuckled as I moved to the door. "I hope I don't need it."

11

I cruised over to the main branch of the library in Old Town. I hadn't been here much since they'd remodeled, and the remodel itself had driven me to use one of the other two branches in town. But this one was closer.

The remodel had, in part, expanded the computer area. They had added more computers and spread the stations out so you no longer felt like you were sitting in your neighbor's lap and he was reading your email when you used one of them. By chance, one of the computers was free when I arrived.

I signed on and punched in the addresses from Vollmer's application, all of which were local. I first searched the phone book, writing down the names that came up with those addresses. Next, I searched property records. Two of the places were indeed rental properties. The third was owned by a Michael Tobin, and it was the only house he owned. If indeed Vollmer had lived there, she could have been renting the basement or a room in the house, but it wasn't a rental property for Tobin.

I'd been hoping for parents or a sibling or some other kind of obvious relative, but I didn't think that was what I'd found. It was a real shame Jamie Vollmer didn't have a Facebook page.

I was half tempted to call Ellmann and ask him to see if Vollmer's Rio had been ticketed anywhere recently. But Ellmann had crossed too many lines for me, and that was over. I'd promised I wouldn't ask him for any more of that kind of information. And since I'd made that promise, I was coming to understand just how much of it there had been, and how useful it had been.

As I left the library, I checked the time. It was only about two, so I climbed back into the Scout and mentally mapped out my next few stops. I had a total of eight more addresses to check out for Jamie Vollmer. I needed to swing by Karen Brickle's house. I also wanted to take a run at Hapner today.

Working my way first north, then west, then south and back again, I first drove out to Brickle's house. She lived in the Waterglen Subdivision way out off Vine Drive, just west of the interstate. I turned around in her cul-de-sac and took in the place with an experienced eye. It was an attractive, well-kept place on a large corner lot. There were no signs or stickers warning of a home security system. The door into the garage was behind a six-foot privacy fence. The front door was visible from about eight different streets in the neighborhood.

I also noticed her next-door neighbor was holding a cookout in his backyard. There were extra cars in the driveway and at the curb, and smoke from a barbeque was rising up over the fence. A couple of times I saw the tops of heads or hats as people walked across what I imagined was the deck. I could also hear animated chatter drifting across the yard and into the street where I sat briefly at the stop sign.

I'd had no intention of breaking into Karen Brickle's house right then, but the party next door made it an absolute no-go. And now that I saw her house with its limited accessibility and high degree of visibility, I knew I'd need the cover of darkness. I'd have to come back later.

After cruising out of Brickle's neighborhood, I started knocking address off Vollmer's list. One after the other, I dutifully knocked on doors or rang bells and asked questions while flashing Vollmer's photo. One after another, I came up bust.

Until I knocked on Michael Tobin's door.

"Yeah, I know her," he said.

Tobin was a big guy, tall with a serious beer gut and double chin. He wore dirty jeans, socks with no shoes, and a filthy t-shirt. His brown hair was a little longer in back, thinning on top, and matted with sweat and grime. His hands and forearms were as dirty as the rest of him, and the scent of motor oil permeated from him.

"She a friend of yours?" I asked.

"You could say that. She's my ex-girlfriend."

"Really? How long ago did you two breakup?"

He leaned against the jamb of the open front door as he thought back. "Guess that'll be about a year and a half now, give or take. Why you looking for her again?"

I hadn't actually told him, but I had given him my card, so it wasn't any big secret.

"She missed her court date. I need to find her so she can get rescheduled." Really, I planned to arrest her, but I'd found that news didn't help folks into a particularly cooperative mindset.

I could see in his meaty face he'd actually cared about Jamie Vollmer, and that he still might.

"What's she in trouble for now? More prostitution charges?"

"Did you know how she made her money when you were together?"

He looked offended. "She didn't do that when we were together. And that isn't how we met, either. I'm not one of her johns. I've never paid for a hooker, ever. I met Jamie at a concert, one of those free concerts they put on downtown in the summer, you know?"

I nodded.

"She was there with some friends, and she was the prettiest girl I'd ever seen. I asked her if I could buy her an ice cream cone." His eyes were kind of distant now as he looked back on a scene replaying in his memory. A small smile tipped up one corner of his mouth. "I never thought she'd say yes, but she said no one had ever offered to buy her ice cream before. We sat outside the ice cream place talking until almost midnight. We were pretty much inseparable after that."

The wistful look morphed into hurt and anger.

"We'd been together about three or four months when I found out what she was doing. I was pissed. We had a huge fight. I couldn't stand the thought of other men . . . *touching* her. I'm not one for ultimatums, but I told her if she wanted to be with me, she had to stop. Because I couldn't even think of touching her knowing she'd been with some other guy earlier that day.

"She cried, begged me not to leave her. She said she'd stop, right then and there. She said she'd find another job somewhere, maybe doing nails, 'cause she used to do that. I said if she really would stop, I'd help support her until she found a job. I make good money; I own my own shop. A couple months later, she moved in here.

"I thought we were happy. *I* was happy. She was . . . perfect. But then I found out she'd been sneaking around behind my back, turning tricks again. When I confronted her, she whined about the money. She said she could make more in one hour from a john than she could make in a week working at the nail place."

He shook his head, and now he just looked sad. "I tried to be understanding about it, really I did, but I just couldn't get past it. Soon I couldn't even look at her. I slept on the couch, wouldn't let her come near me. I had to break it off. I'm just not that kind of guy."

"I don't think many guys are," I said.

"You know, I think she really did love me. But a part of her loved hooking more. Because she couldn't stop. And I can't believe it was really about the money. No one needs that much money."

"I'm really sorry, Michael."

"Thanks. It's stupid, but I still miss her, you know?"

"That's not stupid."

"No?"

I shook my head. "No. I think it's normal."

He seemed to take comfort in that.

"Do you have any idea where Jamie might have gone after she moved out?"

"No. She had a couple girlfriends around town, but I don't know if one of them took her in or what. For all I know, she's shacked up with some john. Or one of them's paying for an apartment or something for her."

"Would you mind giving me the names and addresses of her friends?"

"Sure, what I remember, anyway."

"I appreciate it."

He told me what he could recall, which was three names and two vague locations. I wrote it all down and thanked him again for his time and help.

"Hey," he called as I turned to leave. "You think she's all right?"

I stopped and looked back at him. "I'm sure she's well," I said. "But I think she's unhappy." I had to believe any woman who made her money that way was, deep down.

I couldn't tell if that had been a helpful or hurtful answer. Tobin simply nodded his head once then retreated back into the house and closed the door.

12

I made it to the rest of Vollmer's previous and known addresses. Those I found occupied proved bust. At two of them, there was no one home, which put them on the list for a return visit.

It was after five, so I decided to bag Vollmer for the moment. I cruised past Ruben Medera's condo one more time, stopping to knock on the door. Of course, no one answered and the small splinter of toothpick I'd fit against the doorjamb was still there, so I knew no one had been inside since I'd left earlier. I supposed Medera could have used the patio door, but it had been Charlie barred from inside. Actually, I'd put the Charlie bar down when I'd been in the kitchen earlier, because it was basically impossible to get past one, which meant the front door was now the only way in. Medera might have some mad Marine skill that could get him past a Charlie bar, but I doubted it. Wherever he was, he wasn't at home, and it didn't seem like he planned to come home anytime soon.

I left Medera's and drove north to Amy's house. Amy lives on the far northwest side of town in a quite older neighborhood with huge lots and wide streets. There are always tons of kids playing in yards and riding bikes in the streets, and you always see their parents tending flowerbeds or mowing the lawn or washing the car. Perhaps it's a bit dated, but this has always been my idea of the quintessential American neighborhood.

I turned into Amy's cul-de-sac and saw both her car and Brandon's parked out front. The front door was open and there were lights on inside. I parked and went to the door.

Brandon is Amy's fiancé, and he's pretty much perfect for her. Naturally, I'd been critical at first, scrutinizing everything he did or said, but he'd proved himself to be a standup guy with honest intentions. Which was good, because Amy's crazy about him.

He's also a pretty smart guy. He'd figured out early Amy and I are kind of like a package deal, and that has never seemed to bother him. He and Ellmann had been hanging out a lot recently, too.

Their wedding was planned for January, and I was coming to terms with the idea of Amy being married.

I knocked and went inside. I heard the TV on downstairs and smelled something cooking.

"Hello!"

"Hey!"

Amy poked her head out of the kitchen and smiled. Amy's five six and has lean limbs from a lifetime of martial arts training. Her hair was tied back in a ponytail, though a few pieces around her face had escaped. Today, she wore shorts, sandals, and a tank top, and I noticed just how tan she'd gotten over the summer.

"You're just in time," she said. "Are you hungry?"

I'd been hoping to score dinner.

"Yes," I said. "Smells good."

The house is a tri-level and very similar to mine, the primary differences being that it is much bigger and had been updated and remodeled over the last few years. Since Amy had purchased it four years ago, she'd been working on one project after another, and the place looks great.

Brandon came up from the basement where he'd been watching TV. He kissed my cheek as he headed for the kitchen. "Hey, Zoe. How was your vacation?"

Amy chuckled as she ducked back into the kitchen.

I shot her a dirty look, but she'd already gone.

"It was great," I said, following him. "Very relaxing. We had a lot of fun."

"Good. You guys deserved it. You know, I tried to talk Amy into California for our honeymoon, but she flat out refused." He chuckled.

"Why would anyone chose California over Hawaii?" she asked.

"No idea," I said. I was actually slightly envious of the honeymoon trip they had planned. I'd been helping Amy with some of the details, and they had a fantastic week planned hopping all over the Hawaiian Islands. They were going to love it.

While Brandon and Amy moved food from the stove to the table, I got out plates and silverware. Soon we were seated and filling our plates with spaghetti, salad, grilled veggies, and garlic bread.

"Did you get your school schedule figured out?" Amy asked me.

I nodded. "Yeah, before I left town."

I'd recently decided to go back to school. The first time around, I'd left after my second semester for a relationship that had blown up badly, and had never gone back. I'd always regretted that I hadn't finished, though I had no idea what I would study. Originally, I'd been on track toward a nursing degree with Sadie. But that probably worked out for the best, because I didn't think I was well suited to a nursing career.

Amy had also been taking classes, working toward her own degree. After high school, she'd jumped right into work, establishing her own cleaning business with her friend Jody.

Running your own business, getting it up off the ground, was more than a full time job; Amy just had never had time for anything else. Now, however, her business had grown into something substantial, and neither she nor Jody had to work all the time. Mostly they just managed things from the office a couple days a week.

A few weeks ago, I'd gone to Front Range Community College and signed up for a full class schedule that fall. Once sense had returned to me, I'd dropped down to just two classes, one of which I was taking with Amy. Classes started next week.

"Did they let you return the books?"

I rolled my eyes. "That was a battle, but they did take them back. What a joke."

"I've started buying all my books elsewhere," she said, "because those bookstore people are so rude."

"I'm going to have to do the same. Hey, the hotel called me back. We're all set for the weekend of the wedding. But they say we'll need at least ten reservations."

"We'll have at least that." She looked at Brandon. "Don't you think?"

"With just my family alone." He shook his head. "Small wedding. Yeah, right."

Their guest list had gotten a little out of control. They'd wanted to have just fifty people, but they soon realized that accounted for just Brandon's family, and none of their friends or what few of Amy's family would attend.

Amy smiled and squeezed his hand across the table. "It's going to be fine. Fifty, a hundred—what's the difference?"

"About double the cost," he muttered darkly. "I still think we should have cut some people from the list—some of my extended family."

She shook her head and said firmly, "No. It's going to be a special day. It should be witnessed."

Amy and I had never been the kind of girls to sit around dreaming of what our weddings would look like. But since we'd begun planning her wedding, the fever had hit Amy hard. She was wrapped up in dreamy ideas of what the perfect wedding looked like, and the whole thing was becoming more and more detailed and grandiose than she and Brandon had originally discussed. In typical male fashion, Brandon didn't much care about any detail but price; he just wanted to know where to show up, and at what time. But if Amy didn't come to her senses soon, they wouldn't be able to afford their wedding.

"Brandon, did you get your tux yet?" I asked.

He shot an almost panicked look at Amy. "Monday," he said quickly. "I have an appointment on Monday. I'm leaving work early."

"And you're not going to miss it this time," Amy said in what I've always called her scary voice. She doesn't use it very often, but that just means it's scarier when she does.

"No, honey," he rushed to assure her. "I won't miss it. Monday." Then he put his head over his plate and focused on eating.

Geez. I never thought it possible, but my best friend was slowly but surely morphing into Bridezilla.

On the rare occasions I'd briefly thought of my own wedding, I'd mostly imagined a little trip to the courthouse and a small backyard party with my closest friends. Once or twice I'd considered the whole white-dress, walk-down-the-aisle thing, but that just didn't seem to suit me. And I was glad I didn't need to think about it at all; I had way too many other things to figure out.

After helping with the dishes, I thanked them for dinner and whispered to Amy to take it easy on Brandon. She just rolled her eyes at me, but when she next looked at her future husband, her eyes were much softer.

As I drove away from Amy's house, my phone rang.

"Hi there," I said to Ellmann. "Gonna get away for dinner?"

"Not anytime soon. Probably not at all. Do you want to go back on vacation?"

I chuckled. "Sure. Turns out I love the beach."

"Maybe we could try Florida this time. That's farther away."

"Are you at least making progress?"

"Yes, actually. With any luck at all, we'll get things wrapped up in twenty-four hours. I'm hoping for twenty-four hours, anyway. Are you working?"

"Yeah, I picked up three new skips, and I'm looking into something private for Sadie."

"Sounds interesting."

"Too soon to tell."

In the background, I heard someone calling Ellmann's name.

"Shit, I've gotta go. Will you be home?"

"Not for the next couple hours, but I should be after that."

"I'll stop by if I can get away."

The guy in the background was shouting at Ellmann again when we hung up.

Things like that that made me grateful to work alone. I never had anyone shouting at me. Well, apart from the fugitives who sometimes vented their frustrations on me. But since they were usually in handcuffs at that point, it didn't bother me too much.

Since I'd gotten up before dawn that morning, I was beat, and really just wanted to go home and go to bed. But there was one more thing I needed to do first.

It was a fairly short drive to Karen Brickle's house. But I still wasn't getting inside. The neighbor's barbeque was still in full swing. I could hear voices and music drifting over their fence, and there were even more cars at the curb now.

Whatever they were celebrating, they were still at it. And would be for a while, I guessed.

I made another pass by Medera's and then by his mother's. I didn't see him, the Toyota pickup truck the DMV had registered to him, or any sign he'd been either place. I next tried the two places on Vollmer's list where I'd gotten no answer, but still no one was home. The only other skip pending was Hapner, but it was far too late and I was far too tired to go after him tonight.

13

I went home and let myself into the house, disarming and then rearming the security system. I'd never had a security system before, but in the last couple of months, I'd experienced several break-ins. I'd installed the system as a deterrent. I didn't know yet if it was working, as everyone who had broken into my place was either dead or in prison, but it made me feel better. As an added bonus, it lowered my insurance.

I changed out the laundry and went up to my room. I folded the clothes then fell asleep watching a rerun of *Murder, She Wrote*. Sometime later, Ellmann came into the room, flipped off the TV, and crawled into bed beside me. Even in the dark, I could tell he was dead on his feet.

"They're going to let you sleep?" I mumbled as he pulled me into his chest.

"They didn't have a choice. They found me sleeping in the conference room."

Ellmann yawned then went still and quiet, asleep in record time.

I listened to the steady rhythm of his heartbeat as I drifted back to sleep.

My alarm went off at five a.m., but I was already awake. Ellmann had woken me up some time before. Considering how exhausted he'd been, he'd sure recovered fast.

While Ellmann finished in the shower, I turned off the alarm and called Sadie at work.

"Karen still there?" I asked.

"Yes. You're in the clear; no one's leaving early tonight. We're getting hammered."

"Sorry to hear that. I'll catch up with you later for your briefing."

"How about this afternoon? A late lunch?"

"Sure. Sounds good."

I hung up as Ellmann emerged from the bathroom, ducking his head slightly under the doorframe. Ellmann is nearly six and a half feet tall, with broad shoulders and thick muscles. He could probably juggle baby elephants if he wanted to.

"Do I even want to know what you're up to this early in the morning?" he asked as he went to the dresser where he kept some clothes.

His dark, wavy hair was wet from the shower, curling over his ears and forehead. He usually keeps his hair a little longer and is rarely clean-shaven. Since our return home, he hadn't shaved at all, so he sported a short beard. His broad back was still deeply tanned from our days spent on the beach. That was the Italian in him; he tanned easily.

I got up and crossed to the bathroom.

"It's perfectly innocent," I said.

"Yeah, right."

"All right, fine. But it's not dangerous."

"I'll believe that, even if it's only true for the moment."

I twisted on the shower then stuck my head back out into the bedroom.

"You know, you're lack of faith in me is depressing."

He came over and cupped my face. "I have every faith in you," he said seriously. "But I worry about you. You're not invincible, and you tend to attract trouble." His eyes were green, a deeper green than mine, and there was something mesmerizing about them.

"Do you wish I had a different job?" I was kind of surprised. Ellmann had turned me on to bounty hunting in the first place. He was the one who was always telling me how good I am at it.

"No, I think you're in the right field. You have a freakish knack for finding people. Sometimes I just wish you weren't doing it alone, that's all. I felt a lot better when you were working with Blue."

Bounty hunting generally isn't a team sport, especially not for freelance people like me. Occasionally, circumstances dictate the need to team up, but typically in those situations the reward is big enough to compensate both parties sufficiently that it doesn't feel like a waste of time or effort.

I leaned on the doorjamb, and he went back to the dresser to pull out a t-shirt and a pair of socks.

"You know I always try to be careful, right?"

"Yes, but I also know you don't back down from a fight." He shrugged as he sat on the end of the bed and pulled on the socks. "I hate to think of you out there alone engaging with some seriously bad people."

"Sometimes that's unavoidable."

He nodded then pulled the t-shirt on. "I know. But I don't have to like it."

"Fair enough."

He came over and kissed me. He smelled good, like soap and clean laundry.

"Be careful, okay?"

"I will. Go close your case, huh?"

He groaned as he turned away. "God willing." He went out of the room calling, "Love you!" over his shoulder.

I tried not to let that rattle me too much and got in the shower.

Twenty minutes later, I was in the Scout headed back to Karen Brickle's house.

The sky was dark, sunrise still about an hour away. At this time of day, I hoped I didn't have to worry about the neighbors.

Mercifully, the neighbor's house was dark and quiet, and most of the cars had vacated the curb. I turned around in the cul-de-sac, eyeing Brickle's house, the next-door neighbor's house, and the other houses with any line of sight on Brickle's. I saw no signs Brickle's house was occupied, the party neighbors were probably sleeping it off, and it was too early for anyone else to be up and about.

I made a right and parked down the street. I climbed out of the Scout and eased the door shut quietly. Then I walked back to Brickle's place.

The only real option for entry, even at this time of day, was the door to the garage. The front door was out; the porch light was on and the door sat in plain view of passersby on six different streets and nosey neighbors from two dozen homes.

I strolled along the sidewalk in front of the house then cut across the yard between Brickle's house and the neighbor's. I let myself in through the gate and tried the knob on the garage door. It was locked. I used my bump key and slipped inside.

I put my shoe back on and flicked on a flashlight. The two-car garage was empty aside from some boxes and a lawn mower. The door to the house was unlocked. Inside, I paused to listen.

The garage opened into a laundry room with a long hallway beyond. To the left were bed- and bathrooms. To the right, the kitchen. I heard nothing, and was fairly confident I was alone. However, I didn't want to find out I was wrong by surprise.

I made a left and peeked into the bedrooms. Then I took a quick turn through the common areas of the house and the basement. I was indeed alone. I next turned my attention to what had brought me here.

The house looked as if Brickle was still in the process of moving in; there were boxes in most rooms, and several of the rooms in the basement were serving as storage. The kitchen, living room, and master bedroom looked obviously lived in. The kitchen counters held a few random food things, a stray piece of mail, and a few other miscellaneous items. There was a dirty pan on the stove and dishes in the sink. There was a glass on the coffee table in the living room and a blanket strewn across the sofa. The counter in the master bathroom was cluttered with items every woman has in her bathroom.

Brickle had a fairly boring movie collection, overrun with romances and chick flicks, but her TV was expensive. Actually, her entire entertainment system was expensive. Seemed a shame to use such a system to watch *Fried Green Tomatoes* and *The Notebook*.

Her decorating style leaned toward modern with neutral colors, clean lines, and lots of glass. She hadn't gotten around to hanging anything on the walls, and half the living room furniture was still in the basement. The sofa was white leather, which made it just about the ugliest thing I'd seen in a while.

The guest bathroom was unused, as were two of the bedrooms. One of them had an extra bed and dresser, but the bed was bare and there were boxes stacked along one wall. Aside from the master bedroom, the most used room was the study. A shiny new Mac computer sat on top of a genuine maple secretary desk. I ran my finger over the trackpad and the screen blinked on, asking for a password. What an untrusting world we live in that everyone password protects their computers.

I sat at the desk and looked through the papers and mail. In the closet, I found a small wooden two-drawer filing cabinet. It was locked, but I picked it open. Every document I found was in the name "Karen Brickle." If she'd kept anything from her past life, it was hidden well.

I used my phone to take photos of her cell phone bill and a bank statement. I'd look through the phone bill later. The bank statement caught my eye because she had a six-figure balance.

According to Sadie, nursing didn't pay *that* well, so I wondered where Brickle's money was coming from.

The master bedroom had a heavy, expensive, dark six-piece furniture set. The pieces were too big for my taste, and too big for the space. The king-sized canopy bed seemed to dominate the entire room.

There was nothing hanging on the walls in this room, either, and very few personal items. The bed was unmade, there were dirty clothes on the floor in the bathroom, and the oversized walk-in closet was stuffed to bursting with clothing and accessories that were largely very expensive. I poked around a bit for any hidden secrets, but found nothing. I did note that a few of the labels would have made Sadie drool, however.

In the bedside table drawers and in a box under the bed, I found an impressively varied collection of unmentionable items. More interestingly, Brickle had a gun under the mattress. I made a note of the serial number and put it back.

The rest of the room yielded little. I found nothing with anyone else's name on it. Short of pawing through every box, I'd found everything I could find. In reality, seven years was a long time to assume another woman's name. By now, her former self was likely so far behind her she had little left. And this far into the game, whatever she may have had, she would keep it somewhere else, somewhere safer and farther away.

I let myself out the same way I'd come in and returned to the truck.

14

I wanted coffee, but I made myself go to the gym. With the running program, it wasn't good to run every day, or so said Sam. Apparently, it was better to run every other day and let your body recover in between. Since the program seemed to be working, I tried not to think too hard about it. I'd run yesterday, so today I lifted weights for a while then swam laps until I was bored out of my mind. I always try to count my laps, to stave off the boredom and for a better measure than just time, but I always lose track about thirty times and never have even the faintest idea how many laps I swim. Today was no exception.

I was starving when I left the gym, but I didn't have time for breakfast. Instead, I choked down some protein shake thing that had to be good for me because it tasted like sawdust and drove back to the neighborhood near Rossborough Park.

Yesterday, the house had cleared out at around eight thirty. It was nearing eight when I parked down the street, and only one car was in the driveway. The boredom of waiting seemed to exacerbate my hunger, so I drained my water bottle and ate a Cliff bar I dug out of the glove box. I had no idea how long it had been there, and it was a little melty, but I ate it anyway. It was a blessing I didn't have to wait very long. At just after eight, the homeowner came through the gate, got in his car, and drove away.

As I had the day before, I waited another ten minutes. When the guy still hadn't doubled back, I grabbed my bag and got out of the truck.

I made quick work of letting myself in and retrieving the SD card out of the smoke detector camera. Then I pulled my laptop out of my bag and inserted the card. There was no point in removing the camera if it hadn't caught what I needed.

This little plan of mine was one I'd hoped to play out over the long run, and I'd wanted to leave the camera in place for a week or so before I came back to check it, but Karen Brickle was forcing me to move up my timetable.

The content of the card loaded, and I played it back, fast-forwarding through the long hours of video. This cursory look told me I hadn't gotten the preverbal money shot I'd been hoping for, but I saw enough that I thought I could fake it for now. I downloaded the video off the card onto my computer and cleared the card's memory. I replaced the card in the camera and left the device in place. I'd bluff with what I had now, but all too soon I'd need something real. Maybe tonight would prove more fruitful.

I packed up and let myself out.

I drove to The Egg & I for breakfast. I've always thought of The Egg & I as a seniors' destination, but I like their food.

I ordered an omelet, orange juice, and coffee, then worked at my laptop playing amateur video editor until my food arrived. By the time I was through with my meal, I had something workable. I pulled a couple of still frames from the video and sent them to be printed at Walgreens. Who knew what the kid working the photo counter would think of them. Maybe nothing. Surely people printed stuff that was a whole lot more interesting.

My next stop was Medera's. I wanted to check the door and see if he'd been there anytime during the night. I found that, of course, he hadn't been.

Bond enforcement was like this, one strikeout after another. It took a lot of persistence and perseverance to find the person you're looking for. And then eventually, you got lucky.

So, I returned my efforts to Jamie Vollmer, the girl who lived nowhere.

I had needed to stop by the two places where I'd gotten no answer yesterday. It was now ten o'clock in the morning, so I wasn't sure I'd have any better luck, but I gave it a shot all the same.

The first one was a bust. No one was home. I couldn't determine if anyone had been home since my last visit, but it didn't really matter. So I moved on.

Next up was the home of William Tolliver. This was the address listed on Vollmer's arrest report. Tolliver himself had an arrest report. It seemed he had a proclivity for prostitutes.

William Tolliver was tall, lanky, bald, and very awkward looking. He had ill-fitting clothes, a beer belly, and a moustache. The moustache was so thick it looked like a muskrat was decorating his face, which just served to highlight how very little hair he had on his head.

When he opened the door, his skin was flushed and sweaty, his shirt wet under his arms and down his chest. He didn't have air conditioning, and the weather report lady had guessed right: it was hot.

I handed him a card. "My name's Zoe Grey," I said. "I'm looking for Jamie Vollmer."

He looked surprised. "She's not here."

"When did you last see her?"

"Last week."

My turn to be surprised.

"Does she live here?"

"No. She stayed here briefly, but that was months ago."

"But you're still in touch with her?"

"Yes. Uh, we're friends."

Friends. Right.

"Do you have a current address for her?"

He started to clam up. "I don't think it's a good idea . . ."

"Look, Mr. Tolliver, I think we can come to an understanding here. I'm sure you'd like to keep the details of your private life away from the prying eyes of the police. I would like to know where to find Jamie Vollmer. If you give me her current address, I won't mention to my detective friend that you're still paying for sex. Are those terms agreeable to you?"

Sweat ran from Tolliver's brow. He wiped it away with a quick flick of his hand as he looked at me. He was no doubt trying to decide if I posed a credible threat and if there was any way to give me what I wanted and still see to it I lost.

But it was a short battle. Whatever feelings he may or may not have had for Jamie Vollmer, his interest in self-preservation won out.

"She's living in a house on the south end of town," he said. "A few girls live there full time. After Jamie's last arrest, she went to work for the woman who runs the house. She said it would be less risk for her that way."

"Who's the woman?" I asked. "Where's the house?"

"Her name's Jan Taylor," he said and rattled off an address I already knew.

Surprise, surprise. Someone had lied to me.

I turned to leave.

"Don't tell Jamie I told you!" he cried. "I really like her!"

"It'll be our secret."

I returned to the Scout and headed south.

I couldn't say I was surprised to learn Jan Taylor had lied to me. As a general rule, I operate on the assumption that everyone is lying to me, unless I have a strong suspicion otherwise. The sad truth is, my bounty hunter spiel doesn't bring out the best in people.

I returned to Jan Taylor's house and parked. I took time to write down the number of every license plate I could see, and I made sure I had handcuffs and capture paperwork and went to the door.

Jan Taylor was surprised to see me again, but there was the tiniest bit of fear in her pretty, painted eyes, too.

"Hello again," she said, standing in the open door.

"Ms. Taylor, you and I better go inside. We need to have a different conversation this time."

She began to protest, but I stepped into the house, forcing her back.

"I'm not asking," I said.

She recovered quickly. Straightening her perfectly tailored and pressed top, she turned and led me into the house.

I followed her into the living room, which had been converted into a comfortable and plush lobby. There were nice armchairs and loveseats, several end tables with lamps and magazines, and a large, well-stocked sideboard. The pretty music still played softly. At present, Taylor and I were the only ones there.

She stopped in the middle of the room and turned to face me. She didn't offer me a seat.

"Now, what's this about?"

"I'm going to ask you again about Jamie Vollmer. This time, I'd appreciate it if you didn't lie to me."

"I neve—"

"You've basically got two options at this point." I realized I sounded kind of bored. I guess I was. There are only so many times you can listen to lies and denials before they all start to sound the same. "The first is to tell me which room Jamie's in. I'll go to that one, and Jamie and I can walk out of here quietly, without a lot of fanfare or fuss. The second option is to keep up this game. In that case, I'll go into every room. I'll make sure I flash my badge around and make a lot of noise." I pulled my shirt up and showed her the cheap toy-like badge the state had given me with my bounty hunter course certificate. "How do you think that will be for business?" Didn't matter that I wasn't a real cop; the panic would be real.

I was taking a gamble here. Usually if I got a little tough with people, if I threw out a little threat or two, they would give in. Like William Tolliver. People would predictably and reliably default to self-preservation.

But Jan Taylor wasn't like most people. She was a businesswoman in a hard line of work. She dealt with backhanded, corrupt, greedy, and self-serving men day in and day out. She understood well the value of threats, intimidation, and negotiation. And I could see the faintest outline of a small pistol strapped to her left thigh under her pencil skirt. Jan Taylor hadn't gotten where she was by allowing herself to be intimidated or bullied. I knew I would have to appeal to her business sense if I stood any chance of success with this tactic.

"I don't know what you think is going on here," she began.

"I'm a bond enforcement agent. I only care about locating Jamie Vollmer, who is in violation of her bond agreement, and bringing her back to the court. So long as no one's being hurt here—taken advantage of or held against their will—then I don't really care about the business you're running, and that's the honest truth. That doesn't change the fact that it is illegal, however, and if you don't cooperate with me right here, right now, I will make sure the cops are crawling all over this place within the hour."

She looked at me long and hard, and her shoulders softened a bit.

"Every girl here wants to be here," she said softly, but firmly. "And they are all at least eighteen years old."

"Then it's really none of my business."

Again, she stared at me for a long time, privately evaluating the truth in my statements and debating her next course of action. I stood still under her scrutiny, meeting her eyes, waiting while she thought. Finally, a very expensive clock chimed softly and seemed to rouse her.

"Come," she said, moving around me. "I'll show you to Jamie's room. It might be better if I speak with her."

Taylor led me out of the waiting room and up the stairs. As we traveled the long hallway, the expected sounds could be heard beyond the closed doors. I resisted the urge to stick my fingers in my ears and hum.

Taylor stopped at the last door on the left and rapped her knuckles against it sharply. To my surprise and discomfort, she didn't wait for a response but opened the door and went in. Afraid of what I might see, I hesitated a few seconds. Then I found some resolve and went into the room. I was an adult, after all, and I was on the job.

Jamie Vollmer was in bed astride a middle-aged man with a severe t-shirt tan line and flabby arms. She was wearing a sheer red teddy adorned with feathers and bows, sheer red stockings, and a garter belt. He was wearing socks and a wife beater tank top. She didn't seem particularly bothered by the intrusion. He, on the other hand, looked equal parts terrified and embarrassed.

"Excuse me," Taylor said, as if she were interrupting nothing more than teatime. "Jamie, this woman needs to speak with you. It's urgent."

"About what?" Vollmer asked, her eyes flashing to me.

The man and I both seemed surprised she was willing to hold a discussion just then.

"If you'll step into the hall," I said, waving a hand at the open door. "It's kind of private."

As I moved my arm, my shirt must have shifted. Vollmer's eyes flashed down to my waist, and I knew she'd seen at least part of the badge.

In an instant, she had jumped off the guy and shot for the window. In the blink of an eye, she shoved the screen out and launched herself through.

"Bond enforcement!" I cried, darting across the room. "Jamie, stop!"

All I could figure was that she'd practiced this escape method before, because she used a rope tied to a nearby tree branch to swing down to the ground. She was already halfway across the yard by the time I reached the window.

"Shit!"

Without thinking too hard about what the hell I was really doing, I climbed onto the windowsill and jumped for the tree branch. Not so long ago, I'd suffered a bullet wound to my left shoulder. It had required two surgeries and weeks of physical therapy to heal. And it still wasn't back to one hundred percent, which I became acutely aware of as soon as I found myself hanging from the branch.

As a string of curses flowed from my mouth, I got a hand on the rope and dropped to the ground. Then I took off at a sprint.

Vollmer was ahead of me, tearing straight down the middle of the street. She looked ridiculous in her red lingerie, and I could only imagine what the guys at the detention center would say when I brought her in. I was already something of a joke out there, and I was sure this incident wouldn't improve my standing any.

This little chase here was why I practiced running, and while I still wasn't much good at it, I was getting better, and I knew Vollmer wasn't getting away from me. Probably the thing that really improved my odds was the fact that Vollmer was only about five two and didn't have any shoes on. As she ran, I could see the bottoms of her stockings were ripped from the pavement. But even that wasn't slowing her down much.

She ran straight for the end of the street, and she didn't show any signs of stopping. But I was gaining. And if I hadn't been before, I became a true convert then, and I vowed never to slack on my running regimen.

Suddenly, I saw a car in the street. The car slammed on the breaks and slid to a stop as Vollmer shot out in front of it. But it came close enough to her that she put her hands on the hood as she jumped out of the way.

It was the delay I needed. I sprinted into the street and barreled into her, pulling her away from the car with enough momentum to knock the wind out of her. We crashed to the asphalt in a pile of arms, legs, and curses. (Those were mostly mine.)

I got Vollmer in an arm lock and rolled her over. This wasn't difficult because I had about fifty pounds on her. Then I heard the car's driver's side door open.

"Oh, my word!" A woman cried in a shrill voice. "Are you o— *what* on Earth is going on?"

"Bond enforcement," I barked at her as I pulled the handcuffs from my back pocket. "Stay back. Jamie, stop resisting." Vollmer was kicking and screaming, yanking and twisting, doing her damnedest to get free of me.

"Bond what?" the woman asked, coming closer. "Is she okay?"

"Bitch!" Jamie had obviously recovered her breath. "Get off me! Let me go!"

I clamped the cuffs around her wrists and stood. Vollmer writhed in the road for a while, trying to free herself of the cuffs, I guess. When that didn't work, she tried to figure out how to get up with her hands cuffed behind her.

Another car happened upon our scene. That driver too stopped and came over.

"What going on?" he asked. "Should I call the cops?"

"No need," I said, flashing him my rinky-dink badge. "It's under control."

"Oh, thank heavens," the woman shrieked. "You're the police. I was so worried you were trying to hurt that woman."

Sometimes people see my badge and assume I'm a cop. This can happen even if I identify myself as bond enforcement, as it had here. Usually, I allow people to persist in that misunderstanding. It tends to be simpler, since bond enforcement is poorly understood, and because it usually incites better cooperation. Which is why I didn't bother to correct this woman now.

"Come on," I said, reaching down and hauling Jamie to her feet. "Let's go."

I set her on her feet, and she tried to bolt. I quickly caught her, locking my hand around her upper arm.

"Knock it off," I said. "You're done. It's over."

She must have realized the truth of that. Suddenly, she refused to stand. Like a toddler throwing a fit, she flopped down onto the street.

The woman driver gasped.

I rolled my eyes.

"Need a hand?" the male driver asked.

I was half tempted, but I hadn't been particularly impressed by the way he was eyeballing Vollmer in her ruined teddy.

"I'll manage," I said.

I squatted down and hauled Vollmer up again, this time throwing her over my shoulder like a sack of potatoes.

She gasped in surprise and did her best to resist. But I had my arm locked around her legs, and with her hands cuffed behind her back, she wasn't able to gain much momentum.

About halfway back to the truck, she gave up and resorted to vehemently and creatively cursing me and every family member she imagined I had.

For a pretty girl, she sure had an ugly mouth.

15

I dropped Vollmer off at the detention center in exchange for a body receipt. I'd found an old, mostly clean towel under the seat and wrapped it around her since most the detention center staff were men. Vollmer never said anything, but she seemed surprised when I offered to do this, and she agreed to it. I took that as gratitude.

I was vague about the details when the booking sergeant asked me where I'd found Vollmer and why she was half dressed in lingerie.

"Leave it to you to bring in the strange ones, Grey," he said with a chuckle.

Personally, I don't really care how I bring them in, so long as I bring them in.

I took my body receipt and motored over to Sure Bonds. Marge's office was in a large building with two other retail spaces, one on either side. On one side was a medical supply store distantly associated with the hospital. On the other was an auto glass place.

I parked and went inside. The cigarette smoke hit me immediately, and I started coughing. I backed out of the office and held the door open.

"What's the matter, princess?" Marge's voice called from inside. "You gotta problem with me smoking, too?"

I used the large rock near the door to prop it open. Then I went in.

The office was dingy and dark. I irrationally imagined the cigarette smoke was so thick it was obscuring the light from the open windows. The office was large, and looked larger by the lack of furniture. There was an old brown leather sofa against the wall near the door with a coffee table in front of it. Further back, there were two desks, one of which was occupied by Marge, who sat with her feet up, happily smoking.

Behind her desk was a long worktable that held a fax machine and a large copier. On the same wall, nearer the sofa was another table that held a coffee machine, a microwave, and a toaster. A water cooler stood beside it and a miniature refrigerator was tucked underneath it. A hallway in the back led to other rooms and the rest of the space.

There were local area maps tacked to the walls near both desks. Many of them had red and yellow pins in them, marking various specific locations. Some of them had obviously been up for quite some time. And it became equally obvious Marge, and her husband while he'd been alive, had been smoking in this office every day since she'd moved in. The walls and ceiling were tinged yellow from the smoke; the ceiling tiles were sagging, as if the poison they'd absorbed was just too heavy for them. The industrial carpet, which had likely been there since the building had been constructed, was absolutely trashed.

As far as I could tell, Marge was the only one in the office. I went to her desk and laid Vollmer's body receipt on top of some files she had stacked there.

"Who's that?" Marge asked.

"Vollmer. I take checks."

She exhaled a long stream of smoke as she glared up at me.

"How's it coming with the other two?"

"I'm going after Hapner next. I'm not sure about Medera."

"What's the matter, princess? The big, bad Marine playing hard to get? I thought you were good at this."

"I'm good, but I'm not psychic. If you think you can do better, I'd be happy to give his file back to you."

"Now, now, there's no need to get touchy."

"It's the oxygen deprivation."

She rolled her eyes and reached for a file on the desk. Her ancient chair squeaked viciously with every move. She held the file out to me.

"Just came in," she said. "Ten-thousand-dollar reward. Thought you might be interested."

Before I could say anything, the phone rang, and Marge snatched it up. It was one of those old phones with the rotor dial and a cord. It had probably been sitting on that same desk for thirty years.

"Sure Bonds," Marge answered.

She listened for a beat then rolled her eyes. "Yeah, yeah . . . Yeah, Pauly. I heard ya. Quit whining. You sound like a little girl."

With that, she smacked the phone down.

"Paul Cramer," she said, pointing at the phone. "Idiot got himself arrested again."

"I won't keep you," I said, putting the file down on her desk. "I just need a check for Vollmer."

She took another drag then dropped her feet to the floor and sat up, the chair squeaking as she did so. She snubbed the cigarette out in an overflowing ashtray and looked at me.

"What about that case? You want it? If you do, it's yours."

Not for the first time, I had the distinct sense something was amiss here at Sure Bonds. Marge had not survived this long in the business without a recovery agent. I imagined when her husband was alive, the two of them had done their own apprehensions. But someone had been helping her since his death. So where was that person now?

92

"Who's your regular guy?" I asked. "Why doesn't he want this FTA?"

She looked suddenly uncomfortable. She dropped her gaze to the desk and began straightening the files and papers.

"The other guy, he's, uh, busy this week. It doesn't matter. You want it or not?"

"Too busy for a ten-thousand-dollar recovery? Bullshit."

"Oh! Don't be so dramatic!" She shook her head and reached for a pack of cigarettes. "Idiot newbies. It's not a big deal. He's just not available right now."

She lit the cigarette and inhaled deeply.

"Marge, you smoke too much."

She blew out a lungful of smoke and glared at me.

"You sound like the fucking landlord. What are you gonna do next, tell me I can't smoke in here anymore?" She took another drag and blew out another cloud of smoke. "He already tried that. Look how good that worked out for him."

I guessed this exchange with the landlord had happened recently, since she was still bent out of shape about it.

She rolled her eyes and leaned back in the chair with a squeak. "What's he gonna do anyway, evict me?" She shrugged. "I've been here thirty-five years. And I've smoked the whole time."

Which was why the paint was peeling off.

I bit back a sigh. "Marge, write me a check for Vollmer. I need to get out of this office."

"Don't you judge me, missy," she snapped, pointing a finger at me. "You're not perfect, either."

Overall, I didn't really mind Marge. Near as I could tell, the only real drawback to her was the fact that she was a card or two short of a full deck.

"The check," I said.

93

"Take this case," she said, indicating the file she'd handed me earlier.

"No. Sorry."

"You didn't even look at it."

"The only kind of people who have one-hundred-thousand-dollar bonds are really bad guys. Like murder suspects. I don't need to look at the file to know I don't want the case. You better get a hold of your regular guy and see when he'll be available."

She clamped her cigarette between her lips as she sat forward and pulled open a desk drawer. She was shaking her head, causing a chunk of ash to break off and rain down on the desk.

"Freaking newbie princess," she muttered. "All you newbies, you got some kind of moral objective to everything, like the world's black and white." She slapped a heavy spiral book on to the desk and looked up at me, taking her cigarette between her fingers and pointing them at me. "I'm here to tell ya, it ain't *ever* black or white. Nothing's ever that simple."

I leaned on the desk and met her stare.

"I know. Which is why I don't believe you when you say your regular guy is busy."

She narrowed her eyes at me. "Mind your own business, princess."

She flipped the book open and scribbled out a check. She ripped it free and thrust it at me.

"Since you cleared one, how about you take another from the stack," she said. She picked up a file off one stack sitting at the edge of the desk. "You said you'd take these."

"When I've found the first three, and only if you don't get right with your regular guy."

I folded the check and tucked it into my pocket.

"I'll be in touch when I've got Hapner," I called as I walked to the door.

"Hey! Close that door!"

"No!"

As I angled the Scout out of the lot, I saw the front door was still propped open.

16

Sadie had chosen a Japanese restaurant in Old Town called Suehiro. I found a parking spot only two blocks away, which was lucky for downtown on a Friday afternoon. By the time I walked back, Sadie was seated at a table on the patio.

As usual, she was lovely, her look this afternoon casual, obtained easily, I was sure. Her blonde hair was loose and soft around her shoulders. She wore a light, breezy, knee-length sundress and wedge sandals. She didn't look like she'd just rolled out of bed after sleeping all day because she'd worked all night.

She waved as the hostess showed me to the patio. I confirmed I'd found who I was looking for and went to join her.

"Hi," she said, smiling brightly. "Hope you don't mind if we sit outside. Ugh, why do you smell like an ashtray?"

I pulled my chair further into the shade of the umbrella, lest my weak skin burn in the sun. "Work. Lady I just visited chain-smokes. How was work?"

"Terrible," she said, reaching for her water glass. "I have no idea what was going on at CSU last night, but we must have seen half the student body."

"Probably some start-of-semester bash."

College students don't need much of an excuse to throw a party and drink themselves into oblivion. Any day that ended in *y* seems sufficient.

"Yeah, probably. Anyway, it was a madhouse. And if that wasn't enough, Crazy Karen wouldn't stay away from the drunks."

"What?"

"Yeah. Every time I turned around, she was in someone else's zone with one drunk or another. Someone said she has the hots for one of the security guards." Sadie shrugged. "I only ever saw her with patients."

From past conversations with Sadie, I understood the standard operating procedure in the ER to be to group drunk patients together into one zone of neighboring rooms. This allowed for the consolidation of resources, like security guards, who were required to watch all drunk or mental health patients. Typically, no one wanted to be the nurse with the drunk tank.

"She wanted those patients?" I asked.

"I really don't know. Every nurse last night had drunks; there were just too many of them. Security had to call in their on-call guy. I have no idea what Karen was up to, which is why I'm now calling her *Crazy* Karen."

The waitress appeared at our table. She was a tiny, young Asian woman with long black hair and bright eyes. She wore minimal makeup and the required black uniform and apron. She gave us a small bow.

"Would you like any appetizers?" she asked, with a genuine accent.

Sadie looked at me with question in her raised eyebrow.

I deferred to her. "Whatever you want."

She'd obviously eaten here before, because she knew exactly what she wanted. She ordered something I couldn't pronounce then looked at me. "You have to try it," she said. "I know you'll like it."

The waitress dutifully wrote it all down then asked if we wanted any specialty drinks and if we were ready to order lunch.

We both declined drinks and ordered our meals. The waitress gave another little bow and disappeared, moving almost without sound, gracefully dancing between tables and around chairs.

"So," Sadie said in a tone I knew meant she was turning our conversation to business. "What have you found?"

I'd been debating how much I would tell her during this meeting. I realized, of course, that she'd hired me. But I was new to the whole private investigating thing, and I didn't know if it was customary to show all your cards to the client this early. My natural inclination in life, not just in work, was to keep my cards close and show them to no one.

"I assume you want me to dig all the way to the bottom of Karen Brickle," I said. "You want to know all there is to know, right?"

"Yes. Why?"

"Because I've only begun to scratch the surface. If whatever I tell you now gets around and gets back to Karen, she'll be gone, and this investigation will be over."

She looked at me for a beat, then a wide smile spread over her face. "You're worried I'm going to run around blabbering whatever you tell me."

"It crossed my mind. There aren't a lot of secrets among your group of friends."

"On the contrary, Zoe, there are a great many secrets. It's why we're all still friends."

That was a new twist on the way I'd always viewed Sadie's close-knit social circle.

"Be that as it may, it will be best if you don't say anything to anyone for the time being."

"You can trust me to keep   quiet, I assure you."

The waitress appeared beside our table again, this time holding several small platters of food. She carefully arranged them on the table, bowed, and disappeared.

"This one here," Sadie said, pointing to one of the plates. "You've got to try it. It's wonderful."

I started to ask what it was then thought better of it. Instead I just plucked up a piece with my fingers, foregoing the chopsticks I couldn't use, and put it in my mouth. To my surprise and delight, it was actually very good, whatever it was.

Sadie chuckled. "You look so surprised." I noticed she was emphasizing her Southern drawl. "Why, Zoe, in the span of just one lunch, I'm beginning to think maybe you don't trust me."

By her tone I knew she was just having fun with me. Sadie knew I trusted her, because that trust had been put to the test several times in the past. She'd never let me down.

"I'll trust you to order lunch in a foreign language anytime," I said. My way of apology.

She laughed. "We should have French next time."

French cuisine isn't my favorite, but Sadie will never give up trying to convert me.

She sat back in her chair, crossed her legs, and took a drink of water. "Okay," she said. "Let's hear it."

I wiped my hands, thinking.

There seemed to be only one course of action.

"'Karen Brickle' is not her real name," I said.

Sadie's eyes widened just a fraction as she took that in. "What is her real name?"

"I don't know yet. She's been using this one for a while now, so it's going to take some digging."

"Is that what you found in her house?"

"No. Actually, there wasn't much interesting at her house. Half of it is still in boxes."

"Really? She's been here for months."

"Maybe she's been busy; maybe she's planning to move again; maybe she's just lazy. But there are a lot of boxes."

"Did it look like anyone lived there with her?"

"Not particularly. Why?"

"She's been real close and cozy with this EMT named Jimmy. I just wondered if he was shacking up with her yet."

"Yet?"

She shrugged one perfectly brown shoulder. "He tends to move in quickly. You know, gets a new girl, then next thing you know, he's living with her. They break up, and it's on to the next."

"You think they're dating?"

"No idea, but like I said, they seem cozy."

"What's his last name?"

"Ward, I think. Why?"

"I don't know. Might be something to check out."

We were quiet for a few minutes, both of us munching on the various appetizers. After some time, Sadie leaned back in her chair and looked at me. I could see her eyes faintly through her sunglasses.

"Why do you think she changed her name?"

That was the million-dollar question.

"I don't know," I said.

"But it's probably not good."

"I can't think of a lot of innocent reasons to assume a new identity."

"Do you think she really did have something to do with her friend's disappearance in Boulder?"

"It's really too early to say one way or the other."

"But that possibility has crossed your mind."

"Yes, it has."

"As much as I dislike her, I was really hoping you'd find nothing and she'd turn out to be just a terrible nurse and a nasty person."

"I was hoping the same thing."

17

I needed help getting additional information on Karen Brickle, and I planned to take care of that this evening. But that left me with a few hours to kill and two skips to track. A quick cruise past Medera's told me nothing had changed.

So I decided to take a run at Robert Hapner. In the past, Hapner hadn't proven difficult to find. I thought I could grab him today and cross him off my to-do list.

Timber Ridge Mobile Home Park wasn't too bad, as far as trailer parks go. And I have some frame of reference. Since starting this bounty hunter gig, I've been to every trailer park in town chasing FTAs. I'm not making any correlations, just stating a fact.

I cruised past Hapner's trailer, located in the middle of the block and boasting a six-foot privacy fence. The fence was weird. His was the only fence I saw, and it surrounded the entire lot, not just the yard. Surely the community had regulations against such things, so why had they permitted it?

I parked around the corner and walked back. The neighborhood was quiet, even at this time of day. The few homes that appeared occupied had TVs and radios playing. One man was outside working under the hood of his El Camino. I'd seen another lounging in a lawn chair at the other end of the street.

As I neared Hapner's place from the opposite direction that I'd driven in, I realized the fence was only one of many weird things about it. Second were the blacked out windows I could now see. Suddenly, I had warning bells sounding inside my head.

Maybe he works nights, I thought. Sadie worked nights and had blackout curtains on her bedroom windows.

But Hapner's windows looked covered over with trash bags, not curtains, or even a sheet. And it wasn't just the windows of one room; it was all the windows. There just weren't any good reasons to blackout *all* the windows.

As I got nearer, my footsteps elicited barking from the other side of the fence. Through the wooden slats, I saw enough movement to conclude there were two dogs in there, although only one was barking. Apparently, the BEWARE OF DOG signs were not just for show.

The barking had alerted those inside the trailer, and someone at the end of the block. Two men, neither of which were Hapner, came out onto the front step and looked around, eyeing me with open hostility. They were both dressed in white tank tops and sweating like pigs. They also both had one hand behind their backs, no doubt gripping the handles of guns stuffed into their pants. See? That's where the *bad guys* keep their guns.

I acknowledged them in what I hoped was a neighborly and disinterested fashion and kept walking. They stood on the porch, continuing to watch me with suspicion. As I passed, I caught the distinct scent of burning plastic, which unnecessarily confirmed what I'd already come to suspect.

I strolled to the end of the block and made a right, now under the careful watch of the man in the lawn chair, whom I suspected was a lookout. In an effort to sell the just-out-for-a-walk bit, I walked two more blocks before making another right and heading back toward my truck.

When I was finally out of sight of the corner lookout, I pulled out my phone and dialed Ellmann.

"Hey, I can't talk long," he   said. "What's up?"

103

"I went to pick up a skip and found a meth lab instead."

He didn't seem surprised. "Where?"

I gave him the address.

"Where are you now?"

"A couple blocks away."

"I don't have to tell you not to go back, right?"

"No. I already aroused suspicion. I'm afraid of what they'll do if they see me again. As you might imagine, they're edgy."

"No shit. I'm sending people now. Stay clear until you hear from me."

"Copy that."

I hung up and walked to the end of the street. When I made a right and started back to the truck, I knew I had a problem.

The man who'd been working on the El Camino was standing at the corner, looking at the Scout and talking on a cell phone. He spotted me then reported something to whoever was on the other end of the call. When he spoke again, I was near enough to hear him.

"Yeah, that's her . . . No, she doesn't live around here. Her truck's parked around the corner."

I got on my phone again, this time calling 911. I needed help sooner than Ellmann's guys could get themselves together.

I quickly reported a gunman and my current location. It seemed like a good bet the guy did have a gun, and reports of gunmen always brought the cops running. The dispatcher promised me help soon, and instructed me to stay on the line. I hung up.

The lookout mechanic nodded his head. "Yeah. I'll take care of her." Then he snapped the phone closed.

"Let me leave," I said, still walking toward the truck. "I don't want to hurt you."

Really, I didn't want to kill him, and these things had a way of going that direction in a hurry. Best to avoid them all together.

He snickered as he tucked the phone into his pocket. "That's funny."

He shot a look down the street to his left as he continued striding toward me, now reaching behind him, no doubt for his gun. When he looked back he suddenly froze, his hand out at his side and indeed holding a gun. He was staring at the Browning P22 I'd pulled from the holster at the small of my back.

"Drop your weapon," I said, the Browning steady in front of me as I continued forward.

"You a cop?" the lookout mechanic asked, failing to comply with my instruction. His eyes flicked down to my waist, and I imagined part of the badge was visible.

"No," I said, "but I'm a damn good shot."

He scoffed, but he was beginning to rethink his position. "You won't shoot me."

"I'd shoot you in a heartbeat," I said, stopping twenty yards from him. "Drop that weapon."

I saw his eyes flit to the left briefly and knew he saw something down the street.

He dropped the gun and raised his hands, grinning at me like an idiot. A split second later, I heard a whistle blow. Three more whistles blew in response. The alarm had been raised and acknowledged. Hapner and his buddies were undoubtedly on the move, getting the hell out of Dodge before the cops showed up.

"Son of a bitch," I swore as I charged forward.

The lookout mechanic was still grinning when I clubbed him with the butt of the Browning. I blew by as he fell and ran for Hapner's street a block ahead. I could hear his dog barking again, along with someone, a male, shouting. I tried to remember if I'd seen a car.

I rounded the corner onto Hapner's street as I heard the first wail of a siren. A beat-up Eurovan tore out of the driveway across from Hapner's and shot to the end of the block, barely slowing enough for the corner lookout to jump in. I committed the plate to memory and slowed to a walk. I hadn't seen the driver or anyone else in the van, but I guessed Hapner to be among them.

"Shut *up*! Stupid dog!"

Someone was still at Hapner's.

I was running again. I saw a glimpse of a man coming out of the trailer and heard a car door squeak open on old hinges.

"Move, you! Get back! Get! Sits! Sits!"

An engine fired up, and I ran for the fence, expecting the driver to open the gate. Instead there was an enormous crash as the car, an old Mercury sedan, collided with the fence, ripping a section away. As the car backed crazily into the street, a Pitbull shot through the open fence and ran down the street past me.

I jumped out of the path of the car and caught a look at the driver. Robert Hapner.

I brought the gun up.

"Stop! Get out!"

Yeah, right.

The old boat skidded to a halt and the fence slid off, landing in the street. Hapner shoved the transmission into drive and stomped on the gas. Then he had a gun out the window, aimed not at me, but at the trailer. I immediately understood what he was doing.

"Shit!"

I turned to run and saw the front yard where the fence was missing. A huge German Shepherd was standing at the edge of the yard, watching the scene unfold in the street. Suddenly, a few pieces fell into place.

"*Hierr!*" I ordered the dog, waving him toward me. "*Hierr!*"

The dog immediately complied, but came quickly to the end of a rope that had been lying slack on what was left of the yard. The rope was tied to a stake near the house.

"Shit."

Hapner was now firing, his bullets spraying the side of the trailer.

In a moment of what probably amounted to insanity, I fired off a few rounds at Hapner's car as I started toward the dog. Hapner's fire halted briefly in response to the bullets now flying in his direction.

I sprinted for all I was worth as I pulled out my pocketknife. I slid to a stop next to the dog like a runner sliding into home and swiped at the rope with the knife. The rope separated. I dropped the knife, pushed myself up, and ran.

"*Hierr!*" I ordered again as Hapner's fire resumed. I heard the click of the dog's nails on the pavement as the bullets peppered the side of the trailer, some of them shattering the windows. I fired off a few more rounds at the car, just to buy myself a little time.

As I darted back into the street, feeling horribly exposed, I heard a third gun, the shots coming from a different direction. The sound of the bullets hitting the side of a car registered, and I thought maybe the patrol officer was giving me some cover fire.

I sprinted directly across the street, my eye on a rusting Honda Accord parked at the curb one lot down—the best I could hope for now; even with the suppression fire, Hapner hadn't let up. I flung myself over the hood, the dog leaping right beside me, as I heard another round of fire from Hapner's gun. And he finally hit was he was aiming for.

An enormous explosion pounded my eardrums and shoved me violently over the hood of the Honda, where I landed hard on the sidewalk, the Browning flying out of my hand. I saw the dog land roughly on the pavement and stumble. The windows of the Honda burst, spraying the immediate vicinity with glass. Debris rained down and the smell of ammonia burned on the air.

For a moment, I was stunned. I was overwhelmed by the force of the explosion, the sound of it in my ears, and the choking chemicals in the air. I tried to force my brain into gear, but it seemed momentarily disconnected from my body. All I could do was lay splayed out on the sidewalk.

Finally, sense returned to me, and I could move. With a groan and a cascade of sensation, I pushed myself up and sat leaning against the Honda for a moment while I tried to get my bearings and catch my breath.

The dog hovered nearby. I put a hand on him. Even through my stunned haze, I couldn't help but notice there was no anxiety in his body. He was alert, closely watching me and both directions of the sidewalk, but he wasn't anxious. This confirmed the theory I'd formed a moment earlier.

After a few breaths, I tried to get up, reaching for my gun. I went down hard on my knee, so I crawled to the gun. I got a hold of it and pushed to my feet. I swayed badly and felt a powerful wave of nausea roll through me. I fell back to the ground a second time. On my third try, I used the car, leaning heavily against it as I swallowed the nausea and tried a few more steps. Finally, enough of my senses came back I seemed able to move without falling. I hurried down the sidewalk away from the explosion as fast as I could.

I saw a patrol car turn the corner and head down the street toward me, the officer with a radio mic in his hand. He stopped and got out, hurrying toward me. I knew him. Officer Derek Frye.

"Shit, Zoe, are you okay?" His voice seemed far away, barely audible around the ringing in my ears.

I didn't try to answer. Instead I just nodded my head and kept moving, the dog right beside me. Frye was obviously curious about the dog, but he had bigger things to worry about. He touched my shoulder as I passed, then turned and moved down the street, talking into his radio.

I'd thought about trying to make it back to my car, but made it only as far as Frye's, parked at an angle across the street. I sank down to the pavement, pulled my knees up in front of me, leaned against the car, and closed my eyes. Once again I could feel the dog nearby, and I didn't have to look to know he was once again on guard.

We were still there when the cavalry showed up.

18

An hour later, I was sitting in the back of the open ambulance, a young EMT working on my minor cuts and scrapes. The dog sat on the floor leaning against my leg, ever watchful. He was keeping an eye on the EMT as well as the others outside the ambulance. He had refused to wait outside the ambulance once I'd gone into it, despite the protests of the medics.

I didn't know the dog's name. He wore a collar, but there were no tags. I thought I could feel a microchip under the skin in his neck, however.

I'd been examined by the EMT and her paramedic partner and been found to have nothing more serious than bruises and a few lacerations, nothing that needed stitches, casts, or surgery. Even my eardrums seemed to have survived intact. Which was nothing short of a miracle. The paramedic was now talking to a pretty female patrol officer whose name I couldn't remember, and the EMT was smearing my forearms with antibiotic ointment.

Ellmann wandered over. The dog watched him approach.

When I turned to Ellmann, I saw him wince briefly before he pulled on his neutral cop mask. While I wasn't seriously injured, I knew I looked terrible. And Ellmann had undoubtedly been worried after he'd gotten word of the explosion, knowing how close I was.

"I'm okay," I said to him.

He slowed as he neared the back of the ambulance and addressed the dog.

"I'm coming up there," he said, "and I'm going to kiss her."

Ellmann seemed to have come to the same conclusion about the dog as I had.

With deliberate movements, Ellmann stepped on the bumper of the ambulance and leaned inside, one arm braced on the gurney beside me. Then he carefully kissed my lips and squeezed my hand.

The dog watched him but didn't move, didn't make a sound.

"You had me worried," Ellmann said.

"I'm sorry."

Ellmann turned to the EMT. "About finished?"

She nodded and held up a package of gauze. "Last thing."

"What's that for?" I asked.

"Your arms," she said.

I suddenly envisioned her wrapping me up like a mummy.

I chuckled. "No way." I stood, and the dog jumped up, watching me. I waved toward the open doors of the ambulance. "Let's go," I said to him.

Ellmann backed out and held my hand as I edged past the EMT. The dog jumped down, and I followed him. I instantly regretted it, groaning at the impact. Ellmann perched on the bumper, then pulled me down to sit beside him. He wrapped his arm around my shoulder.

The dog sat beside me again, leaning on my leg. I scratched his head, and he resumed his vigil.

"Did you start smoking?" Ellmann asked as kissed my temple.

"No. I was talking to a tiny, chain-smoking demon earlier."

"Hmm. How you feeling?"

"Not great. They tell me the ringing in my ears will last a day or two."

Ellmann nodded. "I thought we agreed you would stay well clear of Hapner's trailer." I could feel the tension in him, and knew he was working to keep his voice even.

"You know what they say about the best laid plans."

"You could have been killed."

I looked down at the dog. "He *would have* been killed."

Ellmann sighed then resigned himself to the fact that my stupidity would always win out in the end. He reached into his pocket then held something out to me. "I believe this is yours."

I looked down at my pocketknife. Smiling, I accepted it with my thanks.

"So, you've grown attached to the dog."

"Actually, I think maybe he's attached to me."

"You don't say."

I chuckled.

Ellmann asked, "Are you going to keep him?"

"What? No. I couldn't." Even if the thought had maybe crossed my mind once. Or twice. "Anyway," I said, "the humane society is coming to pick him up."

"You remember I told you about those dogs being stolen from the training facility in Colorado Springs?"

I nodded. I was way ahead of him. "The place that trains police and military service dogs? I remember. Why?" I suspected we had the same idea.

"We'll have to check records to confirm, but based on what you told me, I'm guessing this dog was one of those stolen."

That made a lot of sense. It was what I'd come to suspect shortly before the explosion.

I asked, "Why on Earth would Robert Hapner have a dog like this? Do you think *he* stole him from the training facility?"

112

"No, they caught the guys who stole the dogs the following day. But they never recovered the dogs. I have no idea why Hapner would have this one. But this dog has been formally trained."

"With German commands," I said. "Why would an American training facility use German commands?"

Dogs trained in foreign languages typically came from overseas. If they were trained in Germany, for example, they would know German commands. Once they got wherever they were going, like America, it was easier to teach the new handler German than it was to retrain the dog to understand English commands.

After seeing the dog, it was a small leap to guess that I'd heard Hapner trying to give the German command for "sit" earlier. Only Hapner didn't know German, because he'd been shouting, "sits." Really, it is pronounced more like, "zits." The only reason I know this is because a couple of times, when Amy and I were very young, her great-grandmother had come to visit. That old woman was purebred German, like fresh off the boat. She only made German food, she only wore antique German dresses, and she only spoke German. She was always telling Amy and me to "come here," (*hierr*), and "sit down," (*sitz*). I also remember a few food words, but those hadn't ever been useful.

I was glad I'd remembered the German. Otherwise either the dog or I or both of us would be dead now.

"That's a good question," Ellmann said. "I'll be sure to ask when I contact the facility. Actually, I'm sure they'll want to examine the dog for confirmation, so maybe you can ask yourself."

"I can't keep the dog. Anyway, I'm sure the facility wants him back."

"Even if they do, they can't take him. Or at least they can't keep him. For safety reasons, the dog cannot go back to the facility, and he can't be put to work as a military or a police

113

dog. It's too dangerous; there's no way to know for sure what he might have been taught while he was missing. "

So it was off to the pound for this dog. Which didn't sit very well with me, I noticed.

As if on cue, a humane society van cruised up the street and parked a short distance from the ambulance. A greasy-looking guy in a tan uniform got out and stalked over, a dark, beady eye on the dog. The dog sat beside me, looking from me to the humane society guy.

"This the dog?" the guy asked.

His shirt read HARRIS.

I didn't immediately answer. I think because I didn't get a great feeling about Harris. And because I'd sensed a shift in the dog; the dog didn't like Harris.

"If it is," Ellmann said, "what might happen to him after you take possession?"

Harris shrugged. "Dog like that, with military training, that's a dangerous dog. Can't go back to military service, but ain't suited to civilian life, either." He shrugged again. "Probably get put down eventually. Who knows."

Paul Martin, the SWAT commander, walked past the ambulance, his eye on a couple of his SWAT officers gathered near a patrol car half a block away. He spotted the dog and looked at Harris.

"Get that damn dog out of here," he snapped. "Now."

"Yes, sir," Harris said, unwrapping a short leather leash he'd wound around his narrow waist. "All right now, fella, you best come quietly."

He marched forward. The dog immediately stood and began to bark.

Harris had the sense to stop. But his eyes turned dark and mean. This guy sure wasn't much of a dogcatcher.

Harris's hand drifted toward his belt. Then he reached around and pulled a pistol from the waistband at the small of his back. I knew two things instantly. One, the dog was going to attack Harris for brandishing a weapon. And two, Harris was going to fire the pistol at the dog.

Ellmann and I shot off the bumper. I reached one hand down to the dog, near his collar, though I didn't take hold of it. The other I raised toward Harris. The dog was barking, and his body was tensed for action. I wished to hell I knew more German.

Ellmann's eyes were on Harris. "Let's take it easy with that gun."

"It's a tranquilizer gun," he said, like that made it better.

The barking drew the attention of several of the nearby cops who were now quiet and watching the scene carefully, slowly making their way closer with their hands on the guns holstered on their hips.

Ellmann raised his hands to a few of them, warning them not to do anything hasty.

"There's no need for it, Officer Harris." Ellmann was using his cop-negotiator voice. It was a pretty effective one, and it seemed to get Harris's attention. That and the fact Ellmann was showing him respect by using an official title. "Why don't you put it away?"

Harris thought about it for a beat. "That dog's got to come with me, one way or the other." He raised the pistol.

The dog continued barking, and the tension in his body mounted. Now, he was doing little jumps, ready to go.

What a fucking moron. Harris knew the dog had military training. Didn't he have any idea what that meant? I'm not even a dogcatcher, and I know that meant this dog had been trained to attack people holding weapons. A part of me wanted to let the dog attack him. But the smarter part of me knew there was a serious chance someone, maybe the dog or maybe a cop on scene, would get hit with the tranq dart, and that if this dog attacked, it would be harder to keep him from the gas chamber. Or the needle—whatever they did with unruly and dangerous dogs.

I curled my fingers around his collar.

"I think there's been a misunderstanding here, Officer Harris," Ellmann said.

"Yeah?" Harris said, his eyes on the dog and his mouth almost salivating at the thought of using his gun. "And what's that?"

"This isn't the dog we called you about."

Harris's eyes immediately shot up to Ellmann's. "What do you mean?"

Thank you, Ellmann!

"This dog belongs to me," I said quickly.

Harris eyed the dog again. "He don't seem that well trained, lady. And he ain't even on a leash."

"He's had specialized police service training," I said. "He doesn't need a leash. But guns make him nervous. You understand."

"Oh," Harris said, as if he just realized he was holding a gun in his hand. "Well, now, take it easy, big fella. I'll just put this away."

Harris slowly brought the gun around behind his back and tucked it into his waistband. See what I mean about guys who carry guns there?

Harris then raised both empty hands out in front of him. But the dog didn't stop barking. Or hopping.

I stroked his back.

"All right," I said to him. "That's enough now. Stand down. *Sitz.*"

He plopped his butt down and stopped barking, but he was still vibrating with energy and excitement. And he was still watching Harris.

"I'm sorry for the confusion, Officer Harris," Ellmann said, striding forward with his hand out to Harris. He squeezed Harris's hand in an effortlessly crushing handshake, clapping Harris's shoulder with his other hand. Then he steered the guy back toward his van.

"Thank you for coming out," Ellmann was saying. "The dog we're concerned with is a Pitbull. The witness reported it was a full-sized dog and had a brown coat with white markings on the chest and paws. It was last seen running east on this road here. We have had no further sightings since we arrived on scene, so we can't say for sure whether the dog is still in the neighborhood."

As I watched Ellmann redirect Harris onto the search for the missing Pitbull, I was aware of a figure coming up to stand beside me. A sideward glance told me it was the SWAT commander Paul Martin.

Ellmann shook Harris's hand again, then Harris climbed into his van and motored off, talking into a microphone he pulled off the dashboard. Ellmann walked back over, noticing Martin. Even though he had his cop face on, I knew Ellmann well enough to know he wasn't happy.

"Someone care to explain that to me?" Martin asked.

I hated when I got Ellmann into trouble with his coworkers, especially his superiors.

"Martin, look," Ellmann began.

"I thought I said I wanted that dog out of here," Martin said, looking between Ellmann and me.

"That trigger-happy idiot was going to shoot the dog!" I said, indignant.

"It didn't seem appropriate or necessary," Ellmann cut in smoothly, "for the humane society to take possession of the dog." Of course, his way sounded much better than mine.

"I don't care where the dog goes," Martin said slowly, as if talking to a couple of children. "I just want him away from my crime scene."

Technically, this wasn't Martin's crime scene. SWAT was no longer needed, since there was no house to breach and search and no suspects left to apprehend. Really, it was Ellmann's crime scene, since he would be the investigating detective. But neither of us pointed this out. Instead we both simply nodded.

Martin turned and walked away, rejoining the men he'd been speaking with previously.

Ellmann sighed and dragged a hand back through his hair.

"Am I in trouble?" I asked.

"Probably. But what's new?"

19

I needed to get cleaned up, but I wanted the dog looked at first. He didn't seem injured, but dogs have a tendency to hide their ailments. At least that's what my friends with dogs had always told me.

I called Sadie to ask about her vet.

"Did you get a dog?" she asked. The excitement in her voice was unmistakable; she'd been telling me I needed a dog for years.

"I'm not sure," I said. "I'm at a crime scene and there's one here that needs to be evaluated."

"Sounds like the humane society should take him."

"The dog didn't like the dogcatcher."

She chuckled. "I take Lola to Pierce Family Vet Clinic. We usually see Bernie, and Lola seems to like him."

Lola is Sadie's eight-year-old Basset Hound. Lola's spoiled rotten, but she's pretty cute.

"They've got a program going with CSU's vet school," Sadie went on. "They get some kind of grant or something from the school in exchange for letting students intern there. You usually have a student conducting exams and such, but they're always supervised and it means the prices are affordable."

"Okay, thanks. I'll give them a call."

"I want to meet the new boy—is it a boy?"

"Yes. We'll see if he stays   with me."

She laughed again and hung up.

I looked up Pierce Family Veterinary Clinic then called and spoke to a pleasant and competent-sounding woman named Jessie. After I explained the situation, she told me to bring the dog straight over.

I checked out with Ellmann and returned to my truck, the dog following behind my left leg. I pulled the driver's side door open, and he immediately launched himself up and across the bench seat, like we'd done this a thousand times. I couldn't help but notice how incredibly at home he looked there.

I climbed inside and maneuvered the Scout out around various emergency vehicles still clogging up the roads of the small neighborhood.

The vet's office was located on Prospect near Overland, not too far from CSU's equine center. The office was one of several houses along this stretch of road that had been converted into businesses. Another was a daycare next door. The happy sounds of playing children drifted across the parking lot as we made our way to the front door.

The lobby was crowded. I didn't have a leash or anything for the dog, and it hadn't occurred to me I might need one until we went inside. But it became clear the dog couldn't have cared less who was in the lobby.

The dog stuck close to me as I went to the front desk. When I stopped, he immediately dropped into a sit and was soon leaning against my leg.

The receptionist, an eccentric woman with short, choppy, blonde hair with pink streaks and pink cat-eye glasses with rhinestones, looked up from her desk then did a double take, shooting up out of her chair with wide eyes.

"Oh, my word! Are you okay?"

It stuck me then how I must have looked. Which explained the way the others in the lobby had looked at me. I'd shaken most of the glass out of my hair and tied it up in an knot on top of my head, and I'd borrowed a navy blue FCPD t-shirt from Ellmann's gym bag, which was too big but at least in one piece, but I still looked and smelled like I'd been way too close to a meth house when it had exploded.

"I'm fine," I said, trying to give her a reassuring smile. "It looks worse than it is."

"My goodness," she said, settling a hand on her chest. "I certainly hope so, because you look positively terrible."

"Thank you," I said. "I called and talked to Jessie a few minutes ago. She was going to fit us in."

The hand on the woman's chest fluttered slightly as she tried to pull her thoughts from the troubling state of my appearance.

"Right. I'll see if she's available." She moved around the desk and glanced down at the dog as she passed. Then she stopped and stared at me with open accusation. "Your dog must be on a leash in the office."

"I'm sorry, I don't have a leash."

She looked utterly confused. "What do you mean you don't have one?"

"We sort of just met."

"Do you mean this isn't *your* dog?"

"I explained all this to Jessie," I said, my head throbbing. "Maybe I should talk to her."

She took my comment to be an implication that Jessie would permit me to break the rules, and she was offended.

"Your dog—or *whoever's* dog—can't be in here without a leash."

I bit back the response that suddenly formed on the tip of my tongue and took a breath. "Do you have one I could borrow?"

She made a huge show of getting one off a hook on the wall behind her desk. Then she waited and watched while I looped it around the dog's neck.

Finally satisfied, she said, "I'll see if Jessie's available."

With that, she turned and disappeared through a door.

I moved away from the desk and took an empty seat against the back wall. I drew open stares from everyone waiting in the lobby, and an elderly woman, cradling some kind of poodle trembling on her lap, watched the dog and me pass by, as if one of us might suddenly attack her. Once I sat, a woman with two small children and a cat in a cardboard box got up and shooed her kids to seats at the other end of the room.

The dog followed me and sat beside me, leaning against my leg.

"You can lay down," I said to him.

He looked at me, but he didn't move. I really needed to learn more German.

The lobby was painted a pale green color and there was a fish tank in one corner. There were stiff, old, uncomfortable brown chairs around the perimeter, with a couple of end tables holding magazines. The newest feature in the office was the hardwood floor, which was a fairly recent upgrade, I guessed.

The walls were covered with pet-themed posters, a few breed posters, and an advertisement about heartworm. There was also a large bulletin board near the hallway leading to the exam rooms and the rest of the building. Mostly the board held advertisements of animals for sale, flyers about lost animals, and a smattering of pictures of owners with their pets. Near the bottom, though, added more recently than most of the other things, was a missing person poster for Maria Rodriguez, the CSU student I'd heard about on the news.

Soon, the receptionist returned and pointed an accusatory finger at me. The attractive brunette with her smiled and came over to me. She barely blinked at the state I was in, though she clearly noticed. She stuck her hand out to me.

I stood and shook her hand. The dog jumped up with me.

"I'm Jessie," she said, her smile warm. "We spoke on the phone. This must be him." She smiled down at the dog but made no move to touch him.

Her nametag said JESSIE WHITMORE, DVM. I was surprised to realize she was a doctor.

"It is. Thank you for fitting us in."

"Happy to, really," she said, sliding her hands into the pockets of her lab coat absently. "We don't have as many students here today, so I don't have much to do. I'm happy to see him. He's beautiful. Pure bred German Shepherd, I'm sure."

"He is a good-looking dog," I said.

"Oh, yes. His markings are absolutely perfect. Classic. Wow."

I don't know much about this kind of thing and couldn't really speak to it.

"Guess he's lucky," I said.

Jessie chuckled softly. "Well, shall we take a look? Let's get a weight first, if you don't mind." She indicated the scale near the front desk.

I followed her over to it, and the dog followed me. When the receptionist shot me a disapproving look I realized I'd forgotten about the leash, which was just hanging around his neck.

"Step up here," I said to the dog, holding my hand out over the scale. "Come on. *Hierr.*"

The dog stepped up onto the scale.

"Good boy," I told him. "Now, *sitz.* Good boy."

The digital display on the scale ticked up then stopped.

"Shit," I heard myself say. "Is that accurate?"

"Yes," Jessie said. "Ninety-one pounds. He's a big boy."

"Big" was an understatement. The dog weighed as much as some human beings. I couldn't imagine how much he must eat.

"There aren't any open rooms," Jessie said, "but we can use my office. It's this way."

She crossed the lobby, headed toward the hallway. As we passed it, my attention was drawn once more to the bulletin board.

"Excuse me," I said, pointing to the flyer for Maria Rodriquez. "Do you know this woman?"

She glanced at the poster and seemed genuinely sad. "Yes. Maria's worked here for several months, since she started at CSU. We really miss her."

"I'm sorry to ask."

She shook her head. "Not a problem. Please, this way."

She went through a door marked STAFF ONLY, which opened to what used to be the kitchen. It was now a work area with two stainless steel tables, laboratory equipment, and currently occupied by two people in scrubs attempting to draw blood from a cat. The cat wasn't happy.

Behind the kitchen, we passed two small surgical suites, neither of which were currently in use. Behind those, another door opened to a small office. There were three desks crammed into the space, but the area was orderly. And unoccupied.

Jessie waited for us to enter then closed the door. She pulled out a chair from one of the desks and offered it to me as she sat at the desk I imagined was hers.

"Please, sit."

I sat and told the dog to do the same. He sat and leaned against my leg. He suddenly felt heavier to me, knowing the weight I felt totaled a whopping ninety-one pounds.

"So tell me more about what happened," she said, pulling a legal pad from her desk and flipping to a blank page.

I relayed the explosion to her in broad strokes, only going into more detail when she asked for it. A meth lab explosion was not a normal thing, and while not-normal things happened to me with depressing frequency, most people found them unsettling. I'd learned not to talk too much about them.

"So you really know nothing about this dog," she said.

"No. Other than he's been trained. The police are contacting the training facility in Colorado Springs. We may learn he was one of theirs."

"Even if he is, no one can account for the last year—where he's been, what he's been eating, how he's been treated, those sorts of things."

"That's correct."

"I'd like to do a physical exam, check his vitals, really look him over. I'd also like to draw blood. He'll certainly need a heartworm test. And because we can't account for his medical history, I'd like to give him all of his vaccine boosters."

"Okay. I have to tell you, I don't know how he'll respond to all of that. I don't know him very well, and I only know two German words."

She smiled at me, and I had the distinct impression she knew something I didn't. It was the second time she'd had that look, and I was very curious to know the secret.

"Let's just see how it goes," she said.

"I don't think that's a good idea. He's trained to bite people."

"That's true. But he won't bite me unless you command him to."

She said this with absolute trust and confidence. I was not so certain.

She set her notes on the desk and pulled the stethoscope from around her neck.

She looked at me. "He'll follow your lead."

"Right."

I realized I was putting a great deal of trust in this woman, hoping she knew dogs as well as she thought she did.

I pushed my chair back and stood. The dog jumped up. He looked at me expectantly.

"Let's have a look at you," I said to him, dropping to my knees.

I pulled off the useless borrowed leash and took hold of the dog's collar, gently pulling him into my chest. As if he'd merely been waiting for an invitation, he leaned into me, closing his eyes and rubbing his face against me. I automatically wrapped my arms around him and cuddled him close, scratching his neck and ears, murmuring softly to him. In that moment, I realized how easy it would be to forget the dog was a highly trained weapon.

Jessie smiled. "That's what I thought."

"What do you mean?"

"He's rather attached to you."

She was still smiling, and I understood this was the secret she'd been holding.

I shrugged. "I saved his life. I'm sure that's all it is."

She chuckled lightly. "I doubt it."

I wasn't sure how to take that, so I changed the subject. "What happens now?" I was still snuggling the dog, who was still leaning into me.

"I don't want to surprise him," she said, turning to business. "Stay calm and don't worry about me touching him or about him biting me. He'll take his cues from you, and he'll sense if you're anxious. Hey, there, big guy."

She spoke to him a soft voice and reached her hand out. He sniffed it quickly then turned back to me. She began to pet him, and if he noticed, he didn't seem to care.

The doctor moved through the process of her exam, listening to his heart and lungs, palpating his belly, taking his temperature, even looking in multiple orifices with various instruments. The dog tolerated it all, with no reaction more serious than a look of intense displeasure when the thermometer went up his butt.

"He's got a microchip," she said, fingering the small bump in his neck I'd noticed earlier. "Unfortunately, our reader was broken yesterday." She smiled. "That's the only downsides to the students. With so many inexperienced people, the equipment takes a real beating. Anyway, whoever does the evaluation from the training facility will have one."

When it came time to draw his blood, she left and returned with some syringes, some empty blood tubes, and several small vials.

"Normally, I'd have one of the vet techs hold him while I draw the blood," she said as she readied one of the syringes. "But with dogs like this, they don't tolerate that because they're trained against that kind of situation. With these dogs, they'll only trust their handlers to hold them." She looked at me and said, "That's you." Just in case I wasn't following.

"Right."

"I'll give him the boosters first," she said, drawing up the last of the vaccines. "Then we'll do the blood."

She showed me how she wanted me to hold him, and he allowed me to do so. He didn't like it, of course, but he submitted.

She made quick work of the injections, and then I held him for the blood draw. As I did, I realized there was only one reason she was able to get the blood, and that was because he allowed it. Holding him, I could feel the strength and power in him, and I knew had he objected to the blood draw, I would have never been able to hold him still.

"That's a good boy," she gushed as she stood. She set the syringe on her desk and pulled open a desk drawer. She handed me several milk bones.

I gave the bones to the dog, who pretty much inhaled them. When they were gone, he sat and looked at me as he licked his lips.

"No more," I said.

He tipped his head to the side slightly. Jessie laughed.

"That's it," I said, knowing if I'd had more treats to give him, I wouldn't have been able to resist.

"This heartworm test only takes a minute," she said, indicating the small slide she'd already applied several drops of blood to. "The rest of the blood work will be back in an hour or so. I'll call you with results." She used the syringe to fill a couple of small blood tubes, then set them aside and started punching stuff into the computer. "I'll make sure Missy gets you a copy of his vaccination record, and we'll get you a new rabies tag. Do you have any questions?"

"No, I guess not." I looked at the dog. He looked up at me. "I suppose I should get him some food and some toys and some stuff. Maybe a leash."

Jessie pulled open a desk drawer and fingered through some files, finding the sheet she wanted. "This is a list of food we recommend." She marked the page and handed it to me. "Those two brands are the ones most likely used at the training facility. Of course, there's no way to know what the hell he's been eating since he left there. If indeed he belonged to them at all."

"Thanks," I said, smiling. I liked Jessie.

"Looks like heartworm is negative," she said. "That's good. You'll need to start him on meds today."

"I will. Thanks again for fitting us in."

She laughed and waved a hand. "My pleasure."

She picked up the borrowed leash and led us back out to the lobby. I earned another look from Missy the receptionist when Jessie went behind the desk and hung up the leash. After a few instructions to Missy, Jessie shook my hand and went back to work.

Missy got me some heartworm medication, a rabies tag, and a current county pet license. Then she handed me the bill, which wasn't as affordable as I'd hoped.

20

The meth lab explosion had eaten up a lot of time, so now I was worried about making my next appointment, though I was tired enough I could have just crawled into bed and slept twelve hours. Getting blown up really takes it out of you.

After leaving the vet's office, I hurried home for a fast shower. I let us in the front door and the dog stood beside me, suddenly eager, alert. He looked around the house, eyeing the opening that led back to the kitchen and the stairs to the second floor. Then he looked back at me, wagging his tail, waiting, as if for a command. I wished like hell I had one for him.

"This is home," I told him. "I live here. I guess you live here now, too."

He stomped his feet as he looked from me to the house and back. He wagged his tail. He kept looking at the kitchen and the stairs. Did he want to clear the house?

My brain began to tingle with the possibilities.

"Okay," I said. "Go on. Go do what you need to do."

He hopped now, wagging his tail, an excited growl bubbling up out of his throat.

"Go," I said, waving my hand. What was the German word for go? "Go!"

Either the dog finally understood me or he wasn't willing to wait any longer for a command. He tore away from me, his massively strong body shooting through the living room. He disappeared into the kitchen. A second later he returned and darted straight up the stairs. His tail wagged the entire time.

A dog that clears houses? Man, I'm gonna love this dog.

I went to the mudroom near the back door and peeled off my clothes. I tossed Ellmann's shirt on the washer and left the rest of my clothes in pile on the floor, destined for the trash bin.

As I was crossing the living room, the dog bounded down the stairs and over to me, wagging his tail and grinning.

"Good boy," I said, scratching his ears. "Good boy."

The dog laid patiently on the bathmat while I showered. He needed a serious scrubbing too, but it would have to wait.

I found clean clothes and we set out again. A glance at my watch told me we had a narrow window of time to make a stop, but because I had no idea how long we'd be where I was headed next, I didn't want to put it off. I pulled up the pet supply store and got out. The dog automatically stood but waited, watching me. I debated then shrugged.

"All right, come on."

He jumped out and followed behind my left leg as we went into the store.

The two young guys working there helped me find everything I needed. I outfitted the dog with a new collar and matching leash. I bought two enormous bags of food. And I filled an entire bag with toys, noticing the dog seemed most interested in the ropes.

The boys rang up our new stuff, and I paid the four-hundred-dollar bill.

"So far," I said to the dog, "you're very expensive."

He just tipped his head to the side and looked up at me, innocent brown eyes wide.

The boys helped me load everything into the truck then waved and went back inside.

I had no idea how long it had been since the dog had eaten, so I opened one of the bags of food and filled one of his new dishes. I set the dish on the bench seat beside me, and the dog immediately inhaled it. Then he sat back, licking his lips, and looked at me.

"No more," I said, putting the empty dish in the back. "You have to wait for dinner."

He tipped his head slightly and unleashed his full-on begging face, with sad eyes and everything.

"Oh, you're good," I said as I started the engine. "You are good."

The dog moved on and contented himself with sticking his face out the open window while I drove.

I returned to the house near Rossborough Park, and this time I parked around the block. The dog and I jumped out and walked back. The driveway was empty; I had arrived in time. I smiled and went through the gate.

The front door was locked, so I used the bump key to let myself in. I stepped inside quietly and listened. It seemed empty.

The dog was once again eager, expectant, as if waiting for a command.

"There's no one here," I said. "But you go check. Go!" I waved him off and he darted away.

He disappeared down the hallway. A minute later he returned and made a quick pass through the kitchen, then he darted straight up the stairs. His tail wagged the entire time.

Best dog ever.

I shut the door and went into the kitchen, checking out the refrigerator. I'd just finished pouring myself a glass of orange juice when the dog returned. He came up to me, ears perked, tail wagging, an unmistakable look of pride on his face. I reached into a bag of chips that had been left on the counter and gave him one.

"Good boy."

He took the chip, crunched twice, and it was gone. He looked up at me again.

"No more."

I sat at the kitchen table, feeling the stiffness and aches settling into my joints. As I pulled my phone from my pocket and dialed Amy, I went to the cupboard where I knew the occupant of the house kept his medicine cabinet. I shook a couple Ibuprofen into my hand then returned to the table and swallowed them with my orange juice.

"An explosion," Amy repeated after I'd told her the story. "Like, in the movies, except it was real . . . and you were there when it happened."

"Yes."

"And you're okay?"

I'd answered that question three times already. But I patiently said again, "Yes."

Amy hadn't been particularly thrilled about my job since I'd been kidnapped in May. Last month, after I'd been duct taped to a chair and tortured with kitchen utensils, she'd asked if I was serious about this job or if I might consider other alternatives. She knew me well enough by now to know there would be no point nagging me about it if I was set on keeping this job, and if I was, she'd support me. But she did worry about me, and I knew her well enough to know that every time I told her how close I come to serious injury, she wished I'd go back into real estate.

"And there was a dog?"

"Yes." I repeated the part about suspecting he was one of the dogs stolen from the training facility. "I talked to Ellmann a little while ago. He reached the facility, and I'm to take the dog down there tomorrow for evaluation."

"What if it is their dog?"

I explained about how they couldn't take him back.

"So you're keeping him?"

I looked down at the dog, who was now lying by my feet. "It looks that way."

"What's your landlord going to say about that?"

The landlord. I hadn't even thought about that. I'd signed a contract expressly forbidding animals of any kind on the premises.

"Uh, well, I don't have that part worked out yet," I said. "I wondered if you remembered any more German."

"Oh, geez, that's been a long time. Let me think."

Over the next ten minutes, Amy and I managed to recall the command for "eat," the word for "grandmother," and six more food words. Which didn't help me at all.

I heard a car pull up outside, maybe two, followed a moment later by the sound of the gate opening.

"Gotta go," I said. "I'll call you later."

I hung up as a key was fitted into the lock and the door opened.

Two men came into the house, both of them dressed in expensive, smart-looking suits with detective badges and Glock pistols on their belts. It took them a moment to notice me. The dog remained where he was, though he was now watching the two men.

Surprise flashed on the face of Detective Colin Topham when he caught sight of me, followed quickly by fear and then anger. The anger stuck.

"What the fuck are you doing in my house, Grey?"

Detective Mario Olvera spun around to see what Topham had. He seemed surprised, and then almost amused.

"Waiting for you, of course," I said. "What's it look like?"

"Is that a dog?" Topham snapped, pointing an angry finger at the dog as he stormed forward. "You brought a dog into my house?"

The dog didn't like Topham's tone or maybe his aggressive posture. He got to his feet, planting himself between me and Topham, a low growl of warning rumbling from his chest.

"When did you get a dog?" Olvera asked conversationally as he strolled over, removing his jacket and carefully draping it over the back of the sofa.

"This afternoon. You boys are home kind of early. No big Friday night plans? Or are you planning a night in? Ellmann and I like those, too."

Topham's already red face flushed crimson and his eyes got wide. "And what the fuck is that supposed to mean?"

The dog growled again.

Olvera clapped him on the shoulder, silently warning him to calm down. "How did you get in?"

"Ah," I said, reaching for my glass. "Secret of the trade."

"This is breaking and entering," Topham snapped. "I could arrest you."

"But you won't."

"And why the fuck not?" He took a step forward, jabbing his accusatory finger at me now. "Grey, you've been nothing but trouble from the day we met!"

The dog growled louder now, curling his lips back. He was obviously making Olvera nervous, but Topham seemed oblivious to him.

"The day we met you were laughing at Ellmann's tragedy," I said with an edge to my voice now. "Did you expect we would become bosom buddies after that?"

For the first time, I saw shame and guilt in Topham's face, and I was surprised. Frankly, I hadn't thought him capable of either, certainly not with regard to Ellmann.

"Why don't we all take a breath here?" Olvera said, the calm in his voice forced now. He put a hand on Topham and turned to him. "Colin, that's not a typical dog. If you don't take it down a few pegs, he'll attack you."

As if noticing the dog's posture for the first time, Topham took an instinctive step back. Then he raised his hands. "Okay," he said, shooting me a dark look. "Fine."

"Zoe, I don't suppose there's any point in asking you to leave?" Olvera said.

"No. I promise I won't stay long, but I have a proposal to make. I think you'll want to hear me out."

"Something tells me we don't have a choice," Olvera said. The faintest hint of amusement had returned to him.

Topham rolled his eyes. "Fine. What do you want?"

Detective Colin Topham and Detective Mario Olvera are partners, in more than one sense of the word. The two had been in Ellmann's graduating class at college and had probably been dating then. After joining the Fort Collins PD, they later became detectives and were partnered on the force. The PD isn't like the military in its view on gay personnel, but Topham and Olvera have worked very, very hard to keep the nature of their relationship secret. I'd spotted it the first day we met, but I'm a better-than-good read on people and so far I'm the only one to notice.

Personally, I don't care about sexual preferences—theirs or anyone else's. Straight, gay, whatever, it makes no difference as far as I'm concerned. Topham and Olvera had taken great care to hide their relationship, however; they did not want their secret getting out. So while it didn't matter to me, it mattered to them. And that meant I could exploit it.

"To propose cooperation between us," I said. "Something I believe will prove to be mutually beneficial."

Topham stared at me. Olvera looked more amused now as he leaned back against the sofa and crossed his arms over his chest.

"Cooperation," Topham repeated. "What the fuck does that mean?"

"There's no hidden meaning," I said sweetly. "You help me out; I help you out. I think you'll find it could be quite useful to have a friend like me, someone who isn't bound in the same way as you are, as police." I tapped a piece of paper I'd laid on the table. "To begin, I need you to run a serial number and a name for me."

Topham didn't even look at the paper. "And you think I'll do this out of some far-fetched hope of cooperation?"

I smiled. "Yes. Well, that and because I asked nicely."

He was not amused or persuaded. "Why don't you have your boyfriend run them for you?"

"Ellmann has crossed too many lines for me. I can't ask him to do that anymore."

"But you can ask us?" Topham said.

"I think you're missing the significance here," I said. "I don't offer my aid and cooperation to just any one, especially not cops."

"We've managed to do our jobs all this time without your help," Topham said. "I think we'll mange without it now."

I sighed. "I'd hoped we could keep this friendly, but I'm afraid now you're missing the point. The point is you want me to be your friend, not your enemy."

My meaning hit Olvera immediately. He rubbed a hand over his mouth as it sank in. Topham was still struggling to catch up.

"Are you threatening me now, Grey?" Topham asked, anger bubbling up in him again.

The dog watched him carefully.

"This isn't personal," I said. "The simple fact is you've got a secret. Because I know that secret, I can use it to extort you." I shrugged. "The fact that I dislike you just means I don't feel as badly about doing it."

Olvera sighed. "And this secret pertains to us both."

"Yes, it does."

The two men exchanged a look, and I knew all three of us were now on the same page. Topham was instantly enraged, his anger now masking his fear. The dog gave him another low warning growl. Olvera held a hand out to his partner.

"Now then," I went on. "I'm only asking for a bit of information. Nothing much. But I do need it, one way or the other. If a carrot isn't enough to entice your cooperation, I will use a stick." I looked between Topham and Olvera. "Get me the information I asked for or I will make sure the true nature of your relationship makes the fucking newspaper."

Olvera once again seemed resigned to his fate. Topham, by contrast, nearly vibrated with rage, frustration, and fear.

"You broke into my house, Grey," Topham spat. "You even think about making problems for me, I'll do the same for you."

"I found the front door unlocked."

"It was locked!"

"Prove it."

"You're bluffing," Topham said, too much hope in his voice for any one of us to believe he thought that was true.

I chuckled. "I think we're a little beyond denials at this point, Detective."

"You wouldn't out us," he said. This was him grasping at straws now. He knew it was over, but he wasn't willing to just lie down without a fight. And I respected that. "Even if you do, it's your word against ours." He threw his arms up. "Who would believe you?"

"The real question is, are you willing to find out?"

He took two aggressive steps forward, and that was all the farther he got. The dog was suddenly standing right in front of him, the most dangerous growl I'd heard yet emanating from him. His body was tense. He snapped his jaws, and Topham immediately backed off, hands held up again.

"Call off your dog!" he squeaked, panic overriding his fear.

I stood and finished my juice. I set the empty glass on the table and picked up my phone.

"I don't speak German," I said.

Topham glanced at me, his eyes dark. "This goes both ways," he hissed. "Do you really want a cop digging into your life? You've got quite a few skeletons in your closet, and you're pretty liberal in your interpretation of the law."

I moved toward the door. The dog kept his body between Topham and me. He really was a cool dog.

"There's no need for this to be a battle. Really, Detective, I think you'll find I'm a valuable friend. Why don't you two relax and discuss it? I think you'll find the positives outweigh the negatives."

I looked from one to the other as I pulled the door open. Topham was seething. Olvera just nodded.

"Don't mind him," Olvera said, trying to sound lighthearted but failing. "He's cranky after work."

"I understand. I've had a long day myself. I'll give you boys some time to think, but not too long. I need that information." I opened the storm door and looked at the dog. "Come on, let's go." He didn't immediately respond. "Come on, boy." I gave a low whistle. "Let's go."

The dog backed toward the door, never taking his eyes off Topham.

When we were outside I told him, "You know, I don't really need a protector, but that sure was fun."

He wagged his tail and grinned up at me.

I scratched his ears.

21

I still needed to find Medera, and Hapner was still out there somewhere. I considered swinging by Medera's place again, knowing one of these times I'd get lucky, but decided against it. And I knew Ellmann and the cops were working to track Hapner down now. They were following up on the two license plates I'd given them, and they were questioning the lookout mechanic, who had just been coming around when the police arrived on scene. Ellmann would call when they had something.

Tonight, I was exhausted. My ears were still ringing, some of my lacerations were stinging, and my entire body ached. I'd managed to keep it together with Topham, but I could barely think straight anymore. I decided to head home. The dog needed a bath, then I could turn in and get some sleep.

On the way, I called my landlord, Stuart Mosley. All things considered, he wasn't a bad guy. I almost liked him. And he was a good landlord as far as I could tell. So we needed to work out this dog thing.

"I'm sorry, Zoe," he said after I'd explained the situation. "I just can't do it. Dogs . . . they tear the place apart. Even if it's not intentional, they are hard on a place. I just can't agree. I'm sorry."

His quick answer, given without taking any time to really consider it, pissed me off. A sure sign my patience, notoriously in short supply anyway, was worn down to the nub.

"Okay, Stuart," I said, trying to keep my voice even and calm. "I'll be in touch."

"Wait. What does that mean? You don't have the dog there now, do you?"

"It means I have a decision to make." I started to hang up.

"Are you going to move out?"

That was one option. The other option was to buy the house. As far as I knew, Stuart wasn't selling, but that might be because no one had made an offer. Really it would come down to how badly I wanted to avoid moving again.

"I'll let you know."

I hung up and called Ellmann. He answered just before the call went to voicemail.

"I'm going to need to stay at your place for a couple days while I work out a dispute with my landlord."

I could hear him smiling. "I believe I said once you shouldn't be renting. Having a landlord just doesn't suit you."

Actually, he'd asked me why I was renting a place instead of living in one of the houses I already owned. At the time, it had been the best move. Now, however, I wondered the same thing.

"Do you mind if I have the dog with me?"

"Of course not. I think I'll actually be able to come home tonight."

"Great. So you wrapped up your case?"

"Mostly. Got a couple things we're pinning down, but we made an arrest."

Ellmann doesn't arrest people unless he's certain of their guilt and he has the evidence to support a case in court. If he'd made an arrest, it meant the case was closed, even if they were still dotting *i's* and crossing *t's*.

"Congratulations."

"I won't have much of a break, however, because I got another case dumped in my lap this afternoon when my girlfriend blew up a meth lab."

"That's hilarious," I said flatly. "I'm sure that's exactly what everyone's saying."

He laughed. "That's just one version. I've heard several. Some of them are pretty creative."

"Yeah. I'm sure." Even I could hear the ugly bitterness in my voice.

"Come on, honey," he said. "Don't worry about what anyone's saying. None of it matters."

"I don't want to be known as Ellmann's loser, fuck-up girlfriend. I mean, trouble seems to follow me around. People must wonder what the hell you're doing with me."

In the rational side of my mind, I realized I was way too tired and battered to be having this kind of conversation. I even realized that if I hadn't been so tired, I probably wouldn't have cared what Ellmann's coworkers thought about me, or the guys at the detention center, for that matter.

"That is not how you're known," he said seriously. "Not to people who know me, who matter to me. We've both had a shitty day. Let's both go home and get some sleep, okay? I'll meet you there as soon as I can."

I silently thanked him for giving me an out, and ended the call.

Ellmann really is a good guy. So, probably, I was projecting, or something like that. *I* wondered all the time what he was doing with me. So I just assumed everyone else wondered the same.

I didn't even bother to stop by my house. I had a few things at Ellmann's, and all the dog's stuff was in the truck. I hauled all that stuff into the house, fed the dog another bowl of food, and brought him into the guest bathroom with a tub. He eyed me dubiously as I stacked old towels on the closed toilet and opened the large bottle of extra strength doggy shampoo I'd bought earlier. As added incentive, I'd stuffed some doggy treats into my pocket.

"Come on," I said, waving him forward. "*Hierr.*"

Dubious or not, he immediately came forward. I gave him a treat and scratched his ears.

"It's going to be fine," I said. "Come on, in you go."

He didn't like it, but he suffered through the ordeal with dignity, standing still, patiently waiting while I scrubbed and washed his thick coat twice. I couldn't believe how much dirt and grime washed down the drain. Who knew how long he'd been staked out in Hapner's yard. Who knew when he'd last had a bath. At ninety-one pounds, he wasn't thin from neglect, and he didn't show any signs of being abused, but he'd undoubtedly been mistreated, and I was glad to have found him. He was a good dog, and he needed someone to care for him.

After he was washed, I sat on the bathroom floor and brushed him out. It took forever and generated a trashcan full of hair. But this part he obviously enjoyed. His eyes drooped to half-mast and he gave little groans of contentment. While I was at it, I trimmed his toenails too. He didn't like this either, shooting me dark looks of disapproval, but a few more treats took his mind off things.

When he was clean and groomed, the bathroom was destroyed. I understood now why those mobile dog wash outfits and the self-service dog wash places stayed in business. You get a clean dog and leave the mess for someone else. I'd keep that in mind for next time. It took thirty minutes to clean up.

I threw the wet towels in the washer and crawled into bed. As soon as I was settled, the dog jumped onto the bed and curled up behind my legs. I tried to imagine how Ellmann would feel about the dog being on his bed, but before I could really come up with an answer, I fell asleep.

22

The alarm was set for six, but the dog woke me up at five. I felt his nose as he nudged my arm. As I began to stir, he jumped his front paws on the bed and nudged my shoulder and then my cheek. When I finally cracked an eye, I saw him standing there, front paws on the bed, one of his new rope toys in his mouth. And I could tell by the gentle twisting of his body he was wagging his tail.

And he was probably the cutest thing I'd ever seen.

I got up, and he darted for the bedroom door with sheer excitement. I shooed him out of the bedroom and closed the door so Ellmann might sleep a while longer. When we were in the hall, the dog turned back to me and bowed, the rope still in his mouth, his tail wagging madly. He wanted to play.

I took one end of the rope and tugged. The dog responded immediately, jerking backward on the rope with an excited shake of his head. As our game continued, he made little grunting sounds, his tail wagging all the while.

I managed to flip the coffee pot on and direct the dog outside, grabbing one of Ellmann's sweatshirts from the back of a chair. We played tug-of-war for a long time. Then I got one of the balls from the bag of toys and we played ball for a while. By the time we came back inside, the dog seemed happy and relaxed, sated with attention and play.

Ellmann was in the kitchen when we returned, showered and dressed. He was filling a travel mug with coffee.

The dog went straight to the water dish I'd filled and set out for him last night and lapped up half of it. I went to the coffee pot.

"Morning," I said.

Ellmann turned and wrapped his arms around me, gently pinning me against the counter. He squeezed me tight and nuzzled my neck.

"Morning."

I curled my arms around his neck. For a long moment, we just stood there, wrapped up together, and for that moment, it felt to me like all was right with the world.

"I wanted to have breakfast with you," he said against my neck, "but I got a call. I have to go."

"I've missed you," I heard myself say, and realized it was true. We hadn't seen much of each other since we'd returned from California, both of us running with work since we got back. But I'd missed him—missed seeing him, talking with him, missed our time to just hang out together doing anything or nothing.

I did a mental eye roll. *Geez, Zoe. You've got it bad.*

"Me, too," he said. "Want to move away? We could go to California, or anywhere else you want. I could teach science to middle schoolers and you could sell real estate and we could be home every evening and every weekend. No more phone calls in the middle of the night, no more working twenty-four hours or more straight, no more explosions, no more bad guys. What do you think?"

"Sounds good," I said. Except for the real estate part, but I kept that to myself. "You'd give up being a cop?"

"I don't know yet, but I've been thinking about it some lately." He looked down at me, brushing my hair away from my face. "I want to spend more time with you."

Ellmann could do any number of things with his life. He has degrees in science and psychology. And he isn't hurting for

146

money, either; he has a smart money manager and some good investments. He's a cop because it's a calling; like all the greats, it's in his blood. He may have been thinking about giving that up, but I knew in my heart he wouldn't be happy for long if he did.

"I'm not going anywhere," I said. "Don't make any hasty decisions." Even if I could see him teaching middle-school science.

He kissed me. It was the kind of kiss that curled my toes and made me forget my own name.

Sometime later, he broke away and growled, "I've got to go." He grabbed his coffee and walked out of the kitchen. Then he stopped and turned back to me. "I love you, Zoe. More than anything."

My brain was still shorted out from the kiss, so I just nodded.

He grinned and left.

When sense returned to me, I poured myself a cup of coffee and had a few sips while I dialed Olvera. Of the two, I thought it best I direct most of my communications to him. He didn't answer. I hung up and sent him a text, asking if he had my information yet. And I made a mental note to stop by Walgreens for the photos. If I could swing it, I wanted to pull the camera out of the house before I used the photos. If I showed the photos first, I'd end up losing the camera, and whatever other information it had recorded. Topham and Olvera were shitty cops, but they weren't completely inept; they would be able to find the camera eventually. If they weren't going to cooperate, I'd have to see if I could get into the house today.

I pulled on running clothes. Normally I went to the gym and ran on the treadmill so I could watch the little TV and pretend I wasn't so bored. But I thought the dog could go with me, so I decided to run outside.

My body still felt battered and stiff, but I didn't want to slack on my training. And I thought it would ultimately help me feel better. So I downed some more Ibuprofen and took my time stretching.

We left the house and did my run/walk thing around the neighborhood. I hadn't even thought about a leash until the dog and I passed an older woman walking some kind of small, yappy dog. The yappy dog barked at my dog as we passed, pulling at the end of its leash. My dog didn't even spare it a glance and stuck to my left side.

When I returned to the house, I saw I had a missed call from Ellmann. I hurried through a shower and called him back.

"We got a hit on that Eurovan plate. I thought you might want to tag along in case we stumble across Robert Hapner."

While there was a great deal of cooperation between the police and bond enforcement agents, this wasn't standard practice. The only reason Ellmann was calling me with this offer was because I had an in with him.

"Hell yes," I said. "The bastard tried to kill me and my dog."

Ellmann chuckled. "*Your* dog, huh?"

I hadn't realized I'd said that until he pointed it out. Seemed I had become possessive of the dog at some point. When had that happened? I hadn't even known him twenty-four hours. Man, I was going soft.

"You know what I mean. What's the address?"

"I'll text it to you. Strictly hands-off. You sit out. If he's there, I'll let you take him in."

Even better if they were willing to do all the work and let me reap all the reward.

"Works for me," I said.

23

I drove to the address Ellmann had sent me and was stopped two blocks away by a uniformed officer and directed to park. I complied, and the officer, Frye, came to my door.

"Ellmann says wait here. They're just about to breach."

"No problem."

Frye looked at the dog sitting on the passenger side. "He's a good-looking dog."

I scratched the dog's ears. "He's pretty smart, too."

Frye smiled. "Dogs are amazing. I ever tell you about my nephew's dog?"

"No, I don't think so."

Frye laughed. "So my nephew, Logan, volunteered at the humane society one summer. One day, my sister goes to pick him up, but Logan isn't waiting for her. One of the employees goes to find him and comes back a while later. He says Logan won't come out of the kennels.

"Of course my sister's worried something's wrong. The guy takes her back, and she finds Logan lying in one of the kennels, curled up with a yellow lab." He laughed again. "She tried everything to get him to come out. Finally, she picked him up and carried him out. But both Logan and the dog started crying. Got every dog in the place worked into a frenzy. She had to adopt the dog."

"Seriously?"

He nodded, still chuckling. "True story. It's been two years, and they are still inseparable. My sister tries to keep the dog busy during the day, but he regularly sneaks out. She'll find him sleeping outside the fence at Logan's school."

"That's unbelievable."

Frye shrugged. "Dogs aren't man's best friends for no reason."

I thought about that and looked at the dog. "That's true."

Frye reached for the radio mic clipped to his shoulder and gave a response to something he'd heard in his earpiece.

"They're breaching now," he said, moving away.

"Copy that," I said, climbing out of the truck.

I stood in the open door loading my pockets with paperwork and handcuffs, just in case.

"Shit."

I looked at Frye, who was suddenly sprinting away, responding into the mic and drawing his weapon.

"Zoe! Stay here!"

He disappeared around the corner and down Duke Lane, the address Ellmann had sent me. I lost sight of him just as I heard gunfire.

I felt my heart lurch and my gut tense knowing Ellmann was involved. But before I could dwell on what might be happening, I saw Robert Hapner jump the fence at the end of the street.

"Son of a bitch," I hissed under my breath as I started after him.

He noticed me almost instantly. He quickly drew a pistol from the front of his pants and swung it in my direction. I darted to my left and dove behind a car as he squeezed off a couple of shots.

I came up on my knees, aiming over the trunk, the Browning in my hand. But I couldn't get a line of sight before Hapner disappeared down the next street. And then I saw the dog streak by.

I got to my feet and hurried after them, sticking to the cars parked at the curb for quick cover. Ahead, I saw a group of children playing in a front yard. They were unaware of the chase in the street, but their presence changed things.

"Hapner!" I called. "Stop!"

I kept the gun in my hand, but I knew I wouldn't use it unless there was no other option. I would never risk a stray bullet finding one of those children. In the end, I hoped it wouldn't be necessary, because the dog was quickly closing in on Hapner. I had no commands to give him, but he seemed to know exactly what to do. I hoped to hell he was as good as I thought he was.

Hapner pushed on, and I saw him look at the children. The kids had noticed us now, and where standing in the yard watching this event unfold with open curiosity and excitement. Hapner looked at the children again, and even from behind him, I swear I could see the wheels of his sick and panicked mind turning.

"Don't even think about it, Hapner!" I pushed myself harder. "Dog! Take him down! Now!"

I wished again I knew German. Why had I studied Spanish in high school?

The dog charged forward, as if he, too, understood the danger to the children, his powerful body eating up the ground between him and Hapner. Then he launched himself into the air. He flew at Hapner, his powerful jaw closing around Hapner's right elbow. The force of the impact knocked Hapner forward, and the two went down.

Hapner cried out in pain and surprise as the dog locked onto him. I could also hear the dog's growls as he did his job. The children all gasped in surprise and awe as they watched the dog take down the bad man.

Hapner hit the ground hard. The dog held his grip on Hapner's arm and kept the man on the ground.

"Drop the gun!" I called to Hapner as I caught up.

"Get the dog off!"

"Drop the gun!"

Hapner jerked his arm against the dog's hold. The dog shook his head, whipping Hapner's arm violently. Hapner screamed, and the gun flew out of his hand. It clattered to the pavement.

"Get him off! Help!"

I hurried over and picked up the gun, tucking it into my belt. Then I pulled cuffs from my pocket.

"Hold still," I told Hapner as I knelt on top of him and clasped the cuff around his left wrist. "Okay," I said to the dog. "That's enough. Let go."

The dog didn't immediately respond, and I knew it was because I didn't know the appropriate command.

I got a hold of his collar and pulled him back. "Enough. Let go. Stop. Release."

I don't think it was any of these words that actually triggered the dog to let go; I think it was me tugging at his collar and pulling him back. But he did let go of Hapner. I quickly closed the cuff around Hapner's right wrist, which elicited a long cry of pain.

Still kneeling on Hapner, I did a quick pat down for additional weapons, finding a pocketknife and a second gun. I took both and stood. Then I noticed all the little faces staring at me. And I saw a woman had come out of the house at some point. She stood trying to huddle the children behind her, her wide eyes on Hapner, the dog, and me.

"Bond enforcement," I said, showing her the badge on my belt. "This man's under arrest."

She didn't say anything to that, but it triggered a barrage of questions from the little people peering around her.

"What did he do?"

"Is he a bad guy?"

"Is that your dog?"

"Are you a cop?"

"What's his name?"

"Did the dog hurt him?"

The questions came all at once. I was relieved to note that while the mom found the whole scene upsetting, the kids were excited and interested, not afraid. They had no idea of the danger that had come so very close to them. Thank God the dog had been there. I had been closing in on Hapner, but he'd have reached the children before I reached him if the dog hadn't taken him down.

"Listen, kids," I said, smiling. They quieted down enough to listen to me. "Do you guys do fire drills at your school?"

There was a chorus of "yeahs," and bobbing heads.

"This was a police drill," I said. "We were just practicing, like you practice your fire drills."

"For when the real thing happens," a little boy said. He was probably six.

"Exactly right. We're going to finish practicing now."

I got Hapner under the arm and by the belt and hauled him up. Then I marched him back down the street before any of the kids could ask questions about why the blood was real if the drill was just practice.

24

Hapner cried and carried on the entire walk to my truck. I wasn't so heartless as to say he had no reason to cry; he would need medical attention for the bite on his arm. But I had no sympathy for him. I could only imagine what he would have done had he been able to get his hands on one of those kids.

As we neared the truck, I heard sirens—ambulance sirens. I handcuffed Hapner to the push bar on the front bumper of the truck and unlocked the toolbox bolted to the floorboard behind the backseat. I deposited Hapner's weapons inside for safekeeping.

I'd just locked it up when an ambulance tore down the street past me and sailed around the corner onto Duke Lane, cutting the siren but keeping the lights going.

The feeling of unease I'd experienced earlier bloomed brighter, and I wanted to know what was going on. In the time I had been gone, radio cars and uniformed officers had been positioned at the end of the street to keep people out. They looked grim, the way cops accustomed to tragedy rarely did. The unease grew, and I had one thought on my mind: Ellmann.

I ran, the dog right beside me.

I bolted down the street one block from Duke Lane. I knew the officers would try to keep me out of the scene they were trying to control. It was best to just avoid them.

I could see through the houses and trees as I ran. I saw various police vehicles. As I got farther down the street, the vehicles were thicker, and I began to see uniformed personnel. The farther I ran, the more chaotic things seemed.

Finally, about eight houses down, I saw a yard with no fence. The houses behind it all had fences, but it was one less obstacle to contend with.

I sprinted through the front yard, past the house, and across the backyard. Without a word of instruction, the dog vaulted the four-foot chain-link fence and waited while I struggled over it. When I landed in the next yard, we were running again.

In the street ahead, I could see police cars with lights flashing. I let us out through a gate and ran into the street.

I wound my way through the emergency vehicles and personnel as I made my way down the street. There were cops and other uniformed personnel everywhere, swarming around the house. But none of them was Ellmann.

One ambulance was packed up and about to leave. I ran over, calling to the paramedic that jumped out of the back.

"Wait! Wait a minute!"

He looked back at me then raised a hand.

"It's okay," he said reassuringly. "He'll be fine."

"Who?" I demanded, shoving past him as another figure emerged from the ambulance.

"Geez, Zoe!"

I nearly collided with Frye. He looked well aside from the bloody gap in the shoulder of his uniform.

"You're bleeding," I said, looking at his shoulder.

"I'm fine," he said. "Just a graze."

I looked past him into the ambulance. Another paramedic was sitting on the bench tending to a SWAT officer lying on the gurney. He had a bullet hole in his left thigh. His name was Charlie Wilkins.

"Hey, Zoe," he said, wincing as the medic applied a dressing to his leg.

155

"Are you okay?" I asked him.

"Through and through," he said. "I'll be fine. Others ended up worse."

I swallowed. "Who?" I managed to ask.

He shook his head. "I'm not sure. Lopez for sure; he's the worst off, I understand."

"Okay. Do you want me to call someone?"

"No, I'll be okay. I'll call my wife from the hospital. Boy, she's gonna be pissed."

I'd met his wife a couple times. I liked her a lot. And she was going to be very pissed.

I moved out of the way and the waiting paramedic closed the ambulance doors. He looked at me.

"There are three cops injured," he said. "One of them is critical, but they're all alive. That's all I know."

I thanked him, and he climbed behind the wheel of the ambulance and drove off, making his way around the other vehicles.

"Don't worry," Frye said. "He's here somewhere."

Another ambulance was parked on the other side of the mess of emergency vehicles, and I made my way toward it. I was almost there when I heard a round of commanding voices behind me.

I spun around and saw a group of men coming out of the front door of the house, a gurney between them. Two EMTs, three firemen, and several cops steered the gurney down the walk. Most of them carried bags of equipment. One fireman was on the gurney, giving CPR while they moved.

I ran toward them, trying to get a look at the cop on the gurney. Then something from the doorway caught my eye: a man ducking under the frame as he strode outside. I stopped and stared at Ellmann as he moved quickly down the sidewalk.

I was dizzy with relief.

Tears blurred my vision, and my legs wobbled and threatened to buckle.

"Get him to the hospital," Ellmann ordered. "I'll meet you there."

Someone answered in acknowledgement. I moved away as the crew flew by me toward the waiting ambulance. They made quick work of loading the gurney and equipment, most of them climbing inside. Then the ambulance was gone, siren wailing.

Ellmann stood in the front yard, conferring with SWAT Commander Paul Martin, the two of them pointing and issuing orders. They were both wearing their SWAT uniforms of navy blue BDUs, black boots, black helmets, black Kevlar vests with dozens of pockets, heavy with equipment, and drop holsters on their legs. As he talked, Ellmann looked after the ambulance, and he spotted me. He spoke to Martin for a moment longer than excused himself and came over to me.

"What—"

I threw my arms around his neck and squeezed him, the crap on his vest jabbing painfully into my chest. I didn't care.

"Zoe, you're trembling," he said, winding his arms around my back.

I choked back a sob.

"It's okay," he said. Then it clicked for him. "Oh, honey, I'm okay. Here, look at me."

He pulled back and looked down at me, cupping my face in his hands. I could smell the gunpowder on them. He used his thumbs to wipe the tears from my cheeks.

He smiled at me. "I'm okay."

I sucked in a breath and nodded, covering his hands with mine. "I see that now." I tried to smile.

"Okay?"

"Yeah," I said, pulling myself together. "I'm okay."

Frye came over. "What happened, man? Didn't someone say 'routine bust' earlier this morning?"

Ellmann shook his head. "No such thing, Frye." He looked at me. "Hapner wasn't in the house. I'm sorry."

I hooked a thumb over my shoulder. "He ran down the street about the same time you guys breeched. I've got him."

Ellmann grinned. "That's my girl."

"Ellmann!"

Paul Martin waved an arm, beckoning Ellmann back over.

"I've got to go," he said. "Frye, get over to—are you bleeding?"

We all looked at Frye's shoulder.

"Just grazed me."

"Get over to the hospital," Ellmann said. "I want regular updates on the statuses of our guys. While you're there, get yourself looked at."

"Sure thing."

Frye turned and hurried back down the street toward his car.

Ellmann petted the dog then moved away. "I'll call you later. Love you."

I heard, "Me, too," fall out of my mouth. I must have looked as shocked as I felt, because Ellmann, when he turned back to me, just smiled and chuckled softly to himself.

25

By the time I got back to my truck, I'd kind of forgotten about Hapner. He was kneeling, hands cuffed behind his back and secured to the bumper, sagging against the restraints and looking downright miserable.

I loaded Hapner into the Scout.

"We need to have a conversation about how you came by your injuries," I said to him as I drove.

"You're fucking dog tried to take my arm off," Hapner spat miserably.

That was the problem. All dog bites treated in the emergency department had to be reported to the humane society. Under the right circumstances, a dog bite could tie a person up in criminal as well as civil court, and may ultimately lead to the destruction of the dog. Since I'd risked my life to save the dog, I was anxious to avoid that outcome.

It was a little different if you were bitten by *your own* dog.

"See, that's where the confusion comes in, Robert. This dog is *your* dog. You left him at your place yesterday. I'm sure you just forgot about him, since you were in such a hurry to blow the place up and leave."

Hapner turned and eyed the dog, sitting in the back seat.

"That's my dog? He looks different."

"Have you forgotten him already?"

"Well, why the fuck did he bite *me*?"

"You had a gun in your hand, which you were using to shoot at me and threaten five innocent children. You'll need to fill out a dog bite report when we get to the ER. How about I help you with that?"

It took two hours in the ER for Hapner to get cleaned up, stitched up, and released with a clean bill of health. When I arrived at the detention center, I handed the secretary a stack of papers. The detention center won't accept a guy with so much as an undiagnosed, untreated hangnail.

"He was treated in the ER?" the secretary asked, thumbing through the papers.

They always talk about prisoners as if they aren't standing right there. I've always found this annoying.

"Treated and pronounced fit for jail," I said, clapping Hapner on the shoulder.

"He needs a note—" She stopped when she came across the doctor's note specifically stating Robert Hapner was fit to be taken to and held in jail. This wasn't my first rodeo. I'd had to go back and get one of those notes once. And this woman was obviously hoping she could use that as a reason to refuse Hapner. (Actually, they're always looking for a reason to refuse prisoners.) When she realized she hadn't found one, her nose turned up slightly. "Wait here."

She left and returned a moment later with the booking sergeant. The booking sergeant was not happy about Hapner's injuries, either.

"Let's see that paperwork."

He stood and read every word on every page of the discharge paperwork from the ER, the doctor's note, and my capture paperwork. When he couldn't find a reason to refuse, he looked just as irritated. He huffed and puffed as he took Hapner away.

When he returned to bring my cuffs and a body receipt to me, he gave me a dark look.

I smiled and wished him and the secretary a very happy day. They both just glared at me.

From the detention center, I drove over to Topham's house. I cruised by and saw one car parked in the driveway. It was Olvera's. I decide to see if maybe the boys had gone out together in one car. I parked around the block, grabbed my bag and got out, the dog following me. We returned to Topham's house, and I knocked on the door. There was no answer. I rang the bell as I tried the doorknob. Locked.

I quickly let myself in and hurried to the bedroom. I made quick work of switching out the smoke detectors and all I could do was cross my fingers I had enough footage to be convincing. I packed up and we left.

I headed back to Ellmann's house. I needed to take the dog to the training facility in Colorado Springs, but I preferred not to take the Scout on the interstate. Ellmann had said he didn't mind if I drove his Jeep since it mostly just sat in his garage.

The dog and I transferred vehicles and made the drive south, stopping by Walgreens on the way out of town. I followed the directions on my phone and arrived at a large, plain building so close to the Air Force Academy I was surprised I didn't have to drive past a guarded gate entrance. The parking lot was full of as many government and military vehicles as civilian ones. And there were more cars that I'd been expecting for a Saturday.

I parked, and we got out. I'd brought the dog's new leash, but I just clipped it together and hung it across my chest. He hadn't needed it so far, and I didn't think he'd need it now.

We went inside and found ourselves in a quiet, perfunctory lobby. It was obvious this facility didn't have a lot of walk-in traffic; the reception desk was perfectly empty and was not the workstation of anyone.

A small, typed sign was posted on the vacant desk beside a bell. It instructed the odd visitor to ring the bell or call the phone number listed for assistance. I went over and tapped the bell. Almost at that same instant, a tall, thin, middle-aged man came down the hallway.

"I was just coming to check if you'd arrived," he said in a thick German accent. He walked over and held his hand out. "Zoe Grey, I presume."

"Yes," I said, shaking his hand. "Thanks for meeting us on a Saturday."

The man just smiled. "Happy to. I'm Dietrich Müller. I believe I spoke to a Detective Ellmann on the phone yesterday."

"You did."

"I was most anxious to have a look at this dog." He gazed down at the dog, who was sitting beside me, leaning against my leg. "Oh, yes," the German man said. "I believe this is indeed one of our lost five." He looked at me and waved me toward the hall. "Come. Let us begin."

Müller led the way down one long, empty hallway and then a shorter one, our footsteps echoing off the industrial walls. He stopped and opened a door, leading us inside. It was a large, open room with little furniture and painted markings on the floor. Along the walls there were hurdles, hoops, stairs, mannequins, cones, and various other training equipment ready for use.

The back wall was made up entirely of windows. Beyond them, I saw a large expanse of grass where multiple outdoor training areas had been separated by chain-link fences. All of the areas were currently in use, filled with handlers, dogs, trainers, supporters, and spectators.

To the far right, I saw a building with several men gathered around it. The men were dressed in military fatigues, green Kevlar vests, and helmets, carrying orange rubber shotguns and pistols. Some men were stationed around the building, at the windows and other exit points. The rest of the men were gathered at what amounted to the front door. One man with a German Shepherd on a leash was at the front, right at the door. The dog was wearing his own Kevlar vest and barking, hopping in anticipation. The man seemed to call something into the house then wait for a reply. A moment later, he let go of the dog and the dog tore into the house.

"Ah, that is a military police group," Müller said. "Many military and police units come here to use the training facilities."

"This facility is bigger than I expected," I confessed, turning away from the window.

Müller stood with his hands clasped behind his back. He smiled at me with patience and good nature evident on his face.

"At any one time, we have approximately sixty dogs enrolled in a full-time training program. We have a staff of twenty full-time trainers and fifteen part-time trainers. Our dogs participate in one of several training programs from patrol and apprehension to drug or bomb sniffing. We also hold training classes, available to military and police personnel as well as civilians, which are held here regularly throughout the week.

"Our graduates are deployed as far away as California, New York, Florida, even Canada. More than once, we have sent dogs overseas to various organizations. We have a two-year waiting list for our graduates."

"Your graduates being the dogs."

He chuckled. "Yes. They are dogs. But they are so much more, no?"

I reached down and scratched the dog's head absently as I nodded. "Yes, they are. They're amazing."

"Indeed." He looked down at the dog. "Well, shall we begin?"

"Yes."

Müller strode across the room. There was a long table against the far wall, and he had several things waiting there.

"I believe I know which dog this is," he said. "Why don't we see if I'm right?"

He picked up an electronic instrument that didn't look totally dissimilar from a metal detector wand security people use. He turned and faced the dog.

"*Hierr.*" He pronounced the word as it was meant to be pronounced, and with gentle but firm authority.

The dog's ears perked up, and he stood. But he looked back at me and did not move away from me.

"Oh, my," Müller said. "That is interesting. How long did you say the dog's been with you?"

"Since yesterday."

"Very interesting, indeed. Uh, very well. Please, if you would, bring him over here."

I walked across the room, and the dog followed me. When I stopped in front of Müller, the dog sat and looked at me.

Müller held the device over the dog's neck and there was a soft beeping. Müller consulted the device and nodded.

"As I suspected," he said, setting the device on the table. "It is indeed one of ours, one of the lost five. His name, Ms. Grey, is Dasch."

The dog glanced at Müller in clear recognition of his name. Then he looked at me expectantly.

"Dasch," I repeated. Of course when I said it, it didn't sound quite the same as when the German guy said it. Still, the dog seemed to understand.

Still looking at me, he began to wag his tail.

I chuckled. "Well that should make things easier, huh?" I scratched his ears.

"Dasch was enrolled in our patrol and apprehension program," Müller said. "I don't mind telling you I was most disappointed when I'd learned Dasch was one of the five dogs stolen. He showed unique promise, from the moment he arrived here, and I had very high hopes for him indeed."

"He was one of your favorites," I said.

Müller chuckled softly as he gazed affectionately at the dog. "Yes, I suppose he was. My dear girl, I believe you will come to learn very quickly just how special this dog is."

"I know you're right."

Müller nodded and turned back to the table.

"Do you think that's why this dog was stolen?" I asked.

He turned back to me, holding a piece of paper. "I honestly have no idea. I have thought about that very seriously, and the truth is, those five dogs seem random to me. They had very little in common from trainers to programs down to the very section of the facility where they were boarded."

"Is this the only dog that has been recovered?"

"Yes. The police apprehended the thieves almost immediately, but they'd already rid themselves of the dogs. And no matter which tactic the police tried, the thieves would not say where they had delivered the dogs, who they had delivered them to, why they had stolen them, or who they had stolen them for. I'm afraid all we know is how they were stolen from the facility, which is a very small piece of the puzzle."

"And how did they do it?"

"In short, they had help. From one of the trainers. Of course, that man no longer works here. And the police questioned him for hours as well, but he gave them no information." Müller shook his head. "These men, they say so little, they remind me of old KGB spies. But this is not war, is it? It is dogs. I fear I will never know the whole story."

Müller looked at the dog then up at me. "I am glad *this* dog has been located. Detective Ellmann led me to believe you may be interested in keeping him. From what I've seen in our brief time together, I must encourage you to do so. He has become very attached to you. Usually, that happens after a bit of time and some training together, but in the case of you and Dasch, it seems to have happened quiet naturally, and very quickly."

"Well, I saved his life," I said. "I think he's just grateful."

"So Detective Ellmann said, but, dear girl, I assure you it is something else entirely. Perhaps you can tell me what you do for work, and how you might see this dog fitting into your life. He was trained for a specific job. We may need to do some training to transition him to civilian life."

"Actually, I'm a bond enforcement agent. I don't have much of a civilian life."

Müller just grinned and said something in German. "A match made in heaven," he said to me in English.

"Well, he has helped me out several times in the last twenty-four hours. He's pretty handy to have around."

"Oh, yes, indeed. I am certain you will be quite amazed at the full range of this dog's abilities. You know, he had nearly reached the end of his program when he was abducted. He was less than a week away from graduation, with a handler lined up in the Miami Dade Police Department. I was ready to sign off on his paperwork when I received notice of the theft."

"So what happens to him now? Since he can't be a real police dog anymore. Is there another training program he and I can do, so that he's okay to work with me?"

"I want to work with you both while you are here today. I wish to see how you two work together, what the dog may still remember, what things might need reinforced. As I said, I was prepared to sign off his paperwork. Depending on what I see today, I may well still feel comfortable doing so. In either case, I can certainly provide you with the necessary paperwork so Dasch may work with you."

"I imagine that paperwork is useful in court."

"An absolute necessity. And I can guarantee you now, if this dog works with you, you will end up in court. In this country, people sue one another over the smallest thing. A dog bite, you may well imagine, is not a small thing."

Robert Hapner would agree, I was sure. Good thing I knew a great lawyer.

Müller handed me the piece of paper. "This is a list of German commands. I was Dasch's primary trainer, so he knows German commands." Müller laughed. "I've tried to train the dogs in English, but the German, it just comes out. All that results is a very confused, semi-lingual dog. Strict German is better."

I accepted the list and looked it over. Then I looked at Müller. "Dasch can do all these things?"

Müller smiled, and his blue eyes twinkled. "Oh, yes, dear girl. All those things and many, many more."

26

Müller spent a long time with us. He taught me German commands and how to control the dog. He also evaluated how much the dog had retained, how well he responded to me, and how he carried out the commands. Then Müller asked me for a list of ways the dogs might be useful to me in my job.

Dasch was put through a rigorous performance that amounted to his final exams. At the conclusion of it, Müller pronounced Dasch a successful graduate.

During the time we spent with Müller, it could not be determined what, if anything, Dasch may have been taught after being stolen from the facility. Müller helped me run Dasch through a long series of exercises designed to trip him up and trigger any unwanted reactions. Either Dasch hadn't been taught anything nefarious or else he was too smart to fall for Müller's tricks now. I didn't know which I thought more likely.

Müller gave me lots of literature on police service dogs and a long list of homework. Dasch's training would need to be reinforced and practiced regularly. Additionally, the new things Müller had helped me start teaching the dog would need to be worked on, as well as anything else I taught him in the future. This dog wasn't like an electronic device that once finished was purchased and set on a shelf, in complete working order no matter when I might point the remote at it. No, this dog was like a muscle that needed regular attention in order to stay useful and strong.

Dasch slept on the way home, spread across the entire back seat, which he made look tiny. The day's events had been hard work, but he'd had fun. In the end, he was a dog and all this stuff was just fun and games to him.

While I was with Müller, Olvera had called me twice. He'd also sent me a text telling me to call him back as soon as possible. I thought this was an unusual degree of enthusiasm to comply with my blackmail demands, so either he'd done a complete one eighty, or something else was going on. I suspected the latter.

I called him back from the road.

"Finally! I was beginning to think you weren't going to call."

"I was busy, Olvera, geez. What's got your panties in a bunch?"

There was a beat of stiff silence. "Is that a gay joke?"

It kind of was. I just couldn't help it. "No, of course not. It's an expression. It means, what's got you so worked up?"

"We've been thinking about your proposal," Olvera said. "Maybe we can use your help after all."

"Wonderful. I told you it would be useful to have a friend like me. Where do you need me to break into? What am I looking for?"

"What?" Olvera gasped. "Is that what you meant?"

"Of course. What did you think I meant?"

He heaved a huge sigh. "That isn't what we have in mind. Meet us downtown tonight. Come up to the second floor of the eyeglasses place on the southeast corner of College and Oak. Come dressed for a night out." Then the line went dead.

I looked at the phone.

"What a prick," I mumbled as I dialed Sadie.

I asked Sadie if she had plans for the evening or if she might want to join me downtown. She did have plans, of course, but nothing she couldn't break. I told her I'd pick her up at nine.

It was still early afternoon; I had some time before I needed to be back, so I decided to return to Fort Collins via Boulder.

Sadie was paying me to get to the bottom of the question that was Karen Brickle, and I hadn't gotten very far on that yet. I needed whatever Topham and Olvera could give me. But I couldn't deny I was basically making up this "investigation" as I went along. I really only have the skills for finding people, but Karen Brickle wasn't missing. And besides the fact that Brickle was using a fake name, the only thing I knew about her was that her neighbor had gone missing shortly before she'd moved away.

Call me a skeptic, but I wanted to know about Walling's disappearance. Brickle may have had nothing to do with it, but it was a strange event. I mean, how many of us have a neighbor just disappear? A strange, and possibly criminal, event occurring next door to a woman who had assumed a false identity raised some serious red flags for me.

I didn't know where this avenue of inquiry might lead, but I wanted to check it out all the same.

The drive was pleasant, and it was a gorgeous day. I'd taken the doors off Ellmann's Jeep, and fresh, warm air blew through it. I had the radio on, singing along as I cruised. When I neared Boulder, I checked my notes, punched an address into my phone, and followed the directions to Frank Walling's house. Dasch sat up in the backseat when I parked at the curb, yawning and glancing around.

There was a Ford Explorer parked in the driveway, and the front door was open. I told Dasch to wait in the car, and walked up to the door. When I arrived on the porch, I could hear the TV playing, and a peek through the open screen door revealed two figures in the living room. I rapped on the door. A moment later Frank Walling peered out at me.

"Yes? Can I help you?"

He had aged even in the few months it had been since his photos had been splashed all over the papers. There was more gray in his hair, more lines on his face, and he had the posture of a man carrying a heavy burden. And he eyed me with open suspicion, no doubt wondering if I was a cop or a reporter or someone else come to harass him and disrupt his life in an effort to do my job. Unfortunately, he wasn't too far off.

"Mr. Walling, my name is Zoe Grey. I'm sorry to bother you on a Sunday. Is that football?" I indicated the TV behind him. "I didn't realize football season had started already."

A football fan I am not, which in Colorado makes me downright un-American, but there it is.

"Preseason," he said absently, eyes still appraising me. "You a cop? A reporter?"

This caused some shuffling behind him and a woman appeared in the doorway beside him. She was perhaps a few years younger than Theresa Walling, and quite pretty, but she projected an air of meekness I found unappealing.

"No, sir. I'm a private investigator. I'm investigating a woman named Karen Brickle. I believe you may have known her."

This surprised both of them, and Walling's expression changed almost immediately.

"What's she done?" he asked.

"I'm afraid I can't discuss why my client has asked me to investigate. I will tell you I am very suspicious about Karen Brickle."

There is an art to knowing what to say to which person and when. Sometimes the truth will serve your purpose better than the cleverest lie. By Walling's reaction to my introduction as a PI investigating Brickle, I suspected this was an occasion for the truth, or as much as the truth as I was willing to share with this man at this point. Walling didn't like Brickle, and I planned to extort that in order to extract from him as much information as possible.

"Would you be willing to answer a few questions?" I asked.

Walling didn't need to think about it. He immediately swung the screen door open and stepped back to let me in.

I thanked him and went into the house, mindful to keep my shirt down over the badge on my belt. I'd had no firm plan for how I was going to approach Walling when I'd walked up to the door, so I hadn't thought to take the badge off. And I wasn't sure if PIs carried badges or not. With Walling being so sensitive to cops, I didn't want to inadvertently flash him the badge and have him get the wrong idea.

"This is my wife, Sheila," he said as we moved into the living room. "Have a seat." He indicated the chair he'd vacated a few moments before as he sat on the sofa with Sheila.

"Thank you. I understand you were neighbors with Karen Brickle."

Walling shook his head. "No, I never was. She lived next door to my ex-wife, Terri. I'd moved out several years before Karen moved in."

"I see. So what was your relationship to Karen?"

"I didn't have one. I used to hear about her through my boys. They would talk to their mother, she would tell them something, and eventually it would make its way back to me. The first time I met her was in February when Terri went missing. Karen helped organize volunteer search parties."

"What kind of stories was your ex-wife telling your sons about Karen? Was Karen a bad neighbor?"

"Strange might be a better word. From what I heard, Karen kept odd hours, had strange visitors, and saw quite a few men." He looked up at me. "You have to understand, that's a pretty serious sin to Terri."

"Are Karen and Terri friends?"

"I find that hard to believe. Terri . . . changed after the divorce. Not so much as to believe entertaining a different man every night was acceptable, but she was different. Still, I don't think she would have become friends with a woman like Karen."

"So why did Karen volunteer her time to the search effort? She must have been pretty fond of Terri."

He shrugged. "I always thought it was strange. After meeting her, I thought she was a bizarre woman."

"In what way?"

He struggled to find the right words for several minutes. "I don't want to speak out of turn," he finally said.

This guy wasn't striking me as the disappear-my-wife type. I wondered if the police had anything more substantial than the argument between Mr. and the former Mrs. Walling to point suspicion at him for the crime. I wondered if he was indeed a suspect in the eyes of the police, or if that was just the sensationalism of the media and the slant of Brickle's Facebook page.

"Please, speak freely, Mr. Walling. I have my own opinion of Karen Brickle."

He seemed to consider this for a moment. While he was, his wife squirmed, and finally blurted, "She seemed to enjoy the attention."

"Sheila."

She immediately sank further into the sofa and bowed her head.

This exchange was an interesting show, but it was a reflection on Sheila, not on Walling. Sheila was timid and overly submissive; Walling was not overly aggressive, and I had a very hard time believing him to be an abusive man. I'd met a few, and Walling wasn't setting off any of my warning bells.

"Do you agree, Mr. Walling? Did Karen seem to enjoy being in the spotlight while helping to search for your wife?"

"Ex-wife," he corrected almost absently. Then he sighed. "Yes. She was . . . almost *excited*. She didn't seem worried at all about where Terri might be or what might have happened to her. She didn't seem to get discouraged when day after day the search parties turned up nothing. In fact, she seemed to be somehow satisfied with that."

He shook his head at the memories. "On the second day, after people had scoured the neighborhood and various other areas, I tried to suggest alternate locations for searching. I wanted to shift the focus out of the neighborhood to the wilderness areas, some of the hiking trails, some of the more remote parts of the county where her . . . *body* might not be found for some time."

He had to spit out the word *body*. Terri might have been his ex-wife, but he did not take any pleasure whatsoever in the idea that she may be dead. It was possible he had actually killed her, and that he found genuine sadness in the fact that she was dead, but I suspected not. I thought what I was seeing in him was an inability to commit such violence. Assuming, of course, Theresa Walling was in fact dead, which I did seriously suspect at this point.

"Anyway," Walling went on, "Karen was angry with me for making suggestions. She accused me of attempting to divert the search and made very loud accusations that I had . . . killed Terri."

Again, he seemed disgusted with the idea. I also detected anger. I suspected some of that anger was directed at Karen for suggesting he could have done such a thing, but I thought some of it was in general at the thought that someone might have killed Theresa.

He clasped his hands in his lap, working them over slightly in his agitation. "She took her loud accusations and made them to the police. And she wouldn't let up. It became a campaign with her, trying to convince the world I had done something to Terri. The police seemed to buy into it. They started to tear my life apart. They were here all the time, asking questions of both of us, bothering my kids, my coworkers, my neighbors, digging into my past. They dragged me down to the police station about four times, interrogated me for hours, tried to use things from my past to say I was guilty of this crime, whatever this crime is. I mean, they don't even know what happened to Terri." He threw his hands up in exasperation and looked at me across the room.

"At this point, I'm sure they're working the case as if she'd been murdered," I said gently, infusing my voice with the right amount of understanding and insult on his behalf.

"Can you believe that?" he asked. "They've totally stopped looking for her. What if she's still alive somewhere?"

He sank back against the sofa. Sheila wrapped an arm around him, trying to comfort him. I was half afraid the guy was going to start crying. But in fairness, I couldn't imagine how impotent he felt, and I didn't envy him his situation.

"You still care about Terri a great deal," I said.

He shrugged. "She's the mother of my children. My boys . . . they're perfect. And that was Terri's doing. She was a perfect mother. She may not have been the best wife, and we may not have gotten along all the time, but she'll always be the mother of my children. My boys . . ." He shook his head again. "My sons need their mother back. They've been a wreck since she went missing. If it turns out she is . . . dead . . . well, then, I guess we need to know that, too. At least the boys would have some kind of closure then, and they would try to move on. If you can move on from something like that."

I didn't know what to say to that. I didn't think a person could just move on from learning his mother had been abducted and murdered, so I didn't have anything comforting to say. And since I suspected Theresa was dead, I didn't have anything encouraging to say, either. So I tried to change the subject.

"What else can you tell me about Karen? How long did she live next door to your ex-wife?"

He shrugged. "A couple years, maybe. She moved away not too long ago, a few months, I think."

I nodded that he was correct on that point then asked, "Do you know where she worked or the names of anyone in her life? Friends maybe, or one of the men?"

"She was some kind of medical professional, a nurse or a doctor—I can't remember. I believe she worked at the hospital. And I wouldn't have any idea about her friends or the men or anything. I think one of her friends may have turned out for one of the searches, but I can't really remember; all of that time is kind of a blur." He looked at his wife for help.

She nodded her head, but glanced at her husband before she spoke, as if making sure it was okay.

For heaven's sake, woman, grow a backbone and spit it out!

"There was a friend there," Sheila finally said. "A woman. I don't remember that she ever said her name, and I can't remember how they knew one another. She was just there once, on the first day."

Great. How the hell was I going to track down some woman with no name, description, or connection?

"Do you remember what she looked like?"

"Oh, dear," Sheila said, wringing her tiny hands in her lap in between glances at Walling. "Um, not really. She was about Karen's age, I think. And she must have been pretty average, because she didn't stick out at all."

Average? Wonderful.

"Blonde? Brunette? Tall? Short?"

"Just average," she said again.

Right.

"Were there any press there that day? The first day of the search?"

Sheila, not certain if I was speaking to her or not, looked at Walling, diverting the question to him.

He thought for a moment then said, "I think there might have been. I remember feeling like the press were everywhere. I mean, they camped out on my front lawn for a while. I'm sure they would have been there for the searches."

I nodded and stood. "Thank you for your time."

They walked me to the door.

"You know," Walling said, looking out at me standing on the porch again. "I have always felt like Karen knows something about what happened to Terri."

"Really? What makes you think that?"

He shrugged. "I honestly can't decide if it's just because she worked so hard to cast the blame onto me, or if it's something else I just can't put my finger on. I'm very glad to know someone is looking into her."

I thought for a beat, then asked a question designed to satisfy my own perceptions of Frank Walling.

"If I started looking into your ex-wife's disappearance," I said, watching him closely, "would you also welcome that scrutiny?"

He didn't blink, didn't flinch, didn't shy away or shrink down. His brown eyes held mine evenly. "I lost faith in the Boulder Police Department more than six months ago. Ms. Grey, if you can find what happened to Terri, I'd more than welcome it; I'd be forever grateful to you. I assure you, no amount of digging will turn up anything more sinister between Terri and me than a long history of marital spats. We were good parents and terrible spouses. But I never harmed her, not in February or any other time. And I never wished any harm on her. I didn't want to be married to her anymore, but I have always wanted her to be the mother of my sons. I still want that."

For the first time since meeting Sheila, I saw something besides meekness in her. At her husband's last words, jealously burned so bright in her face it was almost blinding. Her reaction served as confirmation Walling was telling the truth about his feelings toward his ex-wife. It also made me realize I had pretty much dismissed her as nothing more than ornamentation since I met her. But if I were investigating the Theresa Walling case, I'd want to know more about Sheila.

I nodded to Walling. "Thank you again for your time."

They both stood at the open door while I returned to the Jeep and pulled away from the curb.

27

Since I was in the area, I made Karen Brickle's former house my next stop. I didn't know much about Boulder, beyond what everyone knows about Boulder, which is that Boulder is a hippy-dippy, granola-eating, tree-hugging community full of health and environmental nuts. But the neighborhood where I found Karen Brickle's former house seemed like a blue-collar, lower-middle-class area. There were older cars in the driveways, kid paraphernalia in most yards, and kids playing in the streets. One thing was clear: Karen's move to Fort Collins had been a serious upgrade in status.

I parked at the curb across the street and took in Brickle's house as well as Theresa Walling's. The two sat side by side in the middle of the block. Theresa's looked like it had been lived in for twenty-five years; there were planter boxes on the windows, flowerbeds in the yard, a couple of yard gnomes. The windows needed cleaning, the house needed paint, and the gutters needed to be cleared. But it looked like a house well lived in where two boys had been raised.

Brickle's house, on the other hand, looked so clean and well kept it was devoid of personality. There were no personal touches, no indication anyone lived there really, though I was sure someone did, because there was an SUV parked in the driveway. I couldn't see any lights on or any other indication anyone was home. Still, I got out of the Scout and went to the door, Dasch watching from the passenger seat.

179

I rang the bell and peered through the front window, but the living room was dark and held no occupants. That room looked very much like the outside of the house—clean, neat, well put together, without any personal touches.

No one came to the door, so I rang the bell again and knocked. I wasn't sure what I hoped to gain by coming here or talking to whoever lived here now, but I would feel remiss if I didn't make the effort. And as I waited at the unanswered door, I debated the degree of remissness and whether I should let myself in and take a look around.

I was still debating when I heard some noise from Theresa Walling's backyard. Her front door had been shut, and there was no car in the driveway, so I hadn't suspected anyone would be there. But I knew I wanted to jump on the opportunity. So I walked off Karen Brickle's former porch, cut across her former yard, and went to Theresa Walling's front door. I rang the bell and about three minutes later, a good-looking guy opened the door.

"Hi," he said. His natural inclination was to be friendly and polite, but he was guarded, as Frank Walling had been, no doubt wondering who the hell was ringing a missing woman's doorbell.

"Hi," I said, smiling. "My name is Zoe Grey. I'm a private investigator looking into a woman named Karen Brickle. I understand she used to live next door."

"Oh," the guy said, visibly relaxing.

He was wearing jeans, tennis shoes, and a t-shirt. He had sunglasses on top of his head, and he was covered in sweat and dirt and grass. He'd obviously been working outside in the yard. Perhaps mowing the lawn or maybe getting a jump-start on fall cleanup.

"I'm Tom," he said, offering me his hand. He quickly pulled it back and brushed it off on his jeans, then, seeing it was hopeless, apologized and held it out to me anyway. "This is my mother's house."

I shook his hand, dirt and all. "Nice to meet you."

I'd met this kid's father, and I'd seen photos of his mother, but he was better looking than both of them. I wondered if the same could be said for his brother.

"Would you mind if I asked you a couple questions?" I asked.

"Uh, sure. I really don't know that I can help, but you can ask." He grinned and held the door open for me. "I was working in the yard. Would you mind if we took this out back?"

"Of course not. Thank you."

I followed him through the house to the sliding glass door off the kitchen, taking in as much of the house as I could without lingering. The place looked as well lived in on the inside as it did on the outside. The furniture and décor was not new, but well worn and warm, comfortable like a true home should be. And it was obvious someone was currently living here, even though that someone was not Theresa. I suspected it might be a male. Tom perhaps.

In the backyard, I discovered Tom had indeed been mowing the lawn, as well as clearing the gutters and trimming a few overgrown tree branches away from the house.

Theresa's backyard was large and would have been a great place for boys to grow up. Large trees lined the backyard and the north side of the house. In one of the trees, through the large, leafy branches, I saw the outline of a tree house. Narrow boards nailed to the trunk to provided access. In another tree, a knotted rope swayed gently on the light breeze.

Like the front yard, none of the flowerbeds or pots had been planted—Theresa had disappeared before she'd been able to do it this year. But they were tended, free of weeds, with a few perennials on display.

The deck was large and held comfortable patio furniture. I could easily imagine this family having meals and gatherings out here over the years, and I suddenly felt a profound sadness for the loss of Theresa from her family.

The yard was surrounded by a four-foot, chain-link fence. On the south side, I was able to see over into Karen Brickle's former backyard. It was as impersonally maintained as the front. There was a solitary patio table, but no chairs or umbrella. There were no potted plants or flowerbeds. It was downright sterile compared to the life that seemed to brim in Theresa's yard.

"Nice day, right?" Tom said as he went to the patio table and picked up a water bottle. He downed half of it and looked at me. "Something to drink?"

"No, thank you."

From the birth certificates, I remembered Thomas Michael Walling was Theresa's youngest son, and from his birthdate, he would be twenty-six. His older brother, Brian Franklin Walling, was twenty-nine. I hadn't looked into either boy, so beyond their names and birthdates, I knew nothing about them. I found myself curious about Tom.

I said, "I wondered if you might have known Karen Brickle when she lived next door."

He set the water bottle down then retrieved some work gloves from his back pocket and pulled them on. "Not really," he said, walking over to the waiting ladder. "I remember she used to live next door, and I talked to her a couple times, but I didn't know her."

He climbed onto the ladder and began to tug on a clump of dead leaves and small twigs and whatever the hell else accumulated itself in the gutters of a house.

There was something I didn't like about his response, but I couldn't put my finger on it. I moved around to stand in front of the ladder, looking up at him. He jerked the clump free, dropped it into the trashcan beside the ladder, and tugged on another clump. I hate cleaning the gutters. I will pay a neighbor kid to do it every time.

"Is she a friend of your mother's? Or was she, before she moved away?"

He ripped another clump free and dropped it in the trash. He never looked directly at me, and he wore his sunglasses again, but I saw his nose twitch in genuine disgust.

"They weren't friends. My mom would never be friends with a woman like that."

"I see. How did they get along as neighbors? Were things peaceful or were they warring over anything?"

"As far as I can remember, Karen was a regular neighbor. She kept to herself a lot, didn't bother anyone. She didn't spend much time getting to know the neighbors."

There was something a touch too familiar in the way he said her name.

I said, "I understand Karen had a lot of people in and out of her house. A lot of men."

I saw the briefest flash of jealousy and then anger on his handsome face. Now I had a working theory.

"I wouldn't know about that. I had moved out long before Karen ever moved in next door. I came by the house regularly to see my mom or hang out with my brother, but I didn't live here. I wouldn't know about who was coming or going from her place."

"Do you live here now?"

He glanced at me and ripped a particularly large wad of gutter garbage free. "I suppose you know what happened to my mom."

I nodded. "I'm familiar with the case, yes."

He reached for another clump and said, "I stay here about half time. I still have my own place, near the school where I teach. I'm here mostly on the weekends. We decided it was best to keep up with the place, rather than winterize it and shut it up. My brother helps, too, but he's got kids, so he can't stay here as easily. When we find our mom, if she . . ." He stopped to swallow his worst nightmare and jerked on another clump more violently than necessary. "If she wants to come back here, we want the place to be ready for her."

"I know she'll appreciate that," I said, and meant it.

He just nodded and continued with his work.

"Your dad says Karen helped organize the search parties."

He looked at me in surprise. "You talked to my dad? When?"

"Before I came over here. Do you remember Karen helping with the searches?"

"Yeah, she was there. Why?"

"Do you remember anything strange about Karen's behavior during that time?"

He looked at me again, his work forgotten. "You're not suggesting Karen had anything to do with whatever happened to my mom, are you?"

I thought it was too soon to push this kid.

"No, of course not. I'm just trying to get an idea of Karen as a person." I looked at him pointedly. "Perhaps you could help me in that regard."

"I don't know what you mean. I told you I didn't know her very well."

I decided to put this topic away for a while and come back to it later. "How about the new neighbor? What is he like?"

"It's a woman, and I don't know her either. I never see her. I couldn't even tell you her name."

"Is she the woman who bought the house from Karen?"

"I guess. She's the only one to live there since."

"I see. Well, I thank you for your time, Tom. I'll let you finish with the gutters."

"I'll walk you out," he said, climbing off the ladder.

"Oh, that's not necessary."

"I don't mind."

Well, crap. I'd hoped to have a quick look around Theresa's house unguided, but that was not to be. Either Tom was being an overly committed host, or else he didn't totally trust me. Maybe both. And really, I couldn't blame him. It was too easy to imagine the lies and the shady tricks people had used to get even the smallest morsel of scandal from the tragedy that had struck this family in February. For all I knew, some sleazy reporter had actually tried to have a look around Theresa's house, and Tom had learned his lesson.

We walked back through the house in silence. I stepped out on to the porch, then turned back and told him I was sorry for whatever had happened to his mom, which was the truth. He thanked me and closed the door.

I went back to the Jeep wondering if what I'd learned here would prove relevant or useful.

28

The drive back to town was uneventful, and I didn't notice much of it, my mind chewing on what, if anything, I'd learned from talking to Frank Walling or his son, Tom. I swung by Ellmann's to pick up the Scout before heading on to my house. While I kept a few things at Ellmann's, I did not keep anything I needed now. And just because I could, I let Dasch follow me into the house, landlord be damned.

Dasch checked the house for intruders, and I went up to the bathroom. I made quick work of getting myself ready. My mother had done a brilliant job beating vanity into me from an early age; I can do hair, makeup, and attire for any occasion. While I'd give up nearly all these habits in the only act of rebellion my mother could understand, they are skills you never forgot, so I looked damn good when I was done.

I left the house with my hair curled and my face painted, wearing a slutty black dress I'd worn to a bachelorette party a couple years ago. I hadn't worn the dress since, but I had the feeling it would be appropriate for tonight. Plus, it was cut in such a way it mostly covered all my scars.

Dasch and I loaded back into the Scout and headed north. Sadie lives downtown, in a very pricy controlled-access building located in Old Town, the kind where you'd expect to see a doorman. Her one-bedroom apartment is on the eighth floor, and has great views of downtown. It's one of the most beautiful apartments I've ever seen, with marble and teak and everything else; Sadie had remodeled it herself, and spared no expense.

Still, I've always wondered why Sadie continues to live here. Beautiful as it is, it is only one bedroom. Sadie could certainly afford something bigger, something with a yard for her dog and a second bedroom for guests. But she had no plans to move.

I parked on the street in the ten-minute loading zone outside the front door and called her. Five minutes later, she strolled through the lobby and out the door. I hadn't told Sadie to "dress for a night out," because Sadie is a southern woman, and if there's one thing she knows how to do, it's put herself together for every occasion. I knew when I picked her up I'd find her looking four times better than me, and it would have taken her less than half the time.

And she didn't disappoint.

She was dressed in an equally slutty black and nude dress and her six-inch heels she affectionately referred to as her "hooker shoes." Her hair was curled and sprayed, and her heavy makeup was perfect. When she climbed in the truck, her perfume hit me.

"Hello there, handsome," she said, immediately turning to Dasch. Then she dug a treat out of her clutch. "Here you go, baby doll."

Dasch ate the treat in one bite, and Sadie rubbed his neck, murmuring to him. He licked his lips and swooned at her.

"I knew you'd keep him," she said, grinning as she turned back to me.

"Yeah, yeah. You and everyone else. Sadie, meet Dasch. Dasch, Sadie."

"Dasch," she said, turning back to him. "What an unusual name. But it suits you, doesn't it? Yes, it does. Hey," she said, tearing half her attention away from the dog. "Do you want to park here? We can walk."

"Not with Dasch in the car. I don't want to leave him in your garage."

"I'd offer to let him stay in my apartment, but Lola is getting territorial in her old age."

"That's okay. He's not really a stay-at-home dog."

Sadie continued to gush over Dasch as I drove the few short blocks it was to the eyeglasses place Olvera had named. I drove into the Oak Street parking lot and cruised around, looking for a spot. Since it was Saturday night, there wasn't one. Aside from the handicapped spots. So I took one of those.

"If you've got a handicapped tag," Sadie said to me, "I want to borrow it."

"No, I've got something better. I've got two detectives in my pocket."

We got out and clicked our way down the sidewalk to the building. We used an overlooked door that granted access to the second floor and climbed the stairs. None of these doors were marked, so I had no idea which one Olvera might be behind. I banged on the first one and waited.

A moment later, the door swung open and Olvera stared out.

"Holy shit, I didn't recognize you." He gaped at me, looking me up and down.

"I'll take that as a compliment," I said, pushing past him.

"Who are you?"

"Backup," Sadie said striding in after me. "Or cover. Maybe both, we'll see."

I love Sadie.

Olvera shut the door and glared at me. Topham was standing with his hands on his hips looking particularly put out. I ignored them both and smiled at the third familiar face.

"Frye, what are you doing here?"

"Helping out with the operation," he said, smiling.

188

We seemed to be in some kind of apartment. Many Old Town businesses have residential living spaces above them. The price is usually high and the tenant must put up with excessive amounts of noise, but they don't stay vacant very long.

I wondered how the boys knew about this one and where the tenant was.

We stood in the living room. The entire west wall was a line of windows overlooking College Avenue below. On the left, some kitchen cabinets, a small stove, and a small refrigerator had been installed. A tiny kitchen table sat in front of the windows on the left. The rest of the room was occupied by sofas, a coffee table, and an entertainment center. A small doorway on the left led to the bathroom. A closed door on the right led to what I guessed was the bedroom.

All three men were dressed casually in jeans. Frye wore a t-shirt while Topham wore a polo shirt and Olvera wore a Broncos jersey. And they had taken over the living room. The coffee table was crammed with laptops, cameras with long-range lenses, binoculars, and whatever else. Whatever they were up to, they'd been at it a while.

"You girls look . . . ready," Frye said, still smiling.

"I told you I clean up nice," I said, chuckling. "How's your shoulder?"

He rolled his arm in a circle then pulled his collar aside to show me a small white bandage. "Just a graze. Went right through the strap on my vest. I'm fine."

"I'm so glad. Frye, this is Sadie. Sadie, Derek Frye. He's a friend."

Frye offered his hand to Sadie, and I swear I saw him blush. Sadie has this effect on men.

I turned to the others, hands on my hips. "So what's the deal, boys? Why am I here?"

Frye deferred to the other two. The other two exchanged a look, and Topham turned away. Boy, that guy didn't like me.

Olvera came over and leaned against the back of the sofa. "Colin and I have been working a case that seems to revolve around the Drunken Monkey."

Sadie sighed and perched on the arm of the sofa, draping one long leg over the other. She flashed some skin as she did this and every man present stopped to take notice, gay or not. "I hate the Drunken Monkey."

The Drunken Monkey was a bar in Old Town. It was hugely popular with the college crowd and guaranteed to generate at least one phone call to 911 a night. Sadie had told me more than once the ER sees more people from the Drunken Monkey for fighting than any other bar. I wasn't surprised the bar was the subject of a police investigation.

"Is this about drugs?" Sadie asked.

"No." Olvera looked slightly annoyed at his narrative being interrupted.

"What do you know about drugs?" Frye asked her.

Sadie shrugged one shoulder. "Just what I hear. And that is if you need a score, you should try the Drunken Monkey."

"Any drug in particular?" Frye asked, genuinely interested.

"No idea. Pot, I assumed. But maybe other stuff too, like ecstasy. All these college kids do ecstasy, right?"

"And who told you this?"

"Patients. They come in all messed up and talk about scoring down at the Drunken Monkey."

"Anyway," Olvera said sharply. "We're not working a drug case; we're working an abduction case."

I noticed Frye flinched slightly at this, and I had the clear impression my new best friend Olvera wasn't telling me the whole story.

"Abduction?" I said. "Like kidnappings? I haven't heard about any kidnapping cases." Then I remembered the missing girl, Maria Rodriguez. "Although I have heard about a missing persons case recently."

"This has nothing to do with Maria Rodriguez," Olvera said, pronouncing her name properly. He didn't speak with an accent, but Olvera had grown up in a Spanish-speaking home. "We've been all over her case, and we can find no connection to this bar. Plus, there are some distinct differences."

"Like what?" I asked, glaring at him.

Frye waited a beat while Olvera and I stared each other down, waiting for Olvera to fold and let me in. When he didn't, Frye sighed and reached for a folder on the cluttered coffee table. He pulled out a piece of paper and handed it to me.

"Six college girls have been abducted over the last two months." His tone was grim. "They are taken somewhere, held for twelve to forty-eight hours, repeatedly raped, roughed up, then dumped."

I gaped at him. "How have you managed to keep that out of the media?"

"Guys higher up the food chain than me are doing some serious wheeling and dealing with the media," he said with a shrug. "That's all I can figure."

"Holy shit." I looked at the document he'd handed me. On it were the photos of six attractive, young girls, none of them looking older than twenty. How had they even gotten into the bar in the first place? Sadie reached for the paper, and I gave it to her. "You think they were abducted from here?"

Frye nodded. "None of them has a clear memory of what happened to them during the time they were held, but they all clearly remember being at the Drunken Monkey."

"Oh, my gosh," Sadie said, suddenly pointing at one of the girls. "I took care of her—the night she was found." Sadie put a hand to her full bosom. "Oh, I had no idea what had happened to her, but I remember how she looked. Beaten, bruised, bloody, wearing only a bra and a miniskirt." She looked up at me. "It was bad."

I wanted to tell her we were going to help nail the guy and get the girl justice. But I knew from personal experience there was no true justice to a victim of a crime like that. The best we could hope for now was to find the guy and hope the cops could put together a case solid enough to send him to prison where there were no women for him to rape.

I looked from Frye to Olvera. "Please tell me I'm not bait."

Topham's face twisted in a truly terrible smile. "You're not his type."

"Too tall?" I already knew the answer.

Topham smiled wider. "Too *old*."

Prick. "So what exactly is my role here, boys?"

"We're looking at one of the bartenders," Olvera said, picking up his earlier narrative. "A guy named Frazier. Works every weekend, which is when all of the girls went missing. We've had cops in the bar every night for the last week, but Frazier hasn't made a move. We think he can spot the cops."

That was a safe bet. Cops tend to stand out. And criminals tend to have a sixth sense about them.

"We need someone else to go in," Olvera went on. "Someone who isn't a cop. As far as we can tell, the guy hasn't snatched anyone in two weeks. He's gotta be hungry by now; we don't think he'll wait much longer. The girls have all been grabbed on a Friday or Saturday night. Tonight's Saturday; last chance for another week."

"Are there any other missing girls that could fit, maybe girls that haven't been returned?" I asked, mostly addressing Frye.

Topham rolled his eyes. "This has nothing to do with Maria Rodriguez!" Her name didn't sound as pretty when he said it.

"We've looked," Frye said. "And it's possible. But, Zoe, do you know how many people

192

are reported missing every day?"

I shook my head.

"Over the last ten years, there were an average of seven hundred and fifty thousand missing persons cases per year nationwide. That's more than two thousand people reported every day. Obviously, the numbers for our department aren't that large, but we do get new cases every single day." He looked at me for a beat then added, "Plus, there were a couple of distinct differences in Maria's case. It really is unlikely this case has anything to do with hers."

I believed him. Which was kind of disheartening, because that meant there was more than one predator in town preying on college girls. That wasn't a happy thought.

"All right," I said. "So you want me to go in and keep an eye on Frazier."

"Pretty much," Olvera said. He was still slightly irritated, but he was glad to be back on task. He stood up and moved around to the coffee table. "We'll be set up for audio and visual." He picked up a small black bag off the coffee table. He opened it and pulled out a necklace. "Need you to wear this."

I was tempted to make a crack about him playing dress-up with a real doll, but I managed to refrain. Instead I asked, "This a camera? Or just GPS?" I took the necklace from him.

"A camera," he answered. "We'll be tracking the GPS in your phone. That's expensive, so don't lose it."

I removed the necklace I'd been wearing and put the new one on. Topham moved over from the windows and both he and Olvera sat and turned their attention to their laptops.

"I have visual," Olvera reported.

Topham nodded and reached for a pair of headphones, putting them to one ear. "Say something," he said to me.

"Where is the information I asked for?"

Topham stiffened slightly and glared at Olvera darkly across the table.

"Guess it's working," Olvera said. "And I've got your cell phone." He picked up another file and stood. "This is the bartender we're interested in." He handed me a photo. "He's working tonight; we saw him go into the bar. We'd like to know how he's getting the girls out of the building."

I guessed he was walking them right out the front door, but I tried to give Tweedledee and Tweedledum the benefit of the doubt that they would notice such a thing. Anyway, I thought it might be more important to know where the girls were being taken after they left the Drunken Monkey, but if these two idiots just wanted to know how they were getting out of the bar, then so be it.

I handed the photo back. "Got it."

"If at any point you feel uncomfortable, get out," Olvera said. "I'd be seriously surprised if you became a target, but I could be wrong."

Olvera and his partner made a career out of being wrong, but I didn't point this out.

"Detective, I believe you underestimate me."

"I doubt it. In any case, Frye will be nearby."

I looked at Frye, who looked as unhappy with the assignment as I was.

"Absolutely not," I said to Olvera.

Topham got involved for the first time. He shot off the sofa and turned to me. "Grey, he—"

"He looks like a cop," I said. "No offense, Frye. And that's been your problem all along. Do you want to play *this* card," I asked, waving a hand at myself, "or do you want to throw away another night?"

The pair exchanged a look. Obviously Frye had been Topham's idea.

"It's for your safety," Olvera began.

"Bullshit. You don't trust me not to fuck up your little game here. But let me tell you, you don't need my help to do that."

Sadie chuckled then quickly clamped a hand over her mouth and became interested in her shoe. I saw Frye's mouth twitch as he resisted the urge to smile. Olvera and Topham were both angry.

I held my arms out to the side. "Do you think I got all dressed up like a slut because I plan to half-ass this thing? Give me a little credit. And stay out of the way."

Olvera opened his mouth to reply, but Frye spoke first.

"Bail at the first sign of trouble," he said. "We'll be monitoring from here, so we're thirty seconds away if it goes bad."

"Wonderful," I said. I glanced from Olvera to Topham and back. "Now, if we could just settle the issue of the information I requested, I'll be on my way."

Topham turned away and went back to the window, standing with his hands on his hips and staring down at the activity on the street below. Olvera, who had been more or less resigned to our arrangement that morning, was now distinctly put out. Perhaps because the arrangement was no longer private, but now on display in front of Frye and Sadie. Or perhaps he'd had the day to realize how disagreeable he found the whole thing. I didn't know. And I really didn't care.

He finally pulled some folded papers from his back pocket. I took them, unfolded them, and glanced through them.

"Thanks," I said, folding them again and tucking them into my purse with the photos I didn't need to use yet. I looked at Sadie. "Let's do this."

29

"Your friend Derek is cute," Sadie said when we were on the street.

We stood at the light, waiting for the signal or a break in traffic.

"You know they're all listening, right?"

Sadie just waved a dismissive hand. "Is he single?"

I looked at her sideways. "You don't like cops."

"I could make an exception. If he's single."

"He is," I said. "He just got out of a bad relationship."

Which had been a long time coming. I had no idea where Frye had found her, but she was a mean, mess of a woman who brought nothing to his life but chaos and suffering. I'd hated the way she treated him, and I'd been ecstatic to learn he'd kicked her out.

"What happened with the other guy?" I asked Sadie. "The one from the party last night?"

The light changed, and we crossed the street.

"Mm. I think it went well. But he hasn't called."

"Is this that doctor you were fooling around with?"

She scoffed. "No. *That* guy is old news. And he's a manwhore. No, *this* guy is a *surgeon*." She smiled. "His name is Garrett Pearson."

"A surgeon. So, he's, what, fifty?"

196

She smacked my arm. "He's thirty-nine, thank you very much. He just moved here from Georgia."

"Ooh, a southern boy. You two must be getting along great."

"Well, I thought so. But he hasn't called."

"It's been one day."

"I guess that's true. And he was on call today."

I rolled my eyes as we stopped and showed our IDs to the doorman.

"Give him a break, Sadie. It's way too early to write him off."

"Maybe. But what's his name, Derek, *is* really cute."

"Sadie, you hate cops. Frye is really good-looking, and he's a really great guy, but he is a cop, through and through."

"Well, you're drifting that way, but I still like you. Maybe it wouldn't be so bad."

"Whatever you decide to do, just remember, he is my friend, okay? Be careful."

"I believe that man is capable of taking care of himself, Zoe Grey," she said, exaggerating her drawl. "But I take your point."

The bar was crowded and noisy and reeked of alcohol, sweat, and perfume. Almost the moment we walked in the door, a drunk girl fell off one of the swings they had instead of barstools. The sound of her head cracking against the floor was as loud as a gunshot. Sadie rolled her eyes, grabbed my arm, and propelled me toward the stairs.

"Don't want to be recognized as a nurse," she said. "They'd want me to do something."

A crowd formed around the girl as I followed Sadie upstairs. Over the din, I heard someone say something about 911. I idly wondered if it was the first ambulance call tonight, and if it would be the only one.

Sadie and I toured the upstairs, spotting the bartender, Frazier, at the bar. We ordered drinks from him (how ballsy was that?) then found a table. We chatted and sipped our drinks and turned down dance invitations for a while.

From my vantage point, I had a good line of sight on Frazier, but I couldn't see that he was paying particular interest to any one girl. Mostly he just seemed to be working. It was a Saturday night and the place was packed. The drink orders never stopped coming.

"This guy has to be the most boring guy in the world," Sadie said. "He's not even flirting with these drunk girls."

I'd noticed the same thing.

"Maybe he's gay," I said.

"He's not flirting with the drunk boys, either," she said.

And that was also true.

Around eleven o'clock, a pretty blonde girl walked past our table and went to the end of the bar. She almost immediately caught his eye, and he came straight over to her. He kissed her and grinned.

Sadie, who had also been watching, rolled her eyes. "That girl has no idea how lucky she is. She managed to find the last truly decent guy on the planet."

Frazier fixed his girlfriend a mojito. She grinned at him as she sat at the end of the bar.

I didn't sense anything hinky about Frazier. I thought Sadie's assessment was pretty accurate. I can't even begin to describe how surprised I was to learn Topham and Olvera had been looking at the wrong guy.

Sadie looked as bored as I felt. And since our conversation had drifted off, I felt like we were beginning to stick out.

"Let's dance," I said, scooting to the edge of the booth.

Sadie tossed back the last of her drink. "Hell, yes."

I stood and someone collided with me from behind. And I felt that someone palm my backside. I resisted the instinct to break the hand and turned around. He was a black guy I'd seen several times since we arrived. He was over six feet tall and built like a football player. And he wore a Drunken Monkey t-shirt that said SECURITY on the back. He laughed as he moved past me.

"Excuse me," he said. "I'm sorry."

I gave him a smile and waved it off as some kind of alarm bell rang in my head.

"What was that?" Sadie said in my ear.

"No idea. Let's dance."

We wound our way over to the dance floor and squeezed into the crowd. After a few minutes, Sadie went and made a request of the DJ. She let loose the full power of her southern charm, and hers was the next song to play.

"I love this song!" she said, dancing.

Over her shoulder, beyond the crowd on the dance floor, I saw a young woman stumble out of a booth. She clung to the table as she righted herself and tried to get her bearings. Of course, she was so intoxicated the effort was in vain.

As far as I could tell, the girl was alone. She was petite, probably barely twenty-one, and dressed for a night at the club. Behind her at the bar, I spotted the same security guard. Now he seemed to have his eye on her.

The girl continued to stumble forward, bracing herself on tables and the wall as she went. The security guard left the bar and began to follow her. I was half afraid she'd fall down the stairs, but by the time she reached them, he was already beside her, putting a supporting arm around her waist.

"Let me help you," he said in an easy voice.

"Thanks," she slurred.

He practically carried her down the stairs. I pressed over to the railing and watched over the side as he led her toward the bathroom. He scanned the crowd in both directions as they walked, then pulled his cell phone from his pocket. My gut told me he wasn't calling her a cab.

199

I shoved my way to the stairs and hurried down, hoping to hell Tweedledee and Tweedledumb were paying attention.

I got to the hallway leading to the bathrooms and saw no sign of them. I poked my head into the women's room, but the girl was not among the women inside. I moved on and pushed open the men's room door, ignoring the remarks I earned from the men inside. They were not in there either.

"Shit," I muttered under my breath, hurrying down the hall.

The security guy had definitely led her down this hallway, of that I was certain. Now I was beginning to suspect this hallway led to another exit, and I wished I'd had the forethought to ask about the layout of the building before I'd come in here. And I also wished I'd gone with the bigger handbag so I could have brought my gun.

I came to a small alcove on the right and found an unmarked door. I eased it open and peered inside. It was a long hallway, and it was empty. I charged forward, my heels echoing loudly off the concrete and brick.

The hallway ended in an exterior door that opened into a small parking lot at the back of the building. I pushed outside and saw a white Chrysler 300 pulling out of the lot.

"Shit!" I cried, sprinting across the parking lot and shoving through the flood of people on the sidewalk for the street.

"Watch it, bitch!" a girl snapped and shoved me.

As she did, I caught a glimpse of a glass bottle in the hand of the guy walking behind her. It was still half-full of whatever he was drinking. I snatched it and sprinted for the street, chucking it at the car for all I was worth.

The bottle hit the back window and exploded, drenching the car in yellow liquid and glass. The brake lights winked on and the car screeched to a halt. I crossed my finger the driver that stepped out was the security guy from the club. I wasn't disappointed.

"What the hell?" he cried as he stormed over to me.

"Where's the girl?" I asked.

A crowd had gathered as a result of a bottle vs. car stunt, but so far I'd seen no sign of the cops who were supposed to be watching the camera feed.

"What the hell is your problem?" he bellowed, trying to use fear to back me down.

But I'd had a lot of practice overcoming my instinctual response to fear, and I'd seen confirmation in his dark eyes when I'd mentioned the girl. I was right. He had her. Or he knew where she was.

"Give me the girl and this is over," I said.

He laughed now, looking down his nose at me and sizing me up. "Whatcha gonna do? Make me?"

"Honestly, I'd prefer it not go that way."

He laughed again. And this time when he looked me over, he wasn't sizing me up as competition. I felt my skin crawl.

"I love it when they fight back," he whispered to me.

My belly rolled in disgust.

I toed off my shoes and dropped the bag. "I guarantee you won't like the way *I* fight back."

He laughed again and tugged at his belt, adjusting his pants. I had the sick feeling he found this exchange arousing.

"Feisty," he said, grinning. "I like that."

He swiped a hand toward me, and I knocked it away, landing a couple of blows to his abdomen then striking at the inside of his knee with my foot. He cried out in pain and went down on the other knee, grabbing his leg. Striking while the iron was hot, I spun around with a roundhouse kick to the side of his head, which knocked him off kilter and caused him to wobble, but he did not go down.

Suddenly, he burst out laughing and pushed himself up, wincing at the pain in his knee. When he looked at me, I could see genuine amusement in his eyes now. He was enjoying this.

"Any time you two idiots want to make an appearance, I'd appreciate it," I said, watching the security guy closely.

The guy didn't seem to have any real hand-to-hand training, but he was no stranger to a brawl. And he fought like it—dirty. And he used every last ounce of his size to his advantage.

He landed another blow, this one knocking me off my feet, stunning me. I struggled to stay present, to stay focused. And I saw him lunge at me. I knew if he got on top of me, he'd kill me.

Fueled by desperation now, I threw my legs backward and rolled away from him onto my feet, then charged forward, thrusting hard with my elbow against his nose. I heard it crack and felt warm blood flow over my arm as I collided with him. He got his arms around me, trying to drag me down as he fell. I brought my knee into his gut then lashed out at his groin with my foot. His grip slackened, and I got a hold of his wrist, forcing it backward and away.

He hit the ground, and I threw myself on top of him.

"Stay down," a woman ordered.

I looked up to see Sadie standing five feet away, a .38 special held firmly and comfortably in her hands, the barrel pointed straight at the security guy's forehead.

The security guy looked up at her and grinned.

"We could have fun with that, you and me," he said, eyeing the gun and Sadie's long legs.

"One bullet and you'll be dead," she said. "That will only be fun for me."

Her voice was calm and sure, as if she routinely drew her gun and threatened to kill bad guys.

The security guard didn't like her response, because he suddenly grunted and tried to free himself. I had his arm in a lock behind his back. His movement forced it past its natural extension, fracturing his elbow with an audible *crack*. He screamed and began to flail, his massive bulk bucking underneath me, threatening to pitch me off. Worried about my ability to control him and what might happen if he got free, I slammed his forehead into the pavement. When he stilled briefly, I grabbed his other arm and got it in a lock behind his back.

"Where the fuck is the backup I was promised?" I asked, talking into the necklace I wore. "Frye!"

I wished to hell I'd put some handcuffs in my bag.

A small crowd had formed now, and I imagined at least one of them had called 911. I was trying to calculate how long it would take for a patrol officer to respond to the call, and how I might explain myself when he did. Before I was forced to come up with an answer, I heard a welcomed voice.

"Police! Get back! Police!"

Panting, I looked over my shoulder to see Frye burst out of the crowd, his gun drawn.

"Fuck," he hissed, hurrying forward and pulling cuffs off his belt with one hand.

I snatched the cuffs and snapped them on the guy's hands, heedless of his fracture, as Topham and Olvera emerged.

"I'm so sorry, Zoe," Frye said. "I was in the bathroom. I came out and saw . . . Are you okay?" He offered me a hand.

I allowed him to help me up. "Yeah."

I went to the car and pulled open the back door. The backseat was empty. Before I could panic about assaulting an innocent man, I opened the driver's door and hit the trunk release button. Frye held his weapon at the trunk, but I waved him away and pushed the lid open.

The young girl I'd seen stumbling in the bar was passed out in the trunk, a pile of vomit on the tarp that had conveniently been arranged inside. It appeared she'd wet her pants too.

"Get an ambulance," I said to Frye, feeling for the girl's pulse. He was already dialing.

"She alive?" he asked, the phone to his ear.

"Yeah. Just drunk off her ass."

I turned away from the car. Sadie had put her gun away and now stood holding my bag and shoes.

I pulled the necklace off and tossed it at Topham.

"Nice backup," I said. "Glad I could count on you two."

"Zoe, I—" Olvera began.

"Oh, and you had the wrong guy," I said, cutting him off. I wiped blood from my face and looked at each of them. "To be clear, our cooperation balance is tipped *heavily* in my favor."

Topham had the sense to at least look ashamed. And Olvera looked genuinely upset by my state.

"You assholes better think long and hard before you ask me for cooperation in the near future. And you better answer when I call."

I pushed past them and started for the front of the building, Sadie falling in behind me.

"Uh, Zoe," Topham said behind me. "Are you going to mention this to Ellmann?"

I laughed and didn't slow, didn't turn around. "You wish. But you're not gonna get off that easy."

30

Ellmann was home when I got to his house, watching reruns of *The Twilight Zone* in the living room. He switched off the TV and followed the dog and me into the kitchen, where I fed Dasch dinner.

"How'd it go—"

As I turned to face Ellmann, his jaw clenched, the muscles on the side of his cheek the only indication of his emotion.

"I'm fine," I said.

I'd cleaned up and assessed the damage in Sadie's bathroom. I had a gash on my cheekbone, which was swollen, and I would have several bruises on my abdomen and ribs tomorrow, but I didn't look too bad all things considered. As far as I was concerned, the damage was minimal. The dress hadn't survived, but I hadn't even needed a trip to the hospital.

"The other guy's in the ER," I said. "He may have surgery. Eventually, he'll be in jail. I'm way better off." I tried to smile. But I just felt tired.

He dragged a hand back through his hair as he stared at me from the other side of the bar. Then he deliberately put his hands on the counter.

"Where the hell was Frye?"

I sighed and leaned against the island. "So you knew about Topham and Olvera's little secret spy op."

He snorted. "The whole department knows. The only reason it got approved was because Frye was there to keep an eye on things."

"Yes, well, don't be upset with him. Apparently he was in the john when things went to shit. He came running the instant he saw I was in trouble. I have no idea where the other two were."

"And the dog?"

"Oh, by the way, the dog's name is Dasch. Turns out he is one of the dogs stolen from the facility."

At the sound of his name, Dasch looked up from his food, watching me as he licked his lips. Then he glanced at Ellmann. I think he knew we were talking about him.

"Dasch," Ellmann said, managing a smile for the dog. "Nice to meet you, buddy."

Dasch licked his lips and wagged his tail at Ellmann then turned and dove back into his food.

"Where was he during all this?" Ellmann asked.

"In the car. It was a bar; I couldn't bring him in. Besides, he can't run around biting everyone. If he does, the county will force me to put him down."

Ellmann's jaw flinched again. He knew the truth of what I said, but he didn't like it.

"Is that why you were so supportive of me keeping the dog?" I asked. "You wanted him to protect me?"

Ellmann sighed and lowered himself onto a barstool. "It crossed my mind. I find great comfort in the idea you aren't out there all alone, that someone has your back." He looked at me. "You know how you felt this morning, when you thought I'd been hurt?"

I remembered all too clearly. Suddenly my mouth felt dry and there were tears in my eyes. "Yeah," I managed.

"Zoe, I feel that way about you. When I heard Hapner's trailer blew up, or when you chase down crazy art thieves with a sick fascination with kitchen utensils . . . I hear about these things and I swear, it feels like my heart stops."

I swiped at the tears in my eyes and walked over to him. I wound my arms around his neck, and he pulled me close.

"I'm sorry," I murmured. I hadn't really even taken time to appreciate that I might be wreaking havoc on Ellmann's emotions. And I'd gotten a big dose of that this morning. But that had just been one time. In the few months Ellmann and I had known each other, I'd probably given him ten such moments. "I'm so sorry. I'll be more careful. I promise."

Dasch must have felt left out, because he came over and wedged himself between us. We both petted him, and his tongue lolled happily out of his mouth.

"I would have called him, had I been in real trouble," I said. "But I wasn't. Plus, Sadie was there almost immediately, drawing her gun and talking like Dirty Harry."

Ellmann's lip twitched up. "Tell me she actually said, 'Make my day, punk.'"

I laughed. "No, but it was close enough. She was awesome."

Ellmann chuckled at that. I ran my hand back through his hair. I really was crazy about him.

"Why is Frye babysitting an investigations op?" I asked, turning my thoughts to safer territory. "Why is he babysitting anyone? He's a patrol officer."

"He passed his sergeant's test last week. There was some kind of hang up with Stafford's retirement. As soon as he's gone, Frye will move into his position. Until then, they've been giving him bullshit assignments like this one, because they've already filled his patrol shift."

"He passed?" I beamed. "He was so nervous about it. Why hasn't he said anything?"

"The minute he says anything, people will know he's meant to replace Stafford. Stafford's been around a long time; Frye doesn't want to step on any toes. He's waiting for the department to announce Stafford's retirement and his promotion."

"He could tell me; I don't care about any of the inter-office politics."

Ellmann shrugged. "He probably assumed I told you."

"We'll have to celebrate sometime soon." I plucked at my ruined dress. "For now, I need a shower."

Ellmann caught me with a hand around my waist. He pulled me back into him.

"Why did you agree to work with Topham and Olvera on this thing? Frye said you were their idea, but why would you agree?"

"I will answer that question," I said. "But not right now."

He grimaced. "That means I won't like the answer."

"That means you *can't* like the answer, and I'm giving you plausible deniability."

Ellmann just stared at me. "You drive me crazy sometimes, you know that?"

"I know. I'm sorry."

He shook his head. "I try to remember you can't help yourself."

I kissed him. Then I took a deep breath. "I . . ." The word was right on the tip of my tongue. What was wrong with me? "Thank you for being so good to me."

He was watching me, grinning like an idiot. I stepped away.

"Where you going?"

"Shower," I called back.

Ellmann jumped up and followed me.

"I'll help."

31

The next morning, Dasch woke me up with his rope toy. When I cracked an eye, I saw it was still dark, and I knew before I checked the clock it was five a.m. I groaned and pulled the covers over my head. But Dasch didn't go away; he jumped on top of me, nudging me more forcefully with the rope in his mouth.

"I think your dog wants to play with you," Ellmann said, wrapping an arm around me and pulling me back against him. "But he's going to have to get in line."

Ellmann's lips and hands were moving, but it was very hard to concentrate with the ninety-pound animal jumping on my aching ribs. And Dasch wouldn't be ignored. Every time I booted him off the bed, he jumped back up, and soon he began to think that was a game.

I groaned. "Is it too late to call the humane society?"

Ellmann propped himself on one elbow and eyed the dog. "This dog and I are going to need to have a talk."

Dasch pounced again, his front feet coming straight for me. I rolled away as he landed heavily on the bed.

"Okay!" I pushed him off. He jumped to the floor, his tail still wagging madly. "Okay," I said, wincing as I sat up. "You win."

I dragged Dasch outside behind his rope as he growled and wagged his tail. We played tug-of-war for a long time. While we were playing, we worked on some of the new commands we'd

209

started learning yesterday. He didn't seem to know he was learning; he thought we were just playing.

We were on to a ball when Ellmann came out of the house carrying two cups of coffee. He sat beside me on the deck as Dasch dropped the tennis ball at my feet. I threw it, and the dog tore after it.

"What are you going to do about your landlord?" Ellmann asked, handing me a cup.

That was one more thing I had to figure out. "I have no idea. You tired of having him here?" Dasch brought the ball back again, then stood waiting, eyes wide in anticipation and excitement, tail wagging. I threw it for him.

Ellmann wrapped an arm around me, drawing me into him and kissing my head. "No. It means having you here. And I love that."

"It'll be a few more days at least." I threw the ball again. "Probably longer. We'll see if you're still saying that."

Ellmann chuckled. "You'll probably buy your house from the landlord before you'll move in here, but you're welcome to move in here. This place is plenty big enough for both of us, and I'll even let you keep the dog."

I turned to stare at Ellmann. I hadn't mentioned to him my thought about buying the house. That's how well he knew me.

He just laughed and kissed my head again.

"You want to live together?"

Dasch dropped the ball in my lap and nudged me, trying to get my attention.

Ellmann shrugged and sipped some coffee. "Yes. I really do like having you around; I like us being together, sharing a space. I've felt that way for a while, but I wasn't planning to bring it up just yet. The only reason I am is because the opportunity presented itself. Throw the ball."

I'd pretty much forgotten about the dog. I threw the ball and turned to face Ellmann.

"Ellmann, look, I . . ." I squeezed his arm and drew in a breath. The first time would probably be the hardest, right? Just spit it out. I glanced up at Ellmann. He was grinning at me, amused, the jerk. "I . . . love you." The words were barely a whisper. He grinned wider. I moved on. "I do. I really do. But all of this . . . it scares the crap out of me. And I know we spend a lot of time together and we're either at your place or mine but I'm just not ready to give up my place. I'll get there, I'm just not there yet. I'm sorry."

He closed his big hand over mine. "I'm not pushing, Zoe. I'm just offering. I've told you before, I'm not going anywhere. And I mean it. I just want you to know, as far as I'm concerned, this is an option for you. I know you'll figure it out. And I'm okay with whatever you decide."

Greatest guy ever. I kissed him. "I . . . lo . . . ove you."

Ellmann grinned. "I know." He glanced over my shoulder and said, "Finally."

I looked and saw Dasch lying in the grass, panting happily, the ball in front of him.

Ellmann grabbed my hand and pulled me up. "Come on."

I followed him inside, and Dasch followed me. Dasch dropped the ball and lapped at his water. Ellmann filled Dasch's bowl with kibble then took my coffee cup and set it aside. He picked me up and growled, "My turn." He carried me back to bed.

32

Later, I sat at the bar drinking coffee and reviewing the paperwork Olvera had given me last night. Ellmann had the day off and had gone to meet his buddies at the gym. Today was my day off from the gym, so I swallowed some Ibuprofen and had a second cup of coffee.

The first document Olvera had provided was a printout from the Social Security Administration for babies named Karen Brickle born in the last sixty years. The list was three pages long, with Karen Brickles born in all fifty states during that time period.

That didn't necessarily help me. Unless I could get ahold of the social security number Sadie's Karen Brickle was using with her name, I wouldn't know for sure if she was borrowing her name from one of the babies on this list or if she'd fabricated it entirely.

Second was a printout of a driver's license for a woman named Karen Brickle. Olvera noted there was only one Karen Brickle with the Colorado Department of Motor Vehicles. According to the license, that Karen Brickle was two years younger than Sadie's Karen Brickle was, and I noticed the general stats seemed similar—height, weight, hair color—at least as best I could tell from Facebook. I'd have to check with Sadie.

I shuffled to the third document. The gun I'd found was registered to an Angela Morris out of Phoenix, Arizona. The registration was totally legit, and according to Olvera, all of Morris's information checked out. On the next page I found Morris's driver's license photo. Morris was a pretty brunette woman six years younger than Karen Brickle was supposed to be. Morris's stats were similar to both Karen Brickles.

Naturally, I wondered who Angela Morris was, why Brickle had her gun, and how the two women were connected.

I did a bit of searching myself on Angela Morris, and nothing really interesting came up. And a thorough scouring of Brickle's Facebook page yielded no hints as to who Morris was or how they might know one another. Nor could I find any indication Brickle had ever lived in Arizona, where Morris appeared to have lived her whole life.

The only thing even remotely interesting was the fact that Angela Morris was a registered nurse. Her nursing license had been issued in the state of Arizona, and that was the only state in which she'd ever been licensed. But I couldn't see how that connected anything. Morris had gone to a different nursing school than Brickle, the two had never worked at the same hospital, and they'd never even lived in the same state.

I decided to look into the EMT Brickle had been getting cozy with, Jimmy Ward. James Elliot Ward was twenty-eight years old, and a local Fort Collins guy, which made digging up information that much easier. Ward had graduated from Fort Collins High School and attended Colorado State University where he studied fire sciences. During his sophomore year, he'd also taken the EMT course at Front Range Community College and obtained his Emergency Medical Technician license. Clearly, Ward aspired to be a firemen, like every other guy in this town, according to Sadie.

Ward's Facebook page was more limited, and I couldn't get much information from it. According to county records, Ward was not married, owned no property, and had no children I could find. His name was connected to a police report, however.

I couldn't get enough detail from what I saw to know what the report was about, so I sent Olvera and Topham a text asking for it. Then I texted Sadie, asking her for the names of Ward's most recent ex-girlfriends.

The DMV had record of Ward. He had two vehicles registered in his name, to the same address. And that address matched the most current one on his credit report. It was one I recognized. Ward lived in an apartment complex southeast of Harmony Road. Terra Vida Apartment Homes, they call the place. It's all modern art deco, flashy colors, straight lines, and pomp. It's also very expensive. According to Ward's credit report, he was not overextended. So how could he afford such a place on his salary? I had to admit I wasn't certain how much EMTs made, but I knew what the apartment complex cost, and they didn't seem to add up. Unless he had four roommates. But then, Terra Vida only offered one- and two-bedroom apartments.

One other inconsistency: Ward had had the same address for two years, since they'd opened the apartment complex. But according to Sadie, who was tapped into the ER gossip line, Ward shacked up with his lady friends. So why did Ward have a reputation for such a thing, if he'd had his own place all along?

I shifted gears and looked up hospitals in Boulder. After a bit of searching, I managed to learn Boulder Medical Center had an urgent care, but no emergency room. I also learned Boulder Community Hospital and Foothills Hospital both had ERs. This was relevant only if Karen Brickle had worked as an ER nurse prior to her ER position in Fort Collins.

I wrote down phone numbers and put the list away for tomorrow. There would be no point calling on a Sunday.

I turned my attention to Thomas Walling. In a short time with minimal effort, I was able to learn Thomas Michael Walling owned a house and possessed a teaching license. According to the all-knowing keeper of the secrets, Facebook, Tom was single, a middle school teacher, and the track and basketball coach. His interests seemed largely slanted toward fitness, sports, and outdoor activities. His friends seemed to share similar interests, and I learned a few of them were also teachers. He also seemed very close with his brother and very involved in the lives of his niece and two nephews.

I could see no connection on Facebook between Tom and Karen Brickle. Whatever had taken place between them, it had been kept off of Facebook. But that was always the best practice if you truly wished to keep your secret.

Tom's brother Brian was a nerd. His Facebook page was covered in photos of his kids and math-related jokes. Some of them were kind of funny, but some of them I didn't understand. I did think Brian had good-looking kids, though. And in answer to my earlier rumination, I could now see Brian was every bit as handsome as his brother. They actually looked very similar to one another—not twins, but very obviously brothers.

Brian and his wife, Tonya, owned their house, had been married for ten years, and had their names on the birth certificates of their three children. Brian worked at IBM, and I suspected he was an engineer of some kind. Tonya was a physical therapist, and my goodness was she fit. Looking at her photos made me want to give up food and move into the gym. If someone told me Tonya could do one-arm pushups from a handstand, I would have believed it.

Anyway, I got no red flags or warning bells from anything I saw about either of Theresa's children. They both seemed to be regular, normal, healthy guys. They obviously missed their mother, and wanted to know what had happened to her, but that was all normal too. Neither of them gave any indication on Facebook they suspected any specific person of the crime, nor did they speculate as to what exactly that crime had been.

I had briefly looked at Theresa Walling when I began my investigation into Karen Brickle. Now, however, I looked into her in earnest. I returned to her Facebook page. She didn't seem to use Facebook for much outside of staying current on her children and grandchildren. There were two posts that now caught my eye, however.

One was from last December, the other from last January. Both of them indicated to me Theresa Walling was seeing someone. The December post was a comment about how Christmas had come early—in the form of this new man, I guessed. In January, she lamented how fickle relationships could be. I might have been reading into it a bit, but that was my take.

No one had mentioned Theresa had a boyfriend. That little fact hadn't even been in the newspapers. So who was he? Seemed like he would have been a better suspect in her disappearance than her ex-husband.

I made note of her top friends, four women who seemed to have posted to her page the most. A brief search told me two of the women lived out of state. The other two lived in Colorado, but only one lived in Boulder. That one happened to also be a teacher, and, as luck would have it, she taught at Boulder High School, the same school Theresa taught at.

Next I looked into Sheila Walling, Frank Walling's new wife. Meek and mild as she appeared to be, her emotions seemed to run deep, and she was clearly jealous of Frank's lingering respect and affection for his first wife. That didn't necessarily make Sheila guilty of anything, but it certainly raised a few red flags.

Public records indicated Sheila Walling had previously been Sheila Adams, but her marriage license to Frank was the only thing with her name on it in Boulder County. She wasn't even on the title to Frank's house. I found that interesting, and wondered what it said about their marriage.

It took me a while to find her Facebook page. Ultimately, I'd had to find her on Brian Walling's page, as one of his friends. And I barely recognized her from her photo; she didn't photograph well.

And after all that, her Facebook page yielded nothing of substance. She seemed to spend a fair amount of time on Facebook, but she largely reposted photos and memes other people posted. She rarely posted anything original, and while she was a prolific commenter, her comments were all benign and expected.

So I turned to my second greatest search tool: Google. It took some digging and sifting, but I eventually hit paydirt. Sheila Walling, originally from Oregon by way of California, was on her fourth marriage. Initially this struck me as odd, given her personality. Then I learned her first three husbands were dead, and my curiosity burned into suspicion.

Husband number one, Carl Evans, had successfully committed suicide some twenty years ago. He and Sheila had been married about eight years when she found him dead in the garage. He'd shot himself with a handgun registered in his name. According to the newspaper, one possible explanation for Carl's suicide was his impending indictment. Apparently, the police were ready to arrest him for embezzlement, theft, fraud, and some other stuff after discovering he'd been dipping into the company coffers and "borrowing" money from unsuspecting, non-consenting clients. The police couldn't find the money, but they did find evidence proving Carl stole it.

Sheila then married a man named David Adams, who, interestingly, was a partner in the same investment firm where her first husband had worked. From what I could tell, they were married within a year of Carl's death. And from everything I could dig up, Mr. Adams was a very wealthy man. His company had to have taken a serious hit as a result of Carl Evans's shenanigans, but it obviously withstood the blow and bounced back. He was worth several hundred million dollars when he died, or so speculated the media.

And die he did. About ten years after marrying Sheila, Adams boarded a private company jet that then crashed, killing all on board. The media was all over the crash, slinging wild speculations, spouting rumors, and making open accusations. I found articles blaming everything from innocent mechanical failure to the inexperience of the pilot to deliberate tampering by corporate enemies to espionage. No one seemed to have any suspicions about Sheila Adams, and the media eventually reported the official cause of the crash as mechanical failure that was no one's fault.

Sheila was a very wealthy woman when she married William Coleman a year and a half later. Coleman was apparently some big deal businessman around Southern California, with his fingers in all sorts of pies. He was wealthy in his own right, owning multiple businesses across the southern half of the state. But apparently they weren't all on the up and up.

Toward the end of his life, the newspapers began running stories about his involvement with a politician named Robert Barnes. Barnes was clouded in rumors and accusations of corruption, and eventually he was arrested for a slew of federal charges. But not before Coleman wound up dead.

Coleman had been found shot four times in some shady part of Los Angeles. His car was found at one of his office buildings, the keys on the pavement by the driver's side door. The police concluded he'd been abducted, perhaps at gunpoint, shot, and then dumped. The papers didn't report much about the evidence, but they did report the police tied Coleman's murder to Robert Barnes. The theory was Barnes killed Coleman—or more likely had Coleman killed—because Coleman had agreed to cooperate with the police in their investigation into Barnes's corruption.

Sheila left California about a month after Coleman's murder, moving to Colorado. She first settled in Colorado Springs, where she lived for almost three years. Then she moved to Boulder, and within a year, she was married to Frank Walling.

It was possible this woman had the worst luck life could throw at a person, and had truly outlived three husbands killed by means outside of her control and theirs. The fact that she was unmarried for nearly four years when she married Frank Walling seemed to indicate a break in the pattern, which could suggest it wasn't a pattern at all. Not to mention each guy was killed in a different way—suicide, plane crash, murder. And the plane crash threw me off. Even if suicides could be faked and others framed for murder, a plane crash took planning, access, and an intimate knowledge of aircraft. I could have been wrong in my uncharitable assessment that Sheila was kind of an idiot, but she certainly didn't strike me as the aviator type. And significant portions of her life had been documented in the newspapers, with absolutely no mention of her having any experience with flying or airplanes. Which wasn't to say she didn't have help, I supposed.

Still, it seemed far-fetched, even for me.

Sheila had been a very wealthy woman when she'd married Frank, yet I hadn't seen any indication of money in the house or on her person. How had a woman worth several hundred million dollars gone from the high life to living in Frank Walling's middle-class lifestyle?

To be fair, that was precisely what I'd done a few years ago. I'd left my six-figure income and matching lifestyle and never looked back. And I'd made strides to stay out of that lifestyle since. Perhaps Sheila had done the same thing. Not every woman is cut out for a life like that. Maybe it reminded her of all she'd lost.

I didn't know if this information was at all relevant. If there was something suspicious about Sheila, it didn't seem to suggest she'd had anything to do with Theresa's disappearance. For Sheila, if she was a threat at all, it was to her husbands, not their ex-wives.

I did a property search on Karen Brickle's Boulder house. According to county records, the house was currently owned by a woman named Elizabeth Peters. A quick search told me Elizabeth Peters was unmarried and just starting to climb the ladder at local law firm. I guessed her house looked sterile because she paid a lawn service and had no time to spend at home. I could find nothing to indicate she knew Karen Brickle beyond the purchase of the house, and I considered her a dead end.

I went back through my notes, something bothering me. I paged back until I found my earlier notes on Brickle. My earlier search of public records had indicated Brickle did not own her home. That hadn't struck me as odd earlier, but it did now, because she'd owned her home in Boulder. As I'd noted, she'd certainly upgraded, so maybe she hadn't been able to afford it. But then I remembered her bank balance and knew she could.

I did a search on Brickle's Fort Collins address. It came back to Stephanie Roman. A bit of searching told me Stephanie Roman owned no other property in Larimer County. I ran a credit check and found Stephanie Roman had almost ten years of history connected to the same address in Grand Junction. I ran a DMV search and learned Stephanie Roman had a car registered to the same address. I also checked the state records and found Stephanie Roman had a current nursing license.

What the hell was Karen Brickle up to? I was more convinced than ever she *was* up to something. And for reasons I couldn't quite identify, I had the feeling it was bad, and that Theresa Walling fit into it somehow.

I needed to know more about what had happened to Theresa Walling.

I sent another text to Olvera asking him to pull Stephanie Roman's driver's license information and photo. And whatever guilt I might have otherwise felt at asking for yet more information was immediately washed away by the flash of pain in my ribs as I got up.

33

It looked like my investigation into Karen Brickle would be taking me back to Boulder, and I planned to head down there tomorrow morning. I had a few things to do today, and I would go into my office at White Real Estate for a couple hours, since I wouldn't be in tomorrow. White never cared when I came in, but I needed to make sure there wasn't anything going on that needed my immediate attention.

My first order of business was to swing by Ruben Medera's house. I hadn't been there in a while, and he was currently my only outstanding FTA. I wasn't sure I'd gain anything by stopping by his house again, because I certainly didn't expect him to be there, but as I've said, it's all about persistence.

I didn't see Medera's truck parked in the front of his condo, so I parked right outside his door, in the spot I imagined was his. I told Dasch to wait in the car and went to the door. I tried the doorknob and glanced up at the toothpick. Then I stopped and turned back, looking more carefully. I used two fingers to measure the position of the toothpick from the doorjamb. The toothpick had been moved.

Curious now, I pulled the bump key from my pocket and let myself in. As the door opened, I watched the upper edge of the inner doorjamb, but no toothpick sliver fell. I pushed the door open wide and knelt. Just inside the threshold, lying on the tile of the entryway, was the sliver. I'd placed both when I'd left last. I knew the first was the most obvious and would likely be spotted by a Marine like Medera. So I used a second, smaller one in a less conspicuous location, hoping Medera wouldn't look any harder after finding the first. Apparently, he hadn't. Either that or he wanted me to know he'd been home. Of course, if that were the case, he wouldn't have bothered to replace the first one.

So what had he been home for?

"Dasch, *hierr*."

The dog jumped through the open window and ran over to me.

"*Voran*," I told him as I stepped aside. *Search*.

He immediately went to work, looking through the condo.

I didn't really think Medera was here, but if nothing else it was good practice.

I left the front door standing open and walked slowly through the living room to the open kitchen behind it. Dasch trotted up to me a moment later, smiling and wagging his tail.

"Good boy," I said, scratching his ears. "*Bravy*. Good boy."

Nothing seemed obviously different in the kitchen. I went upstairs, flipping on lights as I did, Dasch trailing behind me. I stood for a long time in the master bathroom, staring at the items in the drawer that belonged to Medera's girlfriend.

I racked my brain trying to remember what the hell I'd seen in that drawer the last time I'd been here. I remember thinking it was all regular stuff, stuff any girl would keep in the bathroom. I also remember thinking whoever she was, Medera's girlfriend didn't often get ready for the day here. Either that or she carried her makeup in her purse. Or she didn't wear any. But, come on, what woman doesn't wear makeup?

I was pretty sure there had been a bracelet in the drawer, a petite and modest gold tennis bracelet with a single, very small gold heart on it. I remembered the bracelet because it had been so modest, so tasteful compared to so much of the jewelry people wore today. I remembered thinking I'd like any girl who would wear a bracelet like that. I know I'd seen it in Medera's house somewhere; I was almost positive it had been this bathroom drawer. But there was no bracelet now.

I looked around the rest of the bathroom and the bedroom for the bracelet, to make sure I hadn't seen it in another drawer. But I couldn't find it. And my search led me to believe nothing else was missing, not even any of Medera's clothes.

I went through the kitchen again, pulling open drawers. Nothing seemed to be missing. I flipped off the light and started for the door. Halfway across the living room, I stopped and turned around. The computer. Medera's computer was also gone. It had been sitting on the bar, but was no longer there.

I couldn't help but wonder what Medera was up to. His mother said he would never have missed his court date if it weren't important. So what was so important he couldn't be in court? What was he doing?

I decided it didn't matter. My only concern was catching him and returning him to the court. It made no real difference to me what he was running around doing while he was very effectively avoiding me.

I shut off the lights, left the house, and replaced both toothpicks, choosing slightly different locations this time.

I opened my door and Dasch launched himself onto the seat, crossing to the passenger side. He panted happily out the window while I drove us out of the parking lot.

My next stop was Sure Bonds. It was Sunday, but I wanted to see if Marge was in the office so I could get paid for Robert Hapner. I needed the money from his bond to cover what I'd spent on his dog so far. When I arrived, I found all three businesses were open. But only one of them had an eviction notice taped to the door.

I made Dasch wait in the truck; I didn't want him to get cancer.

I pulled the notice off the door, then propped the door open and went into the Sure Bonds office. Marge was at her desk, smoking and sorting through a stack of files.

"Hiya, princess. You come for some more files? Got plenty."

She indicated her desk, which now held a concerning number of files. Could all those people have failed to appear in court? How could one small office have so many FTAs? Where was her regular guy?

"What's this, Marge?" I asked, setting the eviction notice on the desk.

She rolled her eyes. "You know how long I been in this building?" she asked me, holding her cigarette between her two fingers as she pointed them at me. "Thirty-five years. And you know how many times this building has changed hands in that time? Eight. I've been here through them all, every kind of landlord you could imagine. This punk," she said, tapping the eviction notice with her two fingers, ash raining down onto the page, "he thinks he's some big deal around here. Says he's got big plans for the building, and he'll never find a buyer with me here. Well, I've got news for him. He can't just kick me out because he doesn't like me. I've done nothing wrong. Anyway, I'll be glad when he sells. He charges way too much for rent."

She flicked her cigarette in the general direction of an overflowing ashtray, sending ash raining down over half the desk, then picked up a stack of files.

"Here, princess, take your pick. All high-class scumbags; no low-class scumbags so as to not offend your delicate sensibilities."

"I came to get paid, Marge, not to pick up new cases." I handed her Hapner's body receipt.

She took it and pulled out the giant checkbook, slapping it onto the desk. "Still no luck with the Marine, huh?"

"No. What's with all these cases? Where's your regular guy?"

"Don't you worry about that," she snapped, ripping off a check. "Take your pick of these recovery fees and leave the rest to me."

I tucked the check into my pocket. "I don't mean to be critical, but it kind of looks like things are falling apart. You've got no recovery agent, you've got more skips than you could possibly track down alone, and you've got three days to get out of this office."

"Now you listen here, princess," she said, again pointing her fingers at me. "I haven't been in the bail bonds business for forty years or in this office for thirty-five because I don't know what I'm doing. You got that? Things look tough now, but I'm tougher. And I've got a plan." She picked up the stack of files. "That plan includes you taking these files and dragging these idiots back to jail."

I couldn't explain what was happening, but I found myself liking Marge more and more. Maybe the old bat reminded me of myself to some degree, which was something to sit up and take notice of, lest I become any more like her than I might already be, or maybe I just respected her tenacity, which others might rightly label stupidity. Either way, I found myself wanting to help her.

"Where's your lease?" I asked, taking the stack of files from her and setting them on the chair in front of the desk.

"What's it to you, princess?" she asked, leaning back in her squeaky chair and blowing smoke at the ceiling. "You think you know a little something about real estate?"

"If you don't know that I do, then you didn't do very good research before you came to offer me a job."

She stared at me for a beat, then grinned. She sat forward with a squeak and pulled open a drawer. After rummaging for a minute, she pulled out an old file. Finding the document she wanted, she handed it over to me.

"I'll try to help you with your landlord problem," I said, setting the stack of files back on the desk. "You find your recovery agent and apologize. You need him to help you with these FTAs."

"What makes you think *I* need to apologize?" she asked haughtily, jabbing a finger at her chest.

"I've met you, Marge."

"You're hilarious, princess, absolutely hilarious." She ground out her cigarette with unnecessary violence, causing the mess in the ashtray to spill over onto the desk. Then she reached for the pack and the lighter and lit another. "Maybe I'll make some offers to some other Sideline guys. Maybe they'd be willing to moonlight, things being the way they are over there now."

She had a point, and I was sure she'd find some takers.

"Get your regular guy back here," I said sharply, rapping my index finger on her desk. "Get your business back together."

With that, I turned and left. When I reached the door, she hollered, "Close the door!"

I called back, "No!" which caused her to unleash a string of curses at my back.

I laughed as I climbed into the Scout and drove out of the lot.

34

I let myself into White Real Estate and Property Management through the back door. White's personal office and the hub of what he's building to be a real estate empire is located in the Key Bank building downtown. He has satellite offices in Fort Collins, Loveland, and Greeley. He had just opened the Greeley office and was already making plans for an office in Windsor. Every time he opens a new office, he asks me to run it. I always refuse.

The Fort Collins property office was located on Laurel Street in Old Town. It had been converted to office space years ago, but after White had purchased it, he'd dumped a serious chunk of change into remodeling it. The result was a beautiful, fantastic workspace that no longer resembled the residential space it had once been.

Dasch followed me in.

"*Voran*," I told him, knowing he wouldn't rest easy until he was sure the place was empty.

While he did his thing, I went down the hall and unlocked the French doors to my office. I went to the windows, raised the shades, and took my plant and watered it in the bathroom sink. It was a miracle the damn thing was still alive. My thumb does not have a hint of green on it, but somehow the little thing was hanging on.

I had just logged onto the computer when Dasch came trotting into the office. I scratched his ears, and he settled in for a nap at my feet.

Before I got into work, I pulled Marge's lease from my bag along with the eviction notice and I looked up her property. I found it was owned by Homeland Group, and I felt a jolt of surprise as a connection formed in my mind.

Homeland Group was owned by Lee Rossler and was the most serious competition White Real Estate had in the area. I remembered I'd met Rossler once, years ago, when I'd attended some stuffy real estate function with Mark White. And I'd seen him again a couple days ago . . . going into Jan Taylor's brothel house.

I read Marge's lease, my heart sinking with every paragraph. It was one of the worst leases I'd ever seen; at every opportunity possible, Rossler had taken advantage of Marge. And Marge, having rented the same space for so long, had probably not bothered to read the lease before signing it. Or if she had read it, not understood a thing she was reading.

According to the eviction notice, Rossler was evicting Marge for a slew of contract violations including non-payment, failure to maintain the property, and damage to the property. He cited the damage as the water damage I'd noticed myself in the wall between Marge's office and the medical supply store, as well as what he considered damage done by her smoking. The water damage was most likely not caused by anything Marge or the medical supply people had done directly, and under a more soundly written lease, it would have been covered by the landlord, for whom the repairs would have been covered by insurance.

I thought for a moment, then dialed Marge's office. She was still in.

"Yeah, Sure Bonds. Who's this?"

"Marge, it's Zoe."

"Hey, princess! You change your mind about some of those recovery fees, huh? Ten grand, that's too good to pass up."

"No. Do you know if anyone from an insurance company came out and looked at the water damage on the west wall?"

"How'd you know about that?"

"I'm good at this, Marge."

"Huh. Maybe so." I heard the violent squeak of her chair and imagined her putting her feet up on the desk. "Yeah, some sleazy guy in a fancy suit came out not too long ago. He looked at the wall, pulled up the carpet and looked at the floor. Real jerk. Too good for the rest of us, you know?"

"Yeah. Remember his name? Or which company he was with?"

"Got his card right here. One of them fancy cards, you know, silky. Prick." The chair squeaked again and I heard some rummaging. Finally she said, "Aaron Ryder. Fort Collins Property Insurance. Want his number?"

"Yes."

I scribbled it down.

"So what gives, huh, princess? You find something in that lease?" She made an ugly sound. "Never had a lease as big as that one. Must be fifty pages."

"Maybe. The eviction notice cites non-payment. Have you been paying your rent?"

"'Course! What do you think I am, some kind of freeloader? I'm a businesswoman; I pay my expenses."

"So why is Rossler saying you haven't?"

"Well, he keeps raising the rent—way past what we agreed on *in that lease I signed*. But no, every month, he wants more and more."

I knew that was because of the bad lease she'd signed. It was taxes and maintenance fees and improvement fees and a bunch of other shit Rossler was bilking her for.

"I've got a couple angles to work, Marge, but just in case, get together your bank statements and be ready to prove your payment history for the entire length of this lease."

"Yeah, sure. Got all the records in back here. I keep everything."

"Great. I'll be in touch."

"Say, princess, any chance I could talk—"

"No." I hung up.

I sat for a minute, my mind working. Then I dialed Mark White.

"Hello, Zoe." White has a smooth voice that both puts people at ease and commands their attention. "You're not working on a Sunday, are you?"

"Afraid I am. Taking care of a few things because I won't be in tomorrow."

"I see. Anything pressing?"

"Not so far. Listen, I wanted to ask you about Lee Rossler."

White made an unfriendly sound. "Disgusting man. Please tell me we're not doing business with him."

"No, this is personal. But I may need to use your name to get me in the door."

"You'll have to, otherwise the self-important runt will put you off indefinitely."

"He sounds positively charming. What else do you know about him?"

"Rumors mostly. I have had very few personal interactions with the man."

"Rumors give me a place to start."

White sighed. "Well, I've heard he plays dirty."

"Dirty? How?"

"From what I've heard, by using information people would rather keep private as leverage to pressure buyers and sellers into deals."

"Blackmail." Interesting. "Know anything about Front Range Property Insurance?"

"Only that Rossler's brother-in-law owns it. It's my understanding it is Rossler's only insurance provider, and that Rossler's accounts make up the bulk of Front Range Property Insurance's business. I've never done business with them, and I don't know of many others who have, either."

"Mark, would you have any interest in an aging commercial building on Riverside that needs some renovations and some water damage repairs?"

White chuckled. "Zoe, you're a hell of a saleswoman."

"It isn't the sale of the century. And I'm not even sure Rossler's selling."

"Oh, it's one of Rossler's, huh? Hm. Well, I'll tell you this, if you agree to manage it, I'll buy it."

"Sight unseen?"

"How much in damages are we talking?"

I thought about the extent of the water damage I'd seen, plus the state of Marge's office, as well as the exterior of the building. "It'll probably take thirty or forty grand to get the place up to snuff; it's been neglected for a while. In the end, with prices what they are right now, it'll be worth eight hundred and fifty thousand, easy. And it's got three established tenants in it now."

"How serious are you about this?"

I thought of Marge and the wrong being done to her. Then I thought of what a truly unique pain in the ass she would be as a tenant. "About an eight on a scale of ten."

"I'll call the bank tomorrow, and I'll get an inspector out to the property so we can start talking in specifics."

"For now, let's keep things quiet. But we need to move quickly; one of the tenants got a notice to evict by Wednesday."

"I can have a contract drawn up by Tuesday."

It was a true testament to how much White trusted me that he didn't even blink at the news one of the tenants had been evicted.

And that he was willing to buy the property at all just because I'd brought it to him.

"Zoe, what are you doing?" I asked myself as I hung up.

Before I could think too hard about that answer, I made a third call. Mickey Sands answered on the fifth ring.

"Zoe. Wes and I were just talking about you."

"All of it good, I'm sure."

"Most of it. I'm concerned about some things Cal Stevens told me."

"Your new office manager and I are having trouble communicating."

"He said you quit."

"Can a freelance person truly quit?"

"He says you refused an assignment and walked out. 'Stormed out' actually was how he put it."

"I'm freelance; I can refuse assignments. I don't chase murder suspects, Mick, you know that. But Cal wouldn't give me anything else. His one at a time method doesn't work for me, so I'm exploring my options."

Sands sighed. "He's an ex-cop, Grey. He has a different method than Amerson did. Give him some time to get adjusted."

"How many times have you had to sing that song the last couple weeks?"

A pause. "Too many."

"How are your numbers these days?"

"Between you and me, taking a bigger hit than they should during the transition of a new office manager. And I've lost three guys, with more talking about it."

"If you want to keep them, you've got to give them someone they can respect." I shifted in my seat. "Listen, Mick, I didn't call because of Cal. I actually called because I need some information about Marge Lewicki. Know her?"

Sands chuckled. "Everyone who's been around more than a few months knows Marge; bail bonds is a small world. Why? You been freelancing for her?"

"Yes, just a couple of cases. What's the deal? Who helps her with recoveries?"

"Guy named Jumbo. Been with them for a while; started helping out when her husband, Rick, took ill. Then he stayed on after Rick died. As far as I know, it's just the two of them. Never heard of her passing cases to newbies before—that's her term, not mine. How'd you get hooked in with her?"

"The timing just worked out. She needs a little help with some overflow, and I'm not getting anything from Cal. I just wondered what her story was. What can you tell me about Jumbo?"

"Nothing special. Guy's been in the business for years, decades. I think he and Marge became an item after the husband died. Last I heard, they lived together."

Ah, now it was coming together.

"Thank you, Mick. That's very helpful."

"Zoe, you're not hooking up with Marge are you? I don't want to lose you."

"Get your office manager problem straightened out and I'll be the first one back. Thanks again for the info."

35

I worked for a couple of hours. It mostly consisted of returning phone calls and consulting lease agreements—this was broken, that needed fixed, so-and-so wanted to paint, so-and-so wanted new blinds, somebody else had called a plumber; somebody wanted to renew, someone else wanted to terminate. What was covered? Who paid for what? Was the lease renewable? What were the clauses for termination?

It was a never-ending stream of droning tedium, and I hated it. But I was good at it. Clients and tenants alike trusted me.

Still, if I could have passed my clients off to anyone else, I would have.

After leaving the property office, I drove to my house. Ellmann had called to say he was getting together with Brandon and my younger brother, Zach, for pizza, inviting me to join them. I begged off, thinking it was better the boys had male bonding time together, or whatever men did, but asked him to bring a slice home.

I packed a bag and emptied the fridge of the stuff that would go bad before I moved back home. I still needed to work out my problems with my own landlord, but I wasn't under the same time crunch. I had looked up the property while I'd been in my office, along with the property values in the neighborhood. And I'd done a little research into Stuart Mosley. I'd learned homes were going for the mid-two hundreds in the neighborhood, and that Mosley was making about six hundred dollars profit from my rent check every month. A mortgage would cost me two or three hundred less than I was currently paying in rent.

But that was a problem for another day. I still didn't know if buying the place would be the solution. I might be better off moving—if I could find a place, that is. Rentals were disappearing the same day they were posted.

I loaded the Scout and motored over to Ellmann's. I hefted my bags and let us in the front door. As usual, Dasch darted off to make his rounds. The difference this time, however, was that he started barking almost instantly.

Leaving the front door standing wide open, I dropped the bags and pulled the Browning from my belt, holding it in front of me as I started forward.

"My dog will bite!" I shouted to be heard over the barking. "Hands up! Don't move! My dog will bite!"

Dasch had shot toward the back of the house in the direction of the kitchen. As I made my way there, I quickly cleared the living room to the right and Ellmann's office on the left. Both were empty. I shot a glance up the stairs, but saw nothing and kept moving. As I came around the corner into the kitchen, I was stunned to see Ruben Medera standing near the kitchen table, feet slightly apart, hands raised above his head. And he was smiling.

Dasch was in front of him, barking, hopping.

"Dasch! *Aus! Hierr!*"

Dasch immediately came back to me, tail wagging, but he watched Medera carefully, and I didn't lower my gun.

"*Platz.*" Dasch immediately dropped to the floor, tail wagging, watching me, ready for another command. "What the hell are you doing here?"

Medera kept smiling at me, his posture and attitude casual, as if he was confronted by dogs in such a manner every day.

235

"Either you managed to train yourself a military dog in two days, or that meth head had a dog that didn't belong to him."

A couple pieces fell into place.

"It was you," I said. "Outside the trailer right before the explosion. You were the second shooter."

He nodded. "Yeah. I saw you go back for the dog, and I wanted to buy you a little extra time. I laid down some cover fire."

"Why?"

He looked down at Dasch. "Because I did the same thing once, in Afghanistan. Only it wasn't a dog, it was a goat. That goat was the family's mainstay. They could never afford to replace it and wouldn't have survived without it."

I sighed. "Thank you for your service."

He nodded. "Thanks."

"And thanks for the help earlier. You probably saved my life. And the dog's."

"Glad I was there."

I lowered the gun, but kept it in my hand. In my experience, people only broke into my house with the most nefarious of intentions. "Okay, now that all the civilities have been covered, how about you tell me why you broke in?"

"We need to talk," he said.

He was more attractive than his booking photo suggested, and taller than I would have guessed after meeting his mother. He was obviously of Spanish descent, but his coloring was lighter than his mom's. His hair was still cut in a high and tight, but he had a couple days' growth on his face. He wore jeans and a red plaid short-sleeved button-down shirt. I didn't see a gun, but I knew he didn't need one.

"So talk."

"Can't we be civilized? I'd like to put my arms down now."

"I'd be more trusting if I knew what you were doing in my kitchen."

"I'm going to put my arms down now."

"My dog will attack if you make any aggressive movements."

"I know." He lowered his arms but kept his hands plainly visible at his sides. He looked at me. "Who are you?"

I pulled a generic bond enforcement card out of my pocket and tossed it onto the island. "Zoe Grey. I work for your bondswoman, Marge Lewicki."

Slowly, with deliberate movement, Medera reached out and tapped at something on the table beside him. I now noticed it was one of the same business cards. "I know," he said. "You gave this to my mother."

"I did ask her to give you my phone number."

"But you're also investigating the woman from the hospital, goes by Karen Brickle. Why? She miss court, too?"

Something about the way he said "goes by Karen Brickle" raised a flag in the back of my mind. But how had he known about Brickle at all?

"You've been following me." And I never noticed. Damn, he was good.

"Not exactly. What's your interest in Brickle?"

"Look, I'm not in the habit of discussing my business with perfect strangers. If you came here for information, you're going to leave disappointed."

"I need you to stop looking for me."

"I can't. I've been contracted to apprehend you and return you to the court."

"I know. But I need more time."

"Time for what?"

"There's something I need to do. And I'm running out of time." There was a note of desperation to his voice I instinctively knew was   uncharacteristic for him.

237

"Whatever this is you need to do . . ." I began, thinking, trying to put things together. "That's why you missed your court date in the first place."

"Yes. I had a lead, a solid lead, and I couldn't let it go. I'm afraid I'm too late, but I can't give up on her."

"Her?"

"It doesn't matter who. All that matters is that I find her. Which means I can't spend all my time ducking you. I'd like to make a deal. Give me time and space, and, once I've done this thing, I'll turn myself in to you."

"The bond company goes to judgment on your bond in four days. If I don't put you back into the system before that time, Sure Bonds is out fifty thousand dollars and you lose your condo."

"It doesn't matter. This is more important."

I sighed. "I've heard this before." I tucked the Browning back into the holster. "Can you accomplish whatever it is you're trying to do in four days?"

"If I can't do it by then, it'll probably be too late anyway." For the first time I saw genuine sadness in his mocha brown eyes.

It was obvious whatever he was working on was serious for him; he wasn't going to let it go without a fight. I also knew now what I'd known from the beginning: unless he agreed to come in, I wasn't sure I could bring him in without one or both of us being seriously injured, even with the dog's help.

"Turns out, I have a soft spot for soldiers."

"I'm a Marine."

"Servicemen, then. And I don't take for granted that you saved my life. I'll make your deal."

He was obviously relieved. "Thank you."

"Please don't make me regret it."

"You won't."

"How can I get in touch with you?"

"I wrote my phone number down on the counter." He slowly picked up the card I'd given his mother. "Thank you."

"Be careful."

"You, too."

He backed slowly to the patio door and slid it open. He stepped out and shut the door. He disappeared from the deck and was gone.

"Good boy," I said to Dasch. "*Bravy*."

I scratched his ears and went to get my things from the front door.

What was I thinking, making that kind of deal with Medera?

I saw clearly the look of real pain and fear in his eyes, mingling with unyielding conviction, and not for the first time I felt something like understanding—understanding that Medera wasn't all that different from me.

Which meant I was starting to like the guy.

36

Monday morning came too early. In a very short time, the three of us had fallen into a comfortable routine and sleeping arrangements had been made. I slept in the middle. Ellmann slept on the right. Dasch slept on the left. We all slept in the bed. If Dasch had even noticed the very plush doggy bed I'd bought him, he had given no indication. And he wouldn't be kept off the bed.

Until five a.m., when some internal alarm seemed to go off for him. He'd get up, find what had become his favorite rope toy, then come back and bother me until I got up.

"Guess you're a morning person now," Ellmann mumbled as I pushed Dasch off and sat up.

"We're never having children."

"Why not? We never sleep anyway." He rolled over and pulled the covers up higher.

Dasch and I went to the backyard where we played and practiced his commands. Then we went upstairs and practiced some more commands. Dietrich Müller had said we were welcome to come to the facility for training anytime, and I knew I would take him up on the offer, but with the facility being three hours away, it wasn't a practical habit. Rather, I needed to find something local. I made a mental note to talk to Ellmann's buddy Jason Wilcox about possibly using the same facility he used with his K-9.

240

Ellmann was still snoozing when I went back into the bedroom for running clothes. I snuck back out, laced up my shoes, then slung Dasch's unneeded leash across my chest and we headed out. The sun was just beginning to rise as we did the run/walk routine. We passed a couple other joggers, and the same woman with the same yappy dog. Dasch never broke stride.

He slept on the bathmat while I showered, then laid on the end of the bed while I dressed. He had more than made himself at home. And I noticed he and I already had our own routines, like we'd been together for years instead of days. I found I seemed to know what he wanted, what he needed, and he seemed able to read my mind.

"Breakfast?"

He leapt off the bed and followed me into the kitchen. Ellmann was sitting at the table, reading the paper and finishing his coffee. I kissed his head as I passed him for the pantry where Dasch's food was, and he wrapped an arm around my waist, pulling me onto his lap. One long kiss later, he set me back on my feet, but I couldn't remember what I'd been doing.

"Feed the dog," he said as he stood, carrying his mug to the sink.

"Right."

Dasch was sitting beside his bowl, patiently waiting, drooling slightly in anticipation.

I filled his bowl and he stuck his face in it, doing his best impersonation of a vacuum.

"I've got to go," Ellmann said. "Will I see you later?"

"I think so. I'm going to Boulder today to run down some leads. Oh, that reminds me, do you know anyone on the Boulder PD?"

I went to the cupboard and got a coffee mug, filling it from the pot.

"Couple guys. Why? Need an intro?"

"I'm looking into something that may connect to a missing persons case. Victim's name is Theresa Walling; went missing in February. I'd really like to talk to whoever's working the case."

He jotted the name down in his notebook and nodded. "I'll make a call." He put the notebook back in his pocket and walked over to the dog. "Dasch, you take care of my girl."

Dasch looked up, licking his lips, and wagged his tail at Ellmann as affirmation.

Ellmann gave him a pat and a scratch and looked up at me. "Love you."

"I love you, too." It was soft, but it was clear.

He grinned and came through the kitchen toward me.

"I've been practicing," I said.

"Good," he said, wrapping his arms around me and lifting me onto the counter. "Because I like the way it sounds."

"Won't you be late for work?" I panted a little while later.

Ellmann glanced at the clock on the microwave to my right. "Yes." He made an ugly sound. "But I almost don't care."

I smiled. "Go. We'll finish this later."

"Tonight," he growled, his darkened eyes pinning mine.

I smiled wider as a flash of heat burned through me. "Tonight."

He tore away from the counter and marched out of the kitchen with clear determination. A minute later, I heard the garage door roll up and then down.

I sat on the counter for a minute more, trying to catch my breath.

I made myself a bagel with peanut butter then took it, an orange, and my coffee to the table. As I munched, I scanned the paper Ellmann had left. The front page led with the headline SECOND GIRL MISSING FROM CSU CAMPUS. The article relayed the story of a junior named Julia Webster who had been reported missing by her roommate Sunday. The roommate, another junior at CSU, had not seen Webster since some time Thursday. After becoming concerned, the roommate called around, checked with other friends and Webster's boyfriend, but no one had seen her. The boyfriend, a senior at CSU, was with the roommate when she reported Webster missing.

The article drew connections to Maria Rodriquez's case, stating the two were similar and speculating they were connected. However, the only obviously connection I could garner from the article was that both girls had been CSU students. There were far more differences—the girls ages and appearances; Maria lived in the dorms while Julia Webster lived off campus; Maria seemed to have gone missing from campus while investigators had yet to determine where Webster had last been seen; Maria was an honor student and a vet sciences major while Webster was a communications major and no mention was made of her scholarly accolades, leading me to believe she had none.

What was a communications major anyway?

My phone rang. It was Sadie.

"You're up early," I said.

"I just left work. I had to call you. There is something seriously up with Karen."

I leaned back in my seat. "We know that already; that's why you hired me in the first place."

"Yeah, but last night, I saw her stealing patient blood."

That got my attention and definitely tipped the weird scale. "Excuse me?"

"Okay. I went into a patient room, and I didn't know Karen was in there. She was starting an IV, drawing blood—perfectly normal. Except as I walk in, I see her slip two full tubes of blood into her pocket. And she times it just right so the patient doesn't see it. Plays the whole thing like nothing happened."

"That's interesting."

"Interesting! Zoe, it's crazy! And scary! What possible reason could the woman have to steal those tubes of blood? And, by the way, I checked; those tubes never showed up in the lab, were nowhere in the department. She *did* take them."

"Something's going on that we don't see yet," I murmured, my mind working.

"No shit," Sadie snapped. "What have you learned so far? Who the hell is this woman?"

"I don't know. But I've been looking into her missing neighbor. My gut tells me the two are connected. I'm going to work on that angle more today. I have a lot of pieces for the Karen puzzle that don't seem to fit together. I'm hoping if I can get somewhere on the missing neighbor, I'll learn something about Karen that will make the other pieces make sense."

"I think it's illegal to steal blood like that. And if it's not, it should be. Maybe we should just turn this over to the police, let them turn her life inside out."

"The only serious problem with that is proving she stole the blood. She obviously did it for a purpose; I'm assuming she doesn't hang on to the tubes. If they are no longer in her possession, the cops will find nothing, and we will have tipped our hand to her."

"You think she's done this more than once?"

"She sounds too practiced to be pulling a one off."

"I ask again: what possible reason could she have to steal blood?"

"I don't know yet. Did she see you looking? Does she know you saw her?"

"No. I'm almost certain she didn't."

"Good. Sadie, steer well clear of her for the time being. Don't mention this blood thing to anyone. And be extra careful."

"You think I'm in danger?"

"I'd rather play it safe. I can't think of too many reasons why Karen Brickle's innocent neighbor has been missing for six months. Whatever this woman is in to, I think it's big, and I think it's dangerous."

"What do you think it is?"

I thought of Brickle's account balance. The first time I'd seen it, I'd immediately thought drugs. That was the easiest explanation.

"I don't know," I admitted. "The blood changes things. Now I'm not sure."

Sadie sighed. "You see the news this morning? About that missing girl?"

"Yeah, I was just reading the newspaper. What about her?"

"Well, this is a total HIPAA violation, but one of the girls I work with was telling me this morning she'd taken care of the girl shortly before she went missing." The accent was really coming on now. "I tell you, Fort Collins is going to hell on a sled. My mama, she keeps telling me I need to move home. Lately, I've been wondering why the hell I don't."

I didn't have any good answer to that. Fort Collins did kind of seem to be falling apart.

37

I spent the next hour making phone calls. I called Lee Rossler's office, got his secretary's name when she answered, and hung up. Then I called Fort Collins Property Insurance, told them I was Rossler's secretary Charmaine, and asked for an update on the water damage claim for Marge's building. I was hoping to be told there was no such claim. Instead, I was told the repairs were scheduled for Thursday; the day after Marge was supposed to be out.

I found the notes I'd made yesterday about Boulder hospitals. I called Boulder Medical Center first and asked for human resources. After being passed around a bit, I finally got a real person on the phone who made me believe she might actually be able to help me.

"My name is Jennifer Brown," I said, starting my spiel again. "I'm the hiring manager at Harmony Urgent Care in Fort Collins. I'm calling to check references on an applicant named Karen Brickle."

"How do you spell her last name?"

I spelled it.

I heard typing on the other end of the line.

"First name Karen with a *k*?"

"Yes."

"Uh-huh. Well, I'm sorry to tell you, but I don't have any record of employment for anyone with that name. Are you sure that's how you spell it?"

"Well, that's certainly how she spelled it on her application," I said haughtily. "I suppose this helps us make a hiring decision."

"I would think so. Anything else?"

"No. Thank you for your help."

"You're welcome." *Click.*

No pleasantries with that woman.

I dialed Boulder Community Hospital. I again asked for HR and was again passed around several times before arriving at a helpful destination.

I repeated my spiel, this time to a guy named Ted.

"Well, let's take a look here," Ted said, tapping on the keyboard. "Okay, looks like a one Karen Brickle was employed here from June 2013 until February 2014. Her manager was Roger Hicks. Hmm, looks like Mr. Hicks is no longer in the ED; he transferred to . . ." I heard some more typing. "ICU. Uh, Ms. Brickle has no formal disciplinary action in her file, though I see a couple notes about informal conversations, mostly related to attendance it seems."

"I see. Would it be possible to talk to Mr. Hicks?"

"I don't see why not. Let me give you his direct number."

Ted recited a number, and I wrote it down.

"Is there anything else I can help you with?" Ted asked.

"No, thank you. You've been very helpful."

"My pleasure. Have a great day."

Ted sure was in the right business. With all his pleasantries and well wishes, people probably loved visiting HR.

I dialed the number Ted had given me for Roger Hicks. The line rang six times before it dropped to voicemail. The message informed me Hicks would be out of the office until tomorrow and gave a number to the main unit should I need urgent assistance. Instead I hung up and pulled out my computer. I ran a couple of searches and came up with an address for Hicks.

I packed up and headed out. Dasch and I were just climbing into the Jeep when Ellmann called.

"Got in touch with a guy I know with Boulder," he said. "Name's Clark. He agreed to meet you. Starbucks. At noon."

He gave me the address.

"Thanks, Ellmann. I appreciate it."

"You can show me how much later. I don't care what comes up, you and I have plans tonight."

I smiled. "I remember." I remembered so well I felt flushed again.

An hour later, I cruised by Theresa Walling's house. I saw no sign anyone was home. I circled the block and parked a few streets away. I told Dasch to stay with the car, then got out and walked back.

I strolled up to the front door and rang the bell. I hoped Tom was at school, but there was always a chance he wasn't. Or that someone else was home. Fortunately, no one answered the door.

I walked around the house and let myself into the backyard through the gate. I checked the garage door and found it locked. I continued on to the sliding glass patio door I'd come through yesterday. It was also locked, though the Charlie bar was not in place. Still, the easier point of entry was the garage door.

I pulled the bump key from my pocket and let myself in. The door from the garage to the house was not locked, so I pushed it open and went in. The house was dark and quiet, and it felt profoundly empty.

I tried not to read into that and made a quick tour through the place to make sure I was actually alone. Then I got down to business.

The kitchen and living room were not well preserved, because they had been used since Theresa left the house for the last time. I checked the drawers and cupboards in the kitchen and found the usual stuff. The living room also yielded nothing helpful.

The master bedroom, unlike the common spaces, seemed to have been preserved. As far as I could tell, it seemed unlikely anyone had used this room since Theresa had walked out of it for the last time. The place was clean, however, and I guessed someone, perhaps Tom, had come in and cleaned up after the police had been through. There would have been fingerprint powder everywhere, to say the least of the mess an investigation team left behind. Other than that, though, the room had not been disturbed.

Theresa made her bed, as most women of her generation did. She'd hung up her towels in the bathroom and pulled the shower curtain. And all of her dirty clothes were gathered neatly in a laundry hamper in the closet. But the bathroom counter and the dresser were mildly cluttered with everyday items such as brushes, makeup, and jewelry. My initial impression was that this woman had intended to return here.

Still, I looked carefully at the items in the bathroom. I mentally categorized the makeup items on the counter and in the drawers, making conclusions about what kind of makeup she'd worn every day, and what she'd kept for special occasions. Then something struck me. There was no mascara on the counter.

Everything Theresa very likely wore every day was on the counter. The reality is most women leave that stuff on the counter. I know I'm guilty of this, as are all the women I know, and all the women whose houses I've searched. But there was no mascara. And no woman wore all the rest of this makeup and no mascara.

I searched the drawers again and found two tubes, but those were bold products, kept with the other special occasion makeup, not the kind of thing Theresa would have worn every day. They didn't complement any of the other everyday items on the counter.

Nothing else seemed to be missing: shower products, toothbrush, deodorant, lotion—all there. I checked the trashcan. Maybe the mascara had run out the last day she'd used it and she'd thrown it away. But if that were the case, I'd never know; the trash had been emptied. Most likely by the police.

I went back into the bedroom and looked through the closet and the dresser drawers. I would have no way of knowing if anything was missing. Instead, I was more interested in finding anything that shouldn't be there. I wasn't sure what, but it didn't matter, because there was nothing. No hidden love letter or death threats, no hidden weapons, no hidden photographs, nothing.

I left the master bedroom and looked through the rest of the house. There were two other bedrooms on the second floor; these had likely been the boys' rooms growing up. Now one of them was a guestroom and the other was an office/craft room.

The guest bedroom quite obviously had someone living in it, and I guessed that to be Tom. He had clothing in the dresser and closet, the bed was unmade, and there was some miscellanea on the dresser and bedside table. The only thing of any interest at all was the pistol I found in the drawer beside the bed. I made note of the serial number then replaced it, but by and large it didn't set off any alarms for me. If the roles were reversed, and my mother had mysteriously disappeared from her own house, I'd take to sleeping with a gun beside my bed as well. Actually, I do sleep with a gun beside my bed, so what does that say about me?

In the office and craft room I learned Theresa had been one to take her work home with her and that she had an interest in scrapbooking. I sat at the desk and woke up the computer. It was, by a small miracle, not locked, but it held no secrets or insights. Tom or someone else had been using it since February, but the search history and associated documents were all benign and largely work-related. Who knew being a teacher was such hard work?

The browser history from before February was even more uninteresting. Theresa had used the computer for nothing besides Facebook, email, and work. From what I could tell, she didn't even bank or pay her bills online. I tried getting into her email account, but that was indeed password protected, and my few feeble attempts to guess her secret code failed.

I powered down the computer and rifled through the drawers. There was nothing interesting in any of them, and instead I found a small filing cabinet in the closet much more fruitful. It was unlocked, and this was where Theresa kept her bills and personal information.

I found her cell phone bill and saw the last one was from March, for which there had been no calls, no texts, no data usage. It seemed the account had been canceled after that. I could find bills for only two credit cards, and there had been no activity on either since February. Even before that, she'd been well under her credit limit and made regular payments.

She had a checking and a savings account, and it appeared she'd had the same accounts since her divorce six years before. And from what I could see, she had kept records for all those years. A quick glance back through the balances on both showed nothing suggestive. Both accounts were modest. Her checking account never wavered much, and her savings account steadily increased each month as she made regular deposits from her paychecks. The only thing even remotely interesting was that she hadn't made her regular deposit in December or January. This could possibly be explained by the holidays. People always increase their spending, and by contrast decrease their savings, during that time of year. A look back showed Theresa had made her savings deposits every November, December, and January going back all six years, but with the soaring cost of goods and food, money was tight for everyone these days. Plus, she'd had a new grandbaby and a boyfriend to buy for this year.

I wasn't sure any of this meant anything, so I closed up the filing cabinet and the closet and returned to the desk. I pulled the in-progress scrapbooks toward me and began paging through them. I wasn't much of an expert on scrapbooks, but Theresa's page layouts were attractive. And she devoted a lot of space to handwritten stories, comments, and notes, making the books immensely personal.

One of them was a baby book for the newest grandchild. One of them was for a family vacation Theresa had taken with her boys last summer. In that book, I stopped and studied one of the first pages. There seemed to be a blank spot. I flipped on the light and studied the page. In the light, I could see the faint marks of adhesive where a photo had indeed been affixed to the page.

In looking at the page, reading the notes, it seemed to me that photo would have likely been a family shot. I flipped through one stack of loose photos, then another, and another. There were photos everywhere. Perhaps in working on that page, Theresa had tried a photo and decided it didn't work after all. She'd obviously been kidnapped before she could finish either of these scrapbooks; maybe that was one page she'd not been able to go back and finish.

In the stacks of photos, I found no duplicates. In this digital age, it wasn't like the days when you dropped off a roll of film and got duplicate or triplicate images back. Today, you printed only the photos you wanted. And Theresa most likely did that on her fancy printer sitting beside the computer. So whatever photo had been pulled from the page, I would have no way of identifying it.

I replaced the photo books and the stacks of photos. Then I leaned back in the chair and sat thinking for a minute. I was trying to decide if anything I'd learned here added up to anything significant. Surely I didn't know anything the police didn't know. And they'd still had no luck tracking her down. That strongly suggested she was missing against her will, and very likely dead, after all this time.

But perhaps an argument could be made that Theresa had left on her own. If she'd kept her savings deposits, she'd have had a bit of cash to get her started. She could have taken her mascara because she'd known she wasn't coming back. Maybe she'd taken the photo with her to remind her of her family.

One thing I was certain of: if Theresa Walling had disappeared intentionally, she'd had help. Theresa was a nice, normal, middle-aged woman who had lived a nice, normal, quiet life. Nice, normal, quiet people didn't have the first idea how to drop off the radar and stay off. They always slipped up somewhere. (Like taking a personal photo with them, for example.) But there had been absolutely no sign of her for six months.

She'd only missed two months' worth of deposits, so she hadn't been planning this for long, if she had indeed planned it at all. Whatever cash she had would be gone by now, so not only was someone helping with logistics, someone was financing her. But why? Why would Theresa Walling decide to disappear? And who would help her do something like that? Theresa had a nice life and a beautiful, loving family. She obviously cared about her job and her students. What would motivate her to walk away from all of that?

Those, of course, were just the questions relevant if she left on her own. If someone did in fact kidnap, and perhaps murder, her, why had she been targeted? What could she have meant to someone that would motivate that person to kill her? Or had she just been in the wrong place at the wrong time?

I needed more information. Hopefully the police had more than I did. I headed out to meet Clark.

38

The Starbucks Clark chose was on Highway 7, a standalone building sharing a parking lot with a King Soopers and a gas station. There were no available parking spaces near the building, so I parked in the King Soopers lot and walked back, Dasch following behind my left leg. I still had his leash draped across my chest where it had been all morning.

I bypassed the front door and walked to the shaded patio on the street side of the building. I immediately spotted the cop. He was middle-aged, bald, and looked a little like Bruce Willis. He wore tan slacks and a white button-down shirt with the collar open and the sleeves rolled up. He sat with his back to the building, scanning the street in such a way he didn't appear to be doing so. When I got nearer, I could see the badge and gun on his belt—on the left side; he was left-handed, also like Bruce Willis.

I made my way over and sat in the chair opposite him. Dasch gave him a glance and sat beside me, leaning against my leg, his gaze behind me.

"You must be Ellmann's girl," Clark said, offering me his hand. "Dan Clark. Nice to meet you."

"Zoe Grey. Thanks for meeting me."

Clark shrugged and leaned back in his seat, deceptively casual. "Ellmann said it would be worth my time. He said you're pretty good at finding people."

"I've had some success."

"Gotta wonder, what's a bounty hunter doing looking into a six-month-old missing persons case."

"I'm actually investigating a woman named Karen Brickle." I saw a flash of recognition, and something else, in his eyes. "I see you know the name."

He was obviously uncomfortable at being read so easily. I wondered if Clark had a narcotics background. He was good at blending, at watching his surroundings without seeming to do so, and better than most cops at keeping his thoughts off his face. But I was better than most at reading people. We all have skills; this is one of mine.

"Of course I've heard the name. I investigated Theresa Walling's disappearance. We talked to Brickle, interviewed her—all the neighbors, actually. What are you looking at her for? She fail to appear?"

"No. This is a private matter."

"I don't recall Ellmann mentioning to me that you're a PI."

I hoped we didn't have to get into technicalities here. "It's private, for a friend. A favor."

He considered that for a beat and decided to let it go. "So why the interest in the Walling case?"

"It's highly coincidental to me Karen's neighbor disappeared within weeks of her moving to Fort Collins. In my experience, there is no such thing as a coincidence."

"So what's your theory, Brickle disappeared Walling?"

"Frankly, I don't have a working theory yet. I still have too many questions. I can understand why you wouldn't want to share information with me about an ongoing case, but since you agreed to meet with me, I'd hoped you'd answer a few questions."

He stared at me for a couple of beats, obviously weighing how much to tell me, if anything. I decided to sweeten the pot.

"I don't know very much, but I'm willing to go tit for tat here, if that helps you make a   decision."

Again, he was surprised I'd been able to know what he was thinking. He thought some more, studying me curiously. I absently petted Dasch's head and waited him out.

He arrived at his decision and pulled a thick brown file from below the table. It had the Boulder Police Department badge emblem on the front. "All right. I'll answer your questions, if you share with me what you know. Ellmann's a good guy, a good cop; I trust him when he tells me you're good, too. Even if it's unconventional, I'll take the help on this one. This case has bothered me from the beginning."

"What bothers you about it?"

"I'm not sure. I've worked a hundred missing persons cases over the years. Mostly it's husbands skipping out on wives and girlfriends, or wives and girlfriends killed by their husbands and boyfriends. And that doesn't include the kids. But talking about the adult cases, it usually doesn't take long to dig up some kind of motivation behind the disappearance—alimony payments, child support payments, pending criminal charges or jail time, cheating spouses, stolen money, new girlfriend, you know, the usual. But not so with Theresa Walling. The deeper I dug, the more of nothing I found. The woman doesn't have an enemy in the world, no reason to run. She might have actually been the nicest, most decent woman I've ever investigated."

I nodded. "I'm coming up with the same. Which makes her disappearance all the more suspicious. I understand the investigation focused pretty heavily on her ex-husband."

"Yeah. As I'm sure you know, initially everyone's a suspect. We looked at him, the sons, Theresa's friends and coworkers, everyone. Frank became marginally interesting when we discovered Theresa had been seen arguing with him outside her home the day she disappeared. We believe she was abducted from her home, so we suspected he had been the last person to see her."

"What were they arguing about?"

"According to Frank, money. She'd asked him for some; he'd refused. She didn't take the news well. But it never went anywhere. The guy had a rock solid alibi for that evening. Not to mention, I don't think he's capable of it."

"I met him, and I agree with you there. I've known some killers in my time; Frank Walling isn't one. Who reported her missing?"

"Frank did, actually."

"That didn't help his case."

"No, it didn't. We always look hard at the person making the report. And a few weeks into the investigation, your girl, Karen Brickle, started making lots of noise, pointing the finger at Frank. Media got wind of it, the brass started putting the pressure on, and we, in turn, were told in no uncertain terms to put the pressure on Frank. We tore apart every statement he'd ever made, every aspect of his life. We couldn't break his alibi, and we never caught him in a lie."

"So naturally your suspicion shifted to Brickle."

He tapped his nose. "But it never went anywhere."

"Why not?"

"As soon as we started looking, we got shut down. From the top."

Interesting. "How?"

He shrugged. "Best I can figure, it had something to do with her boyfriend, the illustrious Dr. Adam Galvin."

"Who's he?"

"Good to know his reputation doesn't really span the globe, as he would have you believe. Galvin's a thoracic surgeon here at Boulder Community Hospital. Got an ego as big as the house he lives in. Bigger. Anyway, Galvin's connected. Donates to certain political campaigns and parties and knows all the right people. Get what I'm saying?"

"Sure. You start poking around in his girlfriend's life, he calls his buddy Mr. Mayor, Mr. Mayor calls the chief of police, and on down the line. I didn't think stuff like that happened in real life."

Clark actually chuckled. "Seriously? You ever hear the expression 'truth is stranger than fiction?' Well, in this case, the truth is darker and sadder than fiction. Money buys a lot of things, political careers among them."

"About the time you backed off of Brickle, she uprooted and moved to Fort Collins."

"Yeah." He eyed me across the table. "The timing of that always bothered me."

My opinion of Clark bumped up a few notches.

"Did you ever look into Sheila Walling?"

"Preliminaries, like everyone else. Guess you know about her string of dead husbands."

"Yes. Granted, the pattern seems to indicate she targets husbands, not ex-wives, but she's fiercely jealous of Frank's lingering feelings for his wife."

"Really? How'd you come up with that?" He was genuinely interested.

"I dropped by their house Saturday, talked to them. Frank doesn't want to be married to Theresa anymore, but he still cares a great deal for her, respects her. Sheila's pretty guarded, but that jealousy is there, burning deep and hot."

"I barely remember her. She didn't stand out for me. She was so reserved, quiet—"

"Meek," I supplied.

"Yeah, exactly. She actually said something to you?"

"No. It was in her eyes."

He looked at me for a beat then said, "Anyone else, I'd probably dismiss that. But you've read me twice since we met, and that never happens. So maybe there's something to what you say. I'll go back to her, look again. Of course, I could never find anything that suggested she was responsible for the death of any of her first three husbands, but that's a hell of a coincidence. And if she's killed once, it's easier to do it again."

"So you're operating on the assumption Theresa is dead."

"It's the most practical line of thinking. Unless she disappeared deliberately, the statistics say she is most likely dead. Six months is an awfully long time to keep an abductee alive."

"But not unheard of."

"No. Just very unlikely."

"What else do you know about Brickle? Were you able to dig anything up before you got pulled?"

He shook his head. "No. It was literally just preliminaries."

I debated telling him what I knew of Karen Brickle, mainly that Karen Brickle wasn't her real name.

"But," Clark went on, "I did some digging on my own. Quietly. I started to learn some very interesting things."

My opinion of Clark jumped up a couple more pegs. I thought I might actually respect the guy by the time our conversation was over.

"Like Karen Brickle isn't really Karen Brickle."

He nodded. "Like that. Turns out, there is a real Karen Brickle. Woman lives in Denver."

"Let me guess, she's a nurse."

"Yep. Works at St. Anthony's. Our Brickle seems to have stolen her identity."

"More like she's impersonating her."

"Yeah. And I can't figure out why."

I wasn't sure either, but I thought Brickle had done the same to Angela Morris and Stephanie Roman.

"I don't suppose you were ever able to get a print, find out who she really is?"

"Get this. By the time I got this far, she'd already left for Fort Collins. I knew she'd sold the house, and after a little checking I learned there would be about a week before the new owner moved in. I went over there one night, thinking I'd print the place. I knew it would never hold up in court, but it might tell me who she is, what she's up to. Only, I get over there, and there isn't a single print in the house. Not anywhere."

I gaped at him. "It had been sterilized."

"Way beyond a move out clean. Every single surface of the house had been wiped—doorknobs, window locks, cabinet handles, even the walls. I've never seen anything like it. Not once. Even the best wipe down leaves something—smudges, partials, something. Not here. And not just the prints; the whole place had been cleaned. Like, deep cleaned. There wasn't a speck of dust or a foreign fiber anywhere—even the drains had been cleaned out. I was there for almost six hours, and I found zip."

"Suspicious. No way she was that thorough just because she'd sold the place."

"No. People only do something like that if they want to make damn sure they leave nothing behind. And the only people who do that are those with something to hide."

"So what's she hiding?" I mused aloud.

"That's a question I never made much progress on."

"Did you ever turn up Theresa's boyfriend?"

He looked at me. "What boyfriend?"

"I think she was seeing someone around December, January. I don't have a name, nothing concrete. Wondered if anything came up while you were digging into her life."

"No, nothing. No one said anything about any boyfriend."

I didn't necessarily find this surprising, and it didn't mean there wasn't one. It was possible Theresa had been keeping it private, or else no one thought to mention it. Of course, the third possibility was that someone had lied. The simple truth is everyone lies to the police, even innocent people, and they usually lie about the stupidest shit, the stuff no one cares about.

I'd need to ask my own questions, see what I could come up with.

"Did you guys collect the trash from her bathroom when you searched her house?"

He gave me an odd look. "Why?"

"Wondering if she'd thrown away an empty tube of mascara that morning."

"Mascara?" He stared at me strangely for a beat, then shook his head and flipped open the file. He found the page he wanted then scanned a short list. "No mascara. Why?"

I looked at Clark. "Do you think there is any chance Theresa Walling disappeared voluntarily?"

He stared at me for a long time. Finally he said, "If she did, she would have needed help, but I didn't find anyone in her life capable of helping an inexperienced woman disappear. She would have needed ID, money, a place to go. I didn't find any of that. Why?"

"But you considered it."

He took a beat too long to answer. "Of course I considered it. An investigation like that, you've got to consider every possibility."

I leaned forward. "No bullshit here, Clark. Tell me what made you think it was possible."

"Fuck," he hissed, irritated. "You must clean up at the poker table."

I shook my head. "I never play."

"You should. You'd make a killing."

"It's boring. Now answer my question."

261

He thought for a long minute then finally leaned forward. "The money."

It was official; I respected Clark.

"Her savings account money."

He was obviously surprised I knew about that, but nodded. "Yeah. In December and January, Theresa withdrew the amount she normally stocked away in savings. She also made several regular withdrawals from her savings account. We could never find any record of where that money went. It was only about five thousand dollars, but that would be a great start for a woman on the run." He eyed me. "Why do you ask? Do *you* think it's possible?"

"I've considered it. The theory has a lot of problems, as you pointed out. A woman like Theresa Walling would never have been able to remain undetected this long without help."

"What tipped you?"

"The mascara."

He blinked at me. "The . . . mascara."

"I think she took it with her when she left. I caught on to the money, too, and that bolsters the theory. I think she also took a picture of her family. But the mascara almost seals it for me."

He pulled a card from his pocket and passed it to me. "I'll need something more significant than that if I'm to take this case forward. I'd appreciate it if you kept me updated."

I handed him one of my cards. "I'll bring you in when I've got something solid. I'm not done digging into Karen Brickle."

He slid my card into the breast pocket of his shirt. "Ellmann asked me to meet with you as a favor. Then he told me I'd owe *him* a favor after you found my missing person."

I couldn't help but smile. "He should have made it two."

"Help me find Theresa Walling and I'll happily owe you *both* two."

I offered him my hand as I stood, Dasch jumping up with me. "I'm going to find Theresa, but I'm doing it for her family. Her sons deserve to know what happened to their mom."

39

After Clark had left, I sat on the patio and connected to Starbuck's free Wi-Fi (without buying a drink—take that corporate coffee conglomeration!) and searched for Dr. Adam Galvin. As expected, Galvin wasn't listed in the white pages, lest some disgruntled or overly satisfied patient get his home number or address, but Galvin did own property in Boulder County. In about a minute, I found he owned three properties. Two were residential; one in Boulder, a second with an Allenspark address. The third was a commercial lot he owned with three other men. I guessed these were doctors and the building housed their medical practices. I jotted down the addresses and checked the time.

From Starbucks, I drove to the address I'd found for Roger Hicks. I let the map function on my phone navigate me there, since I didn't know one end of Boulder from the other.

The neighborhood was a quiet, middle-class place with kids everywhere. It was what I would expect for a nurse and his family, especially if the kids were a bit older now and the wife also worked.

I found Hicks's house without any trouble and parked at the curb. When I arrived, a minivan was backed into the driveway, all the doors open, and a man was pulling a suitcase from the back. I told Dasch to wait in the car and walked up the driveway.

"Hello," I called and waved.

The man set the suitcase on the driveway and looked around the van at me. He was mostly what I expected: late forties, graying and thinning hair, expanding waistline, pale complexion. He was wearing jeans, tennis shoes, and t-shirt. Everything seemed slightly wrinkled.

Before either of us could say more, a teenaged boy and a woman emerged from the open front door of the house. They looked equally as rumpled, and the woman looked just as affected by middle age as her husband. Both of them eyed me curiously.

"Hello," the woman said cautiously, obviously wondering who the hell I was and where I'd come from.

"Hi there. I'm sorry to bother you. My name is Zoe Grey. I'm a private investigator from Fort Collins." This little lie was coming more and more easily to me, and it was so much more concise than the truth. "Mr. Hicks, I need to ask you a few questions about a former employee, if you don't mind."

He was obviously surprised. His wife looked at him like she wondered if he'd known about this all along. Their son just looked curious, while also maintaining the requisite teenage air of indifference and scorn.

"Why?" Hicks asked. "Which employee?"

"Would it be okay if we spoke in private? It'll only take a few moments."

"Uh . . ." He looked at his wife. She looked back, waiting for him to make a decision, and I had the clear impression, as he must have, that there was a right and wrong answer, but she gave no hint as to which was which.

Yikes. What a tough broad to live with.

He finally looked back at me. "Sure." He sighed, not sure at all if this was the right response or not, according to his wife. "Of course." He passed the suitcase to his son. "Take this inside, Jeremy. Then you and your sisters get unpacked."

"Whatever." But Jeremy took the handle from his father and rolled the suitcase to the door, then disappeared inside.

Mrs. Hicks crossed her arms over her chest, making clear her intention to stay. Obviously, "private" didn't exclude her. I suddenly felt very sorry for Hicks.

"We'll only be a few minutes, Mrs. Hicks," I said. Then I took a few steps back down the driveway and indicated Hicks should follow me. "Let's go for a walk, Mr. Hicks."

After a moment of internal deliberation, Hicks fell in step behind me. I waited a few paces before I said anything, ensuring the wife hadn't decided to follow us. But it appeared the coast was clear. Poor guy. Who knew how much trouble he'd be in when he got back.

"I tried calling your office, but you were out," I said as we walked.

"We were out of town this weekend, for my niece's wedding in Nebraska. We're just getting back."

"I'm investigating a woman named Karen Brickle," I said. "I understand you were her manager when she worked in the ER at Boulder Community Hospital."

"Karen?" Hicks said, again surprised. "That's what this is about?"

"Yes. Why does that surprise you?"

He shrugged. "I haven't seen Karen in months, and she didn't work for me very long. I can't imagine why you came all this way to speak to me."

"My investigation began because Karen got into some trouble at work." This was a lie, but I wanted Hicks to give me the dirt on Brickle. People usually found that easier if the person they were talking about was already dirty. "Now I'm looking into her employment history, trying to get a sense of her. What can you tell me?"

He stopped and looked at me, then quickly looked away. He was obviously uncomfortable, but there *was* something, something had come to mind for him.

I was quiet for a few beats, letting him work up to it on his own. Then I gave him a little push.

"You're not the first of her bosses, managers, or coworkers I've spoken to," I said. "You likely won't tell me anything I haven't heard already. Speaking to you is a bit of a formality at this point. So please, just tell me."

That clearly lifted some pressure from him, and he took a breath, seeming to relax a bit.

"In a situation like this," he began, "the tiniest things can be blown way out of proportion. I obviously have no idea what sort of incidents you've heard about, or how whatever I could tell you might paint them. I never found myself too concerned with the few things that made it back to my office. If it turns out they were indeed precursors, indications of bigger things to come, I will feel as if I should have done more at the time, though what I could have done I have no idea."

"Let's not get caught up in what could have been, okay? Let's just stick to the facts. I assure you, whatever Karen has done, she is the only one responsible."

He sighed again, and looked down at his shoes as he stuffed his hands in his pockets.

"She was an average nurse. Not brilliant, not highly motivated, not especially hard working, but not stupid, dangerous, or lazy either. In today's workforce, she was average. Sadly, maybe even above average.

"She seemed to get along well with everyone at first, but then I started to hear some feedback that people disliked her. The reasons varied so greatly I assumed it was personality clashes. There are a lot of women in an emergency department, and women are never quiet about who they like and who they don't. And sometimes they dislike one another over the stupidest things." He seemed then to remember he was talking

267

to a woman. He looked up and said, "I'm sorry. I mean no offense."

"None taken," I assured him. "I completely agree with you."

"Anyway, that was all there ever was to it."

"There were never any specific complaints?" I pressed. "About her or her performance?"

"No." He was being honest. "Is that what you're investigating?"

"Frankly, yes. Accusations have been made against her, and in my experience, people Karen's age don't wake up one morning and decide to misbehave. They work up to it, have a history. Are you sure there's nothing more you can remember about Karen?"

He shrugged and looked past me, the wheels of his mind turning back through his memory. "No, I can't remember anything. But Ms. Grey, the truth is, part of the reason I left the ER was the number of complaints. The ER is a stressful environment, flush with a very unique kind of person. They make their opinions and thus their dissatisfactions known. With healthcare changing the way it is, there are lots of things coming down from on high—budget cuts, reductions in staffing, fewer bonuses and benefits, higher expectations, emphasis on patient satisfaction. I left shortly after Karen resigned, so my memories of that time are a bit jumbled. Mostly what I remember is wanting to find a job where people visited my office for reasons other than to complain or be formally disciplined."

I could hear so many of the conversations I'd had with Sadie in recent years echoed in his statements now, and I felt for him.

"I understand, Mr. Hicks. A good friend of mine is an ER nurse. Do you remember why Karen resigned? Did she give a reason?"

He thought for a moment, trying to recall a letter he'd read more than six months before. Then he shook his head. "I'm sorry, I really don't remember. She might not have given one at all; she certainly wasn't required to. You know, some folks resign and they give you their whole life plan, telling you why they have to quit and what they're going to do next, and how their mother-in-law feels about it. Karen wasn't like that. She was a very private person. She was friendly, not shy or anything, but when she talked, she never really said anything— does that make sense? You know the kind of person I'm talking about?"

"I know exactly what you're talking about," I said. And I did. Yet more light was being shed on the picture that was the woman Sadie knew as Karen Brickle, and the image was beginning to look interesting. "She probably didn't have any friends, then? No one she seemed close to?"

"Actually, that's the weird thing. There were two people. One of the techs and a security guard. If I'd had to pick friends for her, I'd never have guessed it would have been those two."

"What do you mean?"

"Well, for one thing, as a general rule, my staff hates the security staff."

This must be a universal truth, because it was true in Sadie's ER too. It was something we'd talked about often.

"My friend says the same thing," I said. "I know what you mean."

He chuckled softly for the first time, and I saw a hint of the younger, happier man he'd once been. Despite everything the years had layered on top, there was something attractive about him there.

"I'd hoped it was just our hospital," he said, "and that security was of a higher caliber other places."

I smiled. "Guess the grass isn't greener."

"Too bad. Anyway, the tech Karen seemed to latch onto was a bit of a loner. Kind of an odd guy, fairly young, not many

269

friends of his own within the department, though he'd worked for us for almost three years."

"Did their relationship seem romantic?"

He shook his head. "No, honestly neither of them did. They seemed . . . cooperative. You know, like partnerships."

"Like they were up to something together?" I ventured.

He considered that. "Strangely, yes. I'm sure this is just my own suspicions and prejudices coloring my memories. Please, don't take any of my suspicions as hardened truths."

"I won't. I would like to talk to those men, however, see if I can get a more direct story from them. Do you remember their names?"

"Sure. Charles Thompson and Andrew Miller. Andy was the tech."

"Was? Has he left?"

"Yeah, resigned a few months ago. More than that, I suppose. Toward the beginning of the year."

"Around February?" I threw out.

"Yeah, maybe. Pretty close anyway."

"And Thompson? He still around?"

Hicks thought for a moment. "Come to think of it, I don't think I've seen him lately. But security staff is managed by an outside company, and I had very little contact with them. Not to mention, I'm not in the ER anymore. I have no idea if he's still employed, when he might have left, any of that. I'm sorry."

"That's okay. I'll find him."

The interview was wrapping up, so I turned us back for his house. We stopped at the end of the driveway. The van had been emptied and closed up. The front door was still open, but no one waited for us.

"What was your impression of Karen Brickle personally?" I asked. "Just your gut impression."

He looked down at the sidewalk for a few beats as he kicked around a small pebble with toe of his shoe. Then he looked up at me.

"I always felt like she was holding back."

"Holding what back?"

He seemed to struggle for the right words, then he said, "She always struck me as intelligent, but her performance didn't really reflect that. Which doesn't make any sense, I know. But I always thought she was holding herself back."

"Playing dumb."

"Yeah, pretty much. Bizarre, right?"

"Yes, it is." I offered him my hand and a card. "Thank you for your time, Mr. Hicks. You've been very helpful. Oh, one more question. Do you know what time high school lets out for the day?"

His eyebrows pinched together at the oddness of the question. "My daughter's a sophomore; her school lets out at three twenty."

I smiled. "Thank you. Please call me if you think of anything else, even something small."

He said he would, wished me a good day, then disappeared into his house to face the woman he'd married. I got into the Jeep, gave Dasch a scratch of greeting, and drove away.

40

I had about an hour, and I wanted to make the most of it. I typed Adam Galvin's Boulder address into my phone and followed it to what turned out to be a massive estate west of town. The house wasn't clearly visible from the street, and a long, paved driveway led through a white gate marked only with the house number on it. As I cruised by, I could clearly see a plowed hayfield to the south of the driveway, perfectly square bundles of hay waiting to be stacked and stored. To the north, visible through the trees, was an enormous barn and three separate, gated corrals.

There didn't seem to be a good way to approach, so I turned around and angled into the driveway. I'd been hoping to take a private tour of Galvin's place if he wasn't home, but with a private driveway and expansive grounds fronting a major street, there would be no way of approaching that both drew no attention and did not seem out of place.

The driveway was over a quarter mile long, leading to one of the biggest, most sprawling estates I'd ever seen. The drive circled an elaborately landscaped centerpiece outside the front door. There was no fountain or statue, but it was grand nevertheless.

To the left was a huge, attached six-car garage bigger than my house. Farther to the left, on the other side of a paved service road, was the barn, which was twice the size of the garage. A couple of horses grazed in one of the paddocks. I don't know much about horses, and it might have simply been the opulent surroundings, but these seemed well kept.

I parked the Jeep in the shade of some thick evergreen trees lining the drive. I had seen no one—no one tending to the horses, no groundskeepers, no farmers in the fields. But there was clearly someone here—one of the garage doors was up, the barn was open, and one of the horses was saddled. I wondered if Dr. Galvin had the day off.

"Wait here a minute," I told Dasch as I climbed out of the jeep. "*Warten.*"

I walked back to house and climbed onto the wide front porch spanning the expansive length of the house and disappearing around the corner to the right. The sidelights on either side of the polished oak front door were frosted glass. I rang the bell, fully expecting a woman in a maid's uniform to answer the door. While I waited, I walked along the porch, peering in the open windows. I nearly choked—the décor was hideous. The windows to the right of the door overlooked the expansive sitting room, and it featured loud, floral wallpaper, floral patterned sofas and chairs, matching floral print, floor-length drapes, and a downright obnoxious area rug. The prevailing color theme was rose pink, with splashes of yellow and green thrown in for a truly nauseating experience.

When I recovered from my shock, I realized the door had still not been answered. I walked back, rang the bell again, and checked the windows to the left. These overlooked an enormous dining room, featuring a long, heavy wooden table and twelve chairs. There was a huge red chintz rug on the floor, which clashed loudly with the puffy, gold floor-length drapes on these windows. The fabric on the chairs was a yellow and brown pattern that matched absolutely nothing. The dark walnut of the table didn't complement the white oak of the chairs or the built-in maple cabinets or the huge cherry china cabinet. The decorative scheme of the room was downright schizophrenic.

I walked back to the door, which had still not been answered. I tried the knob and, as expected, found it locked. I whistled to Dasch, who jumped through the open window and streaked across the driveway and up onto the porch. I was just rounding the corner on the right side of the house when he caught up to me.

"Good boy," I murmured. "*Bravy.*"

He sniffed around some as I peered into some more windows. I saw the living room from the other side, the dining room beyond, and not much else. The place was just too big.

The porch swelled to a little rotunda on the southeast corner and was crowded with green whicker patio furniture adorned with green and white striped cushions and solid green pillows. A couple of stairs led off the porch to a paved path that ran to the west and behind the house.

I followed the path and found the lawn swept down to a large outdoor pool, complete with diving board and slide, surrounded by heavy chaise lounge chairs. Behind the pool was another structure. My distance vision isn't great, but I could clearly make out a covered outdoor bar. I guessed the rest of the building was either a clubhouse or a guesthouse, most likely the former.

But really, the most interesting feature of the grounds was the wide clearing in the numerous trees beyond the clubhouse. It didn't take great vision for me to clearly make out the helicopter sitting on a paved helipad.

"The doctor has his own helicopter?" I said aloud.

Dasch just wagged his tail and grinned.

I peered in some more windows, discovering a more informal family room done overwhelmingly in red with an eight-piece sofa set that, through the window, looked like red velveteen. Farther north, I looked in at the kitchen and an informal dining area. The schizophrenia continued here—blonde butcher-block counter on the island (contrasting badly with the rest of the brown marble countertops), maple cabinets, knotty pine floor, and oak along the windows and trim. This room was green, a too-bright hunter green painted on two thick pillars at either end of the long center island, and green tiles on the backsplash, with vine-patterned wallpaper above the cabinets.

I couldn't help but wonder if the good doctor had done the decorating himself.

I rounded the northwest corner of the house and saw a man dressed in Wrangler jeans, worn cowboy boots, long-sleeved, dirty, blue work shirt, and cowboy hat. He was tall, with long legs and a lean frame, fit from physical labor. He saw me as he crossed the road from the barn to the garage. He was clearly surprised to find me here.

"Can I help you?" He veered off toward me, his legs eating up the distance in easy strides.

I took a wild guess there was no way this guy was Dr. Adam Galvin.

"I'm Zoe Grey, a private investigator from Fort Collins," I said, continuing toward him.

He glanced from me to the dog and back again. He didn't seem the least bothered by Dasch, and Dasch had no issue with him. "Long way from home, aren't you?"

He had a casual, self-assured way about him I found myself liking. He pushed the brim of his hat up, wiped at his forehead with his sleeve, and pulled the hat back down. His brown hair was wet with sweat. I didn't know what color his eyes were behind his sunglasses.

"I'm actually investigating a woman who used to live around here. Karen Brickle. Know her?"

He stopped a few feet from me and shook his head. "Doesn't ring a bell. This house belongs to Dr. Galvin. No woman has ever lived here so long as I've been here, which is about four years now."

I pulled up a picture on my phone, one I'd saved from Brickle's Facebook page. "Does she look familiar?"

He pulled his shades off and slipped them onto the brim of his hat in a practiced gesture. As he studied the photos, I saw his eyes were coffee brown.

"Sure," he said. "I saw her around here a couple times. Been a while, though."

"Do you know why she was here, or the nature of her relationship with Galvin?"

"No. But then, I make it a point to have as little interaction with Galvin as possible." There was an edge to his voice.

"The good doctor isn't a good boss?"

"If you don't mind my saying so, the man's a royal prick. Only reason I stay is he pays well, pays on time, and doesn't charge me to board my horses here. But we don't socialize. I do my work, and he doesn't bother me."

"Sounds generous. That kind of goes against the picture I've been forming of him."

He shrugged, but the casualness of it was forced. "I don't know what to tell you."

"It's not generosity, is it?" I saw the answer flash on his face. "What is it? Why does the man pay you so well? Something tells me he's the kind of guy who would only pay so well if his own ass was on the line."

Bingo.

He clamped his hands on his hips and looked down at the grass.

"Is he paying to keep you quiet? Or compliant?"

"Look, it happened a while ago." He was obviously upset at the memory.

"What did?"

He heaved a sigh, glancing up at the house. "There was a maid here when I first started, her name was Yolanda. She was young, and here illegally, I learned. Galvin always seemed to pay her a little too much attention, you know? Then one night, one of the horses started acting up, carrying on in his stall. I went down to check on him and found him stomping around, banging against the door. He was starting to get the others riled up. And then I heard the scream.

"I ran out of the barn, to the house. I went to the back door, which is almost always unlocked. I saw through the windows Galvin had Yolanda pinned against the counter and he was ripping at her clothes. She was screaming, crying, trying to fight him off, but she was much smaller than he was.

"I ran in and grabbed him around the neck, threw him halfway across the room. He was drunk; he reeked of whiskey. He crashed into this really fancy china hutch that used to be in the kitchen, cut himself up pretty bad on the glass, destroyed a bunch of antiques, or so he claims.

"Anyway, the crash seemed to sober him a little. He hurried out of the kitchen and then left. I probably shouldn't have let him drive, drunk as he was, but I just wanted him gone. I tried to get Yolanda to go to the police, but she wouldn't, because she was afraid they would deport her. So I got her hooked up with my sister, down in Oklahoma. She'd been wanting a nanny, and Yolanda couldn't stay here.

"The next day, Galvin came home, swept up the mess in the kitchen and carried the broken hutch to the trash. He never asked where Yolanda was, if she was coming back. But that next night he came to me, told me he had adjusted my salary, given me a raise, and dropped the boarding fee. He never said as much, but I knew it was in exchange for keeping my mouth shut.

"Normally, something like that wouldn't sit well with me. The only reason I haven't said anything is because Yolanda flat out refused to report it, and she was gone two days later. So I stay, investing all the money he pays me with my brother, who's pretty good with numbers, and I keep an eye on the way he acts toward the female staff. All the maids since Yolanda have been much older, though, like forties or fifties. I figured he didn't trust himself. I don't trust him either."

That was not the kind of thing I'd been expecting to learn about Galvin, and it cast him in a decidedly suspicious light. Rape was no small matter. And men who could commit rape tended to have an overdeveloped sense of entitlement. Men who believed they were entitled to whatever they wanted were dangerous, in more ways than one.

"So the pay isn't the only reason you stay," I said.

"No. Actually, my investments have done really well. A part of me, a big part, is ready to leave here, buy my own place. But the timing doesn't feel right yet. I care about Cindy, the maid he's got now. He hasn't even so much as looked at her sideways, but I don't know if that's because he wouldn't touch her or if it's because I'm here and he doesn't dare touch her."

"That's noble," I said. And meant it. Not many people would have done what this one had. "But how long are you going to stay? You can't act as protector to all those in Galvin's life for the rest of yours."

He shrugged. "I don't think I'll have to. Guys like him, they always fuck up—excuse my language. If his dick don't bring him down some day, his ego will. He's got plenty of money, and his hands in lots of pockets, but eventually, he'll get into something he can't buy his way out of."

"You have phenomenal faith in our system."

"No, I just have faith."

Geez. I'd managed to find one of the last decent men on Earth. I should probably buy a lottery ticket on the way home.

"I didn't catch your name."

He offered his hand. "Travis Tidwell."

"Nice to meet you, Travis. Do you know, was Cindy working here whenever Karen Brickle would have come around?"

"The lady in the photo?"

278

"Yes."

"Well, let's see. Probably. Cindy's been here about a year. Year's about all the longer they last in there with him, even though he isn't here much."

"Is Cindy here now?"

"No, I saw her leave about an hour ago. Gone to the grocery store or for other errands in town, I'd guess."

"Anyone else work here?"

"No, just the two of us."

"Does Galvin have any other regular visitors?"

A shrug. "Not really. Well, a couple folks make use of the helicopter, but they don't ever go in the house. Why? What's Galvin done?"

"I don't know, but he's connected to a woman I'm investigating. That helicopter get a lot of use?"

"Yeah, damn near every day."

"Does Galvin fly it?"

"No. I usually see the same guy come get it or drop it off. Ex-military looking guy, you know, buzz cut, muscles, a frown."

I nodded. "I know the type. Why's a guy like Galvin have a helicopter at all?"

"Reason he gave when he bought it was that it made going to his place up in Allenspark easier. It's about an hour's drive, and some of the roads suck. It's about twenty minutes or so by air. But he doesn't spend as much time up there as the use of the chopper would suggest. So I have no idea what they're using it for. Like I said, I pretty much keep out of his business."

"You ever been up to his place in Allenspark?"

"No. None of the maids ever go up there, either. But I don't imagine he cleans or cooks for himself up there, so I've always assumed he pays someone local to keep it up."

"Travis," I said, offering him my hand. "You've been a big help. Thank you for talking to   me."

He squeezed my hand and looked at me. "Is Galvin into something illegal?"

I thought for a beat. "I have no proof of that whatsoever . . . but my gut tells me yes."

He accepted that answer, and I moved around him. His voice turned me back.

"I let him get away with something once; I don't want to see him get away with anything else. If you need anything from me, if I can help in anyway, you let me know."

41

It was three thirty when I parked in the lot outside Boulder High School. The place was crawling with kids sporting all the latest statements in fashion and coolness. There were groups of kids gathered around various cars in the parking lot, others along the sidewalk outside the school. A few teachers and a uniformed school resource officer also stood out front, chatting to students, parents, or one another.

Geez. I did not miss high school. I hadn't been suited to high school, and had graduated early, but I'd hated what I'd experienced of it. The cliques and the rumors and the bullies and the kids far more interested in who was doing what to whom than anything any teacher had to say—it was cruel and unusual.

With so many kids around, I didn't want to leave Dasch in the Jeep. I trusted him fine, but I didn't trust a bunch of teenagers with so many hormones soaking their brains they shorted out on logical thinking. The last thing I needed was one of them reaching in to pet the pretty dog and getting their hand bitten off. But I didn't think the school resource officer would just let me waltz into the building with the dog, even if I put the leash on him.

I wished I had something to identify Dasch as a working or service dog. I'd have to work on that.

In the meantime, I would need to resort to subterfuge.

I scratched Dasch's ear. "You remember your hand signals?" I asked him, a vague plan forming in my mind.

His tongue lolled out of his mouth as he leaned into my scratch.

I got out, Dasch jumping down after me. I skirted the parking lot to the far edge and approached the building entrance away from and slightly behind the cluster of teachers, whom the school resource officer was now talking with. I stopped, told Dasch to sit, then gave him a hand signal to wait.

Before I could even take another step, glass shattered somewhere to the right, followed by a shout of, "Oh, shit!" It drew the attention of everyone in the immediate area, including all of the teachers and the officer. The officer honed in on the culprits immediately, a group of boys gathered around a Honda Civic with a busted driver's side window. One of the boys was holding a homemade slim jim and looked equal parts confused and surprised.

"Whoops," I muttered, striding for the front door. "Not as easy as it looks on YouTube."

I waved Dasch forward, and he was immediately at my left heel.

Inside, only a few straggling students remained, leaving the hallways almost eerily quiet. I found the front office and went inside.

Several of the chairs were occupied and the receptionist, who looked as stern as she did loving, was on the phone at her desk. I'd spent a fair amount of my own time sitting in chairs like these, waiting to talk to the principal or the vice principal or the school resource officer.

Two of the kids were obviously a couple, sitting so close they were practically on top of one another, their foreheads together, their hands entwined, whispering incessantly to one another about who knew what. There was a trio of boys who had dressed up as gangsters that morning, all baggy pants, dark hoodies, and bad attitudes. Two of the other students who were sitting alone, one boy and one girl, looked fairly normal, and very nervous. I had a bit of fun imagining what they might have been in trouble for. Finally, there was a very nerdy kid sitting as far removed from the others as possible, his heavy backpack on the floor at his feet, a book open on his lap. He wore glasses, a button-down shirt, khakis, and he was bent over the book, a pencil between his teeth.

The receptionist concluded her call and glared at the couple, who were millimeters from making out.

"Would you two give it a rest?" She sounded weary. "Why do you think you're here in the first place? Sit up, both of you."

They reluctantly complied, like two magnets struggling to pull apart. It was obvious whatever space they'd gained would be gone again within a few minutes. Ah, to be a teenager again.

The receptionist smiled at me and flicked a glance at Dasch. "Good afternoon."

She really was very pretty, kind of plain, but pretty.

"Hi," I said, returning her smile. When I stopped at her desk, Dasch immediately plopped down to sit beside me. This earned an impressed look from the receptionist. "I'm looking for Cynthia Moore. I understand she's a teacher here."

"Yes, she is." If the receptionist found any of this strange, she gave no indication. "She's—"

The phone rang, cutting her off.

"Oh." She looked at it, then quickly glanced around the room, eyes settling on the nerdy kid reading a book. "Tommy! Would you please show this woman to Ms. Moore's classroom? Then come right back, please. I'll keep an eye on your backpack."

The kid stood and looked at his bag, as if he was reluctant to leave it. Then he made his way over to me, clutching his book, which I now saw was Stephen King's latest, checked out from the library. The boy glanced from me to the dog then back.

"This way," he said, moving toward the door.

283

The receptionist was busy on the phone again and paid us no attention as we left.

Tommy looked a little young for high school, but he didn't carry himself like a kid, and I guessed he had some serious weight on his still-narrow shoulders. My heart went out to him; I knew better than most what that was like.

"So, what are you in for?" I asked.

"Fighting." His tone was flat, matter of fact.

"Someone picking on you?"

He glanced up at me, surprised in my instant understanding. "What makes you think I'm not the bully?"

I couldn't help but smile. I liked this kid. "Can I tell you something?"

He rolled his eyes. "Is this more trust-me-I'm-an-adult life advice?"

"Fuck no." This time my language surprised him, and he looked up at me again. "What good would that do you? This is a true story."

He shrugged, trying to play indifferent, but I could tell he was really paying attention. "Fine. Tell me."

"I went to high school with a kid named Gary. Gary was four years younger than everyone else because he was so smart he'd skipped a bunch of grades. All the 'cool kids' used to pick on Gary, because he had tape on his glasses and his pants were always too short and sometimes he'd forget to comb his hair. You know how the 'cool kids' are."

He bobbed his head, even as he reached up to smooth his hair. "Yeah." He voice was sullen.

"Anyway, Gary was so smart, and he worked so hard, he finished high school in about half the time. He was good with computers, really good. He could do anything with a computer. After high school, he got a job with a really big computer company in California called Google. Maybe you've heard of it." By now he was watching me, and his eyes got big. "He worked there for a couple years, then he started his own company. Now, he's a multi-millionaire. He lives in a mansion, drives an Aston Martin, and has his own airplane. You know where the cool kids are now?" He shook his head. "Nowhere. They're in the same town, working the same dead-end jobs, fighting with their wives and husbands because they don't really like each other and only got married because they were pregnant."

He stopped outside a closed classroom door. "That's a true story?" His skepticism was obvious, but underneath it was unmistakable hope.

I raised my hand. "Hand to God, it's a true story. Gary was a pretty cool guy; he was a friend of mine. He used to help me with some of my homework and I used to teach him some self-defense stuff. He got picked on pretty bad. Kids can be very mean. But all this shit here," I waved a hand around the building, "high school, it doesn't last. It feels like it will never end, but it does, and then it's over forever. And believe me when I say it's the nerdy kids who go places. The cool kids peak in high school; high school is all they'll ever have."

He grinned. "Really?"

"Cold, hard truth, kid."

He eyed me. "You're not like any adult I've ever met."

"I'll take that as a serious compliment."

He sighed. "It's too bad you can't teach me some self-defense stuff."

He pulled up his shirt and showed me a nasty darkening bruise on his ribs. I felt my gut tighten even as my blood ran hotter. I couldn't tolerate innocents being hurt; nothing in the world made me angrier. It was a good thing whoever had put that bruise on Tommy wasn't standing nearby.

I pulled a card from my pocket and handed it to him. "You ever get up to Fort Collins?"

"Yeah," he said eagerly. "My dad lives up there."

"You call me. My best friend teaches karate at a dojo there. We'll set you up for classes or private lessons, whatever it takes. If your dad says no, you call me, and I'll come have a conversation with him." I pointed at his ribs. "That's going to stop."

"What about this weekend?"

"You're on. Now, listen, when you go back to the principal's office, you be sure to show her that bruise. Tell her the truth about what happened."

"She won't believe me," he said, crestfallen. "The other kids said I started it."

"Kiddo, unless your principal is a total idiot, there is no way she's going to believe that story."

He looked at the card again. "Is this your cell phone?"

I pulled the phone from my pocket. "It is. And I always have it with me." I tucked the phone away. "Listen, Tommy, high school fucking sucks. It just does. But I'll help you get these bullies off your back. And then it'll just suck, it won't hurt." I offered him my hand. "Sound like a deal?"

He shook my hand. "Deal."

"You better get back to the office before they think you skipped out. Put some ice on those ribs when you get home, and take some Ibuprofen. That'll help. I'll plan to see you this weekend."

He tucked the card safely into his pocket. "I don't have one of those uniforms or anything. I've never done karate before."

"I'll take care of that."

Before he left, he gave Dasch's head a pet and I got his dad's name and address. At the end of the hall, he looked back and waved at me. I waved back. Then he disappeared around the corner.

"Okay," I murmured to myself as I knocked on the classroom door. "Enough saving the world. Now to business."

A woman working at a desk on the far side of the room waved me in through the window even as she stood and came over. I pushed the door open and went in, Dasch at my heel. The woman faltered slightly at the sight of the dog, but recovered quickly.

"Hello."

"Hi," I said, smiling. "Sorry to bother you. My name's Zoe Grey. I'm a private investigator from Fort Collins. I have a few questions for you."

"Oh." She was surprised, and then guarded. "What about?"

"Actually, I wanted to ask you about Theresa."

"Did someone hire you to look into her case?"

I nodded. "Indirectly, yes. I understand you're a good friend of hers."

She softened at that, but only slightly. "Yes. We're very close."

"You must miss her."

Tears swelled in her eyes. She turned and walked back to the desk, plucking a tissue from the box and wiping at them. "I do. At first, all I wanted was for her to come back, you know, but now . . . Now I just want to know what happened."

"Please, let's sit down." I indicated the chair behind the desk and pulled the nearest desk a bit closer. I slid into it, the Browning at my back uncomfortable against the hard plastic of the chair.

Cynthia Moore took up her seat again then eyed me across the desk. "What are you investigating, if it isn't Terri's disappearance?"

"Were you ever aware of Terri's neighbor, Karen Brickle?"

"Sure. Terri mentioned her a couple times, and I saw her occasionally when I was at Terri's house. Why? What'd she do?"

287

"Honestly, I'm not sure yet. But I was hired to investigate her. The thing is, in the course of that investigation, Terri's name and her disappearance keep coming up."

"You think they're connected?"

"I think I want to know for sure, one way or the other. What do you know about Karen?"

Moore shrugged. "Nothing really. Terri mentioned her in passing, just comments about her strange hours or strange visitors, things like that."

"Did you ever see anything strange when you were over there?"

She shook her head. "No. I'd just see her coming or going from her house. I remember having the distinct impression the woman was a bit weird, but that was it. I couldn't even really tell you why; it was just a feeling."

"Around the time of Terri's disappearance, had she mentioned anything about her neighbor?"

She thought about that, a slight frown of concentration on her mouth. "No, I don't think so. Not that I recall."

"Around that time, had Terri changed at all? Was there anything different about her?"

"The police already asked these questions."

"Hang with me, please, Ms. Moore. I think you'll find mine will be a little different."

She sighed but answered anyway. "No, there was nothing different."

"Terri wasn't acting sad or remorseful or wistful? Maybe reminiscing or saying things wouldn't matter anymore? Did she give any of her things away?"

Moore turned sharp eyes on me. "Are you suggesting Terri went missing on purpose?"

I held up a hand. "I'm not saying anything. I'm just asking questions. The police conducted their investigation under the assumption Terri had been abducted, and that led nowhere. Rather than running down that same path, I'm trying others."

"I can't believe Terri would do that."

"Why not?"

"Because of her sons. There are other things too, school, her friends—Terri really loves her life, and I just don't think she could ever leave her sons."

"Let's put that aside for a minute. How was she acting around the time she went missing? Was she reminiscent? Sad? Did she give anything away? Did she ever say something wouldn't matter in the future? Did she ever give you or anyone else any kind of instructions or plans for the future, in case she wasn't around?"

She sucked in a tiny breath and stiffened slightly.

I waited her out, giving time for the memory to solidify in her mind.

She looked at me, eyes a bit wider.

I nodded. "What did you remember?"

"One of her students, he was on a special learning plan. His home life isn't very good, so Terri did a lot of work with him herself. I remember now she made sure I knew about the plan and where it was in her desk. She laughed it off, saying she wanted me to know in case she ever got sick or anything—the kid couldn't afford to miss even a single day. Of course, when she went missing, I took over working with that student." She sat up and leaned forward. "You don't think she knew, do you?"

"When did she show you that?"

"January. We'd just come back from Christmas break. You don't think . . ." I could see the wheels of her mind spinning in overdrive. "If she knew, then . . . she's okay. If she did this herself, then she's okay."

"Whoa." I held up my hand again. "I'm going to caution you about getting too far down that line of thinking. Even if Terri is alive, and after all this time, that's a very big *if*, she is not okay.

289

Whatever she would have been mixed up with that would have caused her to run like that would be too big and too dangerous to say she's okay. Do not get your hopes up, Ms. Moore."

She nodded and swallowed. "You're right, of course."

"Can you think of anything in Terri's life that would have been that big? What could she possibly have been mixed up in?"

"Nothing. And I'm not just saying that. Terri was as kind a person, as straight an arrow as there is. Even to the point of being a little naïve. She was always shocked when one of the students was busted with pot or pills in their bags or lockers."

"Who was Terri seeing around December and January?"

The abrupt change in topic was deliberate, and it worked. I saw surprise flash on her face, and she stared at me with hard eyes.

"I don't know wha—"

"Cut the shit, Ms. Moore." She snapped her mouth shut and watched me, her mind working. "Who was he?"

She started to say something but stopped. After a long beat she asked, "How did you know? Terri kept it quiet, and you're the first one to ask."

"The police didn't ask if Terri had a boyfriend?"

She shrugged a shoulder. "Sure, but they were just asking. They didn't know. You seem to know."

My turn to shrug. "I'm good at this. Who was he?"

"I honestly don't know. Terri never said much about him. I think they met sometime in late November, early December. I don't know how or where. I didn't even know his name."

"Why all the secrecy?"

"I got the impression Terri wanted to keep it from her sons, in case it turned out to be nothing. And I think she was worried it would turn out that way, so she was trying to keep herself from becoming too excited, you know what I mean?"

I nodded. "She liked him."

"I think so, yes. And she was either unsure of his feelings or maybe there was something else in the way."

I eyed her carefully. She was now playing with a pencil. "Like maybe he was married?"

"Well, what other explanation could there be?" She was almost defensive now. "But I can't understand how Terri could be involved with a married man. She's very . . . I don't know, proper."

"Her ex-husband said she'd changed after the divorce. Not dramatically, but enough to be noticeable. And lonely people will justify lots of things to themselves."

Moore dropped the pencil. "I don't know that she was lonely. Her marriage to Frank had never been wonderful. They were great parents, but terrible spouses. After the divorce, she told me she felt free. I think she enjoyed that freedom. I never got the feeling she was looking to settle down again, and she had male company. Nothing overly serious, but dates and dinners here and there."

"So you didn't notice she was different after her divorce?"

"Well, sure. She was more . . . I don't know, adventurous might be a good word. She wanted to try new things and go new places. Like I said, she felt free—*unchained* was the word she used once. To Frank, I'm sure that did look very different. To me, I thought it looked healthy."

"Okay, so if she was feeling adventurous, it's not outside the realm of possibility she was seeing a married man. There's nothing more exhilarating than the chance of being caught, or so I'm told."

"I just don't see it. Adventurous, yes, but still proper. I mean, Terri's kind of old fashioned. She thinks making out is for couples going steady and that sex is for married people only. You know? I really can't see her with a married man. Actually, I can't imagine her sleeping with anyone, so then, what other

291

interest would a married man have? The whole thing never made any sense to me. But she wouldn't talk to me about it."

"Was that unusual?"

"Yes, and no. Terri's pretty private about the deep stuff. We've been friends a long time, and she confides a lot in me, maybe more than most, but she's still private. Still, I always did feel she was hiding something about the guy."

"Why didn't you mention this guy to the police? Did you never suspect he could have had something to do with her disappearance?"

"Of course I did," she said, overtly defensive now. "But . . . I never brought it up because . . . I thought maybe he was a cop."

My brain spun off instantly as the full implication of that struck me. "Why did you think that?"

She shrugged and picked up the pencil again. "It was something she said once, about the guy carrying a gun. Then she said it was for work and that she didn't want to talk about it anymore. Terri hates guns."

"Cops aren't the only ones who carry guns for work."

"I know. But that was just what popped into my head, and it kind of stuck. So when the cops came around after she'd gone missing, how was I to know I wasn't talking to the one she'd been seeing? What if he was the one who did it? I know it's cowardly, but I thought it best if no one knew I'd known about him. Plus, I thought maybe the cops would look harder if they didn't have a boyfriend to focus on, you know?"

It was twisted, broken logic, and it may well have crippled the investigation into Theresa Walling's disappearance. But I didn't say any of this. Because I was sharing one of Cynthia Moore's thoughts: how did I know I hadn't been talking to the cop Theresa had been dating?

42

I'm a suspicious person, always have been. That's the natural result of growing up in a home with a physically abusive father and a wildly bipolar mother. So while Clark had seemed on the level with me, I was now thinking he was a pretty attractive guy, he was about Theresa Walling's age, and maybe he knew a little too much about Karen Brickle.

Maybe he had been better at hiding his true thoughts than I'd given him credit for.

Dasch and I sat in the Jeep outside the school, and I dialed Ellmann.

"I'm leaving here in two hours," he said by way of greeting. "Maybe three. When will you be home?"

"I'm not sure. What do you know about your buddy Clark?"

I could feel him slip into cop mode over the airwaves. "Why? What are you working on?"

"I really don't know yet. Nothing makes sense right now. Is he married? How long has he been a cop?"

"Not married, I don't think. No girlfriend, last I knew, but, Zoe, this guy and I went to a SWAT training thing together three years ago; we're not buddies."

"Okay, I understand. Just tell me what you know."

"Well, he does SWAT, or he did. Lifelong cop, with BPD about ten years at the time of the training. Worked the streets, if I remember right—narcotics."

Score one for me. "Here's what I really want to know: is he a stand-up guy?"

Ellmann was quiet for a beat. "I don't know. I really don't know; I barely know the guy. What struck me about him back then was how good he was. He knew how to handle himself, he didn't make rookie mistakes, he didn't even make expert mistakes. And he was cool the whole time, never got flustered or hung up.

"But I also remember thinking he was a typical narc guy. Played things close to the vest, had a tendency to go off on his own, take risks, things like that. Those guys are a different breed of cop; they're hard to read. So, I really can't answer your question. I want to say yes, because he's a cop, and because I like to think cops are stand-up guys. We both know that isn't true.

"Where's all this coming from? Did you pick up on something when you talked to him earlier?"

"No, actually, he came off to me as totally on the up and up. But a witness just said something that's got me thinking. Even if the idea is right, I might have the wrong guy. I just wanted to ask."

"A witness said something to make you suspicious of a cop? Zoe, what are you working on? If you've got bad cops in the mix, you shouldn't be out there on your own on this anymore."

"I know, but I'm not quite there yet. I'll bring you in as soon as I know something. Promise."

"I trust you," he said. "Please don't push whatever you've got until it's too late to avoid an explosion."

"I won't. At least, not intentionally." I wished I could offer better, but he and I both knew I couldn't.

"Okay. Now, when will you be home?"

I smiled. "I've got a couple more people to see down here then I'm headed back. I think I'll be home by eight."

"I'll hold you to that."

I was still smiling as I used my phone to look up Charles Thompson and Andrew Miller, the two people Roger Hicks had mentioned Karen Brickle had seemed chummy with. Not surprisingly, neither man was listed in the white pages. Andrew Miller owned property, however, and I mapped the address.

It was a short drive to Miller's place, which was a stunning, remodeled house in what I judged to be one of the oldest parts of Boulder. I wondered again how much EMTs made these days.

I parked on the street in front of the house and told Dasch to wait in the car. I let myself in through the scrollwork wrought iron fence and walked to the front door through the landscaped front yard. The place was gorgeous.

I rang the bell and stepped aside to wait. There was a Land Rover in the driveway, so I guessed someone was home. Land Rovers were pretty expensive, too.

The door opened and a tall, well-muscled man looked out. He was in his late twenties, had short dark hair, brown eyes, and was dressed like an Abercrombie & Fitch model.

"Yeah?"

"I'm looking for Andrew Miller." I saw his answer on his face before he brought up his guard and hit me with a head-on defense.

"And who the fuck are you?" he snapped, surging out of the house toward me.

I was no stranger to confrontation, and this guy didn't scare me. So I didn't plan to move, but I heard Dasch give a dark growl of warning, and knew without looking he was out of the car.

I'd barely had the thought when I heard his claws on sidewalk. Miller looked over my shoulder, his eyes going wide with fear.

I stepped back and put a hand out. "Dasch! *Anhalten! Fuss!*"

Dasch launched himself onto the porch, but slid to a stop, plopping down at my left heel. His eyes were fixed on Miller, and for the first time, his tail wasn't wagging. That single detail caused a wave of unease to roll through me.

"What the fuck is that thing?" Miller demanded.

"Guard dog," I said. "Now, Mr. Miller, would you kindly answer a few questions for me? I'd like to know why you don't work at the hospital anymore."

He turned his dark eyes to me. "What's it to you?"

"I'm a private investigator." I'd repeated that lie so many times now I was starting to believe it myself. "I'm looking into a couple things, and your name came up. So, why'd you quit? Or were you fired?"

The anger was back, flaring in his dark eyes. Dasch rumbled a low growl. "I wasn't fired, okay? Whoever said that is fucking lying. I work for the ambulance now. Got tired of the ER."

"You seen your pal Karen lately?"

The anger was still there, but underneath it, I saw a flash of something else—fear.

"I don't know who you're talking about."

"Karen Brickle. Way I hear it, the two of you used to pal around. Close, someone said."

He raised a finger and jabbed it at me, dark eyes burning. Dasch jumped up, growling. I stilled him with a hand signal, and I held Miller's gaze.

"Another fucking lie," he said, his tone dark, threatening. "Whoever you've been talking to is full of shit. Bad source . . . copper." His left hand tapped the badge on my belt through my shirt. How he'd even seen it in the first place, I didn't know.

And I didn't try to correct him.

Dasch was growling incessantly now, body ridged, ready to pounce.

I grinned at Miller, giving him my best I'm-on-to-you smirk. "I'll be in touch."

I backed toward the stairs. "Dasch, *zurück.*" He crept backward, still watching Miller like a hawk. I went down the stairs and called Dasch off. "*Hierr. Fuss.*" He readily complied, but he never looked away from Miller long.

When we were off the porch, Miller smirked. And glared. Then he went back in the house.

Dasch and I climbed into the Jeep.

"Holy shit," I said, letting out a breath I'd been holding. "What the fuck was that?"

Dasch didn't answer, he just leaned over and licked my face.

"I'm okay," I told him, scratching his ear. "You did good. Good boy. *Bravy.*"

But I thought I'd finally stumbled onto a corner piece of the puzzle. Andrew Miller was worked up about something. I just needed to figure out what it was.

I started the Jeep and pulled away from the curb. I needed to do some serious digging into Andrew Miller.

I'd just left Miller's neighborhood when my phone chimed. It was a text from Olvera.

You've got mail.

It was about time. At the next stoplight, I opened my email and saw two from Olvera. I'd have to look at them when I got home. I was tucking the phone away when it rang. This time it was Sadie.

"You know how you asked me for some names of Jimmy's ex-girlfriends?"

"Yeah. You got a few for me?"

"Better. I just ran into one of them downtown. I mentioned Jimmy's name and she started saying some pretty interesting things. You're going to want to hear them. Where are you?"

"Boulder," I said, thinking. "Uh, headed back now. It'll take me an hour."

"Fine. We're at Zquila."

I'd have to come back to Boulder later, probably tomorrow. And maybe that was for the best. It would give me time to learn more about Andrew Miller and locate Charles Thompson. Miller was worried about something, and Roger Hicks had said it always seemed like Brickle, Miller, and Thompson were up to something. After meeting Miller, I was very keen to chat with Thompson.

43

Zquila in Old Town was located on the west side of College, north of Olive. Given the time of day, I didn't even bother looking for a spot on the street. Instead, I went around to the back of the building and parked in the public lot on Remington. I told Dasch to stay put, and went inside.

The place was crowded, with a line of people waiting to be seated. I spied Sadie in a booth and slipped past the busy hostess.

Sadie was looking lovely with her blonde hair curled, dressed in jeans, brown knee-high boots, and a cute, navy blue top. She had several shopping bags beside her. Her companion was a knockout in her own right. She was on the shorter side, with sleek, shiny, perfectly highlighted brown hair cut in a shoulder-length bob. She had big, light brown eyes, and absolutely flawless skin. She wore a sleeveless summer dress, a jean jacket on the bench beside her.

"Ashley, meet my friend Zoe Grey. Zoe, this is Ashley Ringle."

I offered my hand to the woman, who was probably about twenty-five, my age, but she seemed younger somehow. She seemed surprised by my gesture, but grasped my hand with a flash of her gorgeous smile.

"Nice to meet you," I said, sliding in beside Sadie.

The remnants of their meal were still on the table, and I snagged a chip. I remembered now I hadn't eaten lunch.

"You, too. Sadie says you're a private investigator."

Why stop lying now?

"That's right. Sadie tells me you know James Ward."

Ringle rolled her eyes and reached for her margarita. "Unfortunately, yes."

Her glass was half-full, but I guessed it wasn't her first.

"Why unfortunately?"

"Guy's a dick. Total player."

"So you weren't the only one?"

"No. I mean, I knew he sort of had a reputation before we got together, so I guess it's my own fault, but I believed him when he said I was the only one." She shook her head. "Naïve, right?"

It was. "No," I said. "Hopeful."

She scoffed. "That's sweet. But this is real life. In real life, he gave me the clap and slept with my roommate—in *my* bed. Then he dumped me, if you can believe that. I didn't even have the satisfaction of dumping him. I only got to kick my roommate's skank ass out of my house, but that just didn't feel like enough."

"On the bright side," Sadie put in, "he probably gave her the clap, too."

"Unless she gave him something worse," Ringle said, shuttering. "I got a new mattress. Bitch was a skank."

"Well, then," Sadie said, reaching for her own drink, "he's still a grown ass man going by the name *Jimmy.*"

Ringle nodded. "True. Should have been a clue." She looked to me again. "Sadie says you want the dirt on Jimmy. He in trouble?"

"He might be. Does Jimmy have dirt?"

Ringle shrugged and leaned back in the booth, her hands in her lap. "I'm not sure. Guy always had money to burn, and that's weird to me. I mean, I'm a nurse; my salary is probably twice what his is, but he lives probably twice as well as I do. Those apartments he lives in, those are super pricey. I can't afford the smallest place they've got; he's got one of the biggest. And he lives alone."

"Did you ever see the apartment?" I asked.

"Sure. We stayed there a lot."

"I've heard there's a rumor Jimmy moves in with his new girlfriends. But he's always had a place of his own. Know what that's about?"

Even before I finished the question, she was waving a hand. "I've heard that rumor, too. I don't know how it got started, but as far as I know, it's bullshit. He would stay over at my place sometimes, but he liked to be at his place. I always thought it was for privacy, since I had two roommates, but now I wonder if it was just because his place was nicer than mine. I don't know. But I've never known him to live with anyone, though he's slept his way through most of the department."

That answered one quandary. "Where's the money coming from, you think? Family money, maybe?"

"Anything's possible, but Jimmy never talked much about his family. I brought up meeting my parents once, and he was totally cool with it, conman that he was, but he never mentioned his parents. When I asked him about it, he said they weren't close. I could tell it was a sore subject, so I didn't push. He never once mentioned a sibling or any other family member."

"Could he have another job on the side?"

I saw something flash on her pretty face. To cover it, she shifted in her seat and reached for her glass. After a long drink, she glanced at Sadie.

"What is it, Ashley?" I pressed. "It's clearly just speculation on your part, and you're not sure about it, but there is something. What is it?"

"I don't know anything for sure," she began, more uncomfortable now as doubt crept in around her mind.

"Listen, honey," Sadie said. "You wanna stick it to that fool of a man, you tell her everything. Then you can sleep easy tonight knowing payback's a bitch."

That clearly appealed to Ringle. Poor, dumb Jimmy had finally screwed over the wrong woman.

"I don't think it was a job," she said to me. "But he was into something."

"Into what?"

"I don't know. But he would be busy two or three nights a week usually—and I don't mean busy with other women. At least, I'm almost positive. He'd always wear his uniform and meet up with his partner, but I don't think they were working."

"Why do you say that?"

"Well, once, toward the end of our relationship, I was talking to my friend Andrea—she's a paramedic—about what a crazy night EMS had had. I remember it was a Monday, and it was one of those nights when Jimmy had told me he was working. Except, when I said something to Andrea, she told me Jimmy and his partner weren't on that night."

I tried to keep my face neutral, which wasn't hard. Most people are bad liars; I'm not. "And you're certain this wasn't about the other women?"

"I did think that at first," she admitted. "But then a couple weeks before we broke up, we were at my place and he got a call in the middle of the night. It was like one or two in the morning, something like that. I don't know who called, and the conversation was short. Mostly all I heard him say was that he didn't have his uniform—it had been his night off. Then he hung up, got dressed, and left. His partner picked him up at my house in an ambulance. He told me he'd be back for his car later." She looked at me. "I don't think they were on duty, but they were using the ambulance. And I think it happened more than once."

Sadie looked at me significantly; I kept my face neutral.

"Okay, here's a question for both of you," I said. "How is it possible these two were able to borrow an ambulance without anyone noticing?"

Ringle glanced at Sadie then said, "I don't think it's possible."

"Let's not overlook the fact that this EMT seems to have more money than he should," Sadie said. "If there is enough money involved, the ambulance use doesn't have to go unnoticed."

That was along my line of thought. "Who's Jimmy's partner?"

"Back then, it was Dominic Weeks," Ringle said. "But they just redid their schedules, and I think he's riding with someone new now." She looked at Sadie. "Do you know?"

Sadie shook her head. "No. Haven't seen him around lately. Guess that's because he's got a new shift."

I looked at Ringle. "Jimmy seem tight with anyone else? Talk about anyone?"

"No, not really. I could never really figure out who his friends were, except Dom; those two are tight. I did sneak a look at his phone once, though. That's how I found out about my roommate."

Sadie grinned. "Ashley, honey, there is more to you than meets the eye." An unmistakable note of pride rang in her tone.

"What else did you see on the phone?" I asked.

"Besides all the texts from girls, most of the texts were either from Dom or some guy named Galvin."

I resisted the urge to sit up straighter, but she did have my attention. "No more to the name?" I asked. "It was just labeled Galvin?"

"Yeah. And I don't know if that's a first name or a last name. Whoever it is, I've never met him."

"What did the messages say?"

"Weird shit like 'delivery tonight' or 'usual time on Thursday' or 'full load Saturday. Tight window.' I mean, what the hell is that supposed to mean?"

I didn't know. "Did you see the number for this Galvin?"

"No."

"What about the messages from women. Did you look at any of them? Were any of them anything beyond flirty?"

"Honestly, I didn't look that closely. I saw the ones from Roxy—my skank roommate—where they talked about fucking in my bed like rabbits and how good it was and making plans to do it again. I was pretty much done after that."

She did her best to hide it, but hurt bloomed in her eyes as she reached for her drink. Whatever kind of loser Jimmy Ward was, Ashley Ringle had had genuine feelings for him, and she'd been seriously hurt when he'd screwed her over. I knew what she was feeling, and I felt bad for her.

"I understand," I said. "Tell you what, when I meet Jimmy, I'll break his nose for you."

She smiled a little at that. "Wouldn't that be nice?" she said.

Sadie chuckled. "No, honey, she's serious."

Ringle looked at me.

I just shrugged. "And I'll make sure no one mentions to him that he should get himself checked for STDs."

Ringle's grin turned wicked. "Awesome."

The waitress buzzed over, a tray of dishes in one hand. With the other she fished the bill out of one of the pockets in her apron. "Anything for you tonight?" she asked me.

"No, thank you."

She set the bill on the table. "I'll be your cashier when you're ready." And she was gone.

Ringle fished in her bag for her wallet, but Sadie plucked up the check. "I've got this, honey. My treat."

"Oh, no, you don't have to do that," Ringle said.

"I want to," Sadie said with a tone of finality I recognized. "It's no consolation for the way that fool Jimmy treated you, but I was happy to commiserate. Next time we get together, I'll tell you what my last boyfriend did to me. It won't make you feel better, but at least you'll know you're not alone and that all men are pigs."

Ringle smiled a little. "Okay, thanks. And thanks for dinner."

"You bet, honey. Thanks for the information."

Ringle looked at me. "You're really going after Jimmy?"

That sounded so gangster movie.

"I'm going to investigate him, yes."

"I hope he fries in hell," she said, gathering her purse and jacket, "but I'd really like it if he rotted in prison first."

"I'll do my best." I handed her a card. "Call me if you think of anything else."

She tucked the card into her purse and slid to the end of the booth. "I need to run. It was nice meeting you, Zoe. I hope you find something."

Sadie and I watched her walk away, drawing the looks of more than a few men she passed. She really was a looker.

"I kind of like her," I said, snagging another chip.

"Me, too. Pretty little thing, isn't she? I happen to know one of the night shift nurses has a serious thing for her. This business with Jimmy is still pretty fresh, but once she's put a little more distance there, I'm going to get them together. He'd be good for her."

I chuckled. "Always playing matchmaker."

"Well, what can I say? We all have talents." She slid a card into the black folder with the bill and set it on the end of the table.

"That was nice of you, by the way," I said, pointing at the bill.

Sadie grinned, her blue eyes blazing. "I'm deducting it from what I paid you."

44

I beat Ellmann home. I fed Dasch dinner and fixed a sandwich for myself. I ate at the bar with my computer open in front of me. I read Olvera's emails. The first was a copy of Stephanie Roman's Colorado driver's license. The Grand Junction address on it matched what I'd seen on her credit report, and the other information was similar to that of Angela Morris and the real Karen Brickle.

According to Sadie, Angela Morris looked vaguely similar to the woman Sadie knew as Karen Brickle. All of this fit with my working theory that Karen was impersonating these other women. And I didn't think it was a coincidence all three of them were nurses, with valid nursing licenses in the State of Colorado; indeed, I thought that, along with their physical descriptions, was why they were chosen. Following that line of reasoning a bit further, I speculated Karen had intended to assume the identity of Stephanie Roman when she'd moved to Fort Collins, and that was why she'd purchased the house with that ID.

I wasn't sure what had gone wrong. Perhaps with the disappearance of Theresa Walling and the subsequent investigation by the police into Karen, she had fled Boulder in something of a hurry, and hadn't been able to get all the pieces of the Stephanie Roman ID in place in time. I didn't know, and maybe it didn't matter.

The second email was the police report Jimmy Ward's name had been associated with, or at least part of it. It was just a scan of the first report of incident. Ward had been one of about fifty men busted when the FCPD hit an illegal poker ring downtown a few years back.

I thought about that for a minute and came up with three possible conclusions. One, Ward was an exceptionally skilled poker player and was using the profits from his illegal gambling to pay for his extravagant lifestyle. Two, Ward had been mixed up in whatever he was up to now for a while, the profits of which allowed him to gamble. Three, Ward's gambling habit made him an ideal participant for whatever he was mixed up in now.

I was leaning toward number three.

I searched Dominic Weeks. He was a paramedic, thirty-one, and living as well as his partner seemed to be. Weeks was unmarried but, according to Facebook, was in a relationship with a nurse who worked for Air Link, the helicopter service associated with the hospital. They lived together, according to their credit reports and DMV records, in a place in Old Town. Pricey real estate.

I ran a credit report on Andrew Miller. There were three, but I found the one I wanted by his expensive Boulder address. His credit was excellent—low balances on his credit cards, on-time payment histories, no more inquiries than would be considered normal, and an ideal debt to income ratio. So just like before, and just like with Jimmy Ward, I wondered where the money was coming from.

From my earlier property search, I knew the place I'd visited was the only property Miller owned. And his name hadn't popped up in connection to anything else—birth, death, or marriage certificates, criminal records, nothing. So I tried Facebook. It was a no-go; his page was totally private.

But my motto was: When the secret-keeper Facebook faileth, turneth to the all-knowing Google. Google didn't yield a whole lot, either. Miller had been featured in the Boulder newspaper in high school as a star athlete (wrestling), and his name came up in an obituary for his grandfather.

I couldn't deny I was bummed; I'd been hoping to find something more, something that would give me some idea what Miller was up to, or something I could use as leverage to pry the guy open.

Frustrated, I pounded Charles Thompson's name into Google. And my frustration melted away.

I opened a story in the *Boulder Daily Camera*, the headline announcing LOCAL MAN KILLED IN CAR CRASH. I learned Charles Thompson, thirty-eight, employed as a security guard with a local company, was killed instantly when his car swerved off the road and plowed into a tree in January. It was a single-car accident, blamed on the icy conditions of the road and that Thompson had been driving too fast. There was also speculation Thompson had been drinking.

As interesting as that was, the article went on to say the police had previously been looking at Thompson as a suspect in the disappearance of a local man named Harvey Kellerman. Kellerman, fifty-five, was an accountant at Seagate Technology and went missing in early December. The police had taken an interest in Thompson, who'd been working security in the ER at Boulder Community Hospital at the time, because he'd been working the night Kellerman had come in for treatment after being struck by a car while on his bicycle. Kellerman's injuries had been relatively minor, but there was speculation the two men had gotten into an argument.

Another missing person, I thought. I wondered if Kellerman had any connection to Theresa Walling.

I typed Harvey Kellerman into Google and got back more newspaper articles. I read those detailing his disappearance and learned he was divorced with three grown children. His live-in girlfriend had reported him missing when he didn't come home from work. The article went on to say he had been

309

at work that day, so he'd been intercepted somewhere on his way home. He'd been on his bike, which he routinely rode to work, even in foul weather, and neither he nor the bike had been found. According to the dates, Kellerman went missing about a week after he'd been treated in the ER.

Nothing else about Kellerman was particularly interesting. He'd had the same job for almost twenty years; he'd been married for almost thirty years; his kids were normal, productive members of society. His ex-wife spoke out when he went missing, addressing the media alongside the new girlfriend, both of them pleading for anyone with information to come forward. He didn't have any debt or obvious bad habits or enemies. He'd lived in Boulder most of his adult life and was an established, well-liked member of the community.

With the information I had access to, I couldn't see an obvious connection to Theresa Walling, which wasn't to say they hadn't run into one another somewhere random, gotten to talking, and hit it off. I didn't think he was her mystery boyfriend, however, because last I checked, accountants didn't carry guns to work. But cops did.

I ran the basic searches on Detective Daniel Clark. His credit report was about what I would expect for a cop, and it didn't look anything like the credit reports I'd seen lately. There was nothing on it to indicate he had more money than cops earned.

I checked public records in Boulder County. There wasn't a marriage certificate, but there was a divorce decree from about eight years ago. I didn't see any birth certificates, either, so either Clark and his ex-wife didn't have kids or else they'd been born somewhere else. I also found Clark owned a house, and I wrote down the address. It was the only piece of property with his name on it, and a bit of searching told me his ex-wife had been the one to move out, later buying a new house with her new husband. Such was the life of cops.

Not surprisingly, Clark didn't have a Facebook page, and there was nothing about him on his wife's. On her page, though,

I saw she had young kids, so young they most likely belonged to the new husband. Nothing popped on a Google search, either. If Clark was Theresa Walling's secret boyfriend, I couldn't find anything to indicate it. There was nothing suspicious about Clark at all, actually.

I thought some more about the gun-toting boyfriend. Cops weren't the only ones to carry guns for work. Military guys did too. And so did some security guards.

I got back on Google and looked up the security company Thompson worked for. Peak Security Services had a website, which outlined the lengthy list of services provided. I imagined some of those services required officers to carry weapons. I knew the security officers working at Poudre Valley Hospital did not carry weapons, however. I debated calling the company to ask questions, but decided against it and dug out my notes. I flipped back and found Roger Hick's home phone number. I crossed my fingers the wife didn't answer, but, probably inevitably, she did.

"Roger Hicks, please," I said, in my most business-like tone, edging all room for refusal out of my voice.

It didn't work. "Who's calling?" Sharp suspicion in her voice.

"Jennifer, from ICU. Is Roger there?"

"All work calls are supposed to go to his cell phone."

What a bitch. I managed to resist the urge to snap at her. "I'm sorry, this is the number I was given. It's kind of urgent. Is he there? Or could you give me his cell phone number?"

She huffed a huge, annoyed sigh. "Hang on," she spat. There was some shuffling and I heard her snap at him, "It's your work. On the *home* phone."

I felt bad for getting the guy in trouble.

"This is Roger," he said a moment later.

"It's Zoe Grey. We spoke earlier this afternoon."

"Oh, sure," he said, obviously wary of his wife. "I remember."

"I'm sorry for the deception. I didn't mean to upset your wife."

He sighed. "Unavoidable. What can I do for you?"

"I just have one question. Do the security guards in your ER carry weapons?"

He chuckled. "Oh, heavens no. There was some talk about them starting to carry Tasers, but that got shut down early for fear of what patients would do if they could get one away from a guard. And, frankly, that was a real possibility."

"That's what I thought."

"What's this about?"

"Following up on some more leads. I looked up Charles Thompson."

"Oh, uh-huh."

"He's dead. Did you know that?"

"Oh, my goodness. I had no idea. What happened?"

"It happened in January. His car went off the road and hit a tree."

"Oh, that's terrible. My gosh . . ."

"I also spoke to Andrew Miller. He says he's working for the ambulance now."

"Oh, really? I didn't know that. A lot of them do that, you know, start in the ER and work until a job on the ambulance opens up. It's hard to get on with EMS—lots of applicants, few openings. Experience helps. Was he helpful?"

"Actually, no. Do you know anything else about him? Did he have a girlfriend, maybe? Or any other friends? Anything would help here."

"Well, let me think . . . If he had a girlfriend, it wasn't in the department, or, at least, I didn't know about it. As far as friends, I don't really recall. I never had any issues with Andy. He was what I call a middle-of-the-way employee; he didn't underperform or excel, so he never made it on to my radar. I'm sorry, I didn't really know him."

"If you think of anything, will you give me a call? It could be important." My call waiting beeped in my ear.

"Of course. Yes."

"Thanks, Mr. Hicks. Again, I'm sorry about getting you in trouble."

"I appreciate that, but like I said, unavoidable."

I hit a button to answer call waiting. It was Ellmann. As soon as I heard his tone of voice, I knew he was in work mode, calling me as a cop.

"What's going on?" I asked.

"You chasing a skip named Ruben Medera?"

"Yeah. He went FTA Thursday; I got his file the same day. Why?"

"How close are you to finding him?"

I thought of the deal I'd made with the man in this very kitchen not twenty-four hours before. "Not very. Guy's a Marine. I don't think he'll be found until he wants to be."

Ellmann sighed, clearly not surprised by that answer. "I need to talk to him."

"Okay. Is he a suspect?"

I heard some shuffling and the sound of a door closing. "My gut tells me no," Ellmann said, his voice low. "But I need to talk to him. You heard about Maria Rodriguez on the news?"

"Sure."

"Medera's her boyfriend."

45

Dasch and I climbed into the Scout and headed out. Instinctively, I knew I was close. The answer was right around the corner, I just needed to turn the right corner.

I drove over to Jimmy Ward's apartment complex. I parked on the street then Dasch and I walked in. I found Ward's building, but none of the door numbers were visible from the street. Dasch and I walked the sidewalk directly in front of his building, and I glanced in at the doors, set well back within the hallways between buildings, under the stairs. Based on the numbers I saw on the first floor, I figured which apartment must be Ward's, located on the third floor. The windows in his place were lit, and I saw a figure walk past what might have been the kitchen window.

There was no good place to sit on the apartment within the complex, with or without a car. Parking within was assigned, and the nearest lawns had poor lines of sight on Ward's place. The best I could say was that Ward's place was on a corner, and the side windows were visible, barely, through the buildings from the street. I returned to the Scout and drove around the complex, parking on the street so I had a distant line of sight on those side windows.

I'd been hoping to search Ward's place. Now I was debating knocking on his door. The only thing holding me back was what to ask. I had no idea what was going on; I only knew Ward was up to something. If I started asking him questions, it would be a fishing expedition. I already regretted the visit I'd paid to Miller. I'd been unprepared, with no clear direction. I'd tipped my hand by going there. I didn't want to do that a second time.

While I sat there, I got out my notepad and a pen. I needed to sort my thoughts, put them in some kind of order so I could start putting them together, connecting the dots. On a blank page, I wrote key names at various increments, drew lines between the names, and wrote the details of the connection. This didn't spark off any cataclysmic revelations, so I flipped to another blank page and wrote key facts. When I got to the part about Brickle stealing blood, I stopped.

Why would she have done that? The only reason to take blood in small tubes like that was for testing. That was why she'd been drawing the patient's blood in the first place; the doctor had ordered tests. But what could Brickle possibly want to test for? And why do it without the patient's knowledge?

Thinking about patients reminded me of Maria Rodriguez, who'd gone missing shortly after being seen in the ER for food poisoning. Then I remembered Julia Webster, also missing, who had also been seen in the ER recently. And Harvey Kellerman, who'd been treated in the ER a week before he'd gone missing.

Had Theresa Walling been to the ER in the weeks leading up to her disappearance?

I continued writing, reviewing what else I knew. Jimmy Ward, Andrew Miller, and Karen Brickle all seemed to have too much money, more money than their professions could account for. Miller and Brickle had been close when she'd worked in Boulder; Brickle and Ward seemed close now. Both Ward and Miller were EMTs working on ambulances. Ward was connected to paramedic Dominic Weeks, who also appeared to be inexplicably wealthy.

Brickle was reportedly dating Dr. Adam Galvin. Galvin was a not so nice guy who likely raped young women. Galvin had an extremely extravagant lifestyle—to the point of ostentatiousness. Perhaps it could be said he also had more money than his profession could account for. And his name had shown up on Jimmy Ward's cell phone.

The messages from Galvin on Ward's cell phone talked about deliveries and dates. Ward's ex-girlfriend said he worked nights somewhere besides the ambulance service, and suggested he and partner Weeks were borrowing the ambulance off duty. How did this all connect? What use could Ward and Weeks have for an ambulance?

It seemed likely the ambulance, if indeed they were borrowing it, had something to do with the deliveries. But why would they need an ambulance for the deliveries? I thought on that for a while and came up with two possibilities. One, it had to do with *what* they were delivering. Two, it had to do with *where* they were delivering. An ambulance could gain entry almost anywhere; bad guys stole emergency vehicles for this very reason all the time.

I added more words to the page: nurse, ER, blood, ambulance, deliveries, EMT, doctor, helicopter, money, missing persons, abducted. Then an idea began to form in the back of my mind, a dark, disturbing thought that came to life slowly, but steadily.

"Fuck," I heard myself mutter a few minutes later. I didn't like the idea, but too easily the pieces began falling into place. "This is not good."

My phone chimed. I dug it from my pocket, assuming it was Ellmann wondering why I wasn't home. Instead, it was a text from Sadie.

Karen called out sick tonight.

I felt my gut twist uncomfortably.

I sat for a while longer, thinking, working things over, trying them from different angles, and trying to decide what to do.

I still hadn't made much progress when my phone rang. This time it was Ellmann.

"Thought you would be home by eight."

I was just about to respond when an ambulance rolled down the street past me. I watched as it stopped at the end of the street and Jimmy Ward, in full EMS uniform, came out and got in the passenger seat.

"Shit."

"What?" Ellmann demanded, his tone suddenly alert, sharp.

I hadn't realized I'd spoken aloud.

"Change of plans," I told him, starting the truck. "I need to check one thing, then I think we need to talk. Stay by the phone."

"Be careful," was all he said.

I let the ambulance turn the corner before I pulled away from the curb, then I stayed well back. The ambulance was easy to spot, easy to follow. As I drove, I dialed the ER and asked for Sadie.

"What's going on?" she asked. "What's Crazy Karen up to?"

"I don't know yet. I need to you to find out if Jimmy Ward is working tonight. It's important."

"Um, sure. It'll be a little strange, but I'll call the EMS supervisor and ask. Maybe I can come up with some plausible reason to be asking."

"Does the shift supervisor have any say over where the extra ambulances are or who might be using them?"

She understood what I was asking, and why. "Maybe. Let me think. I'll ask someone else, one of the medics or somebody on shift. They should know who's on. There's an ambulance coming in now. When they get here, I'll talk to them."

"Try not to raise suspicion, Sadie, but the information's important. And I need it now."

317

She was picking up on my tone now. "Okay," she said quickly. "They have an ETA of less than five minutes. I'll call you right back."

I followed the ambulance to Harmony, where it turned west on to the interstate. It got on I-25 going south, and I was beginning to get an idea where we were headed. I wished I had Ellmann's Jeep.

We'd made it past the Loveland exit when Sadie called back.

"No," she said, "he's not. I'm sort of friendly with the guys that just came in. I asked about Jimmy, if he was on tonight. They told me no. I also found out he's still partnered with Dom Weeks. Neither of them are working tonight."

"Okay. I appreciate it."

"What's going on?"

"I don't have an answer yet, but I will soon. I need to go."

I hung up and dialed Ellmann. He answered on the second ring.

"Ellmann." He'd slipped fully into cop mode.

"I'm going to give you an address. I need you to drive by and see if anyone's home, without going to the door. Then get on the interstate and head south. I'll call you and let you know where to meet me." I gave him Karen Brickle's address. "Bring your gear. Just in case."

I was pretty certain Ward and whoever was driving the ambulance, most likely Dom Weeks, were headed one of two places. And I didn't know which place would be more ideal.

They continued south to Highway 7, exiting and heading east, toward Boulder. I was pretty sure I knew where we were going.

I dialed Ellmann.

"Come to Boulder. Meet me at that Starbucks where I met Clark this morning."

"Copy that," he said.

I made one more call, then tucked my phone in my pocket and tried to focus on what would happen next. I didn't really see a lot of good outcomes.

The ambulance cut through town to the far west side and turned north. About two blocks from the hospital, it slowed and turned into a parking lot. I noted the address of the building. It was familiar.

I backtracked to Starbucks, finding it just as crowded as it had been earlier, the outdoor patio full of people. Ellmann's navy blue, unmarked Dodge Charger was parked across from coffee shop, next to the car wash building at the edge of the gas station lot. The lights were off, but the engine was running. I pulled in and parked crookedly behind him. We both got out and met at the trunk of his car.

"No one was home," he said, crossing his arms over his chest as he leaned against the car. He was dressed in his SWAT uniform, minus all the gear. "No lights on anywhere. Whose place was that?"

"The name she's using is Karen Brickle. I don't know her real name."

"Is that what Sadie asked you to look into?"

"Yes. Karen's supposed to be at work, but she called in sick."

He considered that a beat. "She could have been home, sick in bed, I suppose."

"I don't think so. We need to talk to Clark. And if I'm right, we're seriously running out of time."

Ellmann stood up. "Then let's go."

46

We rode in Ellmann's car, Dasch in the backseat. On the drive, which turned out to be rather short, I filled Ellmann in, painting my theory in broad strokes. He asked questions, but he didn't interrupt. When I'd finished, he shot me a glance.

"That's a hell of a theory."

"But it fits," I said grimly. "Too well."

"Yes, it does. And I learned early not to doubt you. So let's play this out."

Ellmann turned into Clark's neighborhood, which was older, and slightly rundown. Still, there were bikes and toys in almost every yard, minivans in a lot of the driveways, kids riding bikes in the streets.

Clark's house looked a bit shabbier than its neighbors. Most likely because Clark didn't spend a lot of time here. But he was here now; his unmarked, department-issue sedan was parked in the driveway. A crappy beige Chevy Caprice.

"I was a little suspicious after our conversation earlier," Ellmann said. "So I did a little looking into Clark. I didn't find anything, Zoe."

I nodded. "I know. Same for me. It looks like he's playing straight, but we need to be sure."

"How do you want to do this?" he asked as he parked at the curb.

"I need to see his face when I ask him some very pointed questions. We'll go from there."

We both got out and I opened the door for Dasch, who hopped down.

"And if he's dirty?" Ellmann asked as we walked to the front door.

"Then I hope he doesn't try to kill us."

He eyed me. "You know I had other plans for tonight."

"Yeah, I do." I rang the bell. "And that would have been way more fun."

A minute later, Clark opened the door, obviously surprised and confused to see me standing on his doorstep. He pushed the screen door open, looking from me to Ellmann to the dog.

"What's going on?"

He was dressed in basketball shorts, tennis shoes, and a cutoff T-shirt. The shirt was sweaty, and he'd clearly just come from a workout. Jazz music flowed out the door around him, soft and smooth, but moody.

"We need to have a word, Clark. Right now."

He looked at me. He must have seen something in my face because he stepped back. "Come in."

The living room was sparsely furnished with what I guessed were thrift store finds. If he'd ever had anything nicer, the ex had probably taken it when she'd left. The only thing worth anything was the stereo system on a crappy particleboard cabinet against the wall. The shelves of the cabinet were lined with what must have been hundreds of CDs. Beside it, on a spindly-legged table, was an old record player. On another wall, there were two six-foot bookshelves stuffed with records.

Clark stood in the middle of the room, hands on hips, eying us as we came in. Clark didn't offer us seats. There wasn't enough seating for all three of us, anyway.

"What's this about?" he asked.

"Theresa Walling," I said, watching him closely.

"I don't think so," he said. "That wouldn't bring you to my house."

"Theresa Walling was seeing someone," I said. "She kept it quiet, didn't even really tell her best friend anything, but there was someone. A cop."

Clark just stared at me. "So?"

"Let me run a theory past you," I said. "Theresa meets a man around late November, early December. She likes the guy, but she's sort of new to the dating world, after being married for so long. She decides to keep the relationship private, away from her sons. She doesn't want to introduce the guy to her kids if nothing's going to come of it. But not too far into that relationship, she witnesses something at her next-door neighbor's house, something that scares her.

"Her boyfriend's a cop. Maybe she tells him about what she saw. The boyfriend starts investigating, but the case isn't so cut and dried, evidence is hard to come by. Meantime, the neighbor figures out Theresa knows something, maybe even that she tipped the cops. Now Theresa's in danger. The cop boyfriend helps her out, either helping her fall off the grid himself or maybe putting her in witness protection.

"Now Theresa's missing, and the spotlight's on her. The neighbor has to get out of town before things get too much hotter. Which just leaves the boyfriend, investigating a bogus missing persons case."

Clark stared at me. "You think I'm the boyfriend?" He was stunned, and it was genuine. "What the fuck gave you that idea?"

"You've been looking into Theresa Walling's case for six months and come up with jackshit. I've been looking into her case for four days and I've got a pretty good idea what happened to her. Why didn't you make any progress on her case, Clark? Unless you didn't want it to go anywhere?"

He was angry now, and he took a step forward.

Dasch, who had been sitting beside me, leaning against my leg, immediately stood up and growled.

The sound drew Clark up short. "This is your fucking theory?" he spat at me. "That some mystery cop boyfriend helped Theresa disappear? Are you fucking kidding me? Do you actually have any proof of this? Something besides the fucking mascara?"

"I've got you," I said. "The cop with a reputation for being a good investigator who came up with nothing on her case."

"I don't believe this!" He glared at me then looked to Ellmann. "You believe this?" His indignation was real, and I saw nothing underneath it—no fear, no guilt.

Ellmann shrugged. "I think she's got some pretty good questions, Clark. If you have anything to say, best just come clean now."

"Come cl—There's nothing to come clean about. I never even heard of the woman until the missing persons report landed on my desk. And I never got anywhere on the case because there wasn't shit for evidence. And because within three days, I had four more cases on my desk, and more after that. They never stop coming, and the sad truth is, when we can't make any solid progress on a case, we've got to put it aside and work on the ones we can.

"So I have no idea what kind of crazy theory you're working on here, but it's bullshit. If you just came here to make wild accusations and insult me and my work ethic, you can get the fuck out."

I believed him. Nothing had changed in his face or eyes; he wasn't hiding anything. He wasn't lying.

I let out a breath. "Thank God for that," I said, nodding at Ellmann. "Now, then, let's get down to work. We don't have much time."

Clark blinked at me, obviously confused in my abrupt change in behavior. "What the fuck are you talking about?" His tone was exasperated.

"Organ harvesting."

47

Clark blinked at me some more. "What?"

As we stood in his almost barren living room, the jazz playing on the stereo was almost too loud and too cheerful.

The anger and aggression had gone out of Clark, replaced with stunned surprise and confusion. I scratched Dasch's head and told him to sit. He did.

"Here's the short version," I said. "I believe Karen Brickle and her boyfriend doctor, Adam Galvin, are abducting folks and harvesting their organs. I think a Boulder EMT named Andrew Miller and two Fort Collins EMTs named Jimmy Ward and Dom Weeks are transporting the organs once they've been harvested."

Clark was struggling to catch up now, to put the pieces together. "Karen Brickle's impersonating a nurse."

"And not for the first time," I said. "I think she might actually be a nurse, but for whatever reason, she can't use her real credentials. There may be discipline or complaints against it, who knows. I believe she's using her position in the ER to find donors, by drawing extra blood from otherwise healthy patients without their knowledge."

Clark began to pace, the most outward sign of internal emotion I'd seen from him. "How's Theresa Walling fit in?"

"I think she knew something, or saw something, that made her a threat to Brickle's operation. I can't imagine Brickle was bringing home the victims, but maybe she was. Maybe Theresa saw a missing person on the news, realized she'd seen the person next door, and made a connection. Who knows? But I'm almost certain her disappearance is connected to Brickle's operation."

"Why do you think she was a witness?" he asked. "Why can't she just be one of Brickle's victims?"

"Was Theresa seen in the ER for anything in the weeks prior to her disappearance?"

"Not that I recall," he said, disappearing into the kitchen. He returned with the same file I'd seen at the coffee shop earlier. He dropped it onto the couch and paged through it, shaking his head. "No. I don't think so."

"Then how would Brickle have gotten her blood? I'm not saying it's not possible, in fact, I think that is what ultimately happened, but not initially."

"You were serious with that whole cop boyfriend theory?" he asked, standing upright.

"Theresa's friend said she thought the boyfriend was a cop, based on something Theresa had said. I think whatever operation Brickle's got going here is big, with serious amounts of money involved. She's had to buy off lab personnel, couriers, any number of medical personnel—what's to say she hasn't also bought herself a few cops? That would sure help with all the people they were abducting."

That reality hit Clark full in the face. "So you're saying . . . there could be dirty cops involved."

"Both in your department," Ellmann said, "and mine."

"I think *that's* why your investigation got shut down," I said.

"Shit," Clark muttered, beginning to pace again. "So what the hell do we do now? Do you have any proof of any of this?"

"Nothing that will convince anyone," I admitted. "But I'm pretty sure they're doing surgery tonight. Probably right now."

"Do you know where?" Clark asked, eyes staring hard at me.

"Yes."

Clark turned to Ellmann. "How do you want to do this? If we run this through normal channels, we don't know who we can trust."

"I know. I don't like it, but I think we need to have a look for ourselves. If they're really cutting someone up right now, I don't really want to wait to figure out who we can trust and who we can't. I also don't want to call in backup and risk tipping them off through whoever they've bought off."

Clark held up a hand. "What makes you think they're operating now?"

"Karen Brickle called out of work sick tonight," I said, "but she's not at home. Also, Ward and Weeks are not working tonight but I followed them down here from Fort Collins in an ambulance they shouldn't have."

That was enough to convince him. He looked at Ellmann again. "It's dangerous, going in blind just the two of us."

"It'll be three," Ellmann said, nodding at me. "Plus the dog. Believe me, she can handle herself. And that dog is as good as any police K-9."

Dasch stood up, his ears twitching.

"Actually," I said, as a fourth figure came silently into the room through the open doorway of the kitchen. "There will be four of us."

Clark spun around, staring at the intruder behind him. Ellmann just looked at me. Ruben Medera stood silently, calmly in the doorway, his hands at his side. He was dressed in black BDUs, a long-sleeved black cargo shirt, with a plain black ball cap on his head. I saw one gun, one knife, and a flashlight on his belt, but I guessed the man had more weapons on him than that.

When I'd called Medera earlier and asked him to meet me at Clark's address, I'd thought he'd use the front door. Silly me.

"Zoe, what's he doing here?" Ellmann asked.

327

"Don't stop trusting me now," I said.

"Who the fuck are you?" Clark demanded, having recovered. He shot a dark glance at me. "Who the fuck is this?"

"This is Sergeant Ruben Medera, United States Marine Corps. His girlfriend, Maria Rodriguez, was abducted by Karen Brickle. He's been looking for her since."

As soon as Ellmann had told me Medera was Maria's girlfriend, I'd figured a few things out. Like that he hadn't known I was looking into Brickle because he'd been following me; he'd been following her. He'd figured out Maria had been targeted in the ER and had gotten to Brickle from there. The piece he'd been missing was the connection to Adam Galvin.

"So you want to bring him with us?" Clark gaped. He looked to Ellmann for support. "He's emotionally involved—"

"Detective, I've seen combat on four separate tours in Afghanistan and Iraq," Medera said, speaking for the first time. His tone was calm, cool. "On every single one, I've watched the men and women of my units die around me. It doesn't get more emotional than that. So if you think I can't keep my head in an operation like this one, you're not nearly as good as Zoe led me to believe."

Clark looked again at Ellmann. "Are you seriously considering this?"

"We could use the manpower," Ellmann said. "And it's not like he's an untrained civilian."

"This is unbelievable," Clark muttered.

"Clark," I snapped. "We're wasting time we don't have." I realized I'd raised my voice, but I couldn't help it. I pointed at Medera. "That man has fought and bled for our freedoms, seen and done things no man should ever have to do. The least we can do is give him the chance to help take down the people who kidnapped, and quite possibly *killed*, his girlfriend. It's the right thing to do." I took a breath and deliberately lowered my voice. "Besides, if he doesn't come with us, he'll go on his own, and then we'll just be tripping over each other. So, you don't like it, fine. Your objection is noted. Now get your shit together and let's go."

Clark muttered a string of curses as he stormed out of the room. Barely a minute later, he was back, dressed in his SWAT uniform of green camo BDUs, top and bottoms, and black boots, gun and badge on his belt. He laced up his boots then flipped off the stereo.

"GI Joe, the back door locked again?" he asked, grabbing Theresa's file from the sofa.

"Yes, sir."

"Hit the kitchen light."

Medera complied and we all moved for the front door, filing out.

"So, where the hell are we going, anyway?" Clark asked.

"Galvin's surgery center," I answered.

48

We drove in three cars. Ellmann and I, along with the dog, rode in Ellmann's car and took the lead. Clark followed in his car. Medera brought up the rear in his truck.

The ride across town was tense, quiet. Ellmann and I didn't say much. The most significant conversation was when I asked about EMS.

"Should we call an ambulance now?" I asked. "Or have someone on standby? If they're really operating tonight, we're going to need medical assistance."

"Yes, we should. But what do we say? The hard truth here is that we need to know what we're dealing with before we sound the alarm. And we should prepare for the fact that we're too late for whoever they've got on the table tonight."

I didn't like the point he'd made, but I understood the truth of it. Still, I held out hope. Because that was better than the alternative.

We arrived at the address a couple of blocks from the hospital. The sign on the front of the building read ONE-DAY SURGERY CENTER, and beneath it, Adam Galvin's name was listed along with those of his three partners. Ellmann cruised by and turned around the back of the building, circling the block. Clark and Medera broke off, one of them driving past the front of the building. We met at a predetermined rendezvous point two blocks away.

Once out of the vehicles, all three men began gearing up. Ellmann and Clark donned Kevlar vests laden with pockets full of equipment and emblazoned with the word POLICE on the front and back. They also clipped tactical drop holsters to their legs and secured their weapons in them. Medera had an unmarked vest with fewer pockets, but he was putting all kinds of things into the ones he had.

I didn't have a Kevlar vest, and the only gear I had was the Browning pistol at my lower back and the extra magazine and pair of handcuffs I'd tucked into my back pocket.

"Grey."

I looked up and saw Medera walking over to me. He held an extra Kevlar vest.

"It'll be too big," he said, opening it to put it over my head, "but it'll stop a bullet."

"I don't really expect these guys to have bullets," I said, but I let him slip the vest over my head anyway. He and Ellmann made quick work of fastening the Velcro straps as tight as possible. The thing stuck out past my shoulders two inches on each side and hung four inches past my waist. "I can't reach my gun."

Medera ripped one of the Velcro straps open. "Get it," he said. "Put it here." He indicated an empty pouch on the front of the vest.

I slid the Browning into it and strapped it in as he refastened the Velcro. "That's handy," I said.

Ellmann offered his hand to Medera. "Thanks."

Medera just shook the hand and nodded.

Men could communicate so efficiently sometimes.

"Was the ambulance still out front?" I asked.

Medera nodded, clamping his hands on his hips. "Yeah. It's empty. No one out front at all."

"Probably waiting inside," I said. "That means they're not finished yet." I looked at Ellmann. "There's still time."

Ellmann said, "The good news is this is a standalone building. The bad news is it's probably about fifty thousand square feet, two floors and probably a basement. We've got an unknown number of suspects inside with an unknown number of victims. There are only four of us."

"We need to get in and have a look around," Clark said. "Once we get an idea what we're dealing with, we can call in backup."

"Don't forget we can use the dog," I said. "He's trained for this kind of thing."

I saw Ellmann's look. It had taken me a while to learn to read Ellmann, because he let so little slip by his cop face, but I was getting there.

"You're not worried about the dog," I said. "You're worried about me. He's trained; I'm not."

"Zoe, I—"

"I get it," I said quickly. "And you're right. I haven't had much practice."

"We need to split up," Medera said. "We should go in teams of two, and you two cops should split up, just to cover our asses. I'll guess Zoe wants to go with Ellmann, so that leaves me with you," he said, nodding to Clark. "One team takes the front, the other the back. Slip in nice and quiet, do a little recon, then fall back. No cell phones. You two cops got radios?"

Ellmann and Clark both answered in the affirmative. They quickly tuned their radios to the same, little-used channel Clark identified.

"Clark, you and me take the back," Medera said, continuing to take the lead. "Ellmann, Grey, take the front. Let's fall out."

"Who the fuck put you in charge?" snapped Clark.

"Just try to keep up, old man," Medera shot back, already jogging down the sidewalk.

Clark went with him, mastering his unhappiness and slipping into controlled SWAT attack mode.

Ellmann and I walked in a different direction, headed back toward the front of the office building. Dasch trotted at my left heel. When we reached the open parking lot, Ellmann slipped out his weapon and took everything in with a practiced glance.

"Ready?" he asked.

Night had fallen, but the parking lot was well lit with well-spaced lights, as well as all the ambient light from the surrounding buildings. Inside, lights burned on both floors.

I saw the ambulance parked near a side door at the far edge of the lot. There were two cars parked in the front lot. I guessed there were more parked in a rear.

"We should disable these vehicles," I said, pulling out my pocketknife. "And the ambulance."

"You take the cars," he said. "I'll take the ambulance. Then check the front door. If it's open, we go in there. If not, I'm betting that side door is."

"Copy that," I said.

We ran into the parking lot, each of us running for our objective. Ellmann's long legs ate up the asphalt, and he moved with lithe grace despite his size and the weight of all his equipment.

I reached the first car and plunged the knife into the driver's side front tire. Air immediately hissed out of it, and it was flat before I ever rounded the front fender. I quickly flattened the same tire on the second car, parked three spots over, then tucked the knife away as I ran for the front door, watching for any movement inside the building.

I peered through the clear glass of the front door. The small entryway and the various hallways I could see were all empty. A large sign between elevators told me surgery check-in was on the second floor. That meant the OR suites were most likely also on the second floor.

333

I tried the door. It was locked. I hurried down the sidewalk toward the side entrance. I encountered Ellmann halfway there. I gave a little shake of my head, and he immediately turned around.

The side door was also glass, and behind it I could see two hallways. One led along the front of the building, likely back toward the lobby I'd seen already. The second ran perpendicular to the first, and to the back of the building.

I drew my weapon, the weight of the Browning familiar and comforting in my hand. With my left, I reached for the door handle.

"Dasch, *fuss*," I said. *Heel.* "Stay with me, buddy."

He looked up at me, wagging his tail.

I nodded to Ellmann.

"I'm going forward," he said, his voice low. He used his hand to point while he talked. "You come in right behind me, cover that backward hallway until we're clear."

I nodded again. "Copy. ORs are on two."

He nodded.

I eased the door open and held it with my foot, wrapping both hands around my gun. Ellmann darted into the building. I was right behind him, Dasch right behind me. The hallway was clear, and the building seemed quiet.

I trailed Ellmann down the hallway, his long legs moving at a determined clip, forcing me to almost jog to keep up. At the end of the hallway, we burst into the open lobby. Ellmann covered the front as we continued forward. I brought the Browning up and covered the hallways on our left. Wordlessly, Ellmann passed the elevators and went directly for a door marked STAIRS. Taking the elevator was Dumb Rookie Move Number One.

We climbed with as little noise as possible, Ellmann still leading with his weapon. We paused at the door to the second floor. Ellmann peered through the slit of glass then looked at me. He mouthed, "Lobby." I nodded my understanding. Then he used some more hand signals.

I go first. I go right. You go left.

Again, I nodded. I gave Dasch a quick scratch of praise then the hand signal for heel. He didn't seem to need the reminder, but Dietrich Müller had encouraged such reminders, and I trusted the German knew what he was talking about.

Ellmann opened the door, and we were moving again. We burst outward into an empty lobby, backs together, guns raised. The hallways I could see were empty. When nothing happened behind me, I knew the same was true for Ellmann.

There were more signs here. A sign hanging above the desk in the lobby read SURGERY CHECK-IN. Farther down, on the wall of a hallway, another sign said PATHOLOGY, with an arrow pointing left. A door to the right of the check-in desk declared ALL PATIENTS MUST BE ACCOMPANIED. I thought that one most likely led to the surgery prep areas. The pathology hallway seemed more promising.

Then I felt Ellmann's hand tap my hip. I knew he wanted me to follow him. I put a hand on his back and did.

Toward the end of the building, we arrived at another hallway. As we passed, I saw another sign: DELIVERIES/PICKUPS, with another arrow. The hallway was long, with multiple doors opening to the right. All of them were dark. We passed cautiously but didn't stop to check any of them.

Ellmann paused at the solid wood door at the end of the hall. There was no way to know what was on the other side. Most likely it opened to a semi-public area, but maybe not. Either way, the area could be full of armed bad guys.

One thing was certain: nothing could be gained by just standing there, waiting. So Ellmann opened the door and we shot through it.

The door led to a back hallway. Directly ahead a pair of double doors were marked DELIVERIES/PICKUPS. To the left, I

335

noticed a door marked STAIRS. The hall stretched to the right, with more doors opening from it on each side. Another elevator sat directly to the right. It was obviously a service elevator and marked STAFF ONLY.

Ellmann and I had gone about twenty feet when one of the doors on the left swung open and two men stepped into the hall, both holding cups of coffee. Jimmy Ward and Dom Weeks.

There was a moment of frozen surprise from them, in which they just stared at Ellmann and me. Ellmann and I were still moving forward, more purposefully now. Dasch was beside me, growling, tail wagging in excitement.

"Police! Don't move!" Ellmann barked. Normally, Ellmann's voice commanded compliance. And at first, I thought that would be the case this time, too. I should have known better.

Ward recovered first. He made an exaggerated show of looking around. "I don't see anyone else. Did you two come here alone? That was stupid."

He bent forward, put his cup of coffee down, and pulled up his pants leg, drawing a long knife from a sheath in his boot.

Weeks saw his buddy pull the knife and quite obviously wished he had a weapon of his own. Instead, he threw his cup of coffee behind him down the hall, balled his fists, and squared his shoulders. Weeks was bigger than Ward, strong and solid, and I guessed he didn't often lose in physical confrontations.

Dasch growled louder, his front feet tapping in anticipation.

"*Warten*," I told him. *Wait*.

"How about we keep this peaceful?" Ellmann said, trying his cop-negotiator voice now. "Hurting anyone else will just make things worse for you. And cooperation always goes a long way with the courts. Help yourselves here. Put down that knife."

Ward scoffed. "Nice try, cop. The only way we get out of this now is if we don't get caught. Which means you and your partner here have to die." He smirked. "Dead people are the only people you can trust to keep their mouths shut."

Ward nudged Weeks's shoulder and started forward. Weeks stalked along beside him.

Dasch growled, his eye on the knife in Ward's hand.

"Well, I tried," Ellmann muttered. It had been a long shot, and we both knew it.

I started to respond, but a piercing, terrified shriek echoed through the hall.

I felt my heart kick up a couple beats. Our victim was still alive.

49

The scream rolled away, leaving a horrible, empty silence in its wake. All four of us had stopped moving. For one quick beat, we just stood, frozen, each side staring at the other, waiting, evaluating.

I knew Ellmann and I were thinking the same thing: get to the victim.

Out of the corner of my eye, I saw Ellmann flick a glance at the double doors to our left. The scream seemed to have come from there. He was torn.

"Go check it out," I said. "I'll take care of these two."

Ward's smirk widened.

I'd barely spoken when the scream came again, cut off almost immediately, unnaturally. We both knew there would be no more screaming.

Without much choice, Ellmann pulled a coil of black flexi-cuffs from one of the pockets on his vest and handed them to me.

"I'd prefer them alive."

Ward actually chuckled.

"I'll make every effort," I promised.

Then Ellmann broke off and went left, pulling open one of the doors and disappearing through it.

"Jimmy," I said, "before I forget, a mutual friend of ours asked me to tell you hello."

Ward was almost six feet tall in his black boots and thin, with a wiry physique. He had dirty blonde hair cut and styled into one of those fauxhawk haircuts the pretty boys all had lately. He was clean-shaven with two small diamond studs in his ears. He had brown eyes, full lips, and a strong jaw—I could see the surface appeal. The problem was the malicious gleam in his eyes that bespoke of violence and danger that was too real to be attractive or sexy.

"How do you know who I am?"

"Turns out I'm not a half bad investigator."

His brows knitted together. "What?"

"I not only know who you are, I know what you guys are up to. So how's it work? You guys transport the coolers?"

Weeks flashed a nervous glance at his buddy: a confirmation. Ward just continued to smirk.

I went on. "Maybe you cover ground transport within a certain radius. For longer transports, you probably transport the coolers to a private airfield where they are then flown out. That about right?" I remembered Galvin's helicopter that reportedly got a lot of use.

"Jimmy," Weeks said, "who the fuck is this chick? How's she know all this?"

Weeks was a couple inches over six feet and had the solid, muscled figure of a man who spent a great deal of time in the gym. He had short dark hair, blue eyes, and an olive complexion. He didn't spend as much time grooming himself as Ward did, but he was equally attractive, albeit in a more rugged way. There was also an edge in his eyes, as if he'd seen his fair share of brawls and wasn't afraid to throw in, but his lacked that gleam of violent hunger I could see in Ward's.

I slid the Browning into the holster on the vest and tucked the flexi-cuffs into one of the pockets. "I'm the chick that's about to ruin your lives."

Ward laughed then bumped his buddy's shoulder. "Don't worry about her. The two of us can take her, then we'll dump her downstairs, like all the others."

Personally, I hate knife fights. I'd rather a guy with an itchy trigger finger shove a loaded gun in my face than attack me with a knife. I see a knife come out, and I know one or both of us is going to get cut. The only good thing about a knife fight is that it's over fast.

"Don't suppose you want to put that knife down and go strict hand to hand here," I said, already knowing the answer. "I'll let you both attack me at the same time, how's that sound?"

Weeks laughed now. "We're going to do that anyway."

"Yeah, yeah," I said. "Dasch, *platz. Blieb.*" He immediately dropped to the floor on his belly, tail wagging, watching excitedly. "*Blieb*," I said again. *Stay.*

I moved forward. "Jimmy, you ever been in a real knife fight before?"

By the way he laughed I knew he hadn't. "Sure, bitch. Have you?" He started toward me, Weeks stalking along beside him.

"So then you know both people get cut. And you're prepared for that."

A flicker of unease flashed in his eyes. He gripped the knife tighter. He held it in his right hand, blade pointed upward. This alone told me he was new at this. An attacker truly intent on killing with a knife holds it with the blade down and stabs with downward jabs—*Psycho* style. Not that I didn't believe Ward meant to kill me if he got the chance.

"Shut up," he snapped.

"You're a confusing guy, Jimmy. By day, you're a benevolent EMT, trying to save people's lives. By night, you're a murderer, killing people for profit. Maybe you didn't start out a killer, but you like the lifestyle, don't you? The money, the cars, the women . . . You couldn't say no. And now you're in too deep. Even if you wanted out, you'd never get out."

Ward smirked as he came toward me, entirely too confident in his ability to overcome me. "Why would I say no? I've got nice cars, nice clothes, a nice place to live, and as many women as I could want. Nothing women like better than a man with money."

"Way I hear it, you've got enough money you could have any girl you wanted, but you're not too choosey are you? You'll slip it to anything that'll stand still long enough. I hear some of them are pretty nasty. Which just goes to show money doesn't buy class or taste, does it, Jimmy?"

Anger and embarrassment colored his cheeks now. "Bitch," he seethed, lunging forward with the knife.

He swung the knife toward me in an upward angle. I shot forward with a cross block, catching his forearm between mine. The too-big vest impeded some of my movements, making them somewhat awkward. I immediately bent my arms, bringing his arm into my chest, locking his wrist in my left elbow. I never stopped moving. With my right hand, I grabbed his right shoulder and, using the momentum I still had, took him to the ground, one knee landing on his back, the other on the back of his neck. As we went down, our bodies shifted just enough I felt the blade slice into my left shoulder. With my right hand, I plucked the knife from his hand.

It happened so fast Ward didn't even have time to scream until he was already facedown on the floor. After an initial scream of pain and surprise, he began cursing me as he struggled uselessly against my hold.

Weeks gaped at me, then he attacked, lunging forward, his hands outstretched toward my neck. I heard Dasch growl, heard his nails on the linoleum. But he would be too late. Weeks plowed into me, sailing over his prone friend and barreling into me with all his weight. All I could do was watch the attack come and mitigate the damage.

As Weeks hit me, his huge hands closing around my neck, I flung the knife away and threw myself backward, twisting to the left. We landed hard, more or less on our sides. While he focused on regaining his grip around my neck, I brought a knee into his groin and struck him with an open hand to the face, the vest in my way again. His nose broke as his head snapped back, warm blood suddenly flowing from it like water from an open tap. His grip slacked just as Dasch clamped his jaw around Week's arm.

I heard Ward moving behind me, and had barely gotten to a knee when he slammed into me from behind, snaking an arm around my neck. His mistake was dragging me up to my feet.

He was panting, snarling in my ear. I could barely hear him over Dasch's growls and Weeks's screams.

"Aahh! Get him off! Get him off me!"

"Fucking bitch!" Ward hissed. "You're mine now."

I was already moving, the motions hampered by the vest. I swung my left leg around behind his right, my thigh against the back of his leg. At the same time, I swung down with left hand in a hammer fist, smashing it against his groin, once, twice. He let out a whoosh of air, bending forward in pain. I swung upward then with the same fist, smashing his nose. His head whipped back, pulling his body off balance. I kicked forward with my left hip and thigh. His leg bucked upward and he came off his feet, falling backward.

I spun, grabbing his shirtfront with both fists and forcing him downward, slamming him to the floor. His head connected with a sickening thump and his body went limp.

"That broken nose is from our mutual friend," I said, flipping him over roughly and pinning him a second time. As I went for the handcuffs in my back pocket, I glanced over at Dasch and Weeks. Weeks was struggling, screaming and thrashing. Dasch hopped around, avoiding the worst of the blows while never losing his grip. His tail wagged the whole time.

"Stop fighting my dog!"

The stairwell door at the end of the hall burst open. I looked up to see Andrew Miller step out, followed by a shorter man built like a fucking fireplug. Both of them were in uniform, and both of them looked mean.

"What the fuck?" Miller snapped, angry eyes locking onto me.

"Fuck," I hissed.

I saw Miller's intent to attack flash on his features, and I knew I had time to either snap the cuffs on Ward or rip off the vest. I immediately dropped the cuffs and ripped off the vest.

Miller charged forward, his eyes still locked on me. His partner zeroed in on Dasch. The look in his eyes truly scared me.

"Dasch!" I called as I flung the vest aside and stood, stepping over Ward to meet Miller. "*Aus! Fass!*"

Dasch released Weeks, glanced at me, and turned to the fireplug guy.

I was not afraid of Miller, and only half my attention was on him. I was afraid for Dasch. I knew the dog could handle himself, but that fireplug didn't look like the kind of guy who would be deterred by pain. I didn't have time to do this dance with Miller.

Miller swung at me with his right. I stepped to my left, his fist sailing past me. My attack was brutal.

I swung my left hand up into Miller's elbow, forcing the joint inward, braking bones with audible snaps. At nearly the same instant, I brought my right knee up into Miller's solar plexus as I grabbed his shirt and pulled him forward into the blow. Then I swung my right elbow backward, connecting with the side of his head. He was unconscious before he hit the floor.

As he fell, I was already moving around him, attention now on Dasch. I looked in time to see the dog launch himself through the air as the fireplug swung. Dasch bit his right forearm, hitting the fireplug with such force he swung backward. Pulled off balance, the fireplug fell, landing hard on the linoleum. Dasch landed hard, too, but he never let go.

If the fireplug felt the ninety-one-pound German Shepherd biting his arm, he gave no indication of it. As I ran forward, I saw him getting to his knees, his left hand reaching for something on his belt. I didn't know what, but I knew it was bad.

"Dasch! *Ziehen! Ziehen!*"

Dasch, tail still wagging, began dragging the man backward. The man was too heavy for Dasch to make much progress, but the effort kept the guy from getting to his knees.

I ran and jumped, landing on the guy's back with both my knees. He barely grunted when my weight hit him, and it was like landing on concrete.

"Hold still!" I barked.

I now saw a folded pocketknife in the guy's left hand. He was still trying to open it.

"You were going to stab my dog?" I spat, wrenching his arm behind him with such force I dislocated his shoulder. I ripped the knife out of his hand and threw it down the hall, then savagely snapped the second pair of cuffs on his left wrist. "Bad idea."

I shifted my weight so my knee was on the back of his head. I put significant weight on it, more than I normally would have, and told Dasch to release him. The dog did so, and I worked to twist the guy's right arm behind his back and cuffed it. It was an uncomfortable stretch, and he put up such a fight I almost didn't make it, his brute strength almost overpowering me even from my leveraged advantage, but I got it, and I didn't care that the cuffs were cutting into his wrists.

I got up and turned, finding Weeks crawling on his knees and his uninjured arm in the direction of Ward's knife, still a good twenty feet away.

"It's over," I said, walking toward him. I went around him to the vest I'd discarded earlier, retrieved the flexi-cuffs Ellmann had given me, then went back to Weeks. He'd managed to crawl another three feet. I stopped in front of him. "It's over."

"It can't be," he said, wheezing, his words sounding wet and muffled from the blood running out of his nose. "I don't want to go to jail."

"Too late for that." I kicked his left arm out from under him, and he hit the floor hard, unable to stop his fall. I knelt on his back, slipping a plastic cuff onto his left wrist. "You should have thought of that before you started killing people." I wrenched his right arm back, causing him to scream in pain. I cinched the cuffs and stood.

There was blood all over the floor. Most of it had likely come from Weeks's nose, but his arm was also a bloody mess. Dasch had some on his face, making him look more than a little gruesome.

I quickly slipped plastic cuffs onto Ward's and Miller's wrists, both men still unconscious. Dasch looked on, panting and wagging his tail.

"*Bravy*, Dasch."

I jumped up and went back to the discarded vest. I ripped the Browning free then ran toward the door Ellmann had gone through.

"*Hierr. Fuss.*"

Dasch fell in at my left heel. I pulled open the door and went in, gun up. I hurried forward, down what I discovered was a wide hallway with four sets of double doors opening off it, two on each side. I strained my ears for any sounds that might tell me where Ellmann had gone, where the others were, where the screaming had come from. I heard nothing until the second set of doors on the right suddenly swung open.

I brought my gun to the right, moving carefully to confront whoever was approaching. It was Ellmann, mimicking my

345

stance. We lowered our weapons at the same time. He took me in with a glance, noting all the blood, and the cut on my arm.

"What the hell? Are you okay?"

I nodded and looked at my arm. "It's superficial, and most the blood's not mine. What's the deal?"

"There's only one body up here," he said quickly. "They were just getting started on her. But we've got coolers full of parts. And Karen's not here."

"What—" My head snapped up. "The basement. Ward said something about taking my body to the basement."

"An incinerator," he said, understanding instantly.

We turned and sprinted down the hall, bursting through doors and returning to the back hall. Ward and Miller were still unmoving, Ward bleeding from his face. Weeks and the fireplug were still squirming on the ground. Weeks was crying and carrying on. He, too, was in a puddle of blood. The fireplug was obviously trying to snap the cuffs around his wrists, and I was glad I'd left the metal ones on him.

I didn't stop as I blew through the hall, darting for the stairwell door. Ellmann faltered only slightly as he took in the four figures.

"Holy shit," he said. "Who are those guys? Where'd they come from?"

"Boulder EMS. If there were two bodies, there were probably too many parts for one ambulance to transport."

"Fuck, Zoe. Are those two dead?"

"I don't think so," I said, pushing open the stairwell door. "But I didn't stop to check."

"You scare me sometimes."

"They were going to hurt my dog."

We hurried down the stairs, guns raised, but not worried about the noise we were making. If Karen had gone to incinerate the body, we wanted to intercept her as quickly as possible.

When we reached the basement, Ellmann took the lead and we exited the stairwell as carefully as we had previously. My shoulder to his back, we moved as a unit, Dasch trailing me.

"See anything?" Ellmann asked.

"No." There were no signs down here, nothing to give any directions.

"Then let's see if Dasch can find her."

Hearing his name, Dasch twitched his ears. He looked up at me, tail wagging, tipping his head to the side.

"You're up, buddy," I said. "*Voran*."

He turned and took off, shooting down the hallway and then making a left, like he knew where he was going. His tailed wagged and he slowed occasionally to sniff at closed doors. Ellmann and I ran after him full tilt. It wasn't the best tactical procedure, but it was a calculated risk. Karen was presumed to be the only one in the basement, and it was unlikely she was armed.

Dasch came to a T-intersection. Both sides were blocked with closed double doors. He ran left and sniffed, then turned and ran right, sniffing some more. Then he ran back to the left, barking and jumping up against the door. I ran forward and hit the button on the wall. The doors swung open.

Dasch squeezed through them and was gone. I ran forward and shoved myself through. The door opened to another long hallway with multiple doors. But now I could hear a distant roaring sound, and I imagined we were nearing the mark.

Dasch stopped about halfway down and sniffed at the bottom of a wide door. Then he barked, once again jumping up. I ran forward, Ellmann right beside me.

"Call him off," Ellmann said.

"Dasch, *aus! Fuss!*"

347

He gave a little whimper of protest but immediately came around and sat at my left heel, tail still wagging excitedly.

"Hard and fast," Ellmann said.

"Copy that."

Gun up, he pushed the door open and charged inside. I was right behind him. When he swung to the right, I immediately went left.

We were in an anteroom of sorts. The floor and walls were tile and stainless steel racks lined one wall, holding various cleaning equipment and instruments. Through the huge window of a second door, we could see into another room. And we saw Karen Brickle.

The woman I recognized from Facebook was dressed in green surgical scrubs, still wearing her booties and bonnet from the OR. A narrow, wheeled stainless steel cart was parked beside a long conveyer belt, a bloody sheet wadded up on top of it. Atop the belt was the naked, bloodied form of a woman. The belt led directly into an incinerator, flames roaring inside it. Brickle walked around the machine to a control panel, raising her hand to press a button.

"Go!" Ellmann said, not slowing.

"Take her!" I called as we burst through the door.

"Police! Don't move!" Ellmann barked.

The roar of the incinerator was enormous in this small room, and it was hot. Still, Brickle jumped in surprise. But then she just grinned, the body already being carried forward.

"You're too late!"

"Hands up!" Ellmann snapped. "Back away from the machine!"

As I charged forward, I stuffed the Browning into the front waistband of my jeans.

The body was moving into the incinerator feet first, her feet nearly touching the flames. I shot past the table, and, without really thinking about it, bent over the woman's body, wrapped my arms around her, and flung myself backward, pulling her off the belt with me. As we landed, she came down underneath me, and I found I had instinctively cradled her head, though no such damage would hurt her now.

I sat up, seeing the body more closely. I recognized her from the newspaper. Julie Webster. Her torso was cut open from her throat to her pelvis, and no effort had been made to close her back up. Even in the brief glance I got, I could tell her heart and lungs were missing. I imagined other parts were too. I felt a potent wave of sadness wash over me as I reached up for the sheet on the wheeled cart.

"Zoe!"

"I'm fine!" I said, draping the sheet over the body. "And I got her."

50

Ellmann and I returned to the second floor, Brickle between us with her hands in flexi-cuffs behind her back. She didn't say a word. When we stepped out of the stairwell into the bloody carnage of the hallway, she gasped and her feet faltered.

"What the hell did you do?" she spat at Ellmann, angry, scared.

"This was all me, sweetheart," I said.

She whipped around to face me, taking me in more carefully than she had so far. She was obviously seeing me in new light.

Clark was in the hallway, checking Miller for weapons. I could see he'd already checked Weeks and Ward.

"Let me help them!" Brickle cried, pleading with Ellmann. "Please, they need medical attention! Look at them!" There was genuine concern and fear in her voice that surprised me.

"You just helped murder two people, but you want to help these guys?" he said, his confusion matching my own.

"You don't understand!" she said, starting to cry.

"You sure as hell got that right," I said.

Clark rose and moved over to the fireplug. He glanced at Ellmann. "Your girl did all this? By herself?"

Ellmann shrugged a shoulder. "Told you she could handle herself."

"In all fairness," I said, scratching Dasch's ears, "I had a little help."

"Shit, Grey," Clark said, pulling a second knife from the fireplug's right boot, "remind me never to cross you."

"Don't threaten my dog, or anyone else I care about. I'm not so brutal then." I glanced down the hallway to the left, the doors of which had been propped open. "Where's Medera?"

Clark nodded toward the open hallway. "Back in the OR, asking the doctor a few questions." Finding nothing else on the fireplug, he stood. "I called for backup and EMS," he said, looking at Ellmann. "Better call your people."

"Will do," Ellmann said, passing Brickle to Clark.

As Ellmann pulled his cell phone from his pocket, I walked away, into open hallway. I went to the end of the hall and pushed the button for the second set of doors on the right, the ones Ellmann had come through earlier. I saw now the door opened to another type of anteroom. Another set of automatic double doors at the opposite side opened into the operating suite. Another female was on the operating table, the monitors around her indicating she was still alive.

Medera was already on his way out, his knuckles bloody. Behind him, through the doors that swung open as he approached, I saw two men on the floor of the room. Both wore green surgical scrubs, gloves, booties, and bonnets. One still wore a surgical mask and was lying facedown on the bloody floor, his hands cuffed behind his back. The second was no longer wearing a surgical mask and was slumped against the wall, crying, his face bloody. He, too, was handcuffed, and unable to hold himself upright. I guessed him to be Dr. Adam Galvin.

"Who's on the table?" I asked as Medera stopped in front of me.

"Ellmann recognized her. Susan Wilmont. Says she went missing about two or three weeks ago."

I gaped at Medera, my mind spinning. "Two or three weeks?"

"That what he remembers."

I glanced over Medera's shoulder at the closed OR door. "Did Galvin have anything to say about Maria?"

The only indication of Medera's emotions was the flexing of his jaw. "No. He didn't have anything to say about anything."

That was surprising. I would never have pegged the doctor for being tough enough—emotionally or physically—to keep quiet.

"Maybe they'll have more luck with Brickle," I said.

He scoffed. "I doubt it."

I did, too. Between Galvin and Brickle, I would have thought her the strong one. If he wasn't talking, then she probably wouldn't, either.

I glanced back through the glass of the doors to the girl on the operating table.

"Why hold her for three weeks?" I murmured to myself.

"Maybe lining up recipients," Medera offered.

That was as good an explanation as any. But the fact remained that they'd held her for three long weeks with no one the wiser. Where had they done that? They would have needed something private, where she wouldn't be discovered, and something secure, so she wouldn't escape. And if they'd planned to harvest her organs, they would have needed to keep her relatively healthy by providing her food and water. That wasn't something they'd done on the fly; it took planning.

I knew Ellmann and Clark would search the building from top to bottom once the cavalry arrived, but I seriously doubted Galvin would have risked keeping the girl here, where any number of unsuspecting people could have come across her. He would have needed privacy, seclusion—

I snapped my head up and looked at Medera.

"What?" he asked.

I slapped a hand on his armored chest as I turned and hurried out of the room. "Come on. We need to go."

He fell in beside me. "Do you know where she is?"

"I know where she might have been held," I said carefully. "There's a difference."

"I know. But I'm not giving up on her until I'm certain."

"Fair enough."

We ran back to the hallway where Ellmann now stood alone with five handcuffed prisoners.

"We're leaving," I said, shooting past him for the stairwell. "We need to check something out."

"Zoe, take a cop with you."

"They aren't here yet, and we can't wait. I'll text you the address; have Clark send someone. They can meet us there." I pulled the phone from my pocket.

"Zoe—" Ellmann looked at Medera then back at me. He sighed and dragged his hand back through his hair. "Be careful."

We charged down the stairs and burst through the side door. A Boulder EMS ambulance was now parked beside the first. We ran across the parking lot. Clark, at the front door, no doubt waiting for reinforcements, shouted to us. I waved but kept running.

The small backseat of Medera's pickup was full of stuff; the only place to really sit was in the front. Medera got behind the wheel, I got in the passenger seat, and Dasch stuffed into the middle. He was so big, his head touched the roof and Medera couldn't see well enough to drive. I told him to lie down, and he sprawled across my lap. He was heavy.

"Where are we going?" Medera asked, peeling away from the curb.

"West. We want Highway 7."

I texted the address to Ellmann and mapped it on my phone. I navigated, and Medera sped. I wasn't sure how we'd explain ourselves if we were pulled over—Medera looked like Rambo and I was covered in blood.

The further we got from town, the darker it became, the headlights of the pickup seeming inefficient to their task. We followed the highway past the town of Allenspark where it turned north. Then we made a right, leaving the paved highway for a narrow, unmarked dirt road. As the headlights bounced off the thick trees lining the road, the twin glow of eyes and the quick darts of wildlife could be seen in the night.

Dasch snored until we made another right onto an even rougher dirt road and he was jostled awake. After about a mile, I pointed to the right. "It's about half a mile up that road to Elk Trail Road. The house sits at the end of Elk Trail Road, about half a mile or so in. As far as I can tell, there is only one house on that road."

Medera slowed, looking through the windows out into the night, thinking. "We're going to have to hike in," he said, making the right and flipping off the headlights.

"I know," I said.

Medera eased the truck forward slowly, only the faint moonlight filtering through the thick forest of trees lighting the way. After several minutes, he stopped and pointed to the left. "There's the road."

I squinted but couldn't make it out. My distance vision isn't great in the daylight; it's really not great in the dark. "I'll take your word for it."

He turned the truck off and eased his door open. "Stick with me for now; we'll approach together. Once we do a little recon, we'll make a plan. If there are hostages, there are probably guards."

"Copy that."

"Got a light?"

"No."

He opened the glove box, pulled one out, and handed it to me. "Keep it off."

I nodded.

I swung out of the truck, Dasch jumping down behind me. He stopped to pee on a tree then fell in at my left heel.

Medera and I walked along the rutted, pitted road, making little noise. We could hear the forest alive around us, hear wildlife moving about just out of sight in the dark. Dasch's head was busy, looking from one side to the other, his big ears twitching as he took in all the sounds.

Medera had been right about the road. When we reached it, we made the left and followed it. Medera didn't draw his weapon, and neither did I.

Ahead, I could make out lights, and they seemed vaguely square in shape; I guessed them to be windows. As we got closer, I began to identify the outline of a cabin, and a GMC Acadia parked out front.

Medera pointed to the right side of the road. "Wait here," he whispered. "I'll be right back."

I did as asked and moved off into the tree line, kneeling down behind a tree to wait, Dasch beside me. I watched Medera move off into the trees on the left side of the road and then disappear. I strained my ears for the sound of his boots crunching over pine needles or his clothes brushing against the vegetation. There was nothing.

That's absolutely terrifying, I thought. *Good thing he's on my side.*

About ten minutes later, I knew Medera was nearby. The only reason I knew that was because Dasch had stood and turned to look into the dark to my right, ears twitching. A moment later, Medera materialized out of the dark like a fucking ghost, without making a sound.

I shivered involuntarily. How did they learn to do that?

355

He squatted beside me.

"Front entrance," he said, pointing to the door I could see. "One door around back. Lights on in the first floor and the basement. Only one vehicle, so likely one to four hostiles inside. I didn't see anyone, so I don't know where anyone is in the house. No idea about hostages. I'd prefer a stealth attack, but—"

I nodded. "Dasch doesn't really do stealth."

"So we go in hard and fast. I'll take the back door; you take the front. The back door's unlocked. If the front door's locked, shoot the lock and charge in. As far as the dog goes, I say let him do what he's trained to do."

"Fine. We're ready." I pulled the Browning from its holster.

"Check your watch. We both hit in exactly ninety seconds. Ready?"

I looked at my watch. "Yes."

"Start now."

He rose and once again dematerialized into the woods.

I watched the time. As it ticked down, I moved toward the front door. When I got there, I carefully tried the knob. By a stroke of luck, it was also unlocked. Guess they didn't expect any visitors way out here.

Three . . . Two . . . One . . .

I twisted the knob and threw the door open, bursting inside with my gun up.

"*Voran! Voran!*"

I swung my gaze around what was the front room of the cabin, my gun moving with it.

Dasch shot around me, tearing through the room and down a hallway to the right. I could hear the backdoor crash open. I'd barely reached the hallway when Dasch returned. He darted around me and sprinted back through the living room, disappearing into what I guessed was the kitchen.

356

I ran after him, arriving in time to see the dog sniffing at a closed door that probably led to the basement, Medera standing there ready to open it. I hurried forward, nodding to him. Because of Dasch, I had to go first. Medera yanked the door open, Dasch shot forward, and I tore after him.

"Hands up! My dog will bite! Hands up! Don't move!"

By the time I hit the bottom of the stairs, Dasch was barking. Then I heard the expected sounds of panic.

"My dog will bite! Don't move!"

I ran around the stairs after Dasch, gun raised. Medera was right behind me, covering my back.

The basement opened up behind the stairs. Most of it was unfinished and lit by bare bulbs in the low ceiling. Some of the basement had been finished, however. The back wall was a line of brick, with two metal doors in it. The doors looked like they had come directly from a prison, with a small barred window in the top and a food slit in the bottom.

A man in jeans and a white T-shirt was standing in front of the brick wall. A tray of food sat on a wooden bench off to the left. Dasch stood in front of the man, growling. The man stood frozen, arms out to the sides.

"Whoa!" the man said, his voice shaky. "Are you the police?" His eyes were glued to Dasch.

"Close enough," I said. "Slowly raise your arms."

"I don't want to get bit."

"Then do what I say. Raise your arms. Slowly."

Behind the man, faces appeared in the windows as hands wrapped around the bars.

"Ruben!" A woman in the window on the left began sobbing, her forehead falling against the bars. "Ruben."

I guessed we'd found Maria.

"Stop there," I told the man, who had complied. "Now turn around in a circle. Slowly. I'll tell you when to stop."

He again complied, and I could see no weapons visible around his waist.

"Stop," I said when he was facing away from me. "Slowly take two steps backward." He did, Dasch moving with him. "Stop. Slowly get to your knees. Put your right hand on the back of your head. With your left, lower yourself flat on the floor. Stretch your left arm away from you. Don't move."

I glanced at Medera, who still had his weapon trained on the guy in a steady grip. I holstered the Browning, pulled cuffs from my pocket, and walked forward. When the guy was secured, I began patting him down.

"Where are the keys?"

"What keys?"

I smacked his head with an open palm. It was enough force to bounce his cheekbone off the concrete floor.

"Where are the keys?"

"Upstairs. Drawer beside the fridge."

Medera was moving before the guy ever finished speaking. He was back a few seconds later, fitting the keys into the door of Maria's cell. I heard the lock retract, and he jerked the door open. Maria threw herself against him, sobbing hysterically. Her legs buckled and he held her, lowering her carefully to the ground. He was murmuring to her in soft Spanish, words I didn't recognize but could understand.

I finished patting down the guard, finding absolutely nothing on him, not even a wallet. As I walked toward the open cell door for the keys, a second woman emerged from the cell. She was about ten years older than Maria, blonde, and had a deer-in-the-headlights look. Like Maria, she was dressed in hospital scrubs.

"It's okay," I said, offering her my hand. "It's safe now."

She accepted my hand and stepped out, but seemed unsure what to do next.

"Wait here," I told her.

I opened the second cell and a man stepped out. He was approaching forty, and still wore jeans and a button-down shirt. I guessed maybe he hadn't been here quite as long.

Outside, I heard a siren.

"Good guys are here now," I said.

The man looked just as shocked as the woman.

I looked past them to where Medera knelt with Maria in his arms. I saw him pulling something from the pocket of his pants. It glinted in the dull light, and I knew what it was. It was the tennis bracelet I'd noticed missing from his house. He murmured to Maria as he carefully put the bracelet on her wrist, his big fingers clumsy with the small clasp. Then he brushed the hair back from her tear-streaked face and kissed her forehead.

"I didn't think you'd find me," she said through her sobs.

"I would have never stopped looking," he said, pulling her close. "Never."

Above us, the basement door crashed open.

"Police!"

"I'm Zoe Grey! I know Detective Ellmann sent you. Everything's under control. None of us are armed."

I held my hands up slightly at my sides, so they were clearly visible. Dasch sat beside me. The uniformed officer came around the bottom of the staircase weapon raised, taking everything in. He glanced from me to the guy cuffed on the floor to the hostages to Medera and Maria.

"Zoe Grey?"

"That's me," I said. "Please, lower your weapon. If you'll take this man into custody, I'll help these two out of here. I think they've spent enough time in this basement."

51

It was a long night. Medera and I were on scene at the cabin for hours before we were permitted to leave. More cops were called in, along with crime scene guys to process the place for evidence. EMS was called for the three people sprung from the basement cells. Not surprisingly, Medera refused to allow Maria out of his sight; and she refused to be out of it. A uniformed officer drove the other two victims out of the woods to meet an ambulance, and a second rode with them to the hospital, staying with them until they were picked up by relieved family members.

Finally, Medera and I were driven away from the cabin. Medera was returned to his truck, where he carefully loaded Maria inside then drove her away. He was taking her back to Fort Collins, where she would get checked out in the ER. I'd called Sadie to tell them she was coming, which eased Medera's mind some. And I agreed to meet him later. My ride returned Dasch and me to my truck, which was now the only vehicle parked at Starbucks.

All three people released from the basement of Galvin's cabin were found to be in exceptional physical health. Based on the statements they gave, they were provided three square meals a day, adequate drinking water, clean clothes, and access to clean facilities within the cells, including showers. This last part was confirmed by investigators on scene. All three victims identified Karen Brickle, and the two women also identified Jimmy Ward and Dominic Weeks. Karen Brickle had drawn their blood during emergency room visits. Once the tests were complete on the blood, Jimmy Ward and Dominic Weeks abducted the victims—the female victims, anyway.

Maria had been taken by force after Ward had attempted to pick her up. The blonde had fallen for Ward's charms and gone with him willingly.

The man told a different story. He'd been approached by a man claiming to be a police officer. The police officer produced a badge and told the man he was under arrest, handcuffing him and putting him in the back of an unmarked police car. As a matter of course, the man was shown pictures of Ellmann and Clark, but he did not identify either of them. The case remained theirs.

When Maria was discharged from the ER with a clean bill of health, I met Medera at his mother's house. It was the middle of the night and the woman was dressed in a robe, but she welcomed the couple with fierce hugs. Twenty minutes later, Medera came back out, devoid of all weapons.

"A deal's a deal," he said, climbing into the passenger seat of the Scout.

We drove in silence to the jail. When we arrived, I parked and we walked together to the door.

"They won't like that you're not cuffed," I said as we stood outside the door, waiting for someone to open it.

He held his hands out, and I put the cuffs on. Then he clasped my hand.

"Thank you," he said, squeezing my hand. "For helping me get her back."

"You're welcome. I'm glad we found her."

The door was opened, and we went in. Fifteen minutes later, I left with my body receipt. It was only the second time I'd ever felt remorse about taking someone to jail.

And then I did something I've never done before.

I called Marge and got her out of bed, asking her to come down and bail Medera right back out.

I was just getting out of the shower sometime later when my phone rang.

"You didn't have to do that," Medera said.

"I know. But I thought Maria could use you tonight."

"I owe you, Grey. More than one. And I won't forget it."

"You skip again, Ruben, there won't be any more deals."

"Yes, ma'am." I could tell he was smiling. "Pleasure working with you, Grey."

"You, too, Marine. Take care of your girl."

"Count on it."

I smiled as I hung up. It wouldn't be a happy ending all the way around, but a small part of it had worked out for good, and I was happy for it, happy for Ruben and Maria.

52

Tony's bar is a sad place at two o'clock in the afternoon. The place always has a faint air of desperation about it, but in the brightness of day, without all the college kids to cover it up, it seems stronger, more noticeable. Later, when the downtown scene was in full swing, it would be packed with college kids like every other place, but it was still a dive. If it didn't have fireball whiskey or the cheapest Jaeger shots around, business would be a lot different.

Parking downtown was less of an issue at that time of day, so I snagged a spot right out front of the bar. I told Dasch to stay and went inside. I was greeted with the faint stench of urine as I blinked my eyes to hasten their adjustment to the darkened interior.

Tony's isn't the most upstanding place, and you can't find a lot of stand-up guys in there. Especially not during the day. Today there were four guys drinking at the bar and a few more scattered throughout the room, at a table or playing darts. One or two of them wore suits and ties. Most of them looked unemployed.

Only one of them looked like he could be called Jumbo.

Earlier, I'd dropped by Marge's house, knowing full well she was at the office. I'd been slightly surprised to find her house was well kept and cared for, freshly painted with clean windows and gutters, the lawn tended and the flowerbeds planted. I had envisioned Marge as a workaholic, someone who spent little, if any, time at home. I'd been wrong.

The interior was a different story however, and if I hadn't known it going in, I would have known then whatever had happened between her and Jumbo had hit her hard. The furnishings and décor were all 1980s, but had been as well maintained, until recently. Now the dishes in the sink had been there long enough to stink, and the fridge held nothing but condiments, which I guessed was why Marge had looked a bit thinner every time I'd seen her. The floors were dirty, the bed was unmade, and everything was covered in dust.

Of course, the whole place reeked of cigarette smoke. Ashtrays in the kitchen and bedroom were overflowing, and there were open packs of smokes everywhere. But the wallpaper wasn't peeling from the walls and the ceiling wasn't yellow, so I guessed Marge had only started smoking in the house recently.

I'd also found enough to suggest Jumbo had recently moved out. There was a small gap in his side of the closet, his toothbrush and shower stuff were gone, and the pillow on his side of the bed was long-ways near the middle, where I imagined Marge had been holding on to it every night since he'd left.

The drawers of his bedside table, where there were no cigarettes or ashtray, were full of matchbooks from Tony's. Which was what had led me here.

I walked to the end of the bar and took the stool next to Jumbo. He barely glanced up at me, but I could tell he was paying more attention than he let on.

"I know you?" He was probably six three or four and built like a train. He had a gut starting, and had a layer of softness, but underneath it was solid, unyielding muscle—the kind that would never rot away no matter how much flab got piled on top. He was younger than I had expected, and younger than Marge, probably only in his early forties. His dark blonde hair was long, tied back in a ponytail, and thinning on top. It looked like it needed a good wash, as did his jeans and cut-off Harley T-shirt. He was also several days unshaven, which made him look a little wild, slightly dangerous.

"No," I said. "But we need to meet. I'm Zoe Grey."

He took a long pull on his beer. "I've heard the name. You're one of Sideline's guys—uh, *girls*. So what?"

The bartender came over, nodding a greeting to me. He was young and clean cut with forearms the size of dinner hams. From the way he carried himself and the way his black button-down shirt fit him, I imagined the rest of him was equally well muscled.

"Get you something?"

"No, thanks. I'm not staying."

He looked to Jumbo. "Another?"

"Yeah," Jumbo said, sounding in that single word somehow resigned to the fact that he was now a guy who drank alone in a bar at two in the afternoon. "In a minute."

The bartender walked away.

"Lately, I've been one of Sure Bonds' girls," I said.

I saw that news slap him across the face like I'd hoped it would, but not nearly hard enough. He just shrugged, swallowed some more beer, and said, "So?"

I resisted the urge to slap him myself, and instead took a deep breath. "What the hell is going on between you and Marge?"

Pain pinched his rough features, but he said, "I don't know what you mean. She fired me. Plain and simple."

I rolled my eyes. "Are you fucking kidding me? She kick you out, too, or did you leave on your own?"

He started to eye me then stopped and focused on his beer. "I don't know what you're talking about."

365

"Listen, I don't really have time for all this. Marge is a mess. The office is a mess; the house is a mess. And it's starting to mess up my life. And this all has to do with *you*. So I need you to quit drinking your days away here and get back to work."

"Maybe you didn't hear me," he said, turning slightly on his stool and sitting up to his full height while raising his voice, trying to use his size to intimidate me. "Margie kicked me out— of the house and the office. She doesn't want me. It's over."

I'd learned long ago not to feel intimidated by bigger men. I sat up, raised my own voice, and leaned toward him. "Marge has pretty much been living at the office, probably because she doesn't want to be home alone. And she doesn't seem to be eating—or doing anything besides smoking. *Because she's upset*. That means she doesn't like the way things turned out."

He sunk back onto his stool, the words, "Oh, Margie," wheezing out of him like cries from a wounded animal.

I was suddenly struck with panic that he might start crying.

"I was just trying to help her out," he said, the words beginning to flow out in a rush, as if he'd just been waiting to talk to someone. "She's been so busy lately, and she's the only one writing the bonds. So I tried to help her out. The skips were under control—they always are; she has a sense about people before she ever writes the bond. Anyway, I wrote a few bonds, thinking I could just help her, you know, handle some of the calls, some of the running around, take some stuff off her plate. Only, it didn't really work out that way."

A couple pieces fell into place for me, and I understood why Jamie Vollmer had been bonded out with a 2008 Kia Rio as collateral. And why Sure Bonds had so many skips right now.

"You don't have her same sense about who's going to show up for court and who'll skip, do you?"

"No," he blubbered. "So all these people started skipping. And then Margie got mad at me, because of the way I wrote the bonds, like the collateral and stuff. She said I put us at risk. But I didn't know, and I was just trying to help. Then that stupid prick of a landlord came around and told her she couldn't smoke in the office anymore, that if he found out she was, he'd evict her.

"That was stress on top of all the other stress, you know, and then she started smoking in the house. She's never done that, and she knows it messes with my allergies. So I asked her to stop. She flipped out. I've never seen her so mad. She threw me out."

A part of me kind of felt bad for him.

"Marge didn't really mean what she said. She was stressed, like you said, angry. And she's been torn up over it ever since. If she wasn't so fucking stubborn, she would be telling you all this herself."

He shook his head. "I don't think so. She was serious, madder than I've ever seen her."

"Listen to me, you big, blubbering idiot." My tone was sharp, and it cut through his self-pity and got his attention. "Pull yourself together and go get your girl back. Buy her flowers or a motorcycle or whatever she likes. Tell her you're sorry and you won't write any more bonds. Then get to work on the stack of skips she's got on her desk before she really does lose her business."

I stood and dug a Clean Sweep card out of my pocket. "And call this woman. Now. Today. Ask for the 'referral discount.' Take Marge home to a nice clean house later and make her dinner. It'll be the first meal she's eaten since you left."

He eyed me for a couple beats then fingered the card. "You're sure about this?"

I thought he meant more than just the cleaning service.

"Yes."

"I heard she did get evicted."

"That's being cleared up." I clapped him on his giant, rock-solid shoulder. It was like slapping a boulder. "But if she starts

367

forfeiting bonds, it won't matter, because she won't have a business to run out of her office."

He was nodding now, and I could see some life coming into those big eyes, giving me a hint of what might have caught Marge's attention in the first place.

As I reached the end of the bar I heard Jumbo say, "Forget the beer, Joe. Close my tab."

I smiled and left the bar.

53

I called Dasch and he jumped out of the truck. We walked north on College two blocks to Laporte Avenue, then crossed the street to Pueblo Viejo. I was a little early, but Sadie was already sitting on the sidewalk patio. She wore a strapless summer dress, sandals, and big sunglasses. As usual, she looked lovely, which the waiter had noticed, too.

Sadie loved on Dasch over the wrought iron fence, and I quickly hopped over it, taking the seat across from hers. Then Dasch lay down against the fence near my seat to wait.

"Get any sleep?" I asked.

"Not really. As you can imagine, work has been chaotic with the fallout of Crazy Karen's caper."

"Caper?" I eyed her across the table. "Been reading hardboiled detective novels again?"

She shrugged a perfect, brown shoulder. "What else should I call it?" She had been as sickened as anyone else to learn what Karen Brickle had been up to, but she had enjoyed the adventure of it.

The waiter appeared and delivered a margarita to Sadie with a bit too much flourish. He asked her three times if he could get her anything else, and then, as he was about to leave, he finally noticed me. I ordered myself a margarita, figuring I'd better spend as much of Sadie's money as I could before I tallied expenses and issued her a refund.

"Is Ellmann still making   arrests?"

I nodded. "They're up to nearly twenty between Fort Collins and Boulder. And they've brought in the FBI to look at cases in Phoenix and Albuquerque, where they have learned Karen had lived. Her real name, by the way, is Christine Phillips."

"That's so normal sounding."

"I know. Not hint at all that she's a mass murderer."

The waiter returned, delivered my margarita with no ceremony whatsoever, then asked Sadie twice if she needed anything. He didn't ask me.

"You know," I began when he'd finally left, "if you promised to go out with him, this whole meal would probably be free."

She sighed. "I know. Poor fool."

I tried the drink. It was only mediocre. I bet Sadie's tasted better.

"How's the surgeon?"

An almost giddy smile spread over her face before she could stop it. "He's fine," she said dismissively.

"Good. I'm happy for you."

I saw her roll her eyes behind the dark shades, and she waved a hand at me. "Tell me more about Karen."

"Christine Phillips really was a nurse. She went to nursing school in Utah and worked in Salt Lake until she was fired for diverting drugs."

"Uh-oh."

"Obviously, her nursing license got yanked, but she managed to keep herself out of jail. Based on what Ellmann and Clark have been able to learn, she wasn't using the drugs herself; she was selling them."

"Quite the little entrepreneur."

"Yes, so when she met a doctor with some loose morals and enough mistakes behind him he could be manipulated, her scheme was born. It started in Albuquerque. She'd stolen someone's identity and gotten herself a job at a clinic. She sent the blood of unsuspecting patients for testing and then sold the organs on the black market in Mexico. And it started with just kidneys. They would abduct the victims, drug them, take a kidney, and leave the patient alive, the drug-induced amnesia making it impossible for them to identify their attackers. But one of the operations went wrong, and the patient died. Enterprising young Christine convinced the doctor to harvest all of the organs. That was when things changed.

"The doctor got cold feet. He felt too guilty over what he'd done and wanted to stop. Christine didn't want to stop, because now she saw dollar signs every time she looked at a patient, and she couldn't risk the doctor blabbing to anyone. So he got an injection of potassium one night while he was sleeping. At the time, he was thought to have died from a heart attack, but the FBI has since discovered that wasn't the case.

"From there, Christine moved to Phoenix, starting over in a hospital there with a new ID. That's where she met Dr. Adam Galvin. He was just as greedy as she was and soon partnered with her. Together, they managed to refine the operation down to a cold science. By the time they moved to Colorado, they knew exactly who to recruit and where—a private lab, EMS, pilots and airport personnel, and cops. Not everyone was in on the deal. Actually, most of them had no idea they were doing anything illegal. The orders that went to the lab, for example, all appeared to be completely legit. The airport personnel had no idea the organs hadn't been obtained legally. Then, others were knowing, willing participants."

"Like Jimmy and Dom."

"Yes. And Andrew Miller and his partner Walter Burtch in Boulder."

"I heard Dom had to have surgery for a dog bite on his arm and Jimmy has a closed head injury, a broken nose, and is missing three front teeth." She eyed me through the dark glasses.

"They tried to kill me."

And they'd gotten off easy. Andrew Miller would need a series of reconstructive surgeries on his elbow, which would never be the same, and he had a skull fracture. With the limited strength he'd now have in that arm, he may or may not be able to defend himself in prison.

"The FBI and the local cops are still going through missing persons reports," I said, "and the list of victims is growing. Over the years, in three states and four cities, it's looking like well over a hundred victims were killed for their organs. We may never identify them all, because Christine and Galvin still aren't talking."

"You think Theresa was one of them."

I nodded somberly. "Clark showed photos of every cop on the Boulder Police Department to the man we found in Galvin's cabin basement. The guy identified a patrol officer named Fred Irvin. Clark hit him hard, and the guy cracked. The guy got hooked up with Christine's operation after bringing a suspect for treatment at the ER. Irvin wasn't exactly a by the book cop—he would lift a little dope or cash from suspects, take favors from female suspects, those kinds of things. Christine got onto this and put the screws to him. He may have been recruited by force, but he was soon participating willingly, enjoying the money he was making.

"If they couldn't charm their victims into abduction, then Irvin would 'arrest' them, or tell them a loved one had been hurt and that he would take them to the hospital. He then drove them to the cabin in Allenspark where they would be held for any length of time. According to the guy they had doing guard duty, typical turnover was about three days. The delay came in finding matches for as many organs as possible. See, Christine saw it as a wasted opportunity to just take a kidney when there were so many other perfectly good parts. Then it was a matter of getting the recipients into the country, into hospitals within delivery distance—you know most organs have to be transplanted within a number of hours in order to be viable. Ellmann and the others are learning some of the surgeries were done totally black book in makeshift operating suites, but the vast majority were done in real hospitals by legitimate surgeons. Galvin and his conspirator at the donor alliance were constantly falsifying the donor registry."

"So what happened to Theresa?"

"I'm not really sure," I admitted, sadness returning to me. "And we may never know. Irvin admitted to seeing her; he was the secret boyfriend, and I think Theresa was keeping him a secret not because he was married but because he was younger. He began seeing her after Christine introduced them. For his part, he really did like her, and dated her out of interest. But then, in February, Christine told him to pick Theresa up and take her to the cabin. She wouldn't say why, only that Theresa had become a liability."

"And he did?" Sadie looked appalled.

"He may have had genuine interest in Theresa, but he loved the money more. These people . . . they are the epitome of greed. I think Theresa knew something had gone wrong, and that she was in danger. I think that's why she started pulling cash out of the bank. I think she turned to Irvin for help. When he was told to pick her up, he probably played it like it was time to get her out of town. I think that's why she took her makeup and the picture of her family. Only he didn't help her; he took her to the cabin and locked her in a cell.

"Irvin doesn't know what happened to her after that, and like I said, Christine and the doctor aren't talking. They may have taken Theresa's organs first, but I'm certain they killed her."

I had gone with Clark when he had delivered that news to the family earlier this morning. And when they had cried, I had cried, too. I had dared to hope Theresa Walling had left on her own and that it meant she was alive. Learning she wasn't had been a blow I knew I'd feel for a while to come.

"That's why Karen—or, Christine—tried to shift the focus onto Theresa's ex-husband."

I nodded. "Yes. And why she got out of Boulder so quickly. Whatever Theresa had seen or heard, she was a threat that could have brought the whole thing down. I wish she'd gotten the chance."

"In a way, she did."

I just looked at Sadie.

She said, "I asked you to look into Crazy Karen, but it was really Theresa's disappearance that blew everything open. If you hadn't looked into *that*, you still might not know what Karen was up to."

I smiled, but it was soft, sad. "I suppose that's true. It doesn't really make that much of a difference, though."

54

Jan Taylor had not been thrilled to see me on her doorstep again yesterday, and she wasn't thrilled to see me now. She had not been excited when I'd asked her to help me, and she wasn't excited about doing so now. But she was, because at the end of the day, Jan Taylor was a businesswoman, and she could see she really didn't have a choice.

She led me upstairs to one of the bedrooms. This one was relatively small, with the bed dominating most of the space. It was done in dark colors and had a distinctly illicit feel to it. Clients probably loved it.

"He should be arriving any moment," Taylor said with a glance at her watch.

I nodded and she pulled the door closed.

The girl who used this room had the day off. The bedding looked clean, and I hoped the linens started fresh every day. I chanced it and sat on the edge of the bed to wait.

It was a short wait; Lee Rossler was a punctual man.

I heard footsteps on the stairs and the door opened. Rossler had a slight smile on his face as he stepped in, but it slid off the instant he saw me.

"What is this?" he demanded, fear rising in him.

"Come on in, Mr. Rossler. You and I need to have a conversation."

"I don't know what you think is going on here, but this is a mistake. I'm leaving."

I picked up a few of the papers I'd brought with me. "I've got photo documentation of your visits to this house—your car parked on the street; you coming and going through the front door. I've also got signed affidavits from three of the young ladies you come here to visit, detailing the nature of those visits. My lawyer friend tells me it'll all hold up in court, if the cops ever got their hands on it. So why don't you come in, close the door, and hear me out?"

Rossler was blushing as he stepped in and closed the door, and I thought it was from embarrassment, not anger.

He straightened his tie and tried to regroup. "Who are you?"

"Mr. Rossler," I said in a mocking tone, handing him a card. "I'm offended you don't recognize me."

He snapped the card out my hand and glared at it. "Zoe Grey," he said. "Mark White's top lieutenant. Does he know you're doing this?"

I smiled. "We haven't even gotten to *what* I'm doing."

He nodded. "Good point. So why don't you come to that?"

"I'm so glad you brought it up." I sat up and crossed one leg over the other, as if this were nothing more than a business meeting. "I'd like to discuss the building you own out on Riverside, the one Marge Lewicki leases."

I could see the wheels of his mind turning. "I evicted Marge. She's supposed to be out today. Is that why you're here?"

"No. I'm here to buy the building."

He blinked at me. "Excuse me?"

I pulled a thick document onto my lap. "White Real Estate is making you a very generous offer on the building, and you're going to accept it."

He scoffed. "Why would I do that? It's six thousand square feet of prime retail space on Riverside Avenue. It's worth one forty a square foot, and even more with three tenants in it. Besides, Mark doesn't buy commercial."

"It's five thousand, four hundred and eighty-nine square feet, and with all the structural damage caused by the water leak, it isn't worth more than one twenty a square foot. And Mark's branching out."

Rossler didn't look happy. Obviously, his business dealings didn't often go this way. "That building is worth eight hundred and fifty thousand dollars, easy. Why the fuck would I sell it?"

"In its current state, that building isn't worth seven hundred thousand dollars, but you're going to sell it for six."

He choked, anger coloring his cheeks now. "Wh—"

I stood, reaching for more of the documents I'd brought with me. "You're going to sell it to me, today, for six because you don't want it to get out that you tricked Marge Lewicki into signing a bad lease. You don't want it to get out that you've been charging Marge for damages and renovations to the property she isn't responsible for and that you haven't made. You don't want it to get out that you submitted claims to your insurance company for the same damages you charged Marge for. You don't want it to get out that you've also been charging the tenant next to Marge for the same water damage, pursuant to another poorly written lease agreement. But really, you don't want it to get out that you like to pay hookers to handcuff you to the bed and call you names and smack you with a whip while they fuck you.

"So, you're going to sign this contract I've conveniently prepared. I'm going to call my lawyer, who's waiting on the street outside, and she's going to come in here with a notary public and this will all be finalized. You're going to get a check from White Real Estate. You're going to deposit that check and be glad to be rid of a water-damaged building and a tenant like Marge Lewicki. And then you're going to go about the rest of your life. I don't care if you change your habits or not, and Ms. Taylor has been pleased with your business over the years.

"But you are going to keep one thing in mind. I don't like it when people get screwed over by greedy bastards like you. So the next time you write a lease agreement or the next time you think about filing some kind of bullshit claim with your shady brother-in-law, you better remember this conversation. Because I'm going to hang on to everything I've got here. And if I have to talk to you again about your illegal business practices, I'm going to hand deliver everything I've got to my friends at the police station and the local news media. Even if you somehow manage to escape prison, you can still bend over and kiss your ass goodbye.

"So, Mr. Rossler, what do you say? Have we got a deal?"

A fine sheen of sweat now glistened on his forehead, and his face was so pale he looked anemic. He managed to swallow, then pulled a pen from his jacket pocket.

"You're a very convincing negotiator, Ms. Grey. I believe we have a deal."

55

Marge was in the office when I arrived Friday morning. I propped the door open and went in. She was behind her desk, cigarette hanging from her lips as she spoke to someone on the phone.

"Well, I want to know where he is." She listened some more, then took the smoke between two fingers and used them to point, even though the person on the other end of the phone couldn't see them. "You listen to me, Juanita. I've been fair to you guys over the years, bonding out your idiot husband every time he gets himself arrested. But I'm not just going to bend over here. You either come up with a location for that dirtbag you married by the end of the day, or I make a call to welfare and get half those checks stopped." With that, she smacked the phone down. It rattled into the base with a ring of the internal bell.

"Well, princess," she said, leaning back in her chair with a squeak and putting her feet on the desk. I could see the new black biker boots Jumbo had bought her as an I'm-sorry gift. "What are you doing here?" She blew a lungful of smoke at the ceiling.

"I see Jumbo's getting things back in order around here." I waved at the desk, which was noticeably lighter in FTA files.

"Yeah. Between the two of you and that couple of guys from Sideline, we'll be caught up in a couple days."

I'd agreed to help with a few of the FTAs, taking some of the smaller fish. And Marge had been right about the Sideline guys being open to other opportunities.

"Glad things worked out between the two of you."

She eyed me, and I had the clear impression she knew I'd had something to do with it, though I'd never said as much and doubted Jumbo had either.

She reached for a stack of faxes she'd pulled from the machine. "Got some more skips here, princess. How 'bout this guy? Grand theft auto; no violence, no weapons. Hmm? Fee's five hundred. Guy won't be hard to find. I'll print the paperwork." She sat forward and reached for the keyboard.

"I'm not here for more skips," I said. "I'll bag the ones I've got, and we'll see where things stand."

"Guess you heard Cal Stevens got fired over Sideline."

I nodded. "I did hear that, yes."

"Guess you'll be going back over there."

"Yes, but I'm freelance, Marge. I don't work just one place. Speaking of work." I pulled some papers from my pocket and set them on her desk. "You owe me some money."

She stuck the cigarette between her lips as she pulled the checkbook out and slapped it onto the desk. She scribbled out a check, ripped it off, and handed it to me.

She leaned back, took the cigarette from her lips, and eyed me through the haze. "You're pretty good, princess. For a newbie."

I smiled. "I know." I set the thick document I'd brought with me on the open checkbook.

"What's this?"

"A new lease agreement, this time with White Real Estate. Unlike your last contract, this one is fair to you. White Real Estate now owns this building; I'm the new property manager. You need to read this lease, and sign it. But I'm going to summarize the key components for you. Starting Monday, this building is going to undergo renovations and repairs, both of which are long overdue. The water damage is going to be repaired, and the interiors of all three spaces are going to be updated. What that means to you is new paint, new carpet, new ceiling tiles, all of it. Because I like you so much, Marge, I'm going to let you pick the colors. I'll be bringing a sample book by next week."

I tapped the lease document. "You were right: Rossler was charging you too much for rent. I've set a new rent price. It's fair for the market, and less than you were paying."

"Sounds too good to be true, princess." Her tone was guarded as she eyed me through the blue haze.

"Here's the part you're not going to like, and it's nonnegotiable. Starting Monday, you can't smoke in here."

"I've—"

"I've got a landscaper coming next week who is going to put a courtyard out back. It'll be a nice space with flowers and a waterfall, and whatever furniture you pick out. It'll be the only place you can smoke."

She sat forward, poking her fingers at me, causing ash to fall from the end of the cigarette she held. "I've been smoking in here since nineteen eighty-one—"

"Which is why the paint is peeling off the walls and the ceiling tiles are yellow and why no landlord has ever bothered to replace the carpet you wore through by nineteen eighty-seven. I'm offering you a fair deal, a generous deal. You know it."

"If I want to smoke—"

"Marge, it's two thousand fourteen; no one smokes anymore."

"*I* smoke."

"You smoke too much, but, frankly, I don't give a shit. After Monday, you can't smoke in here. That courtyard will be your space; I'm doing that for you. It's called a compromise. Now, you want to meet with the landscaper next week, or not?"

"Yeah," she snapped. "I wanna meet with him. Geez, princess, don't get your panties in a bunch."

"Great. Read the contract. I need it signed by Monday." I moved away from the desk. "I'll be in touch when I've bagged the rest of my guys."

"Uh, hey, princess."

Her tone caused me to stop near the door and turn back. She was sitting up, leaning her arms on the desk, looking at me with the most serious expression I'd ever seen on her face.

"Yeah?"

"Uh . . . thanks." She looked like she wanted to say more but just tapped a finger against the lease.

I nodded. "You're welcome."

56

"So, are you going to tell me what's going on with you, Topham, and Olvera?"

Ellmann sat at the bar, and I carried our dishes to the sink.

I glanced at him. "Am I talking to Ellmann my boyfriend or Ellmann the cop?"

I saw a brief flash in his eyes, but he said, "Your boyfriend."

Sometimes, it isn't easy for Ellmann the cop to be my boyfriend, I know.

I pulled a thin envelope from my bag and handed it to him as I returned to my seat at the bar.

Ellmann opened the envelope and shuffled through the photos I'd picked up at Walgreens days ago.

"Guess I know what was in the box Amerson gave you."

"Look. I just needed a little leverage. I can't ask you for information anymore, but sometimes I still need a little information. These guys are what you might call an easy target."

"Do they have any idea you'd never really out them?"

"No. And if it ever comes to the point they're taking heat for passing me info, I'll back off. I'm not looking to jam them up."

Ellmann chuckled. "Couldn't have happened to two nicer guys."

I laughed. "Yeah, I don't feel too bad about the arrangement."

"You're something else, Zoe."

"I know."

"Hey, I've got something for you."

Ellmann got up and returned with two small open cardboard boxes. He set them on the bar.

"What's this?"

He grinned as he sat down. "See for yourself."

I pulled one over and reached inside. I came out with something wrapped in plastic. I opened the plastic and saw it was a vest for Dasch. It was tan, with a couple of small pockets, and it had big patches on the sides that said WORKING SERVICE DOG across the top and ALL ACCESS across the bottom.

I smiled at Ellmann. "This is great."

"Now he can go anywhere you go—stores, restaurants, any public place. You'll always have backup."

I called Dasch over and put the vest on him, adjusting the straps. When it was on, he just grinned at me. I scratched his ears.

"He looks pretty good," I said.

"Yes, he does."

I went around the bar and gave Ellmann a hug and kiss. "Thank you for that. Really."

"Happy to. You decide what to do about your landlord? Not that I'm in a hurry for you to leave."

I sighed. "It's cheaper if I buy the house."

"I figured you'd do that."

"I was surprised how easily Stuart agreed. We close next month, but the lease agreement doesn't really matter much now. I can move back."

He squeezed me and kissed my head. "When are you leaving?"

"I don't know. But I'm not leaving, you know . . . I'm not leaving you."

"I know. It's okay. Really."

And he was serious. He may have been ready to live together, but he understood I wasn't, and he didn't hold it against me. Which just made me love him more.

After a long kiss, he said, "Check the other box."

I opened it and found it contained two smaller boxes and a piece of paper. I took them all out, seeing one box contained business cards. "What are these?" I asked, reaching for that box. I pulled out a good-looking card that read ZOE GREY, PRIVATE INVESTIGATOR. I looked at Ellmann. "Did you design these?"

"Yeah." He tapped the document I'd taken out of the box. "In case you decided to make it official. This is an application for a PI license."

I chuckled, but more in confusion and surprise than humor. "I'm not a private investigator. I'm a bounty hunter. I'm good at that."

"You're a pretty good investigator, too. I'm not pressuring you or anything, but I can't help but think if Theresa Walling's family had come to you when she'd first gone missing, you might have been able to find her in time."

It hadn't been his intention, but the comment caused tears to suddenly burn in my eyes. He wrapped an arm around me, and I furiously wiped them away.

Late at night, in the days since the Karen Brickle case had unfolded, I'd often thought about Theresa Walling, and, privately, I'd wondered the same. Would I have been able to find her in time?

"Her family is having a memorial for her tomorrow," I said. "Will you go with me?"

"Of course. Zoe, you're good at your job. You're a natural investigator. It's what makes you good at tracking down skips. And you have an overriding instinct to help people. Theresa's a good example; Tommy's another."

I nodded, thinking of Tommy, who would have his first karate lesson with Amy tomorrow afternoon.

"You could help people as a PI. It's something to think about. I'll support you whatever you decide to do. In the meantime, you'll need this." He tapped the unopened smaller box.

I opened it then gaped at him.

He just grinned. "Thought you could use one."

I pulled the shiny new badge out of the box. It was a round marshal-style badge in silver with an eagle seal in the middle and said BOND ENFORCEMENT AGENT. It looked infinitely more professional than the rinky-dink badge I'd been given after completing the weekend certification course, and it looked enough different from the cop badges most people recognized that maybe there wouldn't be so much confusion about my job.

"I . . . love it," I said. "Ellmann, thank you."

He chuckled. "You're welcome. You know, honey, you're pretty easy to shop for. No jewelry, just tactical gear." He kissed my head.

It was true. Some girls liked diamonds and shoes. Not me.

Ellmann understood that, and it didn't bother him. He loved me anyway.

I looked at him. "Thank you." My voice was soft. I wanted to say more, but couldn't find the words. *Thank you for loving me. Thank you for understanding me. Thank you for supporting me.* I just touched his face. "I love you."

He smiled even as his eyes darkened with desire. "That sounds better and better every time you say it."

He pulled me in and kissed me.

Acknowledgements

Thank you to my friends and family for patiently, even lovingly, tolerating my strange eccentrics and odd habits. Writers are kind of weird, and while you don't always understand me, you support me. I can't thank you enough.

Thank you to the invaluable beta-readers, who read drafts of this story, provided critical feedback, and spent time brainstorming and troubleshooting. Nancy, Mandi, Kacy, my grandmother, Lauren, Deanne—there is no better team than you. I know how lucky I am. Thank you.

Thank you to Sabrina for another beautiful cover. And to Nancy and Patrick, the best cover models ever.

A big thank you to Shonny for putting me in touch with all the right people.

Thank you to John Vander Vliet, twenty-three-year police veteran, EMT, and fireman, for giving me some of your time and allowing me to pick your brain about all things police related. And thank you for your service. Any mistakes, intentional or otherwise, are my own.

Thank you to all I didn't name here. It takes an army to publish a book; I could never name everyone in this short space. That doesn't diminish your contributions or my appreciation. I am honored and so grateful. I've said all along I have the best support and publishing team out there, and I mean it. Thank you.

Mr Frank Harris
7373 E 29th St N Apt E131
Wichita KS 67226-3438

About the Author

Catherine Nelson is a Colorado native. Fort Collins is home to her, and a perfect setting for her novels.

To learn more about her and her books, visit her website at www.CatherineNelsonBooks.com or connect with her on Facebook at www.Facebook.com/CatherineNelsonBooks.

Catherine loves hearing from readers, and responds to all emails personally. She can be reached at CatherineNelsonBooks@gmail.com.

Join Catherine's mailing list for the first-ever Zoe Grey novella, yours free. You'll also learn about free stuff and new releases. (Mailing list signs ups can be found on Catherine's website and Facebook page.)

What did you think of the book? Leave your review on Amazon.

Mr Frank Harris
7373 E 29th St N Apt E131
Wichita KS 67226-3438

71989375R00221

Made in the USA
Middletown, DE
01 May 2018